Honor Among Outcasts

DarkHorse Trilogy, Book 2

ED PROTZEL

Relax. Read. Repeat.

HONOR AMONG OUTCASTS (DarkHorse Trilogy, Book 2)
By Ed Protzel
Published by TouchPoint Press
Jonesboro, AR 72401
www.touchpointpress.com

Copyright © 2017 Ed Protzel
All rights reserved.

ISBN-10: 1-946920-31-2
ISBN-13: 978-1-946920-31-7

This is a work of fiction. Names, places, characters, and events are fictitious. Any similarities to actual events and persons, living or dead, are purely coincidental. Any trademarks, service marks, product names, or named features are assumed to be the property of their respective owners and are used only for reference. If any of these terms are used, no endorsement is implied. Except for review purposes, the reproduction of this book, in whole or part, electronically or mechanically, constitutes a copyright violation. Address permissions and review inquiries to media@touchpointpress.com.

Editor: Kimberly Coghlan
Cover Design: Colbie Myles, ColbieMyles.com

Visit the author's website at EdProtzel.com

First Edition, February 2018

Printed in the United States of America.

DEDICATION

The major travesties depicted in this novel are based on actual events that took place during the Civil War along the bloody Missouri-Kansas border and throughout Little Dixie in central Missouri. Indeed, in what became the most savage guerrilla war in American history, civilians, as well as military personnel, of both sides suffered unspeakable depredations. This novel is dedicated to those men and women, black and white, who valiantly stand to defend the innocent.

SECTION 1

CHAPTER ONE

THE COLOR OF CHAOS

1863. Camp Macon, Eastern Missouri

The April sun performed its slow, irrevocable descent behind the western hills, a miserly ogre hoarding the remaining daylight, leaving the fecund Earth below in shadow. With night falling, the rich green thicket surrounding the Union Army camp rapidly faded to a foreboding forest of horrors infested with malevolent, ghost-like guerrilla bands bearing sudden death and horrendous mutilation.

Activity slowed in the camp, becoming restrained and random, as the clatter of hooves and heavy caisson wheels, the tromping of boots, and the smack of metal against leather died away. Rifles and equipment were abandoned in front of tents. Wood was leisurely gathered, and the air became thick with smoke from myriad cook fires. For the moment, a looming insurgency, more brutal than the soldiers had ever imagined, seemed far away.

At the corral, a worn-out Durksen Hurst closed and tied the gate, relieved to be done with his duties training cavalry horses. After weeks of failed attempts, he was free to make his big move, having arranged to see the general. Luckily, that day no wounded mounts needing attention had returned to detain him. Brushing off his hands and stained civilian work clothes, he crossed the clearing to where Big Josh Tyler sat on a tree stump waiting anxiously for him.

Durk, as he was called, was five-foot-eight of slim, hard muscle made evermore tighter from four years of manual laboring. He had thick, black hair and a strong-set jaw. His high cheekbones, dark eyes, and broad nose reflected his mother's Seminole heritage. Raised by his white father until he was ten, self-educated Durk was well-spoken enough, enabling him to front for his dozen black cohorts.

The strange group of thirteen, Durk and a dozen black men, generally kept to themselves, never discussing their singular arrangement with outsiders, which made the soldiers in camp suspicious. People thought it curious that the others never held back in voicing their opinions to Durk: an oddity that caused rumors to spread. Durk was believed to be a former plantation owner, which none of the thirteen denied. Many suspected he was a fugitive with a price on his head for robbery, or even some dastardly act performed in a dark alley with a pistol or knife. Stories around camp speculated that the odd-looking interloper had never really owned the twelve former slaves with whom he camped, and one popular yarn actually claimed he'd kidnapped them. There was even talk that Durk wasn't white at all, but rather a creature of unknown, profoundly-sinister origins.

Seeing Durk coming, bear-like Big Josh rose to greet him, in no mood to be disappointed. Since sun-up, Josh had been working with a pick and shovel on the camp's earthen fortifications. His neck muscles and shoulders were sore and his temper short. Josh spoke with a stutter. That added to his girth and skin color, and white men paid him little heed. But it wasn't uncommon to see Josh openly reprimanding Durk or issuing what seemed to be orders to him, just as Josh did with the other blacks in their cabal. Such seemingly upside-down interactions made the soldiers scratch their heads… and secure their belongings.

Passing between the rows of tents, Durk and Josh headed toward the general's quarters, speaking quietly. They were hungry, a never-ending discomfort thanks to the meager rations the army supplied its black labor; they could smell brewing coffee and fried fatback wafting in the breeze, yet they ignored their stomachs' urgent cries.

They reached the camp's main road, stepping gingerly over the ruts driven deeply into the mud by artillery caissons, supply and ambulance wagons, and the tramping of marching boots. Nearing the surgeon's tent, Durk slowed in hopes of catching a glimpse of Antoinette, who was working with the medical units, treating the sick and wounded. He hadn't seen much of her lately and missed her terribly. Typhoid was running rampant throughout the camp, and soldiers were falling sick, many dying. She wasn't where he could see her, so he continued on, disappointed.

When they reached the general's tent, an armed guard blocked the entrance.

"Durksen Hurst to see General Sparks," Durk stated formally.

"And who is this?" the guard asked with a sneer, indicating Josh.

"Josh Tyler, my right-hand man," Durk replied.

As the guard left to check with the general, Josh studied Durk's face, which was shadowed in doubt, a very bad sign. Talking the general into permitting them to join the army would be difficult enough, even if Durk tried his best. In this case, Durk had an inbred aversion to violence and didn't necessarily want to succeed.

"Durk, you gotta get us into this army," Josh whispered. "We voted, remember? I knows you c-can do it."

Durk merely sighed, clearly not convinced.

Two years earlier, Durk and his dozen black comrades, accompanied by their women and children, with Antoinette at Durk's side, had arrived at a Missouri Union military outpost, having fled the South under peculiar circumstances, looking to aid the Union cause. They called their strange group *DarkHorse*, but only they knew what that meant. In short order, smooth-talking Durk had gotten them attached as adjunctive labor to the army. Since then, the *DarkHorse* men and their women had worked faithfully and hard for the Federal military, suffering deprivation without complaint. With Durk beside them, sharing their hardships, they'd cut down trees to lay corduroy log road through snake- and mosquito-infested swamp, constructed fortifications, dug ditches, and skinned supply wagons — whatever tasks the army required of them.

To explain their unusual union, Durk's black companions had posed as contraband laborers whom Durk had "liberated" from their masters. At other times, depending on Durk's strategies-of-the-moment, they'd posed as "freed former slaves," based on dubious manumission papers Durk had signed. Actually, Durk had never owned these men, making their documents and their so-called freedman status problematic.

In truth, the men had secretly been partners back in Mississippi, building and working their own plantation together, which they had named *DarkHorse* — a name they'd kept. In the four years since, they'd lived under no formal hierarchy, making decisions by consensus. Nevertheless, with the resourceful Durk to navigate the white world for them, they'd managed to survive together, South and North. Often the group's greatest boons, and occasional stumbles, were a direct result of Durk's wild imagination, which had a tendency to overwhelm his better judgment.

Ironically, when President Lincoln's Emancipation Proclamation became effective in January, its provisions applied only to those states in rebellion, and, technically, Missouri was not one of them. Although the state was under martial law, the proclamation had not freed the state's slaves, not even those belonging to active Confederate soldiers, guerrillas, and Southern sympathizers, making the women and children of Durk's partners officially still property, mere chattel. They could only hope their legal owner, and the damning records branding them such, were hundreds of miles behind enemy lines.

Durk's partners' ultimate dream had been to wear the uniform and fight to free their people from bondage. And just recently, their dim hopes had brightened. At Lincoln's behest, the Union had begun accepting black men as soldiers, both freedmen volunteers and slaves who'd managed to escape their masters and reach an army outpost. But with active slave catchers patrolling the region, any attempt by a slave to take flight was still an extremely risky venture. Throughout the country, the formation of black regiments was hit-and-miss, entirely dependent on the whims of the general commanding any given military district, and no black regiment had yet been established by General Sparks in this region of Missouri.

Durk himself had no military ambitions. He'd never fired a shot in anger, abhorred violence of any sort, and, moreover, was well aware of his own cowardly streak, often noting that courageous rabbits didn't live long. Despite all that, in 1863, colored army units were required to have a white officer. Knowing that many commonly abused their black charges, Durk figured that if he continued to front for his partners, if he took the officer role in the unit, their service might be less humiliating. It could, in fact, be noble and worthy.

The guard returned, and the pair was permitted entry into the dry, musty tent. General Sparks, a quarrelsome man in his mid-fifties, was seated at a table covered with maps with an open bottle of whiskey and a half-filled glass before him. He sported a black mustache and Van Dyke beard, which jutted forward from his chin at a sharp angle. He was a political general, more concerned with his own ambitions than the Union cause: a man whose military incompetence hadn't yet met a situation challenging enough to cause his being assigned to a more appropriate post, where his activities would be less fatal for his underlings.

"Thank you for seeing us, General. My name is Durksen Hurst, and this is my future Number Two, Josh Tyler."

"Oh, yes," the General said, looking up. "I know of you, Hurst. I understand you're quite a horseman. You've done wonderful work with the stock."

"Yes, sir. Thank you," Durk replied. "As my appeal noted, I am prepared to form a cavalry regiment. I already have sixty men willing to enlist, with more coming into camp every week. My men have two years' experience taking care of government mounts, and I've taught most to ride well. We're ready to sacrifice, General, to contribute to our country's glorious victory."

The general scrutinized Josh. Finally, he barked at Durk, "Do you mean to form a regiment of *colored* cavalry, Mr. Hurst?"

"Yes, sir. The men are eager to fight against the rebellion."

"Hurst," the general growled, nodding to indicate Josh, "these people are the cause of my having to leave my family. If it wasn't for them, there wouldn't be a war. I'd be sleeping in my own bed at night."

Durk glanced at Josh to see how he was reacting to such an indictment, but Josh's face remained impassive, stoic, revealing no anger or hurt. "Sir," Durk petitioned, "these men are brave and loyal. I assure you, they'll give the secesh a real whipping."

General Sparks drained his drink and refilled the glass. When he set down his glass, his face glowed bright red. "So, you want me to supply a mob of Negros with uniforms, weapons, and horses, too. Is that what you're telling me?"

"Yes, sir. I have sixty men, enough to start a regiment right now. We'll have a full hundred within a month or two."

The general took a deep swallow, then narrowed his eyes at Durk. "Hurst, understand me; this is not a Negro's war. The rebels would have to spill every drop of blood of every white man in the North before Negros will take up arms. Do you understand?"

"B-but, sir," Durk stuttered, "the rules — the rules have changed now. These men will be as brave as any white man. They just want to prove they're deserving of citizenship..."

"These people haven't what it takes to be soldiers," the general retorted, pointing directly at Josh. "Do they know anything? Why, I'd throw down my arms before I'd fight beside a black man. I'd rather be shot in the back!"

Durk hung his head, knowing there was no sense in arguing. He'd failed his partners. It looked like it was back to being simple camp labor for the *DarkHorse* men.

"Another thing, Hurst," the general continued. "Those people get in the fighting, who knows what they'll demand! Hell, they'll want to *vote* like white men. Can you imagine a more absurd idea? Can you?"

***

The night arrived and nestled in, pulling a blanket of stars and a bright, full moon overhead. For supper, the men had eaten salt-horse, which the women had fashioned into a palatable kind of stew. Supplemented by hardtack fried in fatback, the humble fare had muted their bellies' complaints. But surprisingly, Durk hadn't shown up to join them. They'd almost finished eating when a Missouri State Militia orderly arrived to deliver a note from him, asking them to gather at their regular meeting place in a grove outside camp.

In keen anticipation of the news, the men finished quickly and traipsed the few hundred yards to wait around their modest fire, quietly speculating as to why Durk had called them together out here, especially in a note conveyed by a military private. Had another one of his schemes misfired and gotten them into trouble again?

When they heard Durk's distinctively brisk footsteps approaching at his regular, confident pace, everyone sat up, alert. Jaws dropped as he entered the circle sporting a crisp, new Missouri State Militia captain's uniform.

"Men," Durk crowed proudly, smiling broadly, "we're in the army, in the MSM!"

There were cries of jubilation and relieved laughter. The men leaped up, hugged, and back-slapped each other. It took some moments for Big Josh to quiet everyone down.

"We're going to form our own regiment, the Ninth. Us and all the freedmen volunteers and the contrabands, too. I'm naming it the *DarkHorse* regiment, like we called our plantation. Gentlemen, *DarkHorse* lives again!"

Josh just shook his head in admiration and partial disbelief. Right after work, their friend had disappeared, as he was wont to do, seeking some advantage for them. Sometimes when this happened, he returned with good news. Usually he returned empty-handed, but this time he'd talked his way into an unexpected boon. And Josh couldn't see any potential pitfall in the road ahead... yet.

"Even better," Durk added, pausing for effect, "the MSM Ninth will be a cavalry unit. Cavalry! We'll be riding, not marching!" There was more laughter and hugging, and it took some time for Josh to quiet them.

Josh puzzled over these earthshaking developments. Durk always announced his new conquests like Judgment Day had come, but often, devils hid within the euphoria of his pronouncements. This new revelation brought to mind Durk's announcement in Mississippi that he'd gained title to Chickasaw land on which to build a "plantation" of their own. At the time, Durk's quasi-legal maneuver had struck them like a miracle had happened. That was, until they ran into problems. Now the men were in ecstasy, but Josh knew from experience he'd better ask questions before they found themselves marching, or as cavalry, riding into quicksand.

"B-but Durk," Josh stuttered, "wh-what you mean? The general say he won't allow no colored soldiers in his district."

"To Hell with General Sparks! He's *Federal* Army," Durk replied haughtily. "Fellahs, we're in the Missouri *State* Militia. As of tomorrow morning, *DarkHorse* is the MSM Ninth Cavalry! Now the MSM don't have the equipment the Federal Army has. The horses are broke down, and the weapons are ancient, but we can make do, can't we? Just think, men, tomorrow morning you'll be putting on new uniforms from the quartermaster. I already filled out the paperwork."

"Yes, but the g-general say..." Josh interrupted, recognizing that familiar twinkle in Durk's eyes. He examined Durk's face and could tell his friend was withholding something. His expression evidenced his possession by one of his grandiose schemes, which, crazy as they sometimes sounded, had led to important gains for the group. But his notions had also put their lives at risk more than once. Josh surely didn't want to see Durk's mind flying off just when they were about to get into the war. As soldiers, their survival in this conflict was already going to be tenuous. "You hiding something, Durk. Wh-what's the c-catch?"

"Well, it's not a catch; it's a bonus! See, Josh, we're registered..." Durk quickly devised a way to break to his partners the twisty part of the deal he'd worked out. "We're registered as a *white* regiment. Only way I could do it in this district, right?"

The men groaned as bewildered and distraught expressions supplanted the earlier joy in their faces.

"Listen," Durk said, "the army pays thirteen dollars, right? But it only pays colored troops seven."

"Th-that's right," Big Josh replied. "So?"

"Well, with you on the rolls as a white regiment, y'all will make thirteen dollars, not the seven they would have paid you."

Big Josh merely stared, unsure that he'd heard right.

"See, I got the idea originally from the Chickasaws. The tribe called you 'black white men,' remember? To them, y'all were white men, just *black ones*. So, I figure if I can promote y'all to being white, we'd be a white unit, and I could get you on the rolls at thirteen dollars — maybe better horses and arms, too — maybe better grub. Otherwise, it's going to take an act of Congress to get you that extra six dollars."

"Forget it, D-durk," Big Josh said. "We just gonna have to wait on Congress."

"Listen, Josh, once this war's over, it's still going to be hard to be a black man, no matter what. You know that's true, ain't it?"

Big Josh nodded. "It ain't gonna be harder than being a slave."

"Sure, I know that. That's what we're fighting for. But this idea is about more than the six dollars; it's about years to come. See, if all the freed slaves are promoted to white men, it's going to be easier for people to accept y'all."

"This is you' craziest idea yet, Durk," Josh objected. "What we gonna do, p-paint ourself white?"

"Course not. But..."

"Listen, friend, we ain't getting tangled in none of your tricks. All we s-suffer to finally get in the army, and you think we gonna risk it for six d-dollar? Durk, we proud to be colored troops fightin' for President Lincoln, and that's a fact. That's who we are. Le's just get all the slaves free, and then we just take our chances on getting that six dollar. Sides that," Josh added, "I hear the colored soldiers in the east went on strike for that equal pay. Did you know they hung the black sergeant leading that protest? You heard that?"

"No," Durk said contritely, "I haven't..."

"You want us to chance getting hung for six dollar?"

"All right," Durk said firmly. "Let's take a vote. Forget the money. The paymaster will be happy to pocket the extra six dollars a man. The question is this: should we be a white cavalry regiment, or should I try to get us switched to colored cavalry?"

Bammer, a muscular man with a wife and two children, said, "Listen, we gonna die just like white men. No reason we shouldn't get the six dollar. Our families is hungry."

Josh stood to his full height, and, out of respect, everyone quieted down. "I say get our paperwork switched to be colored," Josh said. "Listen, God, and Durk here," he chuckled, which was parroted nervously by the rest, "has give us this chance to fight for our country, for our people. Some of us won't see the end of this war, making our women and children widows and orphans. Some of us gonna be cripple' for life. If we gonna die, be beggars on the street, let us be proud to be black men fighting for the Union, proud to go into battle to free our slave brothers. I don't wanna be ashamed of what should be the proudest moment in my life, 'specially not for no six dollar."

They went around the circle, and a few others voiced an opinion. There was grumbling, but they voted ten to two to be a colored regiment. Then they came to the last man, Isaac, always angry, who merely spit in the fire and walked off. No matter, ten settled it. As soon as Durk could get their papers switched with the quartermaster, paymaster, and the other authorities, he'd do it... but it wouldn't be easy.

"Well, if that's how you feel," Durk said, disappointed that his partners failed to see his vision stretching off into the decades, with them equal to white men someday. "It's your six dollars," he mumbled, vowing to himself that he wouldn't let his notions get his friends into trouble like they had before, not without their permission, of course.

CHAPTER TWO

PREYING UPON MISERY

Lafayette County, Western Missouri
Beneath the unflinching gaze of a solitary turkey vulture, the anomalous pair of riders traversed the once-pastoral checkerboard of tilled countryside. The local church bell, reserved these days solely as an alarm, no longer tolled regularly because of the fright its ringing proclamations engendered among the populace. Passing a field, beside cows grazing and corralled horses, the riders came upon a scorched brick chimney lording above the blackened ashes of what had been a family farmhouse. Nearby, the ruins of the burned barn sat flanked by neat squares of burnt crops.

The sight was so commonplace that they no longer bothered to speculate on which side had been the perpetrators, which the victims, Union loyalists or secessionists. It was likely that the raiders with their torches and the farmer who lost everything in this conflagration — perhaps even his life — had once been neighbors, sat together on the town council, belonged to the same church, celebrated the same weddings. In Civil War Missouri, only the inexorable flames won victories.

The glaring sun slammed down like a hammer on an anvil, exhausting the harried families straggling toward forlorn hope. Hunger and fatigue coated these refugees like the unrelenting dust as folks became numb and despondent: each day more excruciating than the last. Ahead, the seemingly endless eastbound country road was awash with dazed, ragged men, women, and children — dirty and half-starved, dragging with them what few possessions they owned, each hoping to escape the bloody Missouri counties bordering Kansas. Being vulnerable in transit, mounted Confederate guerrillas, called bushwhackers, and in rare cases Union soldiers, too, plundered these beleaguered souls, robbing what little they'd rescued when their homes and crops were put to the torch. Some had watched in horror as husbands, brothers, and sons were murdered in cold blood by former friends. Many were on foot; but a few had wagons carrying rescued household goods, some drawn by half-starved mules or borrowed oxen, some on makeshift carts pulled by husbands and wives whose livestock had been stolen by the marauders of either side.

Spying the disheveled mass from a distance, the two riders watched for isolated stragglers among the slow-moving stream of fleeing innocents — human wolves singling out calves straying from the herd. At age thirty-five, dressed in her finely-tailored man's linen suit and black bowler hat, Devereau French sat astride her great white stallion. Small in stature, pale, freckled- and peach-faced, Devereau's male disguise was ambiguous at best. Still, she wasn't particularly afraid of discovery. She'd played this perilous game, this absurd masquerade, her whole life. Furthermore, her horse was the best to be had North or South, and she could outride any man.

Beside her on a dark mare sat Robert Sterling, her Indian cohort, sporting a black broadcloth suit coat with a red feather stuck into his trail hat. Strongly built, with dark shining eyes and long, straight black hair, Robert looked every inch the Chickasaw, yet awkward in his city garments as if in a failed disguise. On and off, he'd spent years at Devereau's side, but neither belonged to the other, and that's the only way he would have it. He didn't know or care about the ways the white woman imagined their keeping company to be. He was his own man forever.

Ever alert, the pair silently continued down the main road, disdaining to take extraordinary chances for little return in Union territory as they overtook and left behind one pitiable clump of humanity after another. Finally, they reached a fork in the road where this river of despair broke into tributaries, after which the weary mass thinned out. Loyalists headed north for the safety and provisions at the nearest Union outpost. From there, the more well-connected citizens with money in their pockets would be willing to risk the trek further to the rail station, with St. Louis and the protection of its Union arsenal their ultimate destination. Those without the means to travel farther would camp near the army outpost, to be supplied by the military's largess until the war ended, or until they regained the strength and the will to venture onward… somewhere, anywhere. Pro-secession supporters, many evicted by local officials, took the second branch to flee south toward family in the Confederacy.

After decades of pro- and anti-slavery hostilities culminating in war, the Missouri-Kansas border counties were now plunged into a gale-force storm of violent death, vicious retribution, and unrestrained savagery toward civilians and armed combatants alike. Missouri's war wasn't neat lines of soldiers marching into organized battle as in the East. It was neighbor against neighbor;

deliberate murders and their consequent revenge slayings.

The previous March, General Samuel Curtis had defeated the regular Confederate Army at Pea Ridge and chased them south to Arkansas. As a result, many of the defeated had returned home. But suffering from the depredations of pro-Union Jayhawker Kansas Cavalry, called Red Legs for their red gaiters, who preyed upon Confederate loyalists, many Southern sympathizers joined roving armed guerrilla bands — men beyond law, mercy, or morality. Killing devolved from a braggart's argument to common practice for both sides.

"Slim pickings," Devereau said. "We're getting low on cash."

Robert merely grimaced, making an accusatory face at his companion.

The counties bordering both banks of the west-to-east-flowing Missouri River, which cut the state roughly in half from Calloway County to Jackson County, were called "Little Dixie" for a reason. When the war arrived, most of the state's 115,000 slaves labored tilling bottomland for their masters in this region, growing the cash crops of hemp and tobacco. When harvested, these were shipped to where the Missouri River spilled into the Mississippi at St. Louis. From St. Louis, they were carried downriver on steamboats to New Orleans to be warehoused and shipped overseas. In Little Dixie, pro-Union farmers were in the minority and suffered greatly under constant bloody ravages from their Confederate-sympathizing neighbors. To loyalists' chagrin, Union troops, scavenging for supplies, could be just as predatory, even as deadly. What did it matter who was terrorizing and robbing them? Tomorrow, the other side would finish the job. In Little Dixie, many citizens were forced to make the unenviable decision to scramble away from home for their lives.

Robert signaled to Devereau that they were about to overtake a fresh swarm of civilians. They passed two groups, and, on an isolated stretch, they drew rein beside a tall, unshaven man in his late-thirties stumbling slowly along, leading two young, freckle-faced daughters with long, blond pigtails — one about fourteen, the other about seven. The man's clothing, though soiled and wrinkled, indicated a degree of prosperity. They could see that his face was scarred and purple, with one eye swollen shut. He was in obvious pain, trudging an unsteady gait, holding his side as he dragged himself forward one excruciating step at a time.

Robert slipped his hand to his knife sheath hanging under his coat. He wouldn't need to risk the sound of a pistol shot for these wanderers.

Devereau handed the man her canteen. "What happened to you, mister?"

The man took some grateful gulps and passed the water to his daughters.

"My wife, Rebecca, died back home, in Sibley," the man related, seemingly relieved to be able to tell his tale to anyone. "Then Confederate bushwhackers showed before we'd even buried her: neighbors of ours, damn them to Hell. Farmed by day, then they'd band together and go about raiding people like us by night."

Devereau nodded, attempting as sympathetic an expression as she could muster. "They're no better than brigands," Devereau growled. "Army will hang them. Go on."

"They asked where I hid my money. I said I'd sent it off to Canada, but they didn't believe me. Beat me and kicked me, maybe broke a rib. But I had no money, don't you see? So, they tore the house apart. I was beat so bad, the girls had to drag me into the yard."

"They figured Pa hid his money in Ma's coffin, so they busted it open," the older of the girls related, erupting into sobs.

The younger daughter began to cry. "They cut off Ma's finger to steal her wedding ring!" she exclaimed, clearly still traumatized. The older girl, in great distress herself, wrapped her arms around the youngster to comfort her.

"They let us bury her, but they burned down our house," the man said. "Anything for the girls to eat, mister?"

"Or a doctor nearby?" the older daughter asked. "Pa needs one."

Devereau gave Robert a shrug, suggesting, *These people have nothing.* "There should be a town about five miles ahead, if it hasn't been burned down," was all Devereau would say. Many they'd passed had asked about food, so she'd stopped answering the query. "Maybe they're still helping folks. Did you see any armed parties on the way?"

"They're everywhere," the man said, his bloodshot eyes growing large with fear. "Bushwhackers. Union Army can't keep up with them. I hear some of the army patrols rob people, too. Nobody's safe. Nobody."

"You catchin' the road further up to the Union outpost?" Devereau asked, pointing toward a road branching off ahead.

"Yes, if we make it alive," the man replied.

Devereau felt a pang to help them, but then she hardened. *They may be destitute,* she thought bitterly, *but they have each other, which is more than I ever had.* "Good luck to you," she said coldly and spurred her horse. Robert followed. They continued east, not turning off.

Hours later, Robert noted, "Bushwhacker territory ahead," having a strong instinct for the signs and the types of danger awaiting them.

"I'm ready for the secesh. I forged a letter to Quantrill and signed General Hindeman's name. I just have to remember to reach into this one," she chuckled, patting her left pocket. "Don't want to present the Union documents in my right pocket to the wrong people," she laughed. "Otherwise, we'll have to shoot ourselves free."

"For someone who never drew blood until two years ago, you certainly have come to savor the practice." Robert glanced her direction.

"Nonsense," Devereau retorted. "For me, killing's a necessity. For you, it's your one great passion."

"Well, in these times, it's an easier passion to slake than yours for the long-absent Mr. Dark Horse," Robert said sarcastically.

Her eyes flared with anger. Devereau's hand went quickly to her pistol, but Robert mirrored her movement to his own. For long moments, the pair stared heatedly at each other, tense, muscles tight. Then Devereau spurred her horse into a gallop, and Robert had to follow suit to keep up.

CHAPTER THREE

BLOOD ON HIS HANDS

Camp Macon, Eastern Missouri

"Who y-you k-kill, Isaac?" Big Josh Tyler said, as deep furrows frowned into his brow, his stutter more pronounced than usual under such duress. Big Josh paced the Union Army tent, tugging unconsciously at the sleeves of his crisp, new, blue soldier's uniform with the sergeant patch on his shoulder. Dug from a pile in no order of size, the uniform was uncomfortably tight around his massive arms and chest, and he'd strategically slit the sleeves and legs at points to make it bearable.

It was still dark outside, a half-hour until dawn. Pausing, Big Josh picked up the knife lying on the cot beside Isaac and held it close to the lantern, examining the blade caked in dried blood. Isaac sat in despair, trembling, his head cradled in his hands, his dark fingers, face, and blue tunic also caked in blood. In spite of a steady diet of Union Army food the last two years, boney Isaac was as emaciated as when Big Josh had first run into him in Mississippi in '59. Isaac had been living then in the swamp as a so-called maroon, wearing animal skins over torn clothes, having escaped from his master to live in the forest outside the hamlet of Turkle. There were a substantial number of maroons throughout the South, living in the swamps, forested hills, and woodlands beyond the purlieus of civilization. Rather than live as slaves, these men and women preferred to risk living a wild existence, suffering extreme conditions, courting starvation, and all the while confronting the chance of recapture and severe punishment. To them, no hardship was too great for their freedom.

Sitting across from Isaac on the tent's other cot, wearing his spanking new captain's uniform, Durk studied the top of Isaac's head, its two irregular ridges curving through the black stubble of hair, evidencing the beatings by an overseer who had split his skull more than once. On their perilous trek north, Durk had spied Isaac's naked back, a furious crisscross patchwork of scars that spoke of innumerable lashes, and it had sickened him.

Finally, not lifting his face, Isaac spoke tearfully, in barely a whisper, "I ain't kill' nobody, Josh." He began to sob, his shoulders heaving, and wiped his eyes, tracking red streaks across his cheekbones.

Durk had never seen Isaac contrite like this. Isaac was the one black partner of Durk's who'd always spoken up, expressing what was in the back of everyone's mind, not afraid to confront Durk and identify what was worrying them or making them angry. Durk and Isaac had even come to blows on occasion, but, overall, their heated arguments had generally cleared the air for everyone. Right then, it was as if Isaac's spirit had bled out of him.

In the days since the *DarkHorse* regiment was made official, enough escaped slaves had made the perilous journey, joined by free black volunteers, to build their unit up from a dozen men to nearly sixty, with more arriving daily. Of the freedmen who joined them, a number were fairly well-educated. A few were professional men, determined to face the hazards of war in order to show they were men-in-full, equal to anyone, and patriots worthy of citizenship in the land where they were born. Now Isaac's actions seemed to imperil everything they'd worked for.

Big Josh stopped pacing to stare down at Isaac, then turned to Durk. The two men shared a quizzical, silent exchange. Over the years, the two had bonded, progressing from antipathy to sympathy to trust. Now they felt like brothers, acknowledging and appreciating the other's strengths.

"What you s-say h-happen, Durk?" Big Josh asked.

"Isaac came into our tent," Durk replied. "Woke me up talking all kinds of strange things — crazy things, like his knife is 'Satan's sword' and 'gotta kill them all.' Like that. His eyes were all wild, and he was splattered with blood. His blanket was still rolled up, so he must have been out all night. It don't look good, Josh."

Placing his hands on his hips, Big Josh turned back to Isaac. "And you s-say you don't remember nothin'? The whole n-night just gone out of your head?"

Isaac nodded in confirmation, still not looking up.

"Well, what *does* y-you remember? Come on, Isaac, tells me. I ain't foolin' around. Last night, you goin' to b-bed…"

Isaac's head sunk further down into his elbows, as if he had no muscles in his neck, struggling for composure. Finally, he was able to croak through a constricted throat, "Them voices… they start harpin' on me… harpin' and harpin'… saying mean things. I done heard them before, but not since I join y'all. Now they back," he added despairingly. He thought long and hard, his face twisted with concentration, but nothing seemed to come into his mind. "That's all I 'member, them voices."

"Voices?" Big Josh mumbled to himself, solemnly gazing at Durk. "Isaac's boat done drifted loose from its moorings."

Durk shrugged and sunk his forehead into his palm. "Maybe the thought of having to fight is bringing these voices back. Lately, he's been getting more and more shaky."

"If he killed a m-man, they c-come searching for him. Maybe we all get h-hung," Big Josh concluded. "Maybe lose our uniforms, get kicked out the army. We gots to turn him in, say the man's crazy, see?"

"Isaac couldn't kill any full-size man with a real damn sword," Durk interrupted. He gestured toward him. "Look at this whelp."

"What if he kill some soldier in camp, some white soldier — or maybe he ain't kill no m-man, Durk? What if he kill a w-woman? Or a chile off'n some farm here abouts?"

Hearing this, Isaac began to moan, rolling his head side to side. "Make 'em hang me, Josh. Please, please don't let 'em lock me up. I couldn't stand to be lock up," he pleaded, raising his head, searching their faces for sympathy. "Y'all shoulda just left me in the swamp." He fought to compose himself. "I was born to be alone," he said, lowering his eyes. "Born to be alone."

Durk stood to confront Big Josh. "I'm not turning Isaac in, Josh. He's our friend. He's a partner, too. He's *our* partner."

Yes, Durk and Isaac had suffered countless arguments. Both men were headstrong and outspoken. Yet deep in their hearts, Durk and Isaac shared the special bond of outliers, misfits.

"Durk, this come through the back door 'gainst us, and we protecting him, we be digging d-ditches again. Goodbye, Union Army."

"I'll get us out of it, Josh. You know I will. I always do," Durk said reassuringly, half-pleading.

Big Josh gave him 'the look,' meaning they both knew sometimes Durk talked them out of problems, but sometimes he talked them *into* worse ones. He shook his head no. "I can't conscience nobody innocent hanging for what Isaac done, Durk. It ain't right."

"All the innocent people already been killed by bushwhackers, Jayhawkers, too. Nobody will come looking here for the culprit. So much death everywhere. Besides, whoever he killed, we can't bring him back. We'll take care Isaac don't repeat anything like this. We'll tie him to the tent pole at night."

Josh put his finger to his chin and began to pace again, watched anxiously by Durk. Finally, his mind made up, Josh stopped, hovering over Isaac. "All right, Isaac, on your feet."

Isaac merely stared between his boots.

"I said stand up!" The big man grabbed Isaac under the arms and lifted him bodily like a rag doll, holding him suspended in midair until Isaac's feet were firmly under him.

"You turnin' me in?" Isaac asked resignedly.

"Shouldn't I? They maybe gonna hang s-somebody for this."

"Maybe I just kill a pig… or a dog," Isaac said unconvincingly.

"Maybe he killed a secesh bushwhacker," Durk added. "Isn't that what we signed on to do?"

Big Josh exchanged glances with Durk, then turned his attention to Isaac. "You do what I say," he stated firmly. "Take off your uniform. Take it off." He none too gently helped Isaac remove his clothes down to his skivvies. When that was done, Big Josh wadded the clothing up and stuffed it into Isaac's arms. "Now you take that uniform down to the crick and scrub it with lye soap. Your hands, too. Scrub and scrub till you get ever drop 'a blood gone. Ever drop. You hear?"

"Yes, sir," Isaac mumbled.

"Then you hang it in my t-tent — *my* tent. Then come back here and go to sleep. You been up all night, doing what, nobody know. D-durk will tell the captain you sick today — not that you ever be a d-damn bit of g-good when you well. You hear?"

Isaac nodded, eyes downcast.

"And if I catch you out this tent, I'm gonna break you n-neck and turn in your d-dead body. Hear me?"

"Yes, sir."

"Now, go on."

"What about my knife?" Isaac said.

Josh glared at Isaac angrily. "You ain't never gonna see 'Satan's sword' no m-more, Isaac. You ain't even getting no balls for your musket."

"But my knife," Isaac said urgently. "I gots to have…"

"Get outta here," Big Josh ordered, brooking no lip.

Isaac raised the tent flap and disappeared.

Big Josh thrust the knife deeply into the ground and worked it up and down, side to side, its blade hard against the earth with each movement, then examined

It. Satisfied the blood was gone, he widened the hole with his bare hands and buried the knife, covering it, making sure it left no mark. He stood atop the spot to seal its grave and addressed Durk, "If Isaac try to escape, they hang him."

"For desertion," Durk acknowledged.

Big Josh thought a moment. "If you wants to save Isaac, we gots to get the whole regiment outta here fast as we can."

"But we've got to be doing some kinda duty," Durk said, stating the obvious. "We're not deserting."

The pair thought a while, not hearing the birds chirping outside, welcoming the rising sun, nor the morning activity springing up noisily throughout the military camp. So here it was, time to fight. Durk had been at peace chopping trees and digging in the mud alongside his partners for the past two years. Now though, he struggled to steel himself against the fear screaming in his skull to flee to safety, to follow instincts culled over years of hard rambling. Without those voices of panic and terror directing him, he wouldn't have survived his past. So often during his travels, his feet had spared him from ignoble death, and he knew he would be useless in a fight. Moreover, he had never been one to accept responsibility willingly, but there was no good way to escape his obligation now. To choose otherwise would cut the cord to all he knew and cared about. No, he could never disgrace himself before his beloved Antoinette by quitting. Indeed, that would be worse than death.

In truth, he had only acted bravely — foolhardy, actually — once in his life, and that was his clumsy, albeit successful, attempt to rescue Antoinette from the French family in Mississippi. But now he had her, and any soldiering he did would only take him away from her, perhaps permanently. To join Grant's campaign to take Vicksburg would mean charging headlong into shot and shell. While his partners would willingly risk that, he didn't know if he could bring himself to do it. Perhaps there *was* a way to avoid suicide with Grant's Army.

"The colonel's looking for cavalry to fight guerrillas in Western Missouri," Durk stated their only feasible option. "They're pretty desperate. I think they'd take a colored regiment. They'd ship us by train from Macon City."

"I don't know, Durk. Bushwhackers? That's rough fightin'. You know they ain't gonna take none of us no prisoner if we caught. Didn't they find those two missing regular army pickets in that gulley with their heads smashed in?"

"Not too many of the prisoners our side takes make it to trial either," Durk said. "I hear the patrols talking when they come back to camp. 'Killed escaping. Killed escaping.' Last week, a Company C patrol brought back prisoners, and the captain was furious. 'Why weren't they killed escaping?' he scolded them. To hear him, you'd think the men who captured those rebels deserted in battle."

"They tell me Quantrill be collecting ears. Ears!" Big Josh exclaimed. "And the rebels be taking scalps. It's f-filthy fighting for sure."

"Our men carry scalps on their saddle bows, too," Durk said grimly. "It's rough times, I'll say that." Durk took a minute to think things over. "Look, Josh, we can't stay here. Word gets back to General Sparks that we've formed a black regiment, calling ourselves *white*, there ain't gonna be no more *DarkHorse*!"

"And they prob'ly ain't gonna be no more Captain Durksen Hurst neither. That man be mad at you. He take it personal that you trick' him!"

"See, Josh, if we get shipped to another district now, I can get us switched to a black regiment. That's how we voted, right? I'd just say, 'Well, you can see they're colored, right? Let's just fix up the paperwork.' If we stay here though, no telling what'll happen to us."

Josh shook his head. "I don' know h-how our partners gonna take fighting that b-bushwhacker war. We want to battle in the field, follow Grant, something respectable. Where they train us at?"

"Lawrence. Lawrence, Kansas," Durk answered.

Big Josh rolled it around in his mind, then said, resigned, "Well, don't matter how bad it is. Ain't we sign up to d-die? I think ever'body be willing."

The pair stepped outside the tent and paused to take a deep breath, soaking in the once-pristine, pastoral view of nearby poplar and pine and the plowed fields stretching to the rolling green hills in the distance… but the war had altered the view. The fecund land was pocked by burnt chimneys sunk among the flame-scarred, collapsed walls of abandoned farmhouses, by fields burned by neighbors who'd helped them raise their homes.

Big Josh sighed. "Well, l-le's go down to Hell with the devil."

CHAPTER FOUR

NO TALISMAN AGAINST HEARTBREAK

Antoinette DuVallier stepped from the medical tent into the early morning sunrise, weary and struggling against a dark despondency descending upon her. She had volunteered to sit with the drummer boy through the night as he suffered through his final malarial delirium, cleaning his vomit and listening to his babbling and intermittent cries to his mother. She had held his hand, applied damp cloths to his forehead against his burning fever, and cooed softly to soothe him, knowing he never heard a word as she watched the boy die, a long, long way from home.

She gathered her skirt and sat on the ground, her back against a large oak, bringing her knees to her chin and letting her head sink onto them. The tent-compressed odor of sickness and death, of blood and desiccating flesh clung heavily within her nostrils. The drummer boy's death touched off memories of her own son, Louis Edward, such a sweet child, only three, who died in Mississippi without her by his side to comfort him. He would have been seven by now, had he lived. The desire to cradle him in her arms overwhelmed her still, and the fact that she never would again drove a spike into her heart. She had to put these thoughts from her mind or else — or else she might grow as mad as her mother, as her sister.

Antoinette was heartbroken, yet she knew tears would not bring relief. She had only cried once in her life that she could recall, when she knew that Louie Edward was dead, and that merely consisted of a dry, momentary sob. She had not cried after she shot her husband, forsaking forever her life of privilege. As some cannot find comfort in church no matter how hard they try, no matter their prayers, she simply didn't have the capacity for tears.

She raised her head, trying to compose herself, searching the rows of tents of the newly-forming Ninth MSM Colored Cavalry, finally locating Durk's. At that moment, Durk emerged, looking uncomfortable and out of place in his captain's uniform, with Big Josh stepping out beside him. Both men's faces bore a serious mien. *What was Josh doing in Durk and Isaac's tent?* she wondered. *Especially at this ungodly hour of the morning? Something significant's about to happen.*

Since the *DarkHorse* men first put on their uniforms, she had known things were destined to change, and quickly. She had tried not to think of that certainty, to ignore the coming trials facing them, but Durk's and Josh's expressions meant that drastic exigencies were imminent. With *DarkHorse* now a military unit, she would be separated from Durk. Antoinette, who had lost so much in life — husband, child, position, respectability — was at risk of losing the only person she had left, and she didn't know how to bear their separation.

She studied him in the distance. Of all the men in the world, of whom she generally had her choice, what had made her fall in love with him, a rough, itinerant anomaly? Durk wasn't even handsome in the traditional sense, so what was it? In the past, she'd been pursued by handsome men, well-dressed and -mannered, and she found them all lacking. Far from sophisticated, Durk had become a voracious reader, albeit eclectic and limited to whatever books came to hand throughout his ramshackle life. Just what made her tie her life to his? Why him?

When they'd first met, Durk had been a fugitive, for what he'd claimed was an innocent misunderstanding. In retrospect, having seen the fixes into which his imagination and ambitions had led him, she'd come to accept that.

Antoinette watched Durk and Josh confer gravely, whispering and nodding. Durk hadn't wanted *DarkHorse* to become a military regiment, but he had gone along with his partners' wishes, reluctantly taking on the rank of captain. Now, beset by doubts, he was stuck in a role for which he was entirely ill-suited. She was grateful that Josh would be there to guide him. But knowing she wouldn't be there to steady him made her fear for his sanity and safety, for his life — and for hers, as well.

***

Throughout the camp's orderly rows of tents and haphazardly discarded backpacks and arms, Union soldiers in various states of dress went about their morning business: working cook fires, cleaning their guns, shaving, playing checkers, and making music. The early breeze carried the dense scent of morning's meager fixins to their nostrils, and Durk and Josh suddenly realized how hungry they were.

Durk's eyes scanned the camp for the nearest cook fire, seeking Antoinette. She was not among the dark-skinned women in their headscarves and burlap dresses, busily preparing breakfast, stirring pots, and adding kindling to burning pits. Finally, he spotted her seated near a medical tent and felt the euphoric warmth the sight of her created in him. Thick, long, black hair, large, dark, expressive eyes, rich, broad lips, and her sculpted face, to Durk her refined sophistication belied her simple gingham dress. Antoinette's beauty stunned his inner senses every time his eyes lay upon her or his heart brought her to mind.

Durk shook his head in wonderment. As a woman married to a wealthy public figure in New Orleans, Antoinette had servants to prepare her meals, dress her in the finest gowns and jewels, and organize her expansive book collection: volumes with leather covers bearing gold-engraved titles. She'd read so many in her lifetime, so many. Yet in her youth, she had known hunger and abandonment, worn rags, and slept upon bare floors under torn blankets. He was in awe of her strength but fearful, too, of her vulnerability to bouts of melancholy.

Recently, in the increasingly rare times they had managed to be alone together, he had lain beside her, his lips touching hers, his body melting into her miracle of soft skin, tanned brown by the sun. Now he would have to separate from her, and it hurt. Loneliness, his lifelong tormentor, would return to plague and perhaps cripple him. He hadn't felt pain in his heart like this since his mother's death when he was six. The urge to take Antoinette's hand, to lead her away and escape his promises to his partners of joining the Union Army, to ride west, north, anywhere, pulled so hard at him, he felt sure he would succumb. Until now, the relief of being on the road with Antoinette, free, seemed like a safe port amid a squall at sea. But what would she think of him if he asked her to flee with him?

"What we gonna do with the womenfolk?" Big Josh asked, breaking into Durk's thoughts. "Get them to St. Louie? They be safe there."

St. Louis! Durk knew that a worldly woman like Antoinette would always float to the top, like cream in a milk bucket, as she had in New Orleans. She had no reason to wait for him. In St. Louis, there would be numerous opportunities to abandon him: men of fine breeding, politicians, wealthy merchants, lawyers, generals. Any of them would be gratified to entwine with such a remarkable woman. And who was he? A lowly captain subsiding on soldier's pay, fronting for a company of former slaves.

Big Josh studied the suddenly inarticulate Durk, realizing the man wasn't able to fathom separating from his woman. But they had come this far, had worked hard to thrust themselves into the war, and no woman could share their fate on the battlefield. "Durk, can you get a paper so our women can work for the army in St. Louie? Least they wouldn't starve."

As soon as Antoinette traveled to St. Louis, Durk anguished, *we would be trundled off to Kansas, three hundred miles west of there. Hundreds of ruthless raiding parties would lie between us like gators beside a river. And after we train in Lawrence, who knows where our unit will be sent?*

Big Josh laid his thickly muscled arm around Durk's shoulder and looked him in the eye. "You go on and t-tell her, Durk," Big Josh said in his fatherly manner. Durk shrugged, staring at the ground, resisting even the thought of the terrible duty before him. "G-go on. You got to."

Durk acknowledged his compliance with a reluctant nod, still unable to meet Big Josh's gaze.

"I' t-tell the men where we goin'," Big Josh assured him. "They ain't gonna be happy 'bout it."

***

Sitting on a fallen tree beside a rippling stream, in the shade of a spreading poplar, Big Josh looked into Ceeba's eyes. He saw the hurt there, knowing his decision to send her to St. Louis was the cause.

You condemned to lose every good thing that comes into your life, he thought bitterly — *especially if your skin is black. Every little thing you need, that you love, ripped from your heart.*

Josh remembered the day so long ago on General's plantation when he'd learned his so-remarkable son, a young man of much promise, had been killed trying to protect a woman of dubious white color. He remembered, too, when his wife of eighteen years, the boy's mother, had died, probably from a broken heart. After he lost the two of them — the entire substance of his life — he had accepted that he was doomed to never again know love nor the contentment of companionship. He knew his soul would never heal.

Then stranded in the swamp years later, the others had convinced him to visit the quarters on the French plantation on a surreptitious excursion. And there was Ceeba, a shining light come into his life. Now he knew that even that bit of grace was fleeting, as well. He would likely be separated from Ceeba until the end of the war. In fact, with so many unknowns before them, it was likely he'd never see her again.

He studied the face he had grown to love. Ceeba was a substantial woman, with soft dark skin, tender lips, and laughing eyes that sparkled as with a discovered happiness. She possessed a nurturing soul and an outgoing spirit to embrace the whole world, and him, too.

"I ain't going to no St. Louie, Josh," Ceeba asserted stubbornly. "These women here wants to be with they men."

Big Josh shrugged, picking at bark on the trunk where they sat. Finally, he spoke plaintively, "Do you th-think I don't want you with me?"

"Why can't we go to Kansas with y'all?" Ceeba pleaded.

"The army won't let you stay with us, Ceeba. We soldiers now. We be training to f-fight. 'Sides, we gots to pass through Western Missouri. The whole place swarmin' with bushwhackers that'll kill anybody don't suit them."

"We ain't afraid, Josh. We ain't."

"Honey, word is they planning to attack Kansas. They done it before, kill ever'body in sight, then ride back to Missouri. I just want you safe, Ceeba. You gotta tr-trust me on this."

Resigned, Ceeba kissed him on the cheek, then sat back to gaze at his face, knowing she wouldn't see him again for quite some time… if ever. For her, the future entailed nothing but questions, fatal questions.

Big Josh took her hand in his, and swallowed hard. "I'll think about you ever d-day till this war over," he said mournfully. "And I'll find you somehow."

"Just come back alive," she said quietly, a tear running down her cheek. "That's all I cares 'bout, Josh. Just come back to me."

***

Durk strolled beside Antoinette through the shaded orchard, shyly holding her hand. He was about to lose her. Durk was speechless, an extreme rarity for him. "I don't want to go west," he admitted, "but I can't let them hand over Isaac." He didn't tell her that if they stayed, his wrong-colored cavalry scam might lead him to prison or even a firing squad.

Antoinette stopped in her tracks, and Durk faced her. "I know you don't want to," she said, "but you know you must."

He gripped her hand tightly, urgently. "Let's find the chaplain and have him marry us, right now, before I'm transferred."

Antoinette stared him down. "You know we can't do that, Durk. Not here in Missouri, at least not until the war's over. Maybe not even then. That could mean prison for both of us. But you know how I feel. We're married already. Let's just take each other on our word like we've been doing. We love each other. That should be enough." She studied his crestfallen expression, knowing what troubled him. "I will wait for you until the war's over, of course. Till death do us part. I will, Durk."

Having heard her reassurance, a great weight was partially lifted from his shoulders. He sighed, struggling to convince himself that what she said was true. "Or till my death parts us," he said.

"That won't happen, Durk," she said hopefully, but not convincingly. "Just be careful."

***

"We is all doom to die!" a despondent Old Moses exclaimed to Durk. "Doom."

Old Moses hadn't been at breakfast that morning when Big Josh broke the news that the *DarkHorse* regiment had the chance to begin their military careers in Lawrence. With Durk and Big Josh in agreement, it wasn't long before the entire squad reached a consensus to approve it. That's the way they did things. Now Durk had found the gray-haired old man sitting outside his tent, his hands trembling as he looped and tied string through keys spread out on the table, jabbering some kind of nonsense.

Durk called out to Josh, who left off packing his gear to join the pair. Old Moses was the anomaly among Durk's partners. While the others had worked as field slaves on General's place, Old Moses had been a house servant and bearer of the General's liquor cabinet key and of the General's jug when he traveled. As was typical, the field hands looked down upon the house slaves, and in return, the house servants felt superior to the field hands. Both groups looked down upon impoverished southern whites, some of whom survived on an even poorer diet than did the half-starved slaves. And, of course, whites returned the disdain toward a slave people with black skin. The Old South was a mutually contemptuous society, with repressed anger beneath every encounter, awaiting only a spark.

"Moses," Durk said, "we've been looking for you. Where you been all morning?"

"We g-gonna send you to St. Louie with the womenfolks, Moses," Big Josh said brightly, knowing the old man hated army life and, with only servant skills, had never been much use to the *DarkHorse* cause anyway. His duties, irregular as they might have been, had been mostly as an easily-sidetracked, last-available messenger. He had his own enterprises about the camp, which kept him absent frequently, and he was seldom missed. "St. Louie. Ain't that great, M-moses?" Big Josh added.

"And Bammer liberated a suit for you. You won't have to wear no uniform," Durk said.

"Doom," Moses repeated, terrified. "We is doom."

"What is he ranting about?" Durk asked in frustration.

"Why w-we doom, Moses?" Big Josh asked.

"Cause my keys done lost they magic, is why," Old Moses replied. He reached into his shirt and pulled out a key on a string, displaying it. "Um-hmm. Lost they magic."

Durk and Big Josh exchanged puzzled glances. "Where you get them keys, Moses?" Big Josh asked.

"Back near Fulton, done trade a jug of 'shine to a white man for them. Then had a witch pour spirit water on them. You wear one, the war can't kill you. See? Been sellin' faster than my soap. But now they ain't magic no more, and I ain't seen the old witch since Callaway County. Maybe she fly to the moon and not come back, like she say she will."

Big Josh gave Old Moses his stern look. "You sneak over to see that young girl like I told you not to, didn't you?"

Moses cast his eyes down to the table, unable to withstand Josh's glare.

"And her grandma catch you, ain't that it?"

Moses nodded affirmation. "She tell me to look under my tent flap in the morning," Moses croaked. "She say if it there, we curse. All us gonna die in the war."

"And what you find under the t-tent flap?" Josh inquired, trying to suppress a grin.

Moses held up a straw doll-like figure. "Just like she say, it there this morning. So's my keys done lost they magic."

"I can fix that," Big Josh said. "Durk, spit on this doll."

Durk spit on it.

"If it burn with Durk's spit on it, the curse be gone. Understand?"

Moses nodded, not entirely convinced. Big Josh walked to the nearest cook fire, knelt, and held the straw doll in the dying embers until it caught, then blew on it until it burst into flame. He displayed the burning doll to Moses, then threw it into the pit. Satisfied, he returned to Durk and Moses.

"No m-more curse," he said to Moses. "Now you put on this suit and pack your things right away if you want to go to St. Louie."

Old Moses nodded gratefully.

"Why are you stringing up them keys?" Durk asked.

"I gonna give one of them keys to all our boys come to Missouri together," Old Moses replied, "so's they won't get kill in the war."

Big Josh and Durk made eye contact. *If only it were that easy.* Well, at least they'd find temporary safety in an abolitionist town like Lawrence.

CHAPTER FIVE

A MALEVOLENT HAND

Camp Macon, Eastern Missouri

Devereau French and Robert Sterling cantered swiftly up the neat rows of tents in the Union Army camp, escorted by a mounted, uniformed cavalryman. Devereau's brown tweed suit and bowler hat were in stark contrast to the blue uniforms surrounding her.

Devereau slowed as she approached the colonel sitting with open collar at a table in a clearing outside his tent, which was larger than the rest. Twenty feet from the colonel, she drew rein, her stallion skidding to a halt. Displeased with being stationary, the grand beast restlessly pawed the ground, snorting and pulling at his halter, until he was finally disposed to settle.

The Indian drew rein alongside her and settled back in the saddle, wiping his brow with his sleeve.

Following closely, the Union cavalryman halted near the two interlopers and saluted smartly. "Man from Cairo to see you, Colonel," he said.

An odd pair to be in a Union camp, the colonel surmised. *Who is this foolish-looking dandy?* The young man on the white seemed too small to handle such magnificent horseflesh, but there he was, sitting naturally in the black saddle, in complete control of the animal. The colonel hoped the civilian wasn't connected to any politician or newspaper. You couldn't swat away those pests as easily as you could horseflies. He folded the map before him once so the stranger couldn't see his markings and shifted his considerable weight in his seat.

Seeing they had the colonel's attention, without a word or exchanging a glance, both strangers dismounted simultaneously, as if reading each other's thoughts. Devereau saluted crisply and approached the table, removing her hat to reveal her short-trimmed auburn hair. Her companion stayed behind, sullenly holding the horses' reins, his teeth clinched, a glint of anger in his large brown eyes.

"Let's see your papers," the colonel growled.

Devereau withdrew papers from her jacket, unfolded them, and laid them on the table. "I'm sent by the provost marshal in Cairo, Colonel," Devereau declared with a distinctively slow, Southern drawl. "I'm seeking a man named Durksen Hurst. He sometimes goes by the Indian name of Dark Horse. I am told he mustered into your company with a gang of coloreds."

This man must be a lawyer, the colonel suspected. *This is worse than political falderal or snoops from the press!* Made suspicious by the man's syrupy accent, the colonel pursed his lips thoughtfully and stroked his long black beard. He didn't trust Southerners, especially flowery-dressed ones who were most likely slave owners. And the Indian looked sinister. Reassured by his nearby pair of guards, the Colonel felt safe, so he signaled for the cavalryman to depart. The cavalryman saluted perfunctorily, turned his mount, and galloped off.

"Have a seat," the colonel grunted. "What do you want with this Hurst fellow, Mister..." He studied the documents. "Mr. French?"

"There's a warrant on his head, Colonel. For murder," Devereau warned. "Same for his woman. Goes by the name of Antoinette DuVallier."

Meanwhile, Robert Sterling gripped the reins tightly, his stone face expressionless, as an Indian culturally not given to smiling foolishly as did the white man. Without moving, his eyes surveyed the grounds around the colonel. *Two guards, one vigilant, one half-asleep on his feet from drinking the night before. White men are so easy to read.* He subtly slid his hand to his knife.

Robert did not like that Devereau had insisted they come east into the den of the bluecoats, claiming knowledge of Dark Horse being at the Union camp. It felt like being tied up and thrust into a cage or jail cell. If danger threatened, he would not hesitate to spring onto Devereau's faster white stallion and be off without waiting for her to mount. Let her fend for herself. Besides, riding his mare, she would offer the easier target, like having a shield on his back. A ball from behind would serve her right. After all, she'd made the decision to come to this place.

He would survive this. On the ride to the camp, he'd noted a rich canopy of forest lining both sides of the road. The smell of the earth and the dusty, haphazard brush, the fragrant green leaves and rotting fallen trees had taken him home, to a place natural to him. He knew once he galloped past the perimeter tents, the bluecoats wouldn't have the slightest chance of catching him on foot, especially with him riding the white. If Devereau could keep up, fine. She'd kept up well enough riding the white when they'd fled other dangers, even killers, before. Now she'd have to catch him on the dark mare. He wasn't going to wait for her.

If she was captured and discovered to be a woman, perhaps they would hang her for spying. There were many female spies in Missouri's Little Dixie. That's how the guerrillas acquired most of their intelligence on Yankee movements. No doubt she had a story and a forged document prepared for this scenario. He had warned her that her gambit could result in a noose, but her single-minded pursuit of Dark Horse and his woman knew no reason, no boundaries.

She claimed that when Dark Horse fled Mississippi, he had made off with over a hundred thousand dollars in large-denomination Confederate bonds, now worth a fraction of their value, plus an untold cache of gold coin swindled from her mother. A dubious tale at best. He wondered if this story was a fiction she created to stay his knife when they finally captured the man. Devereau also claimed that, like him, she was possessed by an overwhelming need for revenge against Dark Horse, and he accepted her word on this. Usually.

Yet Robert often found himself troubled, wondering whether Devereau was, in fact, truly motivated by that money and by bloodlust, or by some other notion. Lately, he'd been tormented by nightmares wherein she had some other purpose for pursuing the man: that she secretly harbored a devious, unspoken scheme, but kept it to herself because she feared his knife. Sometimes when he looked into her eyes across the campfire at night, he had the sensation she was seeing Dark Horse, not him. He shared her greed. He embraced her vengeance, too, hungering for the satisfaction of seeing Dark Horse lying dead at his feet. Indeed, were it not for Dark Horse, he and Devereau would be living in comfort right now in the old French mansion in Mississippi, waited upon by slaves, with slaves working the fields for them... with the bonds and gold locked safely away.

If she did have another motive — if she was lying to him — well, his knife had drunk much blood. And like a drunk, its blade was as thirsty for two as it was for one. Sometimes he wondered which of the two he would rather see bleeding in the dirt: Dark Horse or Devereau? When Dark Horse was finally cornered, he would not let Devereau stand behind him, that was certain.

It appeared that Devereau was having difficulty convincing the bluecoat chief about something, and Robert could hear their voices rising in anger. He gripped higher on the stallion's reins, then silently sidled within leaping distance of the sober guard. If the Union chief cried out for help, a single, quick knife-stroke to the man's throat would incapacitate him. If it felt necessary to neutralize the hung-over private, it would be simple to snatch the man's rifle and club him with it. Most likely, he wouldn't have to bother with the weak one. Either way, he would then leap onto the white horse and be gone. He would show Devereau the courtesy of shouting for her to run. But she would have no call to be bitter about being left with the mare. He had warned her.

Gradually the voices, while still tense, grew less loud, less urgent. After a few minutes of heated discussion, Devereau stood abruptly and saluted the white chief, spun around, and stomped angrily back to join Robert. He handed her the white's reins, then swept up briskly onto the mare's back. A frustrated Devereau mounted the stallion beside him.

He wondered what the problem was. Devereau's papers appeared to be official, and white men will always believe the paper, no matter how great a lie it told. Of course, he himself knew better than to trust the white man's papers. He'd learned that bitter truth the hard way.

"They shipped Hurst to Lawrence, Kansas, for training," Devereau spit. "He's already gone."

"Then we must ride west."

***

Central Missouri

They arrived at the small rural bridge where they had planned to cross the Missouri River, only to find it had been burned by bushwhackers, and the army engineers hadn't yet shown up to repair it. Nonetheless, Devereau's Union papers got them across the guarded bridge a half-day father west, near Columbia.

Robert studied Devereau beside him on the stallion, her bowler hat caked with trail dust, her cheeks a blushing apple red in the bright sun. He'd often seen her at night unwrapping and removing the band around her chest, allowing her round breasts to burst into bloom like flowers. Looking directly at her now, he strained to see the woman as she truly was, though she was immediately before his eyes. Rather, as the road stretched endlessly ahead, he envisioned her face transformed into that of a young girl of six, the age he'd first met her. Then her freckled, ivory face dissolved into that of an awkward adolescent, lean and delicate. As they rode together, he saw the many incarnations in which he'd known her, fading in and out from one to the other randomly, like an evil spirit residing in a campfire flame. Deceiving those around her, seeming not to be herself, had always been her greatest power.

The horse's steady rolling pace in the warm sun along the country road lulled him deeper into a dream state. Robert gave in to the rhythm, releasing the bird of his soul to fly above his many years, viewing them as if he were a disembodied spirit. As in an ancient nightmare, in tumbling flashes through the eyes of a small child, he saw his Chickasaw parents murdered, shot bloody with the muskets and pistols of the white men. He tried to remember what his name had been then, but his true name had long ago escaped into the swamp.

He saw the small country church where Reverend Sterling and his wife took him in, a wandering three-year-old near death. He smelled the church's musty books, felt the preacher's switch and rod against his back, buttocks, and face. Heard the woman's harsh voice chastise him, "Robert Sterling! What have you done? Damn you to hell, you ignorant savage!" Yes, Robert Sterling. Though it was not his own, he could not escape that label.

Then he was bought by Devereau's mother to be Devereau's constant companion, her shadow. It had always bothered him that he never knew what Mrs. French had paid for him. How much were his body and his spirit worth to the wealthy widow?

As Devereau's shadow, he was privy to their secrets, mother and daughter, a ghost lurking at the door of their private bedrooms overhearing their never-ending quarrels. As Devereau's shadow, he took supper with them on the rare occasions they ate together, sitting at the foot of the long table in the formal, first-floor dining room. At night, he slept on a pallet in the hall outside Devereau's bedroom, sharing her dreams and her nightmares as she dwelt in the spirit world.

Yes, Robert Sterling had been invisible to the white man and intended to remain that way, an anonymous creature scurrying underfoot. Invisible, yes, and by necessity, absolutely silent about French family matters, even to the house servants. Mrs. French repeatedly warned him that if he ever spoke about French business to anyone, black or white, he would be sold off to work the sugarcane fields in South Carolina. Such a fate would be certain death for him, a mere boy, under the lash and the prevailing hardship, as it was for so many grown black folks far stronger than he. So, he learned not to speak to anyone but Devereau. For all intents and purposes, to others, he was a mute.

Even then, he was more than Devereau's shadow. Far more. Living intimately with her, being her daily companion for six years of her childhood, indeed, for seven of his own, he knew what she was thinking when they were together, as he often did even now. It always felt as if he and Devereau were one soul in two bodies. One spirit in two animals. One spirit at war with itself.

He spurred the mare. They must make haste to meet up with the bushwhacker leaders. Once there, Devereau must bend them to her will, must make them into her pawns in order to trap Dark Horse. They must not waste daylight while the sun was shining warmly on prospects for a profusion of blood.

***

The moon, in its final, darkest phase, drifted behind the rolling clouds as if finding a secluded spot to prepare for death. Devereau French lay upon the twig-covered stream bank under a mature oak, wrapped tightly in her blankets, staring at the night sky. Above, as the clouds arrived, the multitude of stars on the vast black canvas steadily winked out. She glanced aside at the pit, but the fire, hours dead, offered no comfort. Restless and troubled, she shifted her weight, as the twigs underneath her crackled in protest at being disturbed.

It was going to be another endless night of lying awake, unable to sleep, and she was too cowardly to seek the permanent rest she so desired. Her mother had never trusted her with a pistol, fearing she would take her own life. But that precaution had never been necessary. She never had and never would have the courage to kill herself. Death, though always welcome, refused to visit uninvited.

Thoughts assaulted her from every direction that she couldn't fight off. She tried to distract herself, to force her few, wrenchingly rare, warm memories into her consciousness, but inevitably they succumbed to her implacable legions of sorrow, like a handful of peasants against a Mongol horde. Tears began to cloud her vision, and her chest tightened in her attempt to hold back the heaving sobs. She glanced at Robert Sterling to make certain he couldn't hear her. But Robert, his teeth clinched and fists knotted, was thrashing about in one of his frequent nightmare battles against his multitude of enemies — enemies still living and those murdered by his own hand. As his death struggles raged, Robert groaned, twisting, turning, and kicking off his blankets.

Devereau's mind drifted home to Mississippi, to Turkle. She heard the voices of the townspeople whispering that she was 'the loneliest man on Earth.' Walking to church alone, she could almost taste their fear that a wrong word spoken to her could get back to her mother. Because of that fear, she never had a friend, not one.

Then she was standing in the upper hallway of the French family mansion, hearing the creaks and crackles of its ancient wood, the squirrels skittering across the roof, smelling its mold and mildew. She couldn't tell if she'd fallen asleep and dreamed herself there or if she was merely half-asleep, remembering…

She was closeted in her room, which always felt like a prison cell. Freeing herself, she drifted through the dark, empty hallways to her mother's suite, the ghosts of avaricious, lustful French ancestors taunting her the whole way. As she passed, nameless servants smiled at her, their sphinx-like faces grinning masks worn to a funeral. The armed guards Mrs. French kept stationed around the property like wooden chess pieces on a board tipped their hats to her, then quickly turned their backs. She could hear them all laughing. Laughing at her.

Then she was with dear Louie Edward. She could see his sweet face, smell his child's odor, feel his soft skin, hear his melodious voice. She felt his warm hug against her breast. And then just as suddenly, he was gone.

She shook herself awake, suffocating from her hopelessly lonely life. The night she learned he was dead, she knew she was trapped forever in solitude. If only her mother had allowed her a pistol, she might have found the courage to join the boy. *If only.* She tried to dispel memories of the child. She had to, or she would go mad. She wouldn't allow herself to consider Antoinette's feelings either, half-sister or not. She couldn't.

Devereau glanced at Robert Sterling, his hands strangling some haint in his blankets. Her companion now. He appeared to be a strong, well-proportioned man, but she knew he could never save her from the endless longing she was fated to endure.

Her thoughts leapt to that moment back home. She lay on her stomach, hidden by brush in the swamp, peering through her brass spyglass at Durksen Hurst without his shirt, chopping wood into shards for the kiln fire, sweat pouring down his body. He wasn't especially attractive. He wasn't muscular like Robert Sterling, lean but not as tall. His long black hair fell into his eyes. And his suit, which she'd seen him wear in town, was a joke. But in that instant, she wanted him more than anything in the world.

Still restless, Devereau rolled onto her side and felt for her pistol in the dark. When she located it, she fondled it and pressed it to her cheek. Then, as on so many nights, she put it into her mouth, yearning, hoping for it to fire accidently. The pistol was cold, hard, and tasted of metal. She sucked on it like a baby. But as always before, it failed to fire. As always, luck was never with her.

CHAPTER SIX

THE DIE IS CAST

Macon City Station, Central Missouri

Washed by the bright sun pouring onto the Macon City Station platform, Durk gave Antoinette a kiss on the check. He then offered her a hand up into the main passenger car of the Hannibal & St. Joseph, which would take her and the other women to the end of the line at St. Charles, a half day's wagon ride west of St. Louis. She'd purchased her ticket at the window, being the only one of the entire *DarkHorse* group with any money. Union soldiers had robbed all the men during their trek north, but out of courtesy and because Antoinette exuded a sense of intimidating, superior station, she hadn't been searched and robbed of her share of the partnership's gold. Throughout their two years in Missouri, she had husbanded whatever money she had left, reserving it for extreme emergencies. But with a group of thirteen men, a dozen women, and children, she had only a little paper currency left to last until the end of the war. And that distant dawn was not even a speck of light on the darkening horizon. For all anyone knew, the sunshine of peace would never appear again, and the country would remain plunged into perpetual darkness.

Nearby, the white soldiers examined the paperwork held by the black *DarkHorse* women, permitting each, in turn, to board. One by one, the women and children, who had been French family slaves in Mississippi, were waived through the line of soldiers. Unlike Antoinette, they had to scramble onto the train's flatbed car where, because of supplies filling the space, they were packed together so tightly that all of them could not sit at one time. In great discomfort, they grumbled and complained, but the soldiers merely threatened to kick them off if they didn't quiet down. Once aboard, the women and children pressed to the rails of the car, waving their goodbyes and throwing kisses, shouting tearful words of endearment to their men left behind. The men, wearing fresh, new blue uniforms, blew kisses back and waved. It was a bitter parting.

Little Turby's young chin trembled, but his youthful betrothed maintained an erect posture and a strong face to demonstrate her courage, to show him that she believed they would be together again. Someday. But Little Turby couldn't stop the tears from flowing. His eyes grew so full that he could no longer see her, and he had to remove his glasses to wipe his eyes with his uniform sleeve.

Durk regretted that he'd only been able to acquire a limited number of passes. Some of the other black women who had fled to the Union camp recently, many with children and grandchildren in tow, had no papers and only managed to escape Missouri's slave laws because their men were now active in the *DarkHorse* unit's three squads. Now these women pushed and shoved toward the train in an unruly mass, pleading with outstretched arms to be crammed onto the overfull flatbed. But lacking signed papers, they were condemned to remain behind. The soldiers standing in their way were not gentle in suppressing the women's disorderly clamor, using their rifles as barriers, and as clubs when necessary, to deny them access.

When the women realized their fate, they became desperate, frantic, feeling hopeless and deserted, not knowing what to do. Their chance was gone. By enlisting in the Union army, their men were legally free, but these women had no such status. When the eastbound Hannibal & St. Joseph pulled away, the women would be forced to return to the army camp where their lives would be at the mercy of ever-fickle edicts. Just a single order sent by a distant authority could instantly cast them and their little ones to the four winds, like leaves in a gale, to become easy prey in a land beset by horrors. Instant death would be only a drunken soldier or guerrilla away, slow death a matter of gradual starvation.

These women made haste to their men, crying and shouting, but there was nothing the men could do to alter their fate. The men were soldiers now, at the mercy of orders. Everyone surrounded Durk, pleading and shouting at once. Durk was backed against a tree by three of the women and had to be rescued by Big Josh. Within minutes, the remaining *DarkHorse* partners surrounded their two leaders, pushing the mob back, and it took Big Josh to calm things down.

When order was finally restored, the eastbound train chugged out of the station, headed for St. Louis. Durk watched Antoinette through the passenger car window until he could no longer see her face. Then, heart sinking, he remained on the platform, frozen, staring at the empty tracks as the train disappeared around the bend, listening breathlessly as the sound of rolling steel wheels faded. Yet even after the train's smoke had dissipated into nothingness and the locomotive sounds had died, he remained immobile, like some statue dedicated to forlorn forbearance, a tribute to every vain hope that had ever disappointed mankind.

At last, Josh gently took Durk's elbow and led him to where the men were gathering in small groups. There, the two quietly placed a comforting hand on each other's shoulder, sighing deeply, commiserating on what they'd both lost. Everything. Vanished. The women they loved suddenly at the mercy of a dubious fate. They exchanged a final, weary glance and shrugged, then turned to do their duty.

***

Central Missouri

Robert Sterling, crouched on his knees, added another shard of dry wood to the fire, and blew until it took. The night was warm, but when he was planning to stay up all night, he liked a fire to keep him company. A fire would tell him many tales throughout the long, dark hours. Tales as real as the dreams of sleep, and not as prone to nightmare.

He pushed himself upright and sat back against the sycamore, wiping his hands on his britches. Releasing his animal heart into the wilds for its nocturnal hunt, he took a moment to look skyward at the sparkling glitter spots on the black satin background. Comforted that rain would not hinder tomorrow's journey, he then proceeded to fill his pipe. When the bowl was well-packed, he stuck a twig into the fire until it caught and lit his tobacco. His body resting easily, he puffed the pipe into a glow, blowing out thick streams of smoke through his mouth and nostrils.

He studied Devereau, asleep under her blankets, her fair, freckled face resting on her black saddle. How her pale skin glowed in the firelight. He gazed deeply into the burning fire, demanding that its flames reveal their secrets. Would the fire tell him the truth about Devereau? Would it reveal whether, down the road, he'd be forced to kill her? Contemplative, he continued smoking.

He was a boy of eight. Mrs. French's agent appeared one morning bearing a new suit and shoes for him to wear, then took him away from the preacher's cabin in a buggy. It was a long ride through settled country he'd never seen before. They passed planted fields tended by both slaves and farmers, crossed running streams, and skirted thick woodlands. After five hours, the agent delivered him to the FrenchAcres *family mansion. The weathered, neglected monolith fronted by eight great columns was enormous, far exceeding anything in the hamlet from which he'd come, even the courthouse itself. But that was not what impressed him. Rather, when he entered the front door, he was struck by the sheer, cavernous emptiness of the place, as if the gargantuan house had died and its soul departed. His new store-bought shoes, clattering on the wooden floorboards, echoed into the depths of the dead structure. The entrance hall showed no sign of wear, no boot mud or heel scratches, no footprints in the layer of dry dust. The Living had abandoned the French residence.*

He and the agent were led into a parlor and seated on large, ornate chairs, then abandoned by the servant who'd answered the door. This room, too, was dead, with a chess table at its center, like a pit for dog- or cockfights.

Then Devereau's mother entered the parlor and stopped in front of him. Remembering the manners the preacher's wife had beat into him, he stood with hands to his side, studying her closely. She was dressed all in black — the only color he ever saw her wear during his six years there. Her hair was raven black, too, only slightly graying, long and flowing richly down her back. He thought how grand she looked, a woman in her middle years with large dark eyes. Mrs. French said nothing, but merely appraised him critically, as one would evaluate a prize horse or steer. She nodded to the agent, who tipped his hat in thanks and quickly left the house. Then without a word of greeting or instruction, Mrs. French disappeared back upstairs, leaving him confused, frightened.

Robert didn't remember how he learned Devereau was not a boy, nor exactly when, but at some point, he knew. He knew. She had begun to change from a child into a woman. He had grown to love her before the discovery, but somehow when he learned she was a girl, that love changed. And not in a reassuring way.

One night, he was half-asleep on his pallet in the hallway outside Devereau's door, where he always slept. Half drowsing, he listened to the storm and its intermittent lightning overhead. Devereau was thirteen, he nearly fifteen. Then without warning, Devereau called him into her room. Her voice was urgent, strained, unlike he'd ever heard her. He answered her summons in his bare feet, troubled by the fear in her voice.

"Lock the door behind you," she whispered harshly. "Come over here."

She was sitting on the edge of the bed, her feet dangling above the rug, wearing a delicate white nightgown. He had seen her in nightwear like this before. Nervous and confused, he mumbled that he was sorry and made to leave, but she ordered him over again, this time more loudly, more urgently. He walked to where she sat hesitantly, till he was standing beside her.

"Closer," she said. He inched closer, and then she reached out and pulled him roughly to her, until he could feel her cheek pressed to his chest. He was frightened, not knowing what to do, so he remained rigid, like a statue, his hands at his sides. Fears of the sun burning the South Carolina sugarcane fields

flooded his mind.

She stood up, so close he could feel her breath on his face. She took his hand in hers and placed it on the silky material covering her just-emerging, adolescent breast. He pulled his hand away like it had touched a burning stove and stood there trembling.

"Don't be afraid, Robert," she said, taunting him. Then she put her arms around his neck and pulled him to her. She studied his eyes, then kissed him on the mouth. He couldn't react. He didn't like the way she was mishandling him, with so much urgency in her voice.

Then she kissed him again, and he kissed her back, trying hard, obediently wrapping his arms around her, squeezing her body tightly against his own. He had never kissed anyone and felt terribly embarrassed. Their lips separated, and they examined each other's faces, faces they had known intimately since childhood.

At that moment, all the dreams he'd had about her made sense, especially the old ones, but also the disturbing, distorted new ones he'd had since he'd learned her secret. Then he knew. It was not this Devereau he loved; he loved the other one, the one from before. This Devereau holding him in an iron grip was like some animal version herself. He was repelled by her, sickened.

He had learned the truth of himself that night. Even if he could escape to freedom, to where other people lived and laughed, he knew he would always be alone, estranged from both black and white. A beast solitary, with horns or scales, in a world that would despise him.

Later that night, when he was sure Devereau had fallen asleep, he ran silently on bare feet down the long, dark hallways, the closed doors of empty rooms passing on every side. He made it to the back stairs and tiptoed down to the kitchen, where he slipped a big knife into his belt. Then he sneaked out the back, into the rain, shutting the door carefully so it wouldn't slam.

Days later, he was near starvation when he came upon the Chickasaw village, where they took him in. There, he sought a new life. The woman who became his mother named him Wounded Wolf, and that was who he remained while he lived with the tribe.

Yawning, he added more wood to the fire and refilled his pipe.

CHAPTER SEVEN

AN EVIL WIND

Macon City Station, Missouri

Forty feet from the train station, Big Josh completed his instructions to the men gathered under the great oak. When he was finished, he nodded to Durk, who officially dismissed them. Relieved to be at ease, they began to scatter into small, familiar clusters under poplars and maples bordering the railroad tracks, reclining on the grass and sitting on knapsacks.

The break wasn't as peaceful for the recruits from Missouri and adjacent states, who brought their mates and families with them. The distressed women left behind by the train surrounded their men, pleading and crying to accompany them to Lawrence. Tears flowed freely as men, women, sons and daughters came to grips with their last hours together for quite some time. Maybe forever.

Durk stretched out under the oak, his pack a pillow beneath his head, and placed his hat over his eyes to block out the sun, hoping to catch a nap. In short order, the emotional chatter about him merged gently into a meaningless buzz, along with the sounds of songbirds and the military clank of marching feet, and metal slapping leather. Eyes closed, he drew Antoinette's face into his mind, attempting to memorize every detail. Knowing from long experience that even the most cherished memory fades, he was determined to hold her image as long as possible. Fades, yes. His mother, the dearest person in his life, died when he was only six, and her visage was no more than an idea to him now. He didn't remember what she had looked like and probably wouldn't recognize her if she magically returned from where he'd planted her. It had taken a whole day to dig the hole himself with a broken shovel, crying all the while.

Big Josh shook Durk's shoulder, but Durk brushed the hand away. Nonplussed, Josh removed Durk's hat from his face, startling him to consciousness with the mid-day glare.

"What is it, Josh?" he asked, annoyed by the disturbance.

"Get up, Durk. L-look," Josh urged, pulling Durk to a sitting position.

When Durk's eyes adjusted to the light, he saw where Josh was pointing.

Near the stairs to the station platform, two soldiers armed with fixed bayonets, directed by a major, were leading a dignified-looking black man wearing a long, formal, black coat and a white preacher collar. The prisoner shuffled along, hindered by shackles on his feet and hands. He was a man in his sixties, with a strong face and jaw, and mature gray hair. The soldiers sat him on the steps, then took seats above him on the platform.

"Let's see what this is all about," Durk said, rising to his feet. He brushed his uniform free of twigs and dust, and the pair, followed by Isaac and Little Turby, set out to intercept the procession.

Durk and Big Josh saluted the major, a young, clean-shaven man in his late-twenties. "What is this all about, Major?" Durk asked.

"Spy," the major replied. "For the secesh."

"Spy?" Durk exclaimed. "That can't be right."

"Oh, but it is," the major said. "Finally caught the man responsible for the death of my men. This is William Cambridge, Captain. He's the preacher for all the rich white planters around Macon City — has been for many years."

"Is that right?" Durk asked the prisoner. "You're the preacher for the planters?"

The man replied proudly, declaring, "That is correct. 'Let as many servants as are under the yoke count their masters worthy of all honor, that the name of God and his doctrine be not blasphemed.' Luke 6:1."

Josh was taken aback by the vehemence of this wholly unanticipated biblical quotation idolizing the master class. Durk was surprised, too. He'd known of only one other slave who was the preacher for rich planters in Tennessee, and that man, too, had been pro-slavery. The Tennessee preacher, called Bentley's Old George after his late-master, had been an expert in biblical exegesis and could out-debate any white preacher, even respected biblical scholars. The church members had tried to buy him — they'd been paying him seven hundred dollars a year — but Bentley's Old George had refused to be sold from his late-master's estate.

"Is you f-for or against slavery?" a bewildered Big Josh asked the man.

Like some prophet in the wilderness, the man rose and spoke forcefully, his deep voice booming his words to the three dozen uniformed men of the *DarkHorse* squads, then echoing in return from the distant hills. "What do scriptures tell us, brother? Recall Peter 2:18: *Slaves, obey your earthly masters with respect and fear, and with sincerity of heart, just as you would obey Christ.* Ye rebellious servants," he pronounced loudly to everyone, "return home to your good master or surely your immortal soul is in foul jeopardy of damnation and Hell."

Big Josh eyed Durk quizzically, and Durk shrugged. "He's for it," Durk said, shaking his head in disbelief.

Isaac, who had marched in contrite silence from camp to Macon City — a state wholly unlike the voluble firebrand — spoke up angrily. "What do you say, Mr. Preacher, 'bout my master whip me terrible? Even split my head. Is that what God want?" He rubbed the ridges of scars running atop his head.

"Remember Luke 12, my son. *And that servant, which knew his lord's will, and prepared not himself, neither did according to his will, shall be beaten with many stripes.*"

"You say he shoulda beat me?" Isaac screamed, infuriated. Fists flailing, he lunged at the preacher, determined to pummel him, but Big Josh caught Isaac in mid-flight and held him tightly to his massive chest until he calmed down.

The preacher fearlessly stood his ground, oblivious to the physical threat. "Remember your Exodus!" he proclaimed. *"When a man strikes his male or female slave with a rod so hard that the slave dies under his hand, he shall be punished. If, however, the slave survives for a day or two, he is not to be punished, since the slave is his own property."*

Hearing this, Isaac struggled with renewed fury to free himself from Josh's grip, but the big man was too strong, and eventually Isaac ceased thrashing about. Durk laid a sympathetic hand on Isaac's chest, and the hateful fires slowly dimmed from Isaac's eyes.

"These men aren't slaves under the law," Hurst interjected so everyone could hear him. "General Schofield says that any able-bodied colored man, slave or free, who enlists in the army shall forever after be free."

"Read your Leviticus," the preacher intoned. *"And ye shall take them as an inheritance for your children after you, to inherit them for a possession, they shall be your bond-man forever.* General Schofield is an apostate. *Forever*, sayeth the Lord, *forever.*"

But bright young Turby, who had dedicated himself to his books, especially his Bible, stepped forward. "Yeah?" he said. "What about Deuteronomy 23? *Slaves who have escaped to you from their owners shall not be given back to them. They shall reside with you, in your midst, in any place they choose in any one of your towns, wherever they please; you shall not oppress them.*"

The preacher opened his mouth to speak, but Durk held his hand up to forestall the argument. "Listen, Mr. Cambridge, William," he said to the preacher, "do you understand what is at stake for you here? They hang spies. Hang them!"

"A servant shall not betray his master," the preacher said firmly, with calm dignity as he tried to get up. One of the soldiers put his hand on the preacher's shoulder, and the man sat back down on the steps.

"It's very unlikely this old man is some kind of spy," Durk said to the major. "I mean, look at him."

"He is," the major said. "He was in camp preaching last week, trying to get the slaves to return home, trying to make my men kick them out of camp. I just let it pass. But then I sent a squad on a back trail to surprise suspected secesh sympathizers, and my men were ambushed. Murdered to the last man. He's the only one that could have gotten word to the bushwhackers."

"Is this true?" Durk asked the preacher who merely glared at Durk, refusing to reply.

The major spit over the railing. "Maybe he was responsible, maybe he wasn't. If he'd tell us who was, or who the secesh leaders are, I could just put him in prison. That's what I want to do, but he refuses to talk. If you can convince him, you'd save his life."

"Prison," Durk pleaded to the man. "The war will be over someday. You can go back to preaching."

"Remember your Proverbs," the preacher said. "*A friend loveth at all times, and a brother is born for adversity*. I will not forfeit my eternal soul to save my earthly body."

"N-no chance?" Big Josh asked the man.

"You will meet your adored Antichrist Lincoln in Hell," the preacher replied to Big Josh. Then, resigned to his fate, he turned his head away from the gathering, clearly unwilling to speak another word to anyone.

Big Josh eyed Durk, then side-by-side, they returned to the oak tree, unable to speak. Isaac and Little Turby followed in silence. The day no longer seemed bright, the world no longer green and hopeful. None of them glanced back, unwilling to look upon the face of the dignified man who would soon be swinging by his neck. Each knew they had witnessed probably the last black martyr to defend slavery, a man of God ready to sacrifice his life for the South's peculiar institution. And it hurt.

"I wish the train would get here," Little Turby grumbled under his breath.

***

Little Dixie, Central Missouri

The odd pair rode on, the sun directly overhead. The day was growing hotter as Robert Sterling removed his jacket. Devereau French, afraid her breasts might be noticeable, never did so in public. Sweat ran down her face and body, and she could smell herself, which never failed to bother her. They passed a "Jennison monument," a scorched chimney standing above a burnt home, so named after the fanatical Jayhawker leader, Charles "Doc" Jennison, whose men had burned the properties of so many Confederate sympathizers. Lately, with hostilities intensifying, it was impossible to tell whose side had burned which properties, nor whose blood was spilled. They had to be careful.

Under the noonday heat, Devereau and Robert passed exhausted, hungry families resting under shade trees alongside the road. Some ate what little they had; most had nothing. As they passed, the gaunt hollow faces stared blankly at the pair, numb to even the novelty of the two riders in city suits: one appearing to be a frail man on an impressive white stallion, the other a suspicious-looking Indian in shirtsleeves. Devereau rode up to a woman leading five filthy children of mixed ages, boys and girls, and handed her a canteen.

"We've got nothing left to steal," the woman told her, drinking thirstily, before passing the water to the children. "Young ones haven't eaten in two days."

"What happened to you?"

"Red Legs," she said disgustedly. "My husband had a certificate of loyalty issued by the army. Didn't matter. They took everything we had, critters, flour, money. Then they shot Hiram in cold blood and dumped him in the pigsty and set fire to the house. Now we ain't got nothing."

"Jayhawkers?" Devereau eyed Robert, who nodded in acknowledgement. "How long ago was that, ma'am? How far have you come?"

"It's been over a week," the woman replied. "You don't have anything to eat, do you?"

"I'm sorry," Devereau replied sympathetically. "But I saw a farmhouse about three miles ahead. Maybe they'll have something."

The woman shrugged, wiped the sweat from her brow with her skirt, and dragged her children onward. "With so many of us, people ain't so friendly no more," she said resignedly.

Farther on, Devereau and Robert rode up to a relatively prosperous-looking couple on foot carrying satchels, wearing store-bought clothes, wrinkled and dusty from travel. Devereau drew rein, then handed the man a canteen and watched him gulp the water down, before turning it over to his wife. "Where you from, mister?" Devereau asked politely.

"Westport, near Kansas City," the husband answered.

"Nice town. We stayed in your fine hotel there. Remember, Robert?"

"I do," Robert said.

"I owned a dry goods store, name of Joseph's. Maybe you saw it. Then regular Union soldiers came," the man said.

"Quartered themselves in our homes, stabled their horses in our parlors," his wife spit, admonishing God and the world in general. "Now, Westport's really nothing… nothing."

"Headed for the train junction?" Devereau asked.

The man nodded 'yes.'

Devereau stared hard at Robert, then quickly pulled her pistol. But the firearm, and the loud blast it might make, was unnecessary. Robert had already sprung from his horse and grasped the merchant from behind, poised with his knife to the man's throat.

"Red Legs of the Kansas Seventh Cavalry in the area," Devereau reminded Robert. "Take their money, valuables, and any firearms they might have. Then tie them up."

Robert quickly began searching their captive, his bronze face scowling with disappointment. "Red Legs can't question a corpse," he growled.

"Her screams might be heard. You do as I say."

***

Later that afternoon, a squad of eastbound cavalry wearing blue was approaching Devereau and Robert from around the bend. The lead officer, a man in his forties with a shaggy black beard, was clearing the road as best he could for his squad and baggage wagons to pass. He shooed the civilians aside as politely as possible, but his frustration showed through his every word and gesture.

Devereau watched Robert guide his horse into hiding nearby, within close shooting range, then waited in the road to allow the squad to reach her. Bushwhackers often wore the uniforms of dead Union soldiers to catch their prey off guard. This squad looked legitimate, but she wasn't going to show her hand or her papers until she was sure which side they were on. She made a mental note, *Confederate letter in the left pocket, Union documents in the right.*

Coming into view behind the mounted cavalry were six supply wagons skinned by black men and a large disorderly mass of blacks of every age and description. These soldiers were clearly genuine.

Devereau handed her papers to the officer. "What's going on up ahead?" she asked, indicating the direction from which so many were taking flight.

The officer examined her papers, then handed them back. "It's bad, very bad," the officer said. "The whole Missouri-Kansas border is meaner than a violated hornet's nest." He examined the road ahead, noting the number of people resting beside it. "All right!" he shouted. "Vittles! Skinners will distribute food supplies to the civilians first, then the Negros, before they themselves can eat."

The cavalry dismounted and led their horses to a grassy field beside the road. The squad quickly got busy collecting firewood, digging pits, tying up the horses, sending out pickets, and preparing a meal. The wagons followed, rumbling up to where the officer sat his mount. The black skinners then climbed into the wagon beds and waited. Seeing that food was to be handed out, the civilians quickly clamored around the wagons, their hands held out, to be given sacks of flour, beans, and hardtack by the skinners. Everyone would eat.

"Will you join me?" the officer asked Devereau. "We haven't eaten since sunrise."

"Thank you, I will," Devereau replied. She turned to signal Robert, but he was already pulling up beside her. "This is Robert Sterling, my Indian guide."

Without expression, Robert merely tipped his hat brim toward the officer, a gesture returned perfunctorily by the officer with a finger to his own hat. The three made for a large oak to set up in the shade.

Devereau and the officer filled their plates and coffee mugs and, once seated on the grass, began eating. Robert refused all food or drink with a wave of his hand, instead choosing to hold the horses' reins at a distance, near the road, silently watching the soldiers go about their business. He noted a break in the trees lining the east side of the field leading to a stream and determined to ride there on the white stallion in case of trouble. Devereau would just have to talk her way out of things. If they hung her for spying, so be it.

In her chat with the officer, Devereau learned that the man had been a lawyer in Illinois when the war had broken out. He'd acquired his military appointment through a county judge friend of the family who had known the Lincolns.

Devereau claimed that when she finished her business, she would be reporting directly to General Ewing, the man in charge of the region. After that, she hoped to meet Major General Schofield, the man above everyone. She asked the officer about their natures and listened to his exposition on their respective personalities, quirks, and strengths, seemingly enthralled by his contacts and erudition. Then the conversation turned to the war. Devereau asked the man what insights she could pass along to the higher ups.

"In these border counties, about two-thirds of the people are kin to the guerrillas," the officer groused. "Their families feed, clothe, sustain them, and supply them with intelligence about our movements. General Ewing has asked General Schofield for more troops, but every spare man is being funneled to Grant."

"Vicksburg campaign, eh? So what's being done?" Devereau queried. "Just in general," she added. "Mind you, I don't want any details." She figured this desire to avoid sensitive detail would lower the cavalryman's suspicions.

"There'll never be peace in this region," the man said glumly. "The guerrillas know they can't go home and live peaceably because the loyalists have suffered too many depredations at their hands. Yet with their families to support them, they'll never leave. The cycle of violence and revenge between secesh and loyalist civilians has become unbearable for ordinary people."

"What is Ewing doing about it?" Devereau asked.

"He received permission to deport the families of several hundred of the worst ones south, to Arkansas."

"Of course, they wouldn't send them north. The guerrillas would follow them. What about their slaves?" She looked him in the eye, searching for any deceit.

"Well, Ewing asked permission to free their slaves, too. Schofield sent off to Lincoln, requesting approval for the policy. From what I was told by a man who knows Ewing's aide, Lincoln spun one of his stories, naturally. See, there was an Irishman who promised his doctor he'd stop drinking. The Irishman asked the doctor for some soda water, asking that the doctor add a little brandy 'unbeknownst to him.' So, Lincoln's all for the policy if no one knows he's behind it."

"Well, I can imagine how the rebs took that," Devereau said, shaking her head.

"Right. So, Ewing issues Orders Nine and Ten. Under Order Nine, we're providing a military escort and provisions for the slaves of men who support the rebellion, taking them out of state where their masters can't get at them."

"That would explain all the geese in your flock," Devereau commented, nodding toward the collection of blacks eating nearby.

"Order Ten, now, empowers us to escort any loyal citizens to military stations or to Kansas for their safety. We were on that duty a few weeks back."

"That isn't the worst of it, though, is it?" Devereau prodded the conversation.

"No, not by a long shot. The wives and children of known guerrillas, including women who are heads of families and willfully engaged in aiding the guerrillas, are being notified to leave this district and move out of the state forthwith, along with their stock, provisions, and household goods. If they don't leave voluntarily, the local officers will forcibly remove them."

"That's sure to calm things down," Devereau quipped sarcastically.

"That isn't all. Order Ten directs us to arrest any person who aids the guerrillas, including any women not the head of a household."

Devereau whistled in amazement. "That's certainly a loaded shell waiting to explode."

"It *already* exploded. We're just waiting for the shot to tear through our guts."

"Why? What happened?" That got her attention.

"Well, even before the orders were issued, we arrested several women — relations to the guerrilla leaders. Bloody Bill Anderson's sisters, Josephine, Mary Ellen, and Janie; John McCorkle's sister, Charity McCorkle Kerr, and others. They commandeered a house in Kansas City owned by Elvira Thomas, the mother-in-law of George Caleb Bingham."

"The artist?" Devereau wondered aloud.

"That's him. Bingham's in Jeff City. He was selected to be state treasurer."

"Yes, I've met some of the Binghams," Devereau bragged. "What happened?"

"Well, there was a third floor added to the row house, and that's where they interred the women. But cracks in the walls began showing. The Union provost ordered an inspection, but before it was done, the house collapsed."

"And?"

"And the women were simply mangled, crushed. Josephine Anderson and four others were killed. Mary Ellen Anderson had both legs broken, her back injured, and her face was cut up something terrible. She'll never recover."

"The rebs won't be very forgiving."

"It's really stirred up now. We're just waiting for the Sword of Damocles to fall. There's already been a number of raids by the bushwhackers, but they're just beginning. I'm sure they're planning something big. *Big.*"

"What are you going to do?"

"Do? What can we do? There just aren't enough of us, is the problem. Ewing only has about seventeen hundred men spread out across the whole border region."

"You didn't tell me that," Devereau said. "Even though it's me, be careful you don't say anything that might be of use to the rebels."

"Believe me," the officer said, "the rebs know how many men we have and exactly where they're posted… or pretty close to it anyway."

***

Before supper, Devereau and Robert reached the place where the road forked. Robert Sterling turned his horse toward the left branch, but Devereau French told him they were heading to the right.

"Lawrence is that way," Robert stated. "Where are we going?"

"The hills near the Sni-A-Bar River, then on to Jackson County," Devereau stated. "Yes, we're going to Lawrence, but we're going to bring a little firepower with us."

"Maybe kill Dark Horse on the spot?" Robert Sterling asked hopefully.

Devereau French said not a word, her eyes narrowing.

"Or maybe you don't want to kill him," Robert said pointedly.

Hearing this, Devereau turned away.

CHAPTER EIGHT

BLOODY MURDER

Mexico, Missouri

The sunny afternoon was pleasant enough, but still too hot for comfort. Even with the windows down, the train car was oppressive. Antoinette watched the oak trees passing along the tracks, their limbs overhead the only breaks in the cloudless blue sky. The rich farmlands of Eastern Missouri stretched off to the horizon, broken only by scattered homesteads and patches of scrubland. She settled back and closed her eyes, resting her head on the seat, hoping the rhythm of the rolling iron wheels would allow her to find peace. But visions of Durk covered in blood, shot down in battle, continued to plague her.

With so many unknowns before her, a personal darkness returned to torture her again. Terrible memories re-emerged: the loss of Louis Edward, the uncertainties surrounding his death, and scars from New Orleans. She felt an overwhelming sense of abandonment and loneliness that would never heal. New Orleans, where her mother had sold her as a small child to a despicable, twisted man whom she'd been obliged to call Father. She'd only freed herself from him when she was fourteen, a tender age to be without security or any place to live in the Crescent City, with its busy docks and slave trade, yet she survived and prospered.

She thought of the women packed in the storage car, frustrated that she couldn't relieve them from their ordeal. They were her friends, her sisters. She'd spent two years in their company, along with Durk and his partners, but she was helpless to act on their behalf. She considered the irony of traveling in relative comfort in the train car, with her friends packed away like contraband a few cars behind her. What was the difference between them really? The tint of her skin? Of her mother's skin? Of a grandparent's?

She told Durk she would wait for him until the end of the war. But now that her prospects appeared so dim, her dilemmas so profound, could she deny herself relief from the hardship she was sure to encounter by remaining faithful to him? Or would she use all her cunning, all her assets, as a free creature not foresworn to any man? She knew from long experience that men's wills would melt in her presence, with even the most worldly and powerful moved to boyish awkwardness and tongue-tied incoherence by her mere presence. Men would always want to aid her. Would she forsake her high ideals and principled pride — abandon even love itself — and return to being that steel-edged wounded hunter, that hungry scavenger that stalks her victims day and night relentlessly? She had a soothing, reassuring answer to these questions now. But would simple necessity alter her resolve tomorrow?

Unable to rest, much less nap, Antoinette opened her eyes, hoping the bright day would blot out her dark thoughts. She looked around. The car was crowded with uniformed soldiers who had gracefully avoided the seat beside her, leaving her space and privacy. This was natural. She was accustomed to deference. Some of the soldiers were grizzled men in their thirties and forties, but most were fresh-faced boys. No matter, every single one was a veteran by now, hardened from months upon months of hunting guerrillas throughout Missouri and Kansas. Some had fought in campaigns in the border states, as well, in Kentucky and Tennessee. A few bore the evidence of wounds, wearing slings or having crutches leaning against the seat beside them. Their mood was peaceful, serene, clearly relieved to be escaping the fighting — if only temporarily.

The passing pastoral countryside was lovely, with clear rushing rivers and rich, broad fields, but Antoinette was already impatient with the journey, more than ready to arrive in St. Louis. She fixed the pins that held her long hair in a modest bun. Back in camp, she'd nursed soldiers badly wounded in battle after the surgeons performed their initial ghastly work: served them food, talked with them, wrote letters home for them, even cleaned their wounds and changed their dressings. She knew her soothing voice, her mere presence, was good for their morale. Even dressed in plain gingham and calico, her mere proximity gave the shy young men a momentary reprieve, a chance to forget their anguish, their lost hopes. Even so, there had been so much death from wounds, infection, green rot, and disease. *If only so many young men hadn't had to die before their time...* Death in Civil War Missouri was a glutton at a boundless feast.

"You from St. Louis, ma'am?" a soldier sitting across the aisle asked her politely, breaking her reverie.

She examined him. Young and rawboned, with short red hair and an innocent, freckled face, he was very much a rural boy. *He couldn't be more than seventeen.* Like most of the troops, this was probably his first time away from home. *Murder, massacre, desecrated corpses, what a heartbreaking way to experience the world.*

"No. I'm just going there to work with the surgeons," she lied, her words matching her paperwork. Her accent was a possible source of suspicion. "I'm originally from New Orleans."

"That's tough duty," the young soldier said. "I can't picture a lady like you doing that."

"I'm not sure I can either," she said with a chuckle that she didn't mean. "Where are you headed, young man?"

"Home. Nebraska, ma'am. Haven't seen my momma in two years," he said with a catch in his voice.

"I'm very happy for you," she said, her eyes wistful. *The boy should never have had to leave his family for such a dangerous task. He's still just a child.* "Do you mind me asking how old you are?"

"Seventeen, ma'am. But I'm going on eighteen," he said enthusiastically.

"So, you joined up at *fifteen*?"

"Sure did. To be with my older brother, Jim." He paused, growing quiet, then looking out to the countryside, said, "A Confederate bullet laid Jim under the ground near Springfield."

***

The unsuspecting town was easy pickings as the thirty-three mounted bushwhackers broke the still, peaceful afternoon. Dressed in irregular farm gear, a few wore regular army Confederate gray pants with a yellow stripe down the leg; a few sported jaunty, cavalier-like plumed hats. Their gaudy bushwhacker shirts of assorted colors were similar only in their many pockets for carrying ammunition. In a flurry of riding, shooting pistols into the air, whooping and shouting, they loaded up at the general store, savaging what they couldn't take, stole livestock, robbed everyone in sight, burned three homes, and shot three citizens whose looks they didn't much like. It was a hard and fast raid going very well. And then it got wilder. While some of the boys hauled railroad ties to block the tracks, one found a barrel of liquor sitting on the train station platform. Then everybody got drunk. Really drunk.

They wanted to bring some of the whiskey back for the hundred-fifty boys waiting at camp, but nobody could figure out how to carry it. Then another found a store selling boots, so they filled them up and tied them to their saddles. It was a stumbling, frantic exercise, with much spillage and laughter.

After a half-hour of this enterprise, they collapsed to rest a spell, confused and breathing hard: the liquor having made their heads an unquiet jumble. They weren't going to recover quickly from a drunk of this dimension. Then the lookout rode up, shouting that the train was coming. The men rose to their feet unsteadily, sore and stretching, and checked their pistols. Then they mounted up. Time to go to work.

***

When the train braked suddenly, the car lurched, throwing Antoinette and the other passengers forward, then back into their seats. Two men who had been standing went sprawling into the aisle. Soldiers cried out in pain and anger at the disturbance up ahead. Antoinette's wrist hurt after striking the seat in front of her, and it stung.

Without warning, the locomotive gained speed, accelerating rapidly to its limits, and Antoinette pressed her cheek to the window hoping to see what was happening. Without warning, the car jolted to a crashing halt, flinging everyone about. Then she heard gunshots coming from every direction, striking the car and seats. She hit the floor along with everyone else. It was chaos, pure panic, absolute terror.

Lying on the floor, Antoinette looked across the aisle to the red-haired youth, also prone, his long legs beneath his seat. Her eyes urgently sought some direction, but the young man, as terrified as she, could only shake his head and close his eyes to wait… and pray.

The shots ceased, and Antoinette could hear the bloodcurdling rebel cry, along with the rustle of leather saddles and the thunder of hooves surrounding the train. From the doors, she heard the sound of boots as armed men swarmed onto the car, shouting and pointing their pistols.

Peering above the seats, Antoinette watched the Union soldiers on the floor around her rise to their feet, their hands raised.

"We're unarmed," the men called out urgently. "We have no choice but to surrender."

"Don't shoot!" others cried.

A bushwhacker leaned his head out the door and shouted, "Hey, the whole train's full of Federals!"

Then Antoinette heard it: scattered, random shots coming from the cars at the back of the train. She listened closely, trying to determine their exact location. *Are they firing near the car where the women were riding?* Men shouted and fired off pistols, laughing and whooping like maniacs. Then she heard women's screams and knew what was transpiring.

"Like shooting fish in a barrel," a man's voice outside exulted.

Frantic, Antoinette leapt to her feet and made for the front of the car, pushing through the Federal soldiers standing in the aisle. "Let me through," she ordered, pressing ahead. The soldiers cleared out of her path. When she reached the door, she was confronted by four intoxicated bushwhackers, pistols aimed directly at her, men none too willing to let her pass.

"That's my property you're damaging, fools," she asserted. "Get out of my way!" Then she pushed through the armed rebels and rapidly climbed down from the train. Taken aback by her authoritative tone and sudden action, no one shot her. Yet.

Holding her skirt, Antoinette raced to the baggage and freight cars. When she arrived, breathless, her worst fears were confirmed. Two dozen drunk bushwhackers seeking plunder were clawing through the supplies stacked in the train, while two others held pistols on the huddled *DarkHorse* women and children. Pressed together in a trembling mass, Antoinette's friends, in utter panic, screamed, cried, and pleaded shrilly at the tops of their voices to no avail. They clutched their children to them, ordering them to be quiet, holding their hands over the mouths of the little ones. Then Antoinette saw why her friends were so terrified and was instantly consumed by horror and outrage. Lying motionless in a pool of blood was Ceeba, shot multiple times in the chest. Nearby lay Bammer's wife, Melody, also dead. Yards from the group, Turkey John's sister, Marcy Darcy, a small girl barely sixteen, lay lifeless, shot in the back multiple times attempting to run for the woods.

Blocking the women's escape route, a pair of guerrillas joked and guffawed as they reloaded their pistols. Fighting her own terror, her breathing short, Antoinette hurriedly interposed herself between the guerrillas and her friends, confronting the bushwhackers. Her mind raced desperately for a way to stop the shooting, an approach to confuse them. "Look what you fools have done to my property!" she shouted sternly, ignoring the raiders' hardware.

Startled, the older, more sober of the pair replied, "Do these women belong to you, ma'am?"

"Yes. You've killed three of them. You owe me fifteen hundred dollars. Fifteen hundred dollars!" she demanded loudly. "Do you have it?"

Taken aback by the woman's unexpected and insistent demand for payment, the two shooters looked at each other, puzzled, uncertain of what to say or do. Finally, the older of them spoke politely, shyly, slurring his words. "You sound like a Southern lady."

"Of course, I am," she shouted, "and I'm taking my property away from here. You two are pro-slavery men, aren't you? You're not traitors, are you?"

Swaying uncertainly, the younger of the two clumsily waved his pistol in Antoinette's face. "I don't care one way or t'other. I never owned no slave and wouldn't if you gave me a free one, though there ain't many free slaves, are they?" he giggled. "Now outta my line of fire."

"You idiot," Antoinette screamed into his face. "I need these women to get a Confederate officer out of prison, my husband. A real Southern hero, not like you drunken bandits."

The guerrilla band's leader, who'd been overseeing the sacking of Union supplies, noticed what was transpiring and, his curiosity aroused, joined the three. "What's this all about, Jess?"

"This woman claims these slaves belong to her."

The leader turned his gaze to Antoinette. "Is that right, ma'am?"

"Yes, and your fools here killed three of my most valuable women. Fifteen hundred dollars! You ruffians owe me fifteen hundred dollars," Antoinette barked.

The leader, unsteady on his feet from drinking, thought this over a moment. "Jess, search her."

While the older man held his pistol on Antoinette, the younger raider grabbed her handbag and began to rifle through it. First, he took the few dollars she had and stuffed them in his pocket. Then he found her Union Army orders, unfolded them, and looked them over briefly with a quizzical expression.

"What is this?" the leader asked, snatching the document away. He studied the paper with the U.S. imprint on its header but didn't say a word. "Ain't this a Union mark?"

Relieved, Antoinette realized neither of the men could read.

"It's my husband's court order," she replied. "If I don't get my husband out of Union prison in St. Louis, they'll hang him. Hang him, you understand?"

The leader betrayed his disbelief. "Hang? What for?"

"When he was captured at Pittsburg Landing, they put him on parole. Then he got captured again near Springfield. He's scheduled for court-martial next week."

"Violating parole, that's execution, all right," the leader said, bitterness and anger in his voice. Then he stared suspiciously into Antoinette's eyes. "Usually they shoot you right on the spot. How come?"

"*Some* Union men follow the rules," Antoinette said. "After all, he's an officer in the Confederate regular army."

"What do you need all these slaves for?" the leader asked skeptically. "Why shouldn't we just put them to rest right here?"

Antoinette saw the blood lust dominating his face. "Bribe money, fool," she recited, as if instructing a stupid student on simple manners. "I'm going to sell them in St. Louis, for U.S. greenbacks. You know damn well Yankee jailers won't take Confederate script, which I don't have anyway. Sir, my husband's life!"

The leader puzzled over this statement. Then, seeing no flaw in the logic, stuffed the orders for Antoinette and the women in his back pocket. "All right, get them slaves out of here before the boys get rough. We been drinking a bit, you know."

Antoinette pushed aside the pistol the younger guerrilla had been pointing at her chest. Then she moved swiftly to round up her surviving friends. It was a chaotic effort, as the woman and children had already succumbed to hysteria. Once they realized they were out of immediate danger, grabbing their children roughly, the women didn't hesitate to run west to where Antoinette pointed. Behind them, the guerrillas swarmed over the Union supplies, hollering while breaking open boxes, throwing most of what they found into the nearby river.

Glancing over her shoulder, Antoinette could see the Union soldiers from the train now surrounded by armed bushwhackers. Under shouted instructions, the soldiers were removing their uniforms and throwing them in a pile. Guerrillas usually took all the blue uniforms they could find. Wearing Union blue enabled them to travel through unfriendly territory unimpeded and proved useful in getting in close to their enemy to take them by surprise.

Antoinette stopped in her tracks surveying her surroundings. The town was off to her left; to her right, behind the train station, thickly overgrown scrub encroached. Swiftly, she directed her friends to circle the station and head for the woods. As she watched the women scramble ahead, she paused to listen.

"What we gonna do with them?" she heard one guerrilla ask.

"Why, parole them, of course," came the leader's mock-benevolent reply.

"That's what I thought," the first man said, then broke into laughter. At once, the air grew thunderous with continuous volleys of gunshots. Antoinette could hear men screaming and begging, and she knew what was happening. Each shot and scream tore into her heart. A woman shouted an alarm, and all of Antoinette's friends broke into a run for the thick brush.

None of them looked back, unable to witness the horror that was transpiring beside the tracks. As she ran, Antoinette began crying so hard she was blind to what was only feet ahead of her. But that didn't stop her. Tears didn't slow any of them. As they ran, stumbling and tripping through the heavy brush, they could hear earsplitting gunfire and terrified shouting echoing throughout the woodlands for what seemed an endless amount of time. The shots continued long after the last screams of pain and fear had died out, as bullets were fired repeatedly into motionless skulls.

    The women and children hid as best they could, trembling and whimpering, crouched in the forest. But the sounds of bloodcurdling rebel yells and horses galloping continued. Then after a while, the women viewed with horror as massive flames and smoke engulfed the town and the train station. Death, destruction, and desecration were having a field day.

CHAPTER NINE

STRANDED IN A NIGHTMARE

Platte River, Western Missouri

Crowded aboard the U.S. Navy boat heading south down the Platte River, the *DarkHorse* regiment sat uncomfortably on stacks of supply boxes piled around the deck. The hard drizzle hadn't let up for six hours, and by nighttime everyone was wet and miserable. They futilely pulled tarps tightly around their necks with exposed ice-cold hands, waterfalls running from their caps down into their collars soaking their skin, and needles of rain never ceased stinging their drenched faces.

That morning, when first stepping onto the boat, with the weather dry and hot, they learned that Isaac was terrified of drowning. It was all they could do to get him aboard. Shivering, as much from terror as from the chill, Durk and Big Josh seated themselves flanking him, trying everything they could to calm him. They still had a long way to go, but at least Isaac wasn't hearing voices anymore.

They'd begun their journey to Lawrence in Macon City. After seeing the women off on the eastbound train, the regiment took the Hannibal & St. Joseph railroad west to Easton in Buchanan County, where they disembarked and hiked to the Platte to meet up with the navy. In a couple hours, they'd reach Kansas City. There they'd help the crews unload the supplies, which would later be transported by wagon to nearby Westport. That accomplished, they would continue west along the Kansas River to Lawrence. At first, the men had grumbled about the rain, but Big Josh had shut them up with the caution that being on a boat was better than walking. He reminded the *DarkHorse* members of their long trek from Mississippi, a harrowing hike they wouldn't have to repeat.

Sitting in the rain and darkness, Durk ruminated over his doubts and fears, as he was temperamentally wont to do. He was, fundamentally, a man of peace who hated any sort of violence or confrontation. Yet here he was, wearing a soldier's uniform, a pistol at his hip, which he had no intention of ever using to harm another. He tried to reassure himself that his cavalry idea had saved them all from more problematic fates, like being ordered to charge on foot into shot and shell — sheer suicide. He didn't know if he could have brought himself to do that. Yet to refuse such orders meant losing Antoinette and his friends, and along with them, all his hopes and dreams. He was a skillful rider who just felt safer on a horse, had ridden from trouble often before. Often. But he knew eventually there would be circumstances when he could not run, and he dreaded having to face those moments.

Crack! He heard the loud report of a rifle coming from shore, as one of their regiment sitting on the railing fell into the river. Durk rushed to the side of the boat until he located the man floating lifelessly on the black waters. At once, shots poured into the boat from both banks, and everyone began shouting frantically. Naval officers took up rifles and began to fire back, as the captain ordered the stovers below deck to fire up the boilers.

"Get down!" Durk ordered. No longer hearing the hubbub, the cries of fear and pain, the screams and urgent voices surrounding him, Durk watched calmly as his men dove to the deck and scrambled behind boxes or anything solid they could find.

But instead of ducking down, Durk remained silently upright amid the sounds of gunfire and balls whizzing around him. With the darkness alive with chaos and danger, he surprisingly felt within himself a kind of fatalistic peace, a tranquil euphoria, as if he were impervious to the death pouring onto the boat. He knew he should take cover — knew it in the logical part of his mind — but his determination to remain still was somehow reassuring. "Stay down!" he shouted. "Bushwhackers!" Standing tall, he felt free from the fear that had followed him his whole life.

Suddenly, he was struck by a heavy weight, which sent him crashing hard onto the deck, landing on his elbow, the wind knocked out of him. When he recovered his senses, he saw Isaac lying on top of him, shouting into his face, "You crazy? You want to get shot?"

His arm hurt like hell, and he had to fight to catch his breath, but he'd found some inner courage, some reservoir of strength that he'd never imagined he had. Lying on the deck, being pummeled by cold rain, his body aching, inexplicably, he began to laugh… and laugh… and laugh even harder. No, he would never kill another man, but he was no coward, and that gave him great comfort. Great comfort, indeed.

***

Mexico, Eastern Missouri

Dusk descended rapidly as the surviving *DarkHorse* women gained enough courage to leave their hiding places in the woods. Climbing over fallen trees and through thick brush, they emerged to clear ground, only to find horrors confronting them, reviving their terror once again.

Seemingly a lifetime before, earlier that sunny day when they'd first glanced out of the rolling train's supply cars, the town had appeared unremarkable, sleepy, a few wood-frame buildings, mule-hitched wagons, and farm horses lolling in the street. Now the station, general store, and hotel lay in smoldering charcoal ruins, their jagged walls like black burnt fingers grasping vainly at the moonless sky. The bushwhackers had wreaked blind revenge for their frustration at being powerless and inconsequential: their lives at constant jeopardy as their cause tumbled toward inevitable defeat.

At first, the dazed group wandered haphazardly in a frightened mass toward no specific destination. Then their relief turned to shock as they came upon the bodies of local civilians strewn about the streets, being lugged together by weary, surviving townsmen and placed under tarps. Nearby, townswomen and farmwives, dumbfounded and demoralized, talked together in muted tones. Only momentarily distracted by the unexpected appearance of the chaotic group of blacks, the townsfolk soon returned their attention to their own earnest efforts and tearful conversations.

Once oriented to their surroundings, Antoinette and her friends hurried to where the train rested askew off the tracks, like some iron snake that had died in mid-strike. There beside the cars lay the bodies of Ceeba, Marcy Darcy, and Melody, their dresses splattered crimson and covered in dust. Still devastated at having witnessed their friends so brutally murdered, the women and children began to sob and cry out, as the whole group gathered closely together for sympathy and support.

Eventually, one of the women found a military tent tarp and covered the fallen. Only then were Antoinette and her friends settled enough to decide what to do next.

With Ceeba dead, the women had lost their long-time leader. They needed to sort out a new hierarchy. Of course, Antoinette would be an important voice in their future affairs. They'd need her to wheedle their way through the twisted labyrinth of a torn civil society under partial military rule. Her wit and charm — not to mention her beauty — would certainly help them navigate the deadly reefs and shoals of war-torn Missouri. But Antoinette often was off on errands for the women and had little to do with their day-to-day existence, other than to pitch in whenever she could. They needed other leadership.

It was quickly decided that Auntie NeeNee would be their main leader. An ancient, wiry little woman who wore a red headrag, Auntie NeeNee was believed to be in her late-seventies, at the very least. No one was actually sure of her age, not even Auntie herself. She was small, put together like a bundle of sticks, but energetic and tough with an iron will. No one sassed or resisted Auntie NeeNee when her mind was made up, not even the whitefolks way back when. She'd survived a long time, and she knew practically everything about getting along. The other women often sought her counsel, except when they knew what her answer would be and they didn't want to travel the route in which she was sure to direct them.

"Auntie is a ol' woman," objected Sarah, a voluble forty-three-year-old mother of two. "She a good person, but I need to be a boss, too."

There was restrained conversation about this idea, but Sarah quickly gained everyone's support to act with some degree of authority. Sarah was a highly-opinionated woman, a doer who tirelessly pitched in to face every challenge, yet her ideas were not always accepted. Indeed, unlike Auntie NeeNee's notions, they were often a goodly distance from the practical — or even from the logical. But when it came time to get a task accomplished, Sarah was always in the middle of the action, working furiously and helping everyone else out. It was figured that between NeeNee and Sarah, the group had all the ingredients for survival: wisdom, will, and energy.

Auntie NeeNee hushed everyone with a hissing sound between her teeth. "Le's get what we lef' on the train, then see if they's something to eat on it. Or just find anything on that train to help us get by."

Auntie ordered some of the older women to tend the little children, while the rest scavenged the stripped supply cars. Seeing that everyone was distracted by this activity, Antoinette quietly slipped off and circled the train toward the passenger cars, holding her skirt to step over the tracks. No Federal troops had arrived yet to establish order. Rather, a sinister tableau confirmed the sounds she'd heard as she'd fled to the woods. The young federal soldiers she'd ridden with on the train were laying in grotesque poses where they'd fallen, much like the many murdered citizens in town. What had been a group of vital young boys and men were now merely lifeless, blood-drained, desecrated heaps. Each had been shot five or six times in the head, and many of the heads had been bashed in with rifle butts, a useless duplication to blow off drunken frustration. A number of the Federals had been scalped as a prize of massacre.

Antoinette froze, shocked, trembling from head to foot, as she felt some violent, vile, irrepressible force about to erupt inside her. Then she was on her knees, sick, bent over for what seemed a long time until her body finally stopped shaking, until she was empty. Too weak to stand, she managed to seat herself on the dusty ground. Blinded by tears, she fumbled in her handbag until she found her handkerchief to use until she was cried out and her vision returned. Then she saw him, the young man who'd sat beside her, who'd she'd spoken to only that morning, now a twisted, bloody distortion of a human. Her head snapped heavenward and she wailed so hard and so long her body ached.

In '59, after she'd shot her husband, dark emotional tides had risen from deep inside her, driving her toward doing away with herself, but these had been forestalled by her encounter with the *DarkHorse* men, and with Durk. She didn't know why or how, but the partners' common struggle to overcome their seemingly impossible circumstances, their growing faith in each other, their resourcefulness, even Durk's uncontrolled ambition, allowed her to escape the terrible sinkhole into which her spirit had fallen. But now, with so much death surrounding her, these feelings were returning stronger than before. It took some time for her to compose herself. She had to warn the others.

Attempting finally to stand on shaky legs, Antoinette hurriedly stumbled away from the dreadfulness in the dust. She circled the train back to where her friends were. Once on the other side, she ran up to Auntie NeeNee who was busy directing the search for anything salvageable, especially for tin meats or hardtack. "Don't go 'round to the other side of the train, Auntie," she gasped, breathless. "Nobody go there!"

Auntie NeeNee spat disgustedly. "They dead, ain't they," she said like she'd known all along. "All them young mens."

Unable to speak, Antoinette merely hung her head. With a sympathetic look, Auntie NeeNee put her arms around Antoinette who hugged her back, hanging tightly onto the diminutive little woman.

For the moment, Antoinette was able to hold her dark feelings at bay, but Auntie was an awfully small rock to grasp against such overwhelming emotional forces. If she succumbed to them, even Durk would not be enough to save her from drowning.

The remaining *DarkHorse* women climbed onto the train car to rescue what few personal items they had abandoned in their flight. There they found, undisturbed, their castoff pots, pans, tin plates, cups, and utensils tied up in handkerchiefs and rags, the bundles not having been worth the bushwhackers' time to rummage through. To their dismay, the women found nothing but scraps of food in the wreckage. After a day of hiding in the woods, everyone was hungry; the children were especially vocal about it.

Though it was near dark, a number of local white women who were still trying to bring order to the fallen town, ceased their labors long enough to gather the meager foodstuffs to make a hodgepodge meal for the outsiders. The *DarkHorse* women thanked the locals profusely, grateful they'd found enough charity in their hearts to help a ragtag group of helpless black folks after such a disaster. But these gestures of gratitude were waved off, no thanks being needed or accepted. Nearby, an exhausted, emotionally played out Antoinette, unaware of her own hunger, sat on a crate dispassionately watching the commotion, numb, as if the events unfolding around her had no more meaning than a lecture on phrenology. Yet that small bit of humanity amid the smoke and charred rubble of the townswomen's former lives sparked a faint glow of hope in her own troubled heart.

The food was cooked over open fires south of the gutted town. The resultant thin soup had to be parceled out carefully to stretch it for the number of people to be fed. In the end, no one was satisfied. Everyone was still hungry, but no one was starving. Then some of them washed the utensils in the nearby creek as the older women put the children down in a grove, spreading what few blankets they had for them.

When everything was settled, the adults gathered in a circle, knowing one meal was all they were going to get from this town, yet grateful to get that.

"We got to start for the nearest Federal camp in the morning," Auntie NeeNee said. "Them folks in town will know which way it is."

"No, we gots to stay here till they fix the train," Sarah asserted loudly, the distressful circumstances causing her to elevate her pitch. "That's the only way we gonna get to St. Louie."

"An' how long it gonna take for them soldiers to get here and fix it, Sarah?" Auntie NeeNee said disdainfully. "We maybe starve to death before all that done."

The other women grumbled agreement with the old woman.

"It'll be a mighty long walk with the children and no food," Sarah objected. "We aint't gonna be safe till we get to St. Louie!" Sarah looked around the circle of faces. But seeing no one was going to agree with her, she went into one of her infamous sulks. She knew she was right, but Auntie had fooled everyone again, like she always did.

"What you think, Antoinette?" Auntie NeeNee asked.

"I think you're right, Auntie," Antoinette replied. "At least we won't be attacked by guerrillas if we get to an army camp. Perhaps we can stay there until the army can get us to St. Louis." She paused suddenly, a look of doubt crossing her face. "Oh! The bushwhackers took our orders. I'll have to convince the army to let us continue our journey. I don't know what else we can do."

"Well, you can talk to them," Auntie concluded. "We gonna have a hard day tomorrow with no food, doing all that walking. Don't even know how many miles to that camp. Could be days. You best catch your sleep while you can. Now, go on."

Weary from heartbreak at their friends' murder and from hiding in fear all day, the women talked among themselves so as to not disturb the children. Then they stretched out on the bare ground under the night sky to fall asleep, making themselves as comfortable as possible. They'd slept on the ground back at the army camp they'd come from because they couldn't share the tents of their men, so this was nothing new.

Antoinette reclined, shutting her eyes, using her bag for a pillow, but the release of sleep eluded her. Lying awake, her restless mind kept running through one catastrophic possibility after another. She knew that when they reached the camp, the very survival of these women and children would fall on her shoulders. It was a lot to bear, but it gave her a reason to live.

She was jarred awake by the sudden sound of hoof beats rumbling in the town, quite a number. Within seconds, the women were on their feet, in panic, whispering frantically. Auntie shushed everyone to listen... then they were sure, some of the riders were coming their way. Antoinette and Auntie NeeNee herded everyone together, quieting them, while Antoinette stepped front and center to face the interlopers.

Relief! Two squads of cavalry in blue cantered up to them, real pro-Union men, not guerrillas disguised in Federal uniforms. Captain Howard, a tall man with brown hair in his mid-thirties, raised his hand to signal his troops, then drew rein before Antoinette, as the squad pulled up behind him. These guerrilla hunters had spent weeks in the saddle, and the captain's patience was short. He rested his arms on his bow, his brow creased in disapproval, examining Antoinette and the ragged collection of black people.

"What is all this?" he growled angrily at Antoinette, indicating the women.

"They're with me, Captain," Antoinette replied. "Thank God, you've come. We were on the train when the secesh raided it. They massacred the soldiers that were riding with us. It's a nightmare, an absolute nightmare."

"I've been to the train," the captain said grimly. "Bastards." He paused to think of what to do next, then indicated Antoinette's friends. "What do you expect to do with these women?"

"I would hope we could stay by the nearest army camp until the line is opened," Antoinette half-pleaded. "Our orders were to proceed to duty in St. Louis."

"Orders?" the captain said. "Let me see them."

Antoinette shrugged bitterly. "The secesh took my papers."

On hearing this, the captain rubbed his three-day beard, trying to puzzle out the situation, appraising Antoinette with deep skepticism. "Who are these people? Are they someone's slaves?"

Antoinette tried to read the man's face to determine what approach to take with him. The army had three main factions, and the one the captain belonged to would determine her strategy. Was he a "Charcoal," entirely against emancipation? Was he a "Snowflake," in favor of immediate emancipation? Or was he a "Claybank" who believed in gradual emancipation? She studied him, but he remained an enigma to her. Hoping he was a snowflake, she took a chance.

"These women are family members of the Ninth Missouri Colored Cavalry. They've been working for the military, Captain, as cooks, laundresses, everything. If you want to check, I can give you the names and location of the regiments and officers."

"But are they slaves?" he asked more forcefully.

Antoinette had to make a choice. Durk might have read the situation and known what to say, but lacking Durk's instinct for deception, she fell back upon principle to guide her. She would not let the perverse institution of slavery muddy her words.

"These are free women," she stated firmly. "Just as are their menfolk, who are fighting for the Union."

The captain thought this claim over. "And you have no documents," he said.

"As I said, the secesh took them," Antoinette replied.

"The raiders took time to take the papers from every single one of these people?" he questioned skeptically. "And your accent, where are you from, ma'am? What's your name?"

"My name is Antoinette DuVallier. I'm originally from New Orleans. I held all their documents, Captain, but they were all taken from me."

A scowl of disbelief came over the captain's face. "Sergeant!" he called. A sandy-haired young man in his mid-twenties guided his horse alongside the officer's. "I am placing these women under temporary custody."

The sergeant examined the beautiful woman before him, unsure of what to do. "Do you want this woman taken, too, Captain?"

"Her especially," the captain said. "Have a few men lead them back to camp. We'll let the colonel decide what to do with them."

"Yes, sir."

"Arrange to hold them indefinitely. There's something odd about this. Very odd."

"Captain," Antoinette said urgently. "Can you at least send a rider to wire Lawrence, Kansas? Three of these women were murdered in the raid. Their men are in the Ninth MSM. They must be notified immediately."

"I'll do that," the captain agreed. "There's a town with a telegraph office a couple hours up the road." He turned to his second. "Sergeant, get the deceased's names. Send a squad to wire their menfolk from that little town we passed through."

"Yes, sir."

"And Sergeant, keep close guard on that white woman. Don't let her out of our sight."

CHAPTER TEN

GATHERING STORMS

Lawrence, Kansas

Durksen Hurst stumbled weakly out the door of the neglected, weathered farmhouse onto the front porch. The wooden structure, sitting on the purlieus of the Lawrence military post, now served as the Union Army telegraph office. His knees shaky, neither seeing nor hearing the military activity around him, Durk leaned against a support post to steady himself until he could recover his bearings. His head was spinning, like he'd been drinking, but he hadn't touched a drop. With a deep sigh, he nervously, repeatedly slapped a small square of paper against his thigh. Finally, when he was steady enough to continue, he stepped out into the road and angrily kicked at a stone, blowing up a cloud of dust, before venturing further. He had urgent news.

He found the *DarkHorse* regiment drilling in a field a hundred yards away. Ordering the men in his command to take a break from the heat, he pulled Big Josh aside.

Wiping his neck with his bandanna, Josh started to make a joke about the Kansas heat, but when he saw Durk's deadly expression, his smile quickly vanished.

Unable to say anything to prepare Josh for what was coming, Durk reluctantly handed him the paper bearing the cramped, hurried handwriting of a wire transcript.

Big Josh took a moment to read it; then read it again in disbelief. His eyes burned as it fixed on one name: Ceeba. Crestfallen, he angrily crumbled the paper and tossed it aside.

"The train was raided before they could reach St. Louis, Josh," Durk said. "Three of our people were killed. Many others, too. The town mostly burned."

Josh merely looked at Durk in stunned silence, then hung his head, expelling his breath.

Durk paused a long moment to let the news sink in. "Say something, Josh," Durk urged, but Josh remained mute. "Don't get quiet like you do. I need you now. You're going to have to tell the others." Durk placed a hand on Josh's massive shoulder and squeezed it hard until Josh looked up. They were eye-to-eye, tearful. "You've got to tell Bammer Melody was shot, and tell Turkey John about Marcy Darcy. Tell everyone."

"Ceeba? D-dead?" Josh muttered barely above a whisper, bewildered, eyes seeking Durk's for truth. "They kill her? H-how…?"

"Shot, all shot. Bushwhackers. Antoinette wired me from a Federal camp outside Mexico, Missouri. She and the others are safe there for now."

Josh turned his eyes away from his friend and trundled off by himself to the edge of the field, where he sat heavily down on a fallen maple. He stared at the ground and spit between his boots, frozen. Seeing Josh so devastated, Durk followed and sat beside him.

"Josh, my friend, you're their sergeant. You've got to get the men through this. They need to hear from you." Durk swallowed hard, rubbing his forehead. "I can't do it."

Josh stared into space, muttering under his breath, his voice thick, "I ran the plantation back home in Tennessee," he mumbled. "And they k-kill my boy. So young, smart, handsome. And ever day, I ask, 'Why? Why?' I say, 'Take me instead, Lord. B-bring him back and *take me*.' But there ain't no deal I could make with nobody or no thing." He grew thoughtful, remembering his son's smiling, hopeful face.

"Then my wife die of heartbreak. I felt like *I* should be dead. Why didn't God have sense enough to take me? I'm r-ready. 'Stead of l-leaving me alone?'" He paused. "Now…" Tears flowed freely from his bloodshot eyes down his dirt-stained cheeks. "Now C-ceeba. She was all I had left..." He fell silent again, eyes searching the cloudless sky.

Durk put his arm around Josh's shoulders. "You've got us. Don't forget, we're here for a reason." Durk stood and brushed off his pants, taking a deep cleansing breath, determined to see it through.

Josh looked up at him, then resolutely stood, sucking in his gut, wiping his face with the back of his hand. Stretching to his full height, he straightened his uniform. "I tell the men. Le's, le's get this damn war done and over with."

***

Jackson County, Western Missouri

The cool, moonlit night was peaceful, a welcome respite from weeks in the saddle and the constant fear of being detected by armed Union patrols. The steady, twinkling gurgle of the creek flowing through the ravine's thick woods and brush, the horses drinking from its clear waters, their forelegs splashing gently, was as soothing as a lullaby. William Quantrill — his fame, or infamy, making him preeminent among equals — along with his two squad leaders, Dave Poole and George Todd, plus Bloody Bill Anderson, who already wore forty Union scalps on a necklace tucked inside his shirt, talked among themselves. The other bushwhacker leaders and their chief lieutenants stretched out around the large bonfire near Blue Springs in Western Missouri, drinking coffee or whiskey from tin cups. Bushwhacker leaders were determined solely by their ability to raise bands of guerrillas ranging in size from a handful to several hundred at any given time. The pistols they carried tucked in their belts now rested on the ground. Each man carried several into skirmishes and raids because reloading while fighting was complicated: a near impossibility when riding under fire. Scattered throughout the heavily overgrown hills, four hundred of their men rested around small campfires, cooking whatever meal, bacon grease, hardtack, and jerky they'd managed to scrape together. It had taken some time for all the disparate bands to converge here. The men were hungry, weary, and spoiling for a fight.

Rising to her feet, Devereau French reached into her left pocket and pulled out a sheet of paper. Unfolding it, she circled the fire, displaying a letter she claimed was signed by General Hindeman. She paused before each guerrilla, staring fiercely into his eyes, letting him know she meant business. The independent guerrilla bands had the right to refuse or to join in any engagement. If Devereau wanted the guerrillas to take the enormous risk she intended for them, she'd probably need to convince all of them to go or none of them would. She had her work cut out.

"Now this goes no further, gentlemen," she said conspiratorially, "not a whisper, not even to your wife or your best friend. The war may hinge on what we will do next, and the element of surprise is critical." She paused to let that sink in.

The faces of the guerrilla leaders grew skeptical, bitter. They had seen the tide turning gradually against them for some time, like a great ship turning around at sea. As things stood, their minds were unable to make the leap past being merely a nuisance for the Union Army and a terror to the region's citizens, to actually being a catalyst again for winning the war. With a shrug, they turned their attention back to General Hindeman's liaison, a scrawny fellow, but well-spoken, with a thick Mississippi accent. His tailored city suit, too, singled him out from the roughly dressed Missouri raiders in their road-worn britches and guerrilla shirts. They doubted whether they could trust him, letter from the general or no.

"I wish to inform you that General Hindeman has gathered enough troops in Arkansas to invade Missouri," Devereau lied with her most profound gravitas. "Understand, brave warriors, the general is prepared to reclaim our land. The objective is…" She paused for dramatic effect. "St. Louis." The faces of her listeners showed astonishment, and then an exhausted skepticism came over them.

"Just imagine, men," Devereau continued. "The main arsenal in St. Louis in our hands. The guns, the cannon, the munitions, and the means of making more. The city itself is the chokepoint of the Mississippi River. Grant will be cut off from his base, and he'll be forced to pull back. That would save Vicksburg and clear Mississippi and Arkansas of the invaders. We'd be able to get steady supplies from the Gulf of Mexico through Texas.

"Consider this, too: Ewing cut off, has to pull out of Western Missouri." She gestured in a 360 degree circle, indicating the counties around them controlled by the Union Army that they rode through daily as fugitives, evading death at every turn. "Yes, Ewing and his cordon pulled out of our part of the state so we can ride free. We'll be able to gather all the Southern loyalists west of Jefferson City, and build and supply our own army to defeat the Yankees.

"St. Louis! We can turn the war around this year, men. This year! Free our land from Lincoln and his Hell hordes."

That said, pleased with herself, Devereau returned to where Robert Sterling was holding their horses' reins and sat on the ground beside him. There were loud mutterings around the fire as the incredulous guerrilla leaders mused over the improbable claims they'd just heard.

"Take St. Louis?"

"The war won this year?"

"That don't sound likely."

Finally, William Quantrill rose to his feet and everyone quieted down. The former teacher and unofficially acknowledged dominant guerrilla leader was just under six-feet tall and thin, with long sandy hair and a broad mustache. He wasn't overbearing, except in battle when he became a hellion. He waited for complete silence, then spoke with authority.

"And pray tell, what does General Hindeman want us to do to aid his supposed invasion of the cradle of the oppressor, Mr. French?"

Devereau folded her letter, slipped it into back her pocket, and rose to her feet. "Gentlemen, even I don't know if the general intends to invade from Western Arkansas, coming northeast through Rolla, or from Eastern Arkansas, directly north through Cape Girardeau. We are being informed late in the game in order to keep the plan under wraps. Whichever direction he comes from, we have to draw Federal troops to the west of Missouri, as far away from St. Louis as possible. That is our task."

Quantrill tightened his belt and narrowed his eyes at the man wearing the bowler hat. "And how do you propose we do that, sir?"

"Simple. Attack Lawrence, Kansas."

There was a loud gasp from around the fire, then angry voices shouted their disbelief. Bloody Bill Anderson rose and held up his hand for silence, his wild dark mane and beard pouring from his road- and wind-weathered misshapen hat. "Lawrence? Why, that town is a hundred miles of hard riding through the Union wall of outposts."

Quantrill spit disgustedly. "What do you say, John? What do they have?"

John Noland, a handsome, free black guerrilla who had been spying on Lawrence for the Confederacy, tossed aside the stick he was whittling and worked himself to his feet. "I just come back from scouting Lawrence a week or so ago. Folks say the Yankees pulled out their troops three weeks back: needed 'em somewheres else. Guess they got tired of waitin' on us to come."

"Heard anything?" Quantrill asked guerrilla leader Dave Poole sitting nearby.

Dave rose to his feet. "John's right. My man was there just last week. Only Yankees in Lawrence are Missouri Colored Militia, about three or four dozen at most. Untrained, unarmed, unsupported. We'd have no difficulty with them."

Quantrill grew thoughtful. "What do you think, George?"

George Todd worked his way to his feet. "All the plunder the Jayhawkers stole from Missouri will be stashed thereabouts. We can rescue more money in Lawrence than anyplace else. That's what George Todd thinks." He spat in the fire.

"More money and more revenge, too," one of Bill Anderson's men added, then held up his cup in mock toast and drained it.

Every eye was on Quantrill as he crossed his arms and began to pace near the fire. Not a word was spoken. He took off his slouch hat and brushed his hair back through his fingers. "The whole enterprise is almost a forlorn hope, for if we go, I don't know if any one of us will get back to tell the story." He rubbed his chin in thought. "Of course, if you never risk, you never gain."

His eyes searched the faces around him, but he saw his own doubts reflected in them.

Devereau could see that the issue hung in the balance: a possible suicidal gambit, blocked by the well-equipped and -supplied web of Ewing's experienced guerrilla hunters — in total, outnumbering them four to one — versus a rich jackpot in plunder and bloody vengeance for years of relentless Jayhawker ravages against their families and farms. She rose again and planted herself at the center of the inner circle of killers.

"I thought we were men! Men! Fighting for the virtue and sanctity of our poor, innocent womenfolk. Yet, here we sit, our souls fuming with fury at the shameful murder of our own sisters, and what have we done? Nothing. Nothing — yet.

"You, Bill Anderson! Your own sister Josephine slaughtered by those demons overrunning our land like a plague of vermin. Slaughtered! And your sister Mary Ellen, her lovely, milky white face sliced and disfigured, both legs broken, her back crushed so she'll be a cripple for the rest of her life. Four other of our pristine ladies dead, assassinated most foully by Ewing's henchmen. And what holds us back from inflicting reprisals on our sworn enemies, these executioners of Southern womanhood itself? Nothing. Nothing but our own timidity. Nothing but the false belief that the Yankees are invincible. Nothing but despair fostered by temporary setbacks — *temporary* setbacks. Nothing but vacillation from the belief in our Cause. Our Cause, gentlemen. No, sir, our Cause is not dead. If we are strong, if we are brave, if we are audacious, our Cause will yet prevail. Gentlemen, the South and everything it stands for will prevail!"

Devereau paused to catch her breath, shooting a knowing glance to Robert Sterling, whose stern expression betrayed no emotion, no reaction. She grabbed a stick and began to draw a large map in the dirt. "Now, Ewing's troops occupy a series of strong points spread far apart, like immobile pieces on a large chessboard, but there is nothing between these outposts to impede our riders. Nothing, except patrols. Ewing's whole setup is like a few fence poles stuck here and there across a field with no slats connecting them. And we far outnumber any outpost or patrol we might possibly encounter."

Devereau indicated Robert. "I have brought with me the best Indian scout in the Confederacy, Robert Sterling here. The best. He can guide us the hundred miles through the Union cordon without being detected. We'll get there untouched.

"Imagine, men, a beautiful sunrise! We sit our mounts on a hill, pistols loaded, and the slumbering town of Lawrence is laid out below us, just waking. And then we descend, spurring our horses, shrieking like banshees from Hell, guns blazing, taking everything we want, gunning down the abolitionists, wiping out the unarmed colored troops as they flee toward the woods like a flock of quail. A whole colored regiment, a regiment of pitch-black slaves, vanquished forever, wiped out.

"Then, gentlemen, we burn down the whole town. Can you see it? Lawrence in flames! Think of how that'll feel. Complete and utter victory over the source and fountainhead of all our suffering, of all our people's suffering over all these decades of Yankee oppression. Revenge is sweet, men, sweeter than molasses, sweeter than a virgin's kiss.

"Even more, we will know that we are laying the groundwork for the regular Confederate Army to make its move to St. Louis!" Devereau hung her head modestly, as if worn and consumed by her vision.

Bloody Bill Anderson put his hands on his hips, his legs spread. "Even if our raid succeeds, the Yankees may be spread out now. Won't they unite and come after us? We'll be badly outnumbered."

Devereau brushed off her collar, as if shooing away a fly. "First, Bill, we'll cut the telegraph wires. So it'll take quite some time for word of what we've done to get to Ewing's outposts, quite some time. We'll be almost back to Missouri by then. Then we'll split up and disappear into the brush. They may catch a few men, but they'll never catch all of us. Never."

Anderson returned to sit by his gear. "Sounds inspired. Damn, I'll turn loose the fires of Hades upon them."

Quantrill threw a stick into the bonfire. "I'm in. You have my vote." There was a grumbled consensus that spread around the fire.

Seeing her work done, Devereau rejoined Robert Sterling and sat on her blanket. Robert tied the horse's reins to a limb and sat close to her, rocking back and forth, his hands wrapped around his knees. "You are a notable liar," he whispered.

Devereau smiled at him. "I learned the hard way, from the best."

"Yes, your mother. She was the best."

CHAPTER ELEVEN

RUNNING THE GAUNTLET

Lawrence, Kansas

The glaring ball of fire overhead offered no shade, no relief for the *DarkHorse* colored regiment shuffling through the dust in a rough approximation of military drill formation. The oppressive air was so hot you could see it roll away in waves to the horizon, like an ocean of heat. The men sweated and groaned but stamped on, digging their tracks deeper into the dry field. Finally, Big Josh called a halt. "That's it. Rest you up and cool off. Isaac, you come with me."

As the men broke ranks to seek shelter from the blazing rays, Josh and Isaac strolled over to where Durk was barking heatedly at the colonel, who was seated in the only shade within miles. Colonel Daltry was a pear-bottomed, belly-swollen, minor political appointee, condemned to manage colored units on his descent down the military responsibility ladder toward his inevitable dishonorable discharge to civilian life. There his basic incompetence would prove less lethal to those in his charge.

"March, march, drill, drill! What these men need, Colonel, is to learn how to load and shoot," Durk exclaimed. "What good's an army without weapons?"

Colonel Daltry finished picking the pork from his teeth and spit out the pick. He swiped a handkerchief across his face, then blinked rapidly until Durk came into focus. "What do you suggest, Hurst?"

"The last regiment took all the working guns and the ammunition when they cleared out. That's what we need. But they're stacked up at Westport, just sitting *there* and we're *here*."

The colonel wiped his brow. "I told you, Hurst, you men were on the last boat that made it through. That big storm that passed here tore down trees all along the Kansas river. The navy can't ship any supplies to us till the river's clear, and who knows how long that'll take."

"What about overland?"

The colonel shook his head in disgust. "There isn't an escort scheduled to accompany the wagons yet. Now if you're just patient a bit..."

Durk rudely interrupted, raising his voice angrily, "You mean, there aren't enough men willing to risk escort duty to arm colored regiments? Isn't that what you mean?"

Seeing the captain wasn't going to relent anytime soon, Colonel Daltry uncorked his jug and took a swig. "Can you blame them, Hurst? It's extremely hazardous duty. Why, all the raids lately..."

"Listen, Colonel, how about I ride over to Westport with some of my men and escort the guns back myself. My squad skinned supply wagons for two years. You won't find any better."

"So, you intend to ride from here to Westport with hardly a pistol between you? And risk an ambush? I told you, Hurst, just wait for an escort… or for the navy."

"We'll carry the broken muskets the regulars left behind so we'll appear to be armed. And coming back, we really will be. We'll be our own escort."

The colonel waved a fly away. "Riding to Westport would be foolhardy, don't you see? You know very well bushwhackers won't parole a colored squad, *and that includes you, Hurst.* They'll take your scalp and bash your skull in, is what they'll do. Are you willing to chance that? Well, are you?"

The image of being scalped with his head crushed, did not sit well with Durk. The night before, Durk had been one of the three votes against the Westport plan to arm their regiment. Now he looked to Big Josh for guidance, hopeful that the colonel's warning would dissuade his friend. He didn't relish the idea of facing brutal bushwhackers unarmed. But if they carried through with the ploy, Durk, being the white man, would have to accompany the volunteers who made the journey. He was trapped.

Isaac, who had been one of the other votes against, urgently pulled on Josh's sleeve, his face pleading against. If Durk and Josh both went to Westport, Isaac knew he would have to go, too. They wouldn't leave him alone without one of them to keep an eye on him.

Josh's face screwed up in thought, then he subtly nodded approval. Durk reluctantly turned back to the colonel. "We'll take that chance, Colonel."

The colonel merely shrugged. "Your business, Hurst. Nobody's going to say a word about losing a couple dozen of them," he said scornfully, tilting his head to indicate Durk's men. "But goddamn, Hurst, I'll be reprimanded for losing the horses to the rebels, useless as them fleabags are anyway."

Durk, Isaac, and Josh eyed each other, then turned away. Walking together, they were silent until they were beyond earshot of the colonel. Durk whispered worriedly, "Are you sure you want to do this, Josh? I mean, if the rebs spot us..."

Josh fixed his jaw firmly so as to not betray his own doubts. "We voted, Durk. Look, we sitting ducks here, ain't we? Le's go get them guns."

"Sure, we're unarmed, but we're in Lawrence, a hundred miles from any significant body of rebels. Aren't we safe now? Well, aren't we?"

Big Josh merely shrugged. "Ain't no place safe in this war. Not in Missouri or Kansas neither. No place."

***

Eastern Kansas

The isolated country road seemed the perfect place for a bushwhacker ambush. Durk rode beside the four *DarkHorse* partners and twenty volunteers. The number of broken down, converted farm horses available for their venture had been limited, so they had to leave most of the regiment behind. The sun ducked out of sight, making everyone increasingly nervous, frighteningly so. With the moonless night descending, the passing woods on either side of them quickly faded to a depthless blackness, an imposing, impenetrable wall of places for killers to lay in wait. The men knew the journey to Westport might be crawling with rebels. Indeed, the route had become so dangerous in recent months that supplies and mail service to Lawrence had become irregular. Few were willing to ride the gauntlet, and for good reason. Lately, supply wagon trains and mail riders, even those accompanied by troops, had been attacked with increasing frequency.

Regrettably, except for antiquated, single-shot pistols and a haphazard assortment of broken rifles and shotguns, they were effectively unarmed. Neither were their horses the swiftest or most reliable if they had to escape. These practically useless firearms had been left behind when the mounted troops guarding Lawrence had been called away, removing the last trained soldiers in the area. The *DarkHorse* riders hoped their number would deter any smaller bands of bushwhackers who spotted them — hoped — and knew if they ran into larger bands, they'd be defenseless.

Big Josh drew rein and raised his hand for the others to follow suit. The spent, broken-down horses snorted, halting willingly.

Durk rode up beside Josh, his eyes searching the road ahead that disappeared into a limb-covered cave of nothingness. "We get ambushed on this road at night, none of us will live to see morning."

Josh studied the surrounding hills. "We can camp up that ridge where it plateau. At least, we be high up off'n this path to execution. But we best not light no fires."

Durk examined the area, but he could see no better alternative. "Any reb scouts will know we're here already, Josh. I think we should light fires. Show them we're not afraid."

"You crazy," Josh replied scornfully.

"No, listen, Josh. Have the men break into small groups and spread out over the whole flat. Then have each little group build a big fire, big, like for a whole squad. That way, the bushwhackers will think we've got a lot more men than we really have."

Josh thought this proposition over. "Light big fires that can be seen far off? Far off, Durk?" He paused a moment, then relented. "Okay, Durk, le's try it."

***

Western Missouri

Riding a fast horse through dark woods made Robert Sterling feel alive, more alive than slitting an enemy's throat, more alive than anything below the great sky. Feeling the raw power of a beast between his legs, the wind brushing his face, was what he was destined for. The rest of it — talk, dealings with people, feelings — were mere troublesome interludes to enable him to ride.

He found Devereau riding alone near the rear of the winding mass of bushwhackers, looking bored and spent. The ride from Missouri had been a long slog through concealing thick timber and wooded ravines, and this night the four hundred men were half-asleep in their saddles.

Robert galloped up beside Devereau and drew rein. "I found Dark Horse!" he whispered excitedly.

Devereau perked up. "Durk? You saw Durk?"

"A couple miles from here. They're camped out for the night."

"Let's find Quantrill," Devereau said, spurring her horse. Robert did likewise to catch her, and they rode side-by-side, whispering so the riders they passed couldn't overhear them. "How many are with him?"

"Barely a dozen," Robert replied. "Their horses are dog meat. They could never escape us." The Missouri State Militia, the MSM, raised by edict of the governor, were the most poorly armed and trained of all the Union forces. Men who enlisted in the MSM were instructed to bring their own rifles and shotguns and, if they had them, their own horses. With MSM weapons of all different types, ages, and makes, supplying them with ammunition was a nearly impossible task.

Robert studied Devereau's face. Now that she had found her prey, how would she react? Did she truly want to kill Dark Horse or had she some other purpose? Her face gave Robert no clue. She may as well have been an Indian. "Will we kill him?"

Devereau considered her answer, then replied flatly. "Was Antoinette with him?"

"No, just his unit."

Devereau gave Robert a hard stare. "Then we'll need him to draw her in. We'll have to capture him."

Robert's fury and disappointment showed on his face. "We have him, Devereau!" he barked angrily. "Let's finish him. We'll track her down later." He waited for an answer, but his companion was done speaking. The two continued riding in angry silence.

Within a half hour, the pair had caught up to Quantrill and the other leaders at the head of the guerrilla band, their fast approach startling the guerrillas to alertness. Quantrill drew rein, and the others followed suit. "What is it, French? What's so urgent?"

Devereau rode up to Quantrill, as Robert hung back a length, close enough to hear but distant enough to escape unnoticed. His hand went instinctively to his knife.

"Robert spotted a small Yankee patrol camped about a mile from here. Easy pickings."

"How many are there?" Quantrill asked.

"A dozen at most," Devereau said confidently. "A colored unit, shod and armed like the MSM. Thirty men can erase them in a half hour. We'll take care of them, then meet up with you further west."

Quantrill looked to the others for advice. "What do you think?"

Bill Anderson spat, leaning on his bow. "My man just spotted that patrol not a' hour ago. Said there must be a whole regiment, maybe more."

Quantrill weighed the two reports. "Why does your man estimate that many?"

Anderson removed his hat and wiped his forehead with his sleeve. "My man figured they had pickets out, so he couldn't get too close. But he said they're on high ground, that's one thing. The other thing, he said they had a dozen big fires covering well over an acre — well over. Has to be a regiment at least."

Unable to hold his silence any longer, Robert pulled out his knife. "I saw them in the daylight!" he shouted. "In the daylight. There were a dozen at most. At most!"

Anderson's lieutenant shouted, "Watch out! The Indian has a knife!" Three men pulled pistols from their belts, aiming them at Robert.

Devereau put herself between them, holding up her hand to calm everyone. "Sterling is never wrong about these things," she said. "Never."

Quantrill looked from Anderson to Robert Sterling and back again. Then he studied the ground until he'd made a decision. "I believe the Indian," he said, clearing the air.

Robert sheathed his knife, and the others belted their pistols.

"Nevertheless, we'll have to bypass that patrol, easy target as they might be. Lawrence is our objective, gentlemen — Lawrence, don't forget — and we can't chance losing the element of surprise. We don't want to let the Federals know we're coming just to butcher a squad of colored cavalry, tempting as that may be."

"Just give me thirty men," Devereau argued. "They can't escape us on the nags they have."

Quantrill clinched his jaw firmly. "Our horses are pretty tired to be chasing anybody right now, French. We'll continue as planned. No side ventures." He then spurred his horse to the head of the line and his retinue followed.

When they were gone, Robert gave Devereau a threatening look. "I thought you could talk them into anything," he growled, then paused to gather his thoughts. "Perhaps we could sneak into his camp and kill Dark Horse in his sleep."

"Too risky," Devereau said. "We'll get a better chance. Remember, we want both of them."

Robert spat and turned his horse away from her. "Both of them!" he said disdainfully. "You're a coward as well as a liar."

CHAPTER TWELVE

A LAST DESPERATE CHANCE

Eastern Kansas

It was past midnight when an urgent hand shook Durk awake in his blankets on the ground. "Durk, wake up, wake up."

The large bonfire had nearly gone out under the moonless sky. Opening his eyes, Durk fought sleep and the darkness to recognize the silhouette of Long Lou hovering over him. "What is it, Lou?"

"Pickets reported a whole mess of bushwhackers. Hundreds of 'em."

Durk threw off his blankets, rolled over, and sat up. "Hundreds? In Kansas?"

"Hundreds. Headed west."

"West?" Durk scratched his head. "You sure, Lou?"

"Bammer come and get me. I saw the tail end mysef. Over a hundred just in the rear guard. Don't know how many up front."

Durk rose and undid the rope tying his wrist to Isaac. "We'd better go tell Josh." He motioned for Isaac who'd been awakened by the fretful conversation, and the three of them made haste to wake Big Josh, wrapped up in his blankets snoring.

As Long Lou repeated his intelligence to Josh, they were joined by Bammer, who confirmed his sightings.

"Wh-where they headed?" Josh asked.

"Must be Lawrence," Durk said with alarm. "Westport's well-defended. Ain't no other place this far west, not one that would draw so many rebels."

"There been rumors for a long time they g-gonna raid Lawrence," Josh said, rubbing his chin. "Been so long, maybe nobody believe it."

"You know what they planning to do," Bammer said urgently. "It gonna be a massacre. Them poor folks."

"Damn," Durk exclaimed. "The Federals pulled out of Lawrence three, four weeks ago. The only troops there now are the men we left behind, and they haven't any rifles! They're sitting ducks."

"Wh-what should we do?" Josh asked. "They's twenty of us and hundreds of them. And our guns don't even work. What?"

"We've got to get word to the nearest Union camp," Durk said. "It's Lawrence's best chance."

"And warn the t-town," Big Josh added. "Least they'll have a chance."

The four looked at each other anxiously, confirming the urgency and the difficulty ahead.

"Who gonna get through the bushwhackers to Lawrence?" Bammer asked.

"I should be the one to go," Durk said reluctantly, surprising himself that he would volunteer. "I've ridden all my life and spent plenty of time hiding in the wilds. Just give me the fastest horse."

"No, Durk," Big Josh said. "We gonna need you to convince the army of what we saw. They ain't gonna believe none of us. You our best chance."

"I do it," Isaac said resignedly. "It's my fault we in Kansas in the first place. Ain't no loss if they kills me."

Durk and Josh looked at each other, both their faces disdainful of the possible consequences of Isaac being turned loose with so much at stake. Josh patted Isaac's shoulder, then they nodded, accepting the gesture. "Thanks, Isaac," Josh said. "Now, we only got f-four pistols that work, so we need three more men."

The four fell into thoughtful silence.

"I do it," Long Lou uttered reluctantly, sounding like a condemned prisoner. "Somebody got to."

Josh put his big arm around Lou's shoulder and looked into his eyes. "You sure?" he asked intently. "You got a wife and child."

Lou nodded yes.

"Alright, then, get two more v-volunteers, Lou. Tell 'em the truth. Chances are none of you will make it. And tell 'em, if they get caught, it ain't gonna be pretty. Each of you take one of the pistols that fire — you be saving that ball for *you'self*, not to shoot no 'whackers. Understand?"

Lou swallowed with difficulty, then nodded affirmation.

"Now, y'all take different r-routes." Josh's face grew grim. "Le's just hope one of you gets through *in time*. With they head start, ain't much chance, but we gots to try."

"You understand you're going on a suicide mission," Durk said wearily, grabbing Lou's hand with both of his. He then pulled Issac to himself, embracing him, knowing he may never see his friend who'd saved his life ever again. One at a time, the others embraced the pair. Everyone knew it was likely to be the last time they'd see them alive.

The whole unit gathered around the courageous volunteers — Lou, Isaac, a freeman named John Wilkins who had a wife and three children, and Billy with no last name, an escaped slave from Northeastern Missouri — holding the reins to the best horses they had, which still wasn't saying much. The four riders solemnly slipped the pistols into their belts, knowing what they were intended for — and unsure if they would find the will to use them if trapped — said their goodbyes. Eye to eye, Durk and Isaac wordlessly exchanged understandings gained from four years of conflict and compromise between them. Then the four mounted up and rode off, heading west.

"Okay," Josh said to the remaining men. "Le's go. We got some hard riding to do."

Durk mounted a paint, knowing they no longer had any working firearms, but he wanted to make sure there was no chance that any one of them might inadvertently alert the guerrillas. "Keep as quiet as possible. We don't want the rebels to get even a sniff of our horses," he said. "I know our firearms probably don't work, but don't even try to fire a shot, no matter what. Run if you have to, but keep quiet."

***

The Run to Lawrence

As he rode through the forest's night shadows, Long Lou listened intently for the sound of riders. The trees whipped past him, as the trails through them widened and narrowed, and he feared being unhorsed — knocked off by branches or thrown by the beast's lurches and shocks — but he never paused in pursuing his desperate mission. He attempted to keep to the north of where he estimated the column of bushwhackers to be, hoping to circumvent them and to reach Lawrence in time.

As he came over a ridge, Lou felt his stomach drop. With no warning, his horse scrambled down an embankment on the other side, spraying rocks and dirt, whinnying and pulling at its bridle. A novice horsemen, like all of the men except Durk, Lou held onto the reins and saddle horn with all his might as he bumped and jolted about, terrified of being thrown. Finally, when the horse regained its footing, Lou sat upright, steadying his place in the saddle. He turned his head right, then left, but he heard no hooves approaching from either direction. No one had heard his commotion, but he still had a problem. He found himself on the bank of a river. He could tell it was narrow and deep at this point, but the horse couldn't swim across, and Lou wasn't a swimmer. Although it would cause a delay, he would have to find a ford somewhere further north. He turned the horse and spurred it up the embankment, intent on locating that ford. Time was fleeing, and every moment, every second, was precious.

***

On the north side of the hills, young Billy rode his horse down the trail as hard as it would go, reins wrapped around his hand. He hadn't ridden much before, but he'd learned quickly enough to do passably well. Passably wasn't much, but now that he'd volunteered, he had no choice. The animal's bumps and jolts tossed him about, but he managed to stay in the saddle — so far. It was dark, and he was scared. But he and his friends had run away to fight, to wear this uniform, to be a hero against slavery, and Lawrence and the unarmed members of their regiment left behind needed to be saved.

The horse stumbled and caught itself, then rose hard and began to buck and pitch. Billy wrapped his arms around its neck but was flung off like a dead cat, arms and legs flailing every which way. When he hit the ground, his head bounced off a tree trunk, stunning him. He groaned and tried to rise, but fell back… unconscious.

He woke with a painful throbbing in his head, not knowing how long he'd been out, and the horse was gone. He worked himself to his knees, then tried to stand, but fell back. On the second try, he made it to his feet. He was dizzy and confused. It was pitch in the woods — couldn't see ten feet ahead — and he couldn't tell which direction he was facing. There was no sun or trail to offer him a direction. He looked about but couldn't find a clue to where to run next. A sob escaped his throat. The friends he'd escaped with who had joined the regiment, and the others he'd made friends with since, needed him. All he knew was, he had to get to Lawrence and get there fast.

He had to keep moving to have any chance at all. He chose a direction and began to run through the forest. Within a half mile, he was gasping for breath, but he kept running as fast as he could. He couldn't slow, couldn't stop.

He prayed that he was headed the right way, but he was only guessing.

***

John Wilkens rode hard down the most direct road to Lawrence, his path parallel to, but hopefully avoiding, where he guessed the bushwhacker column to be. He knew his blue uniform made him a sure target, but he had to take a chance or he'd never pass the rebel column, which had a head start of hours. He concentrated on the steady rhythm of his horse's hooves rumbling across a wooden country bridge to keep his mind from straying from the task at hand, to focus on his end goal... but a man's mind goes where it wants to go.

His heart ached. The faces of his wife and children back home flooded his mind, dominating his thoughts. He knew the odds were heavily against him, knew very well he might never see them again. Would they understand why he, a free black man, had joined the army? Would they understand that it wasn't just to free their people?

Shock, absolute terror! He could hear the hoof beats of horses and clipped, shouted orders in distinctive Western Missouri twang up ahead. Probably a patrol covering the flank of the guerrilla movement, checking the bridge. He drew rein, pulling as hard as he could until the horse reared. They'd heard him. The guerrillas' horses broke into a gallop, heading directly toward him, spreading north and south to entrap him. He rapidly searched his surroundings. There were woods bordering the road up ahead, but that was the direction from which the riders were coming. He turned the horse back the way he'd come and spurred it. More shouts, a shot! His pursuers were coming after him.

He repeatedly struck the horse's flank. As he rode, he pulled the pistol from his belt and held the heavy, grim, cold metal in his hand. All he could think of was escape, yet he knew in the back of his mind that the rebels would catch him. How could they not? They'd catch up and have him surrounded. If — when — they caught him, he would have to take his own life to preserve his dignity. He wouldn't give them the satisfaction of dying at their hands.

The faces of his family flashed before his eyes. He whipped the horse's flank once more, but the beast was giving all it had and was already slowing. No matter how fast he rode, the pursuit grew louder. They were closing quickly. John Wilkens was preparing himself to die.

***

Isaac reached the riverbank and drew rein. Halted in mid-gallop, his horse pulled back and forth, yanking at its bridal. What could he do? He was blocked. He considered going in search of a ford or bridge, but that would take time. People's lives depended on his speed. He looked upriver and down, but no obvious solution appeared. Finally, he took a deep breath and spurred the mare. The animal resisted his urging, but he kept kicking its ribs. Then the horse plunged into the cold waters, whinnying and neighing.

Partway across, Isaac knew he'd made a mistake. The river was way over their heads. His horse was kicking and splashing, about to go under. He held onto the mare's neck as long as he could, but finally had to jump off the desperate animal in order to avoid being dragged under with the mare and its slashing hooves. He was relieved that he wasn't kicked, but within seconds, the strong waters carried them both away, pulling Isaac under.

He rose to the surface gasping for air, but he was being washed downstream at a rapid rate. Clearing his eyes with his palms, he located the horse, but the terrified animal was under the river's control. Never a swimmer, Isaac splashed and flayed away with all his might back toward shore. As he tried gulping for air, water flooded into his mouth, making him cough and spit. Meanwhile, he, too, was under the current's control, being washed rapidly downstream. It was all he could do to catch air periodically.

Finally, his wild flailing paid off, and he crashed into the rocky shore, where he lay for some minutes gulping and choking, trying to catch his breath. When he recovered enough, he sat up in the shallow water, only to discover he was far downstream from where he'd entered the river, still on the same side where he'd begun. He reached for his midsection, feeling for his pistol, only to discover it had slipped from his pants. Moreover, his horse was nowhere in sight. He stripped off his soaked uniform top to enable himself to run fast and to avoid detection. Uniform coat or no, if the rebels caught him, the military pants he wore were a death sentence. He knew he no longer had a chance to reach Lawrence before the guerrillas who were mounted and had a substantial head start. Realizing his helplessness, he started to cry so hard his whole body shook. People were going to die because of his failure. Fighting back tears, he rose and began to run along the bank. He had to keep going.

Suddenly, the savage voices in his head started taunting him mercilessly. *You killed them! You killed your friends! You killed the whole town, the whole damn town!*

Running as fast as his legs could go, Isaac began screaming frantically. Run as he might, he knew no amount of foot speed could outrun his voices' shrill cajoling… nor could he get to Lawrence in time.

***

Westport HQ, Kansas

Major Danwell, having been awakened, emerged from his tent, pulling his suspenders over his shoulders. It was past-midnight, and he was in no mood for formality.

"I'm telling you, Colonel, there're hundreds of them! Headed straight for Lawrence," Durk exclaimed urgently. Sore from the long, hard ride, he stretched his back and settled himself in the saddle.

"Hundreds? Lawrence?" the major asked, incredulous. He examined the captain astride a poor excuse for an army horse and the ragged group of black mounted men behind him, sitting on animals little better than plow horses. "You say hundreds?"

"Hundreds, sir. We've got to hurry."

"Who saw them?"

Big Josh ordered Bammer forward. "I saw the tail end," Bammer said. "Over a hundred just by itself, and I heard a lot more up ahead."

"But you didn't see the head of the column?"

"I met up with Lou who see the other part of it. Hundreds there, too."

"Where is this Lou?"

"He's riding to Lawrence to warn the folks there," Durk explained. "I sent four men ahead. It's practically a suicide mission, sir, but we had to do what we could. The men who saw them are reliable. I'll vouch for every one of them."

"Hundreds," the major mused, astonished at the terrifying news. He reached into his tent and pulled out his coat and boots. "My Lord, the general pulled the troops out of Lawrence three-four weeks ago. Have Tad blow assembly," he ordered his aide. "We'll try to intercept them on their way back to Missouri."

"I'll take my men to Lawrence, Colonel," Durk said. "We've got to warn the citizens. I've left half my regiment there without any working rifles."

"No rifles? What kind of...?"

"We were on our way to Westport to pick up some weapons. Major, my men are unarmed."

"What a damn mess," the major said. "Okay, Captain, take your men by supply and get what you need. Then you ride straight to Lawrence fast as you can and do what you can. But if what you say is true, I think you're far too little, far too late."

"Right after you sign a requisition form for me. Then we'll be after those bushwhackers."

***

"I want forty of those sixteen-shot Henry repeaters," Durk said, disdaining the muzzle-loaders the supply sergeant had offered him. The sixteen-shot Henrys had begun to give the Union Cavalry a major advantage over the hard-to-load, single-shot weapons Confederate cavalry used. The rebels bitterly remarked that the Union Cavalry "loaded the Henrys on Sunday and shot them all week." But few of the new Henrys were available, with those in inventory precious and closely guarded.

"Can't do that, Captain Hurst," the supply sergeant said, and spit a black stream of tobacco juice into a spittoon beside his desk. "Henrys are reserved for white companies."

"These are for a white company, sir, the Ninth MSM," Durk said in his most friendly manner, holding out his personal papers identifying him as the Ninth's regimental officer.

"I am not blind, Captain Hurst. Case you ain't noticed, your men here is all black as a stew pot."

"Oh, them. These men have merely been assigned to transport the rifles back for my company, the Ninth MSM. That's a white company. Why don't you check your sheet there."

The supply sergeant studied his lists, then looked up at Hurst, surprised. "Yes, I see the Ninth is white. But I'm responsible for these Henrys. Now if you want to wait until I check..."

"Wait?" Durk exclaimed. Then his voice became urgent, higher-pitched. "Sir, you've heard the bugles. You know the rebels are about to ambush Lawrence."

"Yes, I know that. But..."

"The colonel wants me to get these Henrys to the Ninth as fast as we can; it's our only chance. Soldiers' lives are at stake, sir. You don't want me to report to the colonel that you held up weapons for men under attack over a technicality, do you? Lives, man, Union lives!"

"Well," the supply sergeant hesitated, "my list does indicate the Ninth is white. All right, Captain Hurst, sign for them. But any problems, it's your court-martial, not mine. Understand?"

While Durk signed for the rifles, the *DarkHorse* men hurriedly carried the rifles out into the night. Once the whole company was mounted outside, Big Josh grabbed Durk's reins, holding him in place. "Wh-what's this 'bout us being a white company, Durk? A white company?"

"Well," Durk said sheepishly, "I haven't fixed that with the army yet."

"But I tole you we don't want to be no white company, d-didn' I? Didn' I?"

"Listen, Josh, every one of you are still on the rolls as colored, just like you told me, all right? You're still not getting that thirteen dollars. It's just our company that's white — technically. Okay? It got us the Henrys, right?"

Josh glared angrily at Hurst, but he could see no flaw in the logic. "All right this one time, D-durk. But you let me know if you gots any more of your tricks in the works *before* you do them. You hear me? Cause if you get us in trouble with the army, I br-break your neck. Hear?"

"I will, Josh. Promise." Durk turned his horse. "We've got to get to Lawrence, men!" he shouted. "It's our only chance!" He spurred his paint to a gallop, and the rest of the *DarkHorse* soldiers followed suit to keep up with him.

***

Lawrence, Kansas

They waited for the signal at the top of a tree-shaded hill, four hundred horses neighing and pawing the ground aligned single file to either side of them. Robert Sterling pulled the brass spyglass from Devereau French's saddle to get a look at the peaceful, quiet town. It was six a.m., and the sun was rising behind them. Lawrence was just waking up. The night hadn't cooled the air substantially, and every one of the four hundred guerrilla raiders knew the day would bring another hot one. They'd soon be escaping from Union Cavalry under oppressive heat, ameliorated only by the shade of timber, which would also provide concealment from their Union pursuers. But that would come later, about noon, after their business was done. By then, revenge for the humiliating arrests, deaths, and disfigurements of their womenfolk — and for their own powerlessness and personal tragedies — would be satisfied.

The bushwhackers down the line from Devereau and Robert all had their jobs to do. They firmed their pistols in their belts, from four to eight each. Vicious Jayhawker cavalry had plundered and murdered the Confederate sympathizing families of Western Missouri for years, and now they would even scores. Some riders were to go from house to house and call out husbands and sons who would then be shot dead. Some were to put the town to the torch. They'd also brought empty wagons with them to recover the booty stolen from innocent civilians.

And some would surround and slaughter the soldiers, black and white, just outside of town.

***

Robert's perusal of Lawrence's main streets stopped at a building not far from the courthouse. *This must be the bank.* He signaled for Devereau to examine the storefront, passing the spyglass. Devereau studied the building and those around it, then removed the spyglass from her eye and nodded, *Yes, that would be the bank.*

"What is our next move?" Robert asked under his breath.

Devereau thought a moment. "We'll hang back, then help clean out the bank while the 'whackers are busy shooting up the town. Quickly in and out.

And don't shoot it out with the rebels; just grab what you can and be gone. The raid should take three, four hours, so that should give us enough time to put miles between us and the fighting.

"Quantrill ordered his Confederates to assemble on the Wakarusa River after the raid, about three miles south of town," Devereau whispered. "I think he plans to escape down the Fort Scott Road, south and east. So we will merely ride north."

"What if we run into Federal troops?"

"Act frightened and throw them off. 'Trouble in Lawrence. Lots of gunfire. Must be hundreds of bushwhackers. They're fleeing south. We'll go notify the army.' Point south, then ride north."

"If you think it will work."

"Panic will prevail. It always does."

***

Quantrill studied the scene below him. The town was utterly unprepared, with no visible sign of defense or resistance. They'd managed to gain total surprise. He raised his hand. Then his arm swept down as he spurred his horse. A loud rebel cry pierced the morning as the roar of hooves descended from the hills surrounding this western center of abolitionism. Just retaliation was to be meted out in the same measure in Kansas as had been inflicted upon the innocent citizens of Missouri.

CHAPTER THIRTEEN

CONFLAGRATION

Lawrence, Kansas

Like the soldiers they believed themselves to be, the guerrillas initiated their attack with planned precision. The riders swarmed toward Lawrence diagonally like a chess bishop moving across a chessboard, from southeast to northwest. Galloping at full speed, they crossed vacant lots, avoiding obstructions and obstacles so as not to be slowed or ambushed. At Quincy and Rhode Island streets, guerrillas broke off from the main column to form a cordon around the town; others raced to their places on the high ground of Mount Oread, where they entertained a fine, fifteen-mile view. If Federals approached, these latter would give warning.

Like the tide in a winter storm, Quantrill's main force surged toward the town's business district, Massachusetts Street, and continued forward to the two Union military camps south of this main street: one black, the Ninth MSMCC, and one white, the Fourteenth Kansas. Led by Lieutenant Gregg, the guerrillas bypassed the orderly rows of tents belonging to the white troops, many of whom were sleeping a block away on front porches in the warm August morning, and raced into the black camp, firing their pistols at anyone who moved. Awakened abruptly, the unarmed soldiers of the Ninth ran off in every direction, with a few lucky ones making it to safety in the willow brakes along the river until the invasion was over. Most were killed in flight.

Next, reins clutched in their teeth, the secesh charged the tents of the twenty-two white recruits, firing with both hands. They tore through the guy ropes and toppled the tents. The soldiers, whose weapons were stored in a building fifty yards away, had no chance. Most of the unit were massacred.

"On to the hotel!" a guerrilla shouted.

"On to the hotel!" others picked up the cry.

The storm blew on. Quantrill and Gregg galloped up Massachusetts, firing pistols with both hands. When they reached the river, they turned back, like a wave sweeping back out to sea. As the main force followed down the street, columns broke off to flood the back streets until the entire business district was sealed off. Escape was impossible.

Citizens in all stages of undress and work attire dodged the hail of gunfire to reach Palmer's gun shop and the arsenal between Winthrop and Pinckney streets, but they were disorganized, in full panic, and far too late. The massacre continued. Some of the guerrillas dismounted and invaded the district's liquor stores. Once inside, they smashed the ends off bottles and swallowed the harsh liquid. Now fueled by drink, these already hate-filled men became more foul, more angry, seeking bloody revenge for the hardships of two years of war.

Inflamed, the rebels tore up and down the streets at a mad gait, shooting randomly at citizens scattering desperately in every direction. Soon the streets and sidewalks were littered with bodies and blood. When there were no more boys or men to shoot, the horses milled about circling, still breathing hard, their hooves kicking up dust. Then the guerrillas headed to the hotel, ordering the guests to come out front. Rather than invade every business and house in town, they began to set every structure on fire. Anyone inside the buildings would be forced to emerge to an unfriendly reception.

Bushwhackers rifled through the pockets of corpses and broke windows. They stole horses and saddles, guns and liquor. Others loaded spoils into the wagons. Twenty years of raids from Kansas abolitionists on Western Missouri farms and towns couldn't be revenged in a day. But, for the moment, until the Federals began their pursuit, the events of the morning were very satisfactory.

***

Devereau and Robert rode briskly through the thick timber and brush north of town. They hadn't gotten as much cash as they'd hoped, but they'd managed to grab a stack of bills. Enough for now. They paused to listen. They could still hear gunfire, hoofbeats, and bloody cries. Could see the smoke rising from every corner of the once-prosperous town.

Robert shrugged and spurred the mare, followed by Devereau. They had to get further away as quickly as possible.

Reaching the top of a hill, they drew rein to take one last look at the devastation they'd left behind. Devereau shrugged, "War is certainly Hell, and Hell does love the sinner."

Robert pulled the few paper dollars they'd acquired from his jacket pocket. He fingered through them, then angrily shoved them back into his pocket. "Hell may love the sinner, but not nearly enough."

***

Eastern Kansas

Long Lou spurred the horse, frantically whipping its nose with the reins, then cursed and slapped its haunches. After a brief resistance to the rider's urging, the exhausted animal continued up the hill at barely more than a trot. It was late afternoon under glaring sun and broiling heat. Lou had ridden all night as fast as the flea-bit nag could endure. Finally, he was close.

He reached the rise overlooking the town and drew rein. What he saw took his breath away, akin to being punched in the stomach. Below, the town was smoldering, its main streets lined by chaotic blackened beams lying askew amid charred chimneys and ashes of what had once been homes and businesses, the pride of ordinary, well-meaning people. Bodies littered the streets, lying in all manner of grotesque poses. He was too late. Overcome by seeing the horror that was once a thriving town, he leaned on his bow wiping his eyes, trying to remain steady.

Recovering as reality set in, he headed toward the spot where the *DarkHorse* unit had made camp. Reluctant to arrive, he let the animal drift at an unhurried pace, afraid of what he would find. *If only I'd come a day earlier*, he thought. But he knew that would have been impossible. Impossible.

When he reached the army camp, the few members of the regiment that had managed to make it to hiding in the brake were dragging the corpses to form a central pile. Lou did not dismount. Instead, he rode slowly among the bodies of black soldiers in torn bloody blue rags lying frozen in monstrous postures, as if dropped in mid-flight, faces contorted in agony and fear. The bushwhackers had vented years of anger and frustration upon the regiment. Many were unrecognizable, with heads bashed in, their bodies defiled and debased. He was only able to recognize Colonel Daltry by his white hands and his uniform. Then he saw Little Turby, who had hoped to be a schoolteacher or preacher or doctor, lying in a heap, broken glasses beside him, shot down before he could even attempt to run. Others of his original *DarkHorse* partners lay scattered about, their corpses strewn among the new regimental friends from Missouri, Iowa, and beyond. It struck him that they'd survived living under constant threat in a slave land, survived the hazardous trek north, only to have no chance to defend themselves. Dead, dead, dead. Every one dead.

He rode to the lone shade maple at the edge of the same field on which their nascent regiment had practiced their marching and dismounted. He tied the horse where it could nibble on the sparse grass and plopped down onto the ground, but the shade tree offered little relief in the sweltering air.

He was shaking, and his head was throbbing, throbbing, as he let it sink into his hands. All these bodies! What was he to do? As played-out as he was, any action he might take seemed hopeless.

Lou gazed across the field to the heap of inanimate flesh that had once been Little Turby, then lowered his eyes, staring at, but not seeing, the dirt between his boots, unable to look at his lost young friend. He remembered bright Turby, his curiosity always straining at the bit, his hunger for knowledge voracious, his perpetual willingness to help unflaggingly, his glowing smile, his boyish bright eyes…Little Turby had been *DarkHorse's* tomorrow, their future. Covering his face, Long Lou began to cry. Hard. *Ain't nothing to do about it. Ain't nothing left to do but bury them.*

CHAPTER FOURTEEN

HANGMAN BOUND

St. Charles, Missouri, outside St. Louis
U.S. Army General Thomas Barrett paced from room to room in the grand house he'd converted into his headquarters. The home had belonged to one of the wealthiest planters in the eastern portion of Little Dixie, a pro-secession man named Ruggins, and its view of the Missouri River calmed him on nights when he was under strain. Finally, he reached the room where he'd established his office, formerly the home's main dining room. Head framed in curly red hair, bushy sideburns, and a broad, sweeping mustache, the flush-faced Barrett, now in his mid-fifties, fit the nickname his men had given him: Old Cannonball. Certainly, Cannonball matched his rotund shape, but more so his scarlet hair presaging his brash, bullying style and explosive temper.

The general oversaw all of Central Missouri to its western border, where he'd established a string of base camps meant to keep Missouri bushwhackers from raiding Kansas, but the recent tragedy in Lawrence had exposed the holes in this strategy. While the Federals had received a warning of the attack the night before the massacre, the Union response was too late to prevent the Confederate raid, nor to bring justice to all but a few of the guerrillas. Ever since then, the volatile Barrett had been in high dungeon, furious, ranting at those whom he blamed for Lawrence, a massive failure in a territory that was his responsibility. He knew his military career was in jeopardy.

Barrett took a final glance out the window into the garden that bordered the back yard, then turned back, away from the blazing sun. Deep in thought, the general circled what was now his primary office, then sat down on the leather chair behind the enormous carved oak desk that dominated the room. From this vantage point, he could see through the doorway to what had been the parlor, where he had moved the house's large dining table. The polished surface of the table was covered in maps, which were being busily poured over by a pair of colonels and one of his aides.

There was a knock on the door, and the general shouted permission to enter.

Antoinette was led in by two guards, who seated her on the chair across from the general. The soldiers turned to leave, but Barrett insisted they remain. Barrett removed several papers from his desk drawer, inked his pen, and scribbled a few notes. Then, glancing up, he examined the woman before him, his fierce gaze never wavering. The military was certain to investigate the Lawrence fiasco, and his career — if not his freedom — might be in real danger. If he could find extenuating circumstances for the bushwhackers' successful raid, he might be able to use that in his defense to avoid disgrace. Maybe this woman could provide information, or even be culpable in some way?

The general nodded to an aide who poured him coffee from a pot on the makeshift stove, installed by the army for his convenience. A round hole had been cut in the papered wall to fit the tin tube that carried the wood fire smoke to the outside yard. The rich, dark brew was still hot, and the general sipped slowly, holding the cup below his nostrils to take in the rich aroma.

"Would you like a cup, ma'am?" he asked innocently, looking up to examine his guest.

"Thank you, sir; that would be most kind," Antoinette replied in her most gracious New Orleans drawl.

The more he studied the woman, the more his suspicions grew. She was extremely beautiful, somewhere in her thirties, with round, dark-lashed eyes, full lips, and ample breasts. Clearly, she was well-reared, with naturally graceful movements and delicate manners. Moreover, her accent told him she was obviously Southern. Yet here she was in his camp, wearing a plain garment made of rough calico. None of it fit; nothing made sense.

"Now, tell me what you told the sergeant," he said evenly, handing her a cup of the rare liquid, his gray eyes remaining cold, cynical. "First, what is your full name?"

"Antoinette DuVallier," she said, taking a sip.

"And where are you from?"

"New Orleans, originally," she said, nervously pushing a loose strand of hair back into place with her free hand. That morning she'd learned there'd been a massacre at Lawrence, including the Union soldiers stationed there, and she felt as if she'd been struck by a two-by-four. Desperate to check on Durk and his men, she'd rushed to the wire office without finishing breakfast, only to find herself arrested and brought to headquarters to face a general with blood in his eyes. She and her friends had been held at the camp for eighteen days, ever since the train raid, and no one she'd spoken to since, and nothing she'd tried, had moved them an inch closer to being permitted to continue on to St. Louis.

"And when did you come to Missouri, and from where?" the general asked.

"Two years ago. From Mississippi. It's a long story." She placed the remainder of her cup on the desk in front of her.

"Well, I don't have time for long stories, Miss DuVallier — or is it *Mrs.*?"

"*Mrs.*, I suppose, General. I am a widow."

"And the women with you, Mrs. DuVallier, the slaves. To whom do they belong?"

"They aren't slaves, General. They're free women. They came here with me."

A bitter expression crept onto the general's face. He would fight, even die, to preserve the Union, but he never fully cottoned to the idea of freeing the slaves, and he didn't much care for recent proclamations from Washington that were contrary to his beliefs. Still, he was one to follow orders, as well as to give them. "How so? Do you have manumission documents for these people?"

"I'm sorry, I don't, General. When the secessionists raided the train, they took them, along with our orders." Her hands gripped one another in desperation.

Frustrated and growing increasingly skeptical, the general set his cup down heavily on the desk, already not believing her tale. He paused a moment to consider his approach. "So you've been living with this gaggle of Negros for two years, just as if you were *one* of them; is that what you're saying?"

Antoinette nodded.

"Don't you think that's a little odd, a woman of your background?"

"No, n-not at all," Antoinette stuttered, "if you knew th-the situation."

"All right," the general snapped, drumming his fingers against the desk. He paused a moment to think. "Under whose authority did these people become manumitted in the first place?"

"You see, in Mississippi, I ran a plantation for the French family, a place called *FrenchAcres*. As the manager, I sold these women to Mr. Durksen Hurst, another plantation owner. These women were the wives and mates of the men who worked for Hurst, whom he had already manumitted. Hurst freed these women, too. After the war broke out, the whole group of us headed north to aid the Union Army."

"You and this planter, Hurst?"

Antoinette nodded, her heart pounding faster, too nervous to speak.

"So you and this Hurst fellow are abolitionists?"

"That is correct, General."

Clucking his tongue, the general dipped his quill and made notes. He studied what he'd written and shook his head. "So you had approval from this French family to sell their property?"

"Yes."

"How so? That was quite a substantial transaction."

"Not really. The Frenches owned hundreds of slaves. A dozen women and a few children weren't missed."

"So these Frenches allowed an employee to make such decisions. I've never heard of that. How did you come to this authority?"

"You see, sir, Mrs. French was...was my mother." *A child's glimpse of a pink skirt and her mother's face flashed before her eyes, then vanished.*

Angry now, the general slammed his hands down on the desk. This was the most convoluted story he'd ever heard. "Your mother?" he cried. The general took a long, deep breath, swallowed a large swig of coffee, and rose. Clasping his hands behind his back, he began to pace the room. "Madam, how do you explain a woman such as yourself, obviously well-to-do, living with a herd of angus women and children? And Hurst is white, yes? If this Hurst is responsible for them, why aren't they with him?"

"Because Hurst and his men are in the Missouri State Militia. Durk is the captain of the regiment. I tried to explain that to the sergeant and the captain. That's why I've been wiring Lawrence."

"You've been wiring Lawrence back and forth since they brought you in, I'm told. Is that right?"

Antoinette nodded.

"You've used your charms to convince the clerks to send and take messages for you, even though our wire facilities are off limits to civilians, correct? I think that's very suspicious, don't you?"

"As I said, General, their regiment is stationed there."

"Yes? What unit?"

"Ninth MSM Colored Cavalry, called the *DarkHorse* regiment, sir."

"Lawrence! Did you say the Ninth MSM Cavalry? Lawrence, Kansas?"

"Yes, the Ninth MSM *Colored* Cavalry."

"Wait one second, please." General Barrett strode briskly into the parlor and examined the large map covering the table, then returned and sat upright at his desk. "And you say the Ninth is a *colored* unit?"

"Yes, that's correct," Antoinette answered, perplexed at the direction the interrogation was heading.

"The Ninth MSM Cavalry is a white unit. A *white* unit. How do you explain this discrepancy? You say the Ninth is *colored* while I know for a fact it is *white*."

Startled, Antoinette struggled to understand. Had there been some paperwork mix-up, some reporting error? She puzzled this over, then speculated that Durk might have arranged for his men to be registered as a white unit on purpose, perhaps seeing some advantage to it. She couldn't imagine how the slippery Durk had pulled off such a subterfuge, but she wouldn't put it past him.

"Perhaps there's been some mistake," she said haltingly. "If you wire Lawrence, I'm positive they'll straighten the whole thing out. Captain Hurst and his commanding officer will vouch for what I'm telling you."

General Barrett made notes. Then rising abruptly, he began to bellow, his face reddening. "What have you to do with Lawrence, madam?"

Shocked by the aggressive stance and tone the general had taken, Antoinette's face became ghostly pale. "That-that's where the Ninth was transferred. I told..."

"I would have to say," the general continued, "it is unlikely that any wire sent to Lawrence would resolve these questions. The wires to Lawrence are down."

"B-but..."

"Furthermore, Mrs. DuVallier, preliminary reports say the Ninth MSM Cavalry was likely wiped out in the Lawrence raid. In fact, the entire town has been burned to the ground, with most of the male civilian population murdered in cold blood. Now, do you want to change your story before I have you arrested?" General Barrett sat back down, made more notes for himself, and scratched out others.

"Wiped out?" Antoinette exclaimed, her heart sinking. "The Ninth? All of them?"

The general fixed her in his steely gaze, twisting his mustache thoughtfully, once, twice, a third time. "Wiped out. They didn't have a chance."

Tears began to tumble down Antoinette's cheeks, and she began to tremble. The general tossed a handkerchief into her lap, and once Antoinette realized it was there, she used it to wipe her eyes.

"Mrs. DuVallier, did you and Mr. Hurst — Captain Hurst — make your way to Missouri *together*? Along with the slaves?"

"Y-yes," Antoinette sputtered. "But they're *not* slaves."

"And that was when?"

"In '61."

"In '61, with a group of supposedly manumitted slaves? And this regiment, whether colored or white, was recently formed?"

Antoinette nodded, trying to compose herself.

"So, what have you and Hurst and all these Negros been doing the last two years?"

"We were attached to the Federal Fifth most of the time. The men tended the officers' horses, dug ditches, and built fortifications. I worked in the medical tent. The women I'm with did laundry, cooked, all manner of work."

The colonel pursed his lips, a pained expression wrinkling his brow. "And Hurst, what was he doing?"

"Working alongside the other men. He mostly tended and trained cavalry horses, but he performed plenty of hard labor, too."

"By 'others,' you mean the so-called slaves, manumitted or not, is that right? So let me understand this… Durksen Hurst, a Southern planter, spent two years as a common laborer working beside Negros? And, you, the daughter of a rich planter, did the same, except that your duties were more suitable to your sex?"

"That's right, General."

"And why would either of you leave a comfortable life on a plantation, for him to shovel manure and for you to treat wounded soldiers? And both of you living among a flock of crows?"

Antoinette bristled. This wouldn't be easy to explain and might heap more suspicion upon them, but she had to be seen as sympathetic to the Union, and the truth was the best way to do that. Besides, the truth was simpler. If Durk or any of the others did survive Lawrence, there would be less chance of contradictions between their stories. "We were against the war, against slavery, and against secession. We were chased out of town," she explained when she regained her composure.

"So you were abolitionists and came north to support our army? Is that what you're telling me?"

"That's right, General."

Barrett rose again and began to pace, hands behind his back, slapping one into the other. Finally, he stopped to face Antoinette, his bloated face glowing bright red. "So, in essence, you two were in a position to gather all manner of intelligence — troop dispositions, movements, strategy — really anything about the army. After all, who pays attention to a man laboring with the Negros? You say Hurst took care of the officers' horses. Officers talk quite freely when they're saddling their mounts or waiting for them to be saddled, as do enlisted men. You'd know where the cavalry was headed and for what purpose before they even hit the road. Isn't that true?"

Antoinette started to object, but Barrett raised his hand to silence her.

"In addition, you both had access to the officers' tents, their personal correspondence, maps, even to casual conversations among the enlisted men. Being a white man, there was nothing beyond this captain's eyes and ears! Not only that, your group of Negros trusted you, so you had them as a source of information."

The general plopped into his chair and made furious notes. He paused, studied Antoinette, then rubbed his chin thoughtfully. Finally, he said, "And being a nurse, you could come and go from camp any time you wanted. Isn't that true? You were in position to pass information to the outside at will."

"I would never..." Antoinette blurted.

"I don't know what intelligence you contributed to the rebels in the Lawrence massacre, Mrs. DuVallier, but you will find the United States government is not so forgiving in these matters. I am placing you under arrest as a suspected spy, pending the army's investigation into your actions. A fine lady like yourself, plain-dressed like that, can worm her way into many places and find out much about our army. But you slipped up! I caught you in a lie! Your information on the color of the Ninth MSM cavalry was flawed, and, thus, your usefulness to the rebels is now ended. Permanently, I would say. Spying is a hanging offense, madam."

Flabbergasted, Antoinette was unable to speak. Then she sputtered, "But, but will you tell me when you find out if Durk survived? Please..." she pleaded.

"And we'll hold those women, too," the general ordered, ignoring her outburst, then instructed his orderly, "Send a wire to Kansas. Have a Captain Durksen Hurst of the Ninth MSM Cavalry, colored or white, arrested under suspicion for aiding and abetting a female Confederate spy who was likely involved in the Lawrence raid, either knowingly or unknowingly. If Hurst is alive after what happened there, that proves he's a traitor. If not, then good riddance to Southern trash."

The general smiled grimly to himself. He had uncovered a secessionist spy ring, which might prove exculpatory to him. Thus, his ambitions for his post-war political career were not yet dashed. *Why, this pair's entire story is preposterous. Preposterous!* Innocent scapegoats or guilty parties, he was washing his hands of the whole filthy mess.

"I will decide what to do as soon as I hear back from Kansas. Now get this secesh spy out of here. I can't stand to look at her."

The two guards raised Antoinette from her chair to guide her to the prisoner stockade. She tried to speak but was unable to utter a word.

Finally, when the three reached the front porch outside, Antoinette burst into tears, sobbing so deeply she could scarcely breathe. Her knees gave out and, nearly fainting, she fell to the planks, her shoulders shaking, her eyes flooding with grief. *Durk probably dead! Me arrested as a spy!* The world had become a nightmare from which she would never wake. Never!

***

Lawrence, Kansas

Durk dropped the legs of the corpse he was helping Lou carry and scrutinized the field where they'd practiced their marching. Wiping his brow, he watched the others gathering up the bodies of their fallen comrades, cloths and handkerchiefs across their faces to ward off the odor. Then he looked off into the distance toward the town, now a senseless pile of blackened timber.

Next to him, Big Josh dropped the body he was carrying and stretched his back. "Looks like we back on burial detail," he said wearily. "We gonna have a heavy dose of that duty."

Durk merely shrugged.

Digging graves in the barren field under the scorching Kansas sun was suffocating, backbreaking work. Sweat poured down the shirtless torsos and faces of Durk, Big Josh, and the others as they struggled against the unyielding, rocky soil with shovels and picks. There were times when the diggers thought the dirt would win the contest, but, one grave at a time, the men kept on with the gruesome and unwelcome duty of burying their slaughtered and mangled friends. They endured, their only breaks being for water… and for tears.

Josh paused to wipe his brow. Leaning on his shovel, he took deep gulps of air, studying the group's progress. They were getting somewhere, but they had a long ways to go. "When we done here," he shouted, "we got to go into that town and help them people. Gonna be digging more graves. Plenty more."

"Horses!" one of the men shouted. Everyone stopped digging to listen. They watched anxiously as a company of blue-clad cavalry appeared on the road and began approaching.

"Maybe they bushwhackers!" another of the men shouted.

"Too orderly," Josh said. "They ours." The men dropped their shovels and pickaxes and stepped out of the holes they were digging onto flat land. As they watched, a red-haired captain in his early forties led the company of thirty directly up to Durk and drew rein immediately before him.

"Yes, Captain," Durk said, saluting. Following suit, the other surviving *DarkHorse* soldiers saluted the newly arrived authority. Durk's men weren't well-trained, and the impression of the half-dressed laborers attempting a formal gesture appeared irregular and sloppy. "What can we do for you?"

"I'm looking for the Ninth Missouri State Militia Cavalry," the captain said briskly. "Don't know if it's a colored or white regiment."

"That's us. We're the Ninth," Durk said.

"Are you Captain Durksen Hurst?" the captain asked crisply, a threatening look in his eye.

A puzzled look came over Durk's face. "Yes, that's me. I'm Hurst. Why?"

The captain raised his hand and pulled his pistol from its holster, aiming it directly at Durk. Behind him, his mounted men drew their rifles from their saddles and spread around the burial site until all the *DarkHorse* men were surrounded. "Durksen Hurst, I am placing you under arrest."

"Arrest?" Durk stuttered as a murmur grew among the men. "What am I accused of?"

"Treason," came the businesslike reply.

"Treason!" Josh cried and advanced toward the captain.

Immediately, four rifles aimed at Josh. "Hold it right there," the captain said. "Any of these colored soldiers takes a step toward us, don't ask questions. Shoot 'em down."

Josh raised his hands, but continued talking. "That man done risked his life for our country, Captain. He the one warned y'all 'bout Lawrence. Every man here will testify."

"The courts-martial will straighten it all out," the captain interrupted, cutting Josh off. "Each of you will be questioned in good time, I'm sure, but you colored cannot testify on the stand. Now not another word from any of you, or I'll have every one of you shackled and gagged. Understand? Not another word."

Looking around the area, the captain's eyes fixed on the *DarkHorse* regiment's rifles stacked neatly under an elm. "Henrys! What the hell are you doing with all those damn Henrys?" he shouted, flabbergasted. "Those are exclusively for Federal cavalry, not the MSM. And certainly not for colored troops. What exactly is going on here, Captain Hurst?"

"We were given them to protect Lawrence," Durk said. "It was us against hundreds of bushwhackers." From the captain's expression, Durk could see he wasn't believed.

"Well, considering the condition of the town and its citizens, I would hold that claim in dispute. Another issue, Captain Hurst, if the bushwhackers took the trouble to kill every man here, why didn't they take forty fresh Henrys sitting right there? Can you explain that?"

"We got here too late, Captain, as you can see."

"Headquarters will straighten this mess out," the captain said, shaking his head in disbelief. Then he looked the *DarkHorse* soldiers over. "All right. Stack those tools over there for the next regiment that comes and put your clothes on." He turned to his men. "Grab those Henrys up, boys, so we can get them where they belong. Soon as these people are dressed, we'll escort them back to camp. Consider them dangerous. Any sudden movements or other untoward actions, don't hesitate an instant."

"Can we at least finish burying our men? The dogs will get them."

"No time. You do what I say."

"But treason?" Durk pleaded. "What kind of treason are you talking about, Captain?"

"Headquarters will explain. I'm just following orders." He studied the situation, then issued his commands. "Shackle Captain Hurst and keep a close eye on him," he said disdainfully. "He obviously can't be trusted." The captain turned his gaze toward the distant ruins of what had once been a thriving town. "He's got a lot to answer for. And I hope he answers with his neck."

SECTION 11

CHAPTER FIFTEEN

SHACKLES AND ARMED GUARDS

Camp Dusty, Eastern Kansas

His face lined in despair and disbelief, Durk sat slumped in his chair in the parlor of a farmhouse confiscated from a Confederate officer fighting in Kentucky. The room smelled strongly of acrid tobacco smoke, leather, and the sweat of men active in the heat. "What is this nonsense about spying, Colonel?" he asked, incredulous. "Could you please explain this to me?"

The tall, stoop-shouldered Colonel Roland Carter absently ran his fingers through his long, gray-streaked beard, studying the wire from General Barrett. Barrett was the colonel's patron, and Carter knew the general put great store on this Hurst being a spy. He cleared his throat with an angry harrumph. "I will ask the questions, Captain Hurst. You will speak only in reply. Do you understand?"

"Yes, sir."

"All right. Now, Captain, my ear detects a distinctively Southern drawl. What part of the South are you from?"

Durk saw the skepticism spread across his interrogator's face. "Different parts, sir. Most recently in Mississippi, a town called Turkle."

The colonel noted the information on the document he was preparing. "And what did you do in Turkle? What was your livelihood?"

"I had a plantation."

Colonel Carter slammed down his pen in disgust and examined Hurst's features. "A planter! You are trying to tell me you are a planter? You don't look like any planter I've ever seen."

"Yes, it's true, Colonel," Durk pleaded. "Some of the men in my regiment were with me there."

"The men in your regiment, the colored soldiers, is that right? They were your slaves?"

Durk was momentarily befuddled, but he quickly regained his composure. "No, I've never owned slaves, Colonel. I manumitted these men. They were — are — free. Ask them! They'll show you their documents. Signed by me."

This man is devious, a talker, capable of wriggling out of the spy role General Barrett needed him to fill. "So if you've never owned slaves, how could you free them?"

"It's hard to explain," Durk replied and fell silent, calculating his next move. "You see, sir..."

"Quiet!" The colonel insisted, and took his time jotting more notes. "Did these men work for you on your so-called plantation?"

"Yes, yes, just ask them!"

"And being free men, you paid them wages? They were hired hands?"

Durk took a moment to think. How could he explain their partnership without stretching credulity past the breaking point? Finally, he settled on a tiny lie. "Yes, in a sense. I paid them a cut of the profits."

"A cut of the...! Um-hmm. You manumitted them, and they worked as sharecroppers in this plantation you say you owned? No, that's not what you said. They survived on a cut of the profits, is that what you're telling me, Captain?"

"Well, yes, you could say that. Sort of. Ask them to show you their papers."

"Sort of?" A sour, disbelieving expression flooded the colonel's face. He made further notes, then carefully laid down his pen. "Let's forget ancient history for the moment. Most recently, your regiment was mustered into the Missouri State Militia, is that right?"

"Yes, we are the Ninth Colored Cavalry, MSM."

The colonel made a note on his document. "These colored that worked for you in Mississippi, how did they wind up in your regiment? No, strike that. We'll get back to that, too."

"That's not...!"

"Quiet!" Carter interrupted. "I told you not to speak unless I ask you a direct question."

Durk fell silent.

Gathering his thoughts, the colonel made a number of notes, then shuffled through his papers, watched anxiously by Durk. Finally, he slapped down his pen and gave Durk a penetrating look. "All right, Captain Hurst, now what is your connection to this Antoinette DuVallier?"

"She is my — I guess you'd call her my fiancée. We plan to marry after the war."

"And she's been at your side since you left Mississippi?"

"Yes, sir, Colonel."

"So she is a Southerner, too?"

"That's right, Colonel. But..."

"Silence!" Carter fingered through more documents. Then he looked up, shocked. "When you were arrested, the Ninth was in possession of Henry rifles. A colored unit with Henrys! How do you explain all this, Captain?"

"Colonel, we were rushed back to Lawrence to stop the bushwhackers. We would have been badly outnumbered..."

"Enough!" Colonel Carter snapped to his feet again and began to hurl accusations at Durk. "I think you freed some of your own damn slaves as a cover for your activities and accompanied them to Missouri so you could spy on our army. General Barrett wires me that you gathered information and passed it to our enemies through Mrs. DuVallier, who, incidentally, is on her way to St. Louis, under arrest as a spy."

"No!" Durk screamed. "Antoinette's no spy, Colonel!"

"Then prove it," the colonel demanded. He slid a piece of paper and a pen across the desk to Durk. "Write out and sign a full confession."

"But I'm innocent! We both are! Why would I sign up to fight if I were a spy?"

But the colonel wasn't listening. "Hurst, I should hang you now, and it's taking every drop of will power I have not to do it. You *deserve* to hang, and you *will* hang, I promise you that. But for now, I want to know every detail of your spy chain, including everyone involved inside and outside the camp, everything you've done, and every piece of information you've passed to the enemy."

"But I haven't... Look, Colonel, it was me that warned..."

"Shut up, Captain! You say this DuVallier woman is innocent. Explain in your confession how she could possibly be innocent or, by God, you will both hang. Both of you traitors!"

"But, but that's nonsense."

Colonel Carter drew on his beard, contemplating his next action. "This man is a spy," he said to his orderly. "Have him taken under guard to Westport for further disposition."

"But Colonel Carter," Durk objected. "What-what about my men? They can vouch for me."

"They will be assigned to other MSM units. That is all."

The colonel signaled to remove Durk. The guards pulled Durk to his feet and led him from the tent. Once he was gone, the colonel sank heavily into his chair, deep in thought. *This Captain Hurst needs to be executed. His whole story is simply too absurd to be taken seriously. But General Barrett needs the man in St. Louis to prove there were extenuating factors leading to the Lawrence debacle, and our careers are far more important than revenge upon this secesh wretch.* Like General Barrett, his friend and mentor, Carter needed a scapegoat, and this Hurst fellow was a godsend.

He wrote out a brief message and handed it to the orderly. "Wire General Barrett that Hurst has been arrested and will be transported to St. Louis for trial and execution as rapidly as possible."

He stroked his beard thoughtfully, then wrote again. "Tell the general that Hurst as much as admitted guilt but refused to sign a confession."

***

St. Charles, Missouri

Bayonets fixed, a pair of guards escorted Antoinette into the converted dining room in the confiscated plantation house, now General Barrett's office. Her feet were free of shackles, but the steel cuffs on her wrists were heavy and awkward, painful. Hearing the clomp-clomp of boots accompanying a single pair of light footsteps, the general looked up from his paperwork to watch the woman being guided to his guest chair. At his nod, Antoinette was seated.

"General Barrett," Antoinette stated firmly, her tremulous voice revealing an imperfectly repressed desperation, "I ask that you be in contact with the authorities in the Macon army camp. This treatment is undeserved."

Stroking his long, red mustache, Old Cannonball examined Antoinette closely. He had lost sleep contemplating what to do about this woman, but, fortunately, now her plight was beyond his consideration. His report blaming Lawrence primarily on the two spies, her and Hurst, was on its way to General Schofield in St. Louis, and he'd have to wait for higher-ups to determine her fate. Regardless, he was glad to be shipping the woman and her mob of slaves off to be someone else's problem. This way, he would avoid the pangs of hanging such a beautiful creature, misguided as she may be.

"Have you received word about Captain Hurst's fate yet, General?" Antoinette queried anxiously.

"The wires say that the Ninth was wiped out." He watched Antoinette closely for a reaction to this gambit, knowing Hurst was still alive.

Antoinette's shock was immediate and profound. The heartache that she had pent up for two days over her incarceration finally broke, and she burst into tears, sobbing as if there was no end. The general, surprised by the seemingly genuine reaction, thrust a handkerchief toward her. When she finally managed to compose herself, dabbing her eyes, she asked. "Every one of them? Are you sure?"

"No one is sure of anything out there. It's still utter chaos," he lied. "However, the captain's demise is nearly certain. Now, Mrs. DuVallier, I am willing to free you, under one condition."

"And that is?"

"I don't want to hang you, madam. If you sign a full confession, spelling out in detail the late Captain Hurst's spying activities, I would be willing to have you shipped south and released. This is a very generous offer, considering the magnitude of your offence and its consequences."

Antoinette sat straight, holding her head high. "We are both innocent, as I have told you, General. I will not produce a false document which would give you reason to hang Captain Hurst, if he is still alive. Do you understand? And even if I *were* certain he was dead, I would never cast such dishonor on the work he so nobly performed for the Union, a cause he gave his life to preserve. Period."

General Barrett paused, circled his desk, and sat again. "I've sent word to bring Captain Hurst in for questioning if he survived the massacre, so we'll see." This, indeed, was true.

He examined his notes and settled on the issues that still irked him. "So, Mrs. DuVallier, why live with these particular slave women? What have you to do with them?"

"We all came up to Missouri together. I told your men, these women are family to Durk's soldiers."

"The whole lot?"

"Yes, yes, yes, the original group of twelve men. Of course, their regiment's been supplemented by other colored volunteers."

"And these soldiers of Hurst's whom you claim are colored, how did he free so many and not get himself lynched? There've been few manumissions since the Nat Turner revolt."

"They kept their freedman status a secret."

"A secret! So they were freedmen pretending to be slaves? A dozen, and nobody caught on? This is the most farfetched... Madam, if I ever had any doubts about you being a spy..."

"Yes, I know it sounds improbable, General, but it's true. All the men who came with us have manumission papers. Please check."

"Unless they're all dead, of course, in which case any papers, if they did exist, are now rotting underground. And the women? Do they have documentation?"

Knowing that General Barrett could easily disprove any false claim she might make about the *DarkHorse* women's status, Antoinette was unable to answer. She merely stared at her inquisitor pleading... and in vain. "General, these women can vouch for me. If you would..."

"Slave testimony is inadmissible; you must know that. Look, Mrs. DuVallier — or whoever you are — in the aftermath of a major massacre, people are looking to punish the guilty parties that contributed to it. You understand? Amid the groundswell of grief and fury that is consuming the troops at this moment, many of our men are not asking questions. But our president, for whatever reason, has insisted that all executions follow a legitimate court-martial, and I am a by-the-book man. So, in that, you are lucky that I am not having you hanged right here, right now. But I suspect that your luck is only temporary. The powers that be in St. Louis will give you a fair trail and a decent burial. That is more than the people of Lawrence were given by your fellow murderers.

"All right," he said to the guards standing by the door, "I'm not wasting another minute on this travesty. Take this — *this person* from my sight. May she rot in Hell."

The two soldiers flanked her, placing their hands under her elbows. Following their lead, a defeated Antoinette rose to her feet. "But what about the women?" she asked.

"You told me they were slaves owned by a family named French, did you not?" the general asked rhetorically.

"Yes. But that was years ago. Before their manumission."

"Well, that's disputable. Madam, the Union Army has fed them long enough. I am shipping them to St. Louis to be held until claimed by their rightful owner. They're someone else's problem now." He turned to the guards. "That is all."

The men led Antoinette toward the door. Before she reached the threshold, she halted and turned. "Those women are not slaves, I am not a spy, and neither is Captain Hurst!"

"You will have your chance to prove those contentions in St. Louis. Good day." The general returned his attention to signing papers, neither seeing nor hearing the three leave.

※※※

St. Louis, Missouri

The diminutive provost marshal seated himself at his desk and despaired at the thick pile of legal briefs and documents needing examination and further disposition. As the hub of western military district activities, St. Louis was a bustling place, funneling supplies to Grant's Army for his attack on Vicksburg, while maintaining order in Missouri. The guerrilla war especially had backed up the caseload for the courts-martial. His was dreary, boring work, but he was not going to get shot sitting at his desk.

Noting a telegram on top of the stack, he reached for it reluctantly, knowing that missives from General Barrett usually meant additional work and special pressures. Knowing this, he read it carefully:

CPTN DURKSEN HURST THE SPY RESPONSIBLE FOR LAWRENCE STOP ANTOINETTE DUVALLIER LIKELY INFORMATION CONDUIT TO REBELS STOP BOTH TO BE SENT TO ST. LOUIS FOR TRIAL AND EXECUTION STOP INFORM ME OF DEVELOPMENTS STOP GEN THOMAS C BARRETT US ARMY

***

St. Charles, Missouri

The young corporal led five armed privates into what had been the plantation washhouse, now crowded wall-to-wall with nine women and their children. The constricted building was stifling, sweltering on the steamy summer day. Cabin-like, the shack consisted of scrabbled together, unmatched refuse boards, with a dirt floor and leaky walls and roof. "Gather up your things. Let's go," the corporal ordered.

Auntie NeeNee rose from where she sat, brushed off her skirt, and stepped up to face the corporal in charge. "Where you taking us?" the little woman cried out.

"You are being transported to St. Louis. Don't dawdle now, Mother."

"St. Louis?" Auntie asked suspiciously. "What they taking us there for?"

Without replying, the corporal signaled the privates, turned, and stepped out of the shack, a sour look on his face. The privates indicated with their rifles for the women to follow. In a disorderly mass, Auntie and the others hurriedly began filing out the door, watched by the privates, blinking at the bright sunlight as they passed from the dark washhouse. Outside, noting five mule-driven wagons sitting near the Union headquarters, with rough civilian skinners on the seats holding the reins, they began to talk nervously among themselves.

"You will be held there for further disposition," the corporal replied.

"Dis-po-sition?" Auntie exclaimed. "What you mean dis-po-sition?"

"They will have to decide what to do with you people. That's all I know."

A murmur arose as the women looked at each other, trying to figure out what was going on. The small children, seeing their mothers frightened and beginning to panic, began to cry. The corporal turned to silence them, but before he could speak, the women grew quiet. Emerging from the big house where the general made his headquarters, Antoinette, her hands cuffed in iron, was being led to one of the wagons accompanied by two armed guards. Everything stopped, as all eyes turned to watch the three-person procession.

Sarah pushed through the women and confronted the corporal inches from his face. "Why that woman in chains?" she shouted angrily. "Antoinette ain't done nothing but help this Union Army."

The corporal pushed Sarah away, and two privates grabbed her arms. Livid, she struggled to break free, until the corporal shouted, "Bind and gag this woman." While the other women shrunk away in horror, the soldiers quickly pinned Sarah to the ground, clasped her hands in chains behind her, and gagged her with a bandanna. As she thrashed about, the privates dragged her to her feet without releasing their hold on her.

Auntie NeeNee went right up to Sarah and slapped her firmly. "You be still, Sarah. You gonna get us in more trouble than we is." She turned to the corporal. "Why they gots that woman in chains? She a nurse to the Union Army."

"They tell me she's a spy. That's all I know," the corporal replied.

"A spy! Why, that woman couldn't... Look here, Mr. Officer, every one of us can testify for her."

The corporal shrugged. "Maybe so, but you know very well slaves can't give testimony."

"Slave!" Auntie exclaimed, then quieted to think. "Look here, Captain Hurst of the Ninth Missouri Cavalry can speak for her. You gots to wire him."

"Oh," the corporal smirked, "they gonna wire him with good hemp rope. Now, y'all get up in those wagons. Hurry on, or I won't be so pleasant."

Auntie NeeNee grabbed the corporal's sleeve. "Spies? Antoinette and Durk? Y'all done lost your minds, is what you done."

The corporal signaled, and a private grabbed Auntie and began to bind her. The other women objected loudly, but everyone was afraid to stop him. In moments, little Auntie was bound and gagged like Sarah. With their leaders silenced, the women grumbled but were quietly herded onto the wagons. Their fate would have to be determined in St. Louis, along with that of their friend, Antoinette DuVallier.

***

Lafayette County, Western Missouri

The sunny breakfast room was empty except for the last pair in the far corner, away from the kitchen. Devereau French finished whittling the last piece of her steak down to a small cube, stabbed it onto her fork, and examined it from all sides. No major veins of gristle or fat, so with a distasteful frown, she placed it into her mouth and began chewing. Within four bites, she discovered by feel what her eyes had missed: hard deposits of a strange substance that wouldn't surrender to the force of her incisors. Grimacing, she spit the piece into her hand and dropped it onto the pile of fat and waste on her plate, more than half her original steak. Pickin's were slim these days in even the best of these country hotels, and the cattle they served had been near death already before they were slaughtered, cooked, and served to guests. War was cruel on the palate.

She glanced up to see Robert chewing mightily, a grim concentration on his face. Finally, a look of despair overcame him. He spit a large hunk of meat onto his remaining uncut steak and pushed his plate away. He stared accusingly at Devereau and shrugged a question with his shoulders. She merely reflected his displeasure and disappointment with a raised eyebrow, offering no answer or apology.

Devereau picked up the newspaper folded neatly beside her plate and tossed it across the table, to land at Robert's right hand.

"Did the Union catch up to Quantrill?" Robert asked.

"The Federals killed a dozen or so in the rear guard, but most of Quantrill's men dispersed into the Sni-A-Bar. They simply dispersed and vanished."

"Figures," Robert said with a sneer.

"We have had one tiny bit of luck," Devereau said, tapping the newspaper, her sarcastic tone understating her glee.

"Yes?" he replied. "And?"

Devereau looked around, checking that the room was still empty. Through the window to the kitchen in back, she could hear the clattering of dishes and pots being cleaned by the hotel manager. They were alone. "General Barrett," Devereau whispered, leaning forward, "has ordered twenty-six slave women and children to be held in St. Louis until their rightful owner claims them."

"So?" Robert Sterling replied.

"So," she continued, looking around, "these are my slaves from

FrenchAcres," Devereau said with barely restrained glee. "I'm sure of it. 'French family' the papers reads."

A wide grin spread across Robert's face. "French slaves, ha! So we go claim them, take them south, and sell them. That is fortunate."

"That isn't the half of it. The army is reporting that Lawrence is the dirty work of two Southern spies, who have been arrested. A woman named…" she paused for dramatic effect, pointing to the newspaper article, "'Antoinette DuVallier of New Orleans, arrested as a spy for the Confederacy. The army is requesting information on her recent whereabouts and contacts. They have arrested her accomplice in passing intelligence to the local guerrillas. The pair is suspected of having stolen the slaves and bringing them to Missouri for purposes related to their traitorous activities.' How does that sound, Robert?"

"Arrested them both! The 'pair'!" Robert exclaimed. "Sounds like three birds with one stone: Dark Horse, Antoinette, and a couple dozen slaves. A nice day's work."

Grisly revenge spread across Devereau's face. "There are times when the enemy castles queen-side into the teeth of your mating attack," she said. "All right. Let's see how we're going to play this."

Robert rubbed his chin in thought. "Let's not play a straightforward mating position into a complicated stalemate, Devereau, or worse, for us. We need simply to claim the slaves and sell them. Let the army hang Dark Horse and Antoinette."

"No, I think we can parlay our good fortune into a jackpot."

"I don't agree, Devereau," Robert said disdainfully. "Why is it women always have to make things so complicated?"

"Don't you want Hurst and DuVallier in our hands?"

"For what purpose? Devereau, let's take our winnings off the table and head home." Robert stared into his companion's eyes, but all he saw was confusion and indecision. *Perhaps French doesn't want Dark Horse dead after all.* He wasn't going to let her unpredictability deny him thousands of dollars. Thousands! Devereau French was becoming more like her mother every day, and that was a real problem.

He concluded it would be much simpler, and more satisfying, if all three of them were dead. Dispose of the entire corrupt past in one fell swoop and cash in the slave women himself. It was merely a matter of timing. Timing…and the element of surprise.

***

Camp Dusty, Kansas

Colonel Richard G. Edmonds, the collar of his crisp uniform buttoned in spite of the heat of the day, strolled with calm assurance into Colonel Roland Carter's tent, leading a major, a captain, and Carter's own aide. A thin man, Edmonds sported a small, cleanly sculpted mustache. Still wearing his calfskin riding gloves, he flicked his horsewhip rhythmically against his leg. He was a man who meant business and settled for nothing but the best from everyone and everything around him.

When Carter saw Edmonds, he looked up from his paperwork. Why was he being recalled? Even though Lawrence wasn't the least bit his fault, perhaps General Ewing and, above him, Major General Schofield felt they must place blame for the failure to protect it somewhere. And being responsible for guarding Western Missouri and Eastern Kansas, Carter would be the scapegoat. Like his mentor, Old Cannonball, Carter was not a man popular with his superiors. As with Old Cannonball, Carter was too brash and impulsive, never inclined to smooth the edges of his relations with those in authority over him — and highly abrasive to those below him. Further, he was never diplomatic when he disagreed with any strategy, plan, or order that came his way. He was simply not well-liked.

Edmonds strode toward Carter, saluted crisply, and slapped his documents down on the map table. "Colonel," Edmonds said in his clipped voice, "to enable you to prepare your command, I have come to notify you in advance of an important order you can expect to receive within days. I'm also under instructions to carry to St. Louis any intelligence you can provide to General Schofield."

Colonel Carter relaxed so deeply, it was as if the air had gone out of him. *I am not being relieved of command!* He sat heavily in his chair. "Have a seat, Colonel Edmonds. I'd best give you the lay of the land. Would you care for a drink?" He gestured to the guest chair, poured two whiskeys, and set out the bottle. Edmonds sat and took one of the glasses.

While Carter tossed down a slug of the brown liquid, Edmonds sat with rigid back and sipped. "What's the story, Carter?"

Colonel Carter refilled his glass. "About two-thirds of the population in the Missouri border counties are pro-Confederate, so we waste all our time and effort stamping out flames in what is really a forest fire, a damn forest fire. The locals hide the guerrillas, provision them, and supply them with intelligence on our movements. Frankly, Colonel, the border region is completely hostile to the

Union cause."

"I see," Edmonds said, taking another sip of his whiskey. "What is your disposition?"

"Right now we have seventeen hundred men spread among a string of strong points. But it's not nearly enough to control bushwhacker activity. Lawrence is a perfect example. They were able to slip about four hundred men through our lines. I asked for more troops, but every spare man is being funneled to Grant."

"I see," Edmonds mused. "What have you done to repress the rebellion?"

"First there was Order Nine," Carter snarled fatalistically. "Then Order Ten was tougher. We arrested family members of the secesh leaders and deported a few of the major rebel sympathizers to the South. Women not the head of households were no longer exempt. But you see the result. I don't know how much more you can do."

Edmonds's eyes glowed with fierce intensity. "General Ewing is preparing Order Eleven, Colonel Carter, which will be far more effective, I promise you. He plans to clean out this border area." He stared at Carter to let that sink in.

"Clean out? Please explain what you mean?" a bewildered Carter asked.

"If General Schofield approves, we're going to completely evict four or five border counties — everyone — loyal, disloyal, everyone — men, women, and children. Burn all the fields. Wipe out the whole hornets nest. There will be no further support or provision for rebel guerrillas. We'll escort the loyalists to our camps for protection and further disposition and expel the traitors to the Confederacy."

"Can they do that?" a startled Carter asked. "Loyalists *and* secesh sympathizers?"

"Damn right. Lawrence was the last straw. Look, Carter, Order Eleven will protect our right flank. The whole district will be *burnt out*. Any Confederate Army attempting to invade Western Missouri will find no forage to scavenge. The Confederates will be forced to invade through Rolla, right into the teeth of our defenses."

"Well, that should reduce bushwhacker activity," a bewildered Carter mumbled. "But loyalists, too? People loyal to the Union?"

"Yes, the whole region, depopulated," Edmonds said, chuckling. "There is no way to tell one from the other, is there?" He finished off his drink and set the glass neatly on the table, then rose to leave.

"But Colonel," Carter cautioned, freezing his guest in place, "you know as well as I do, our Kansas units seek nothing but revenge. They've been battling Missouri roughnecks for decades. I guarantee, the Red Legs will use this order to visit robbery and bloody murder onto those counties. It'll be a scandal to surpass all scandals."

Colonel Edmonds smiled broadly. "That's part of the order, too, Carter. Any Kansas troopers that cross the border will be shot. Period. We want to fulfill Order Eleven as ethically as possible."

Carter nodded. "I am relieved to be rid of the whole morass."

Edmonds slapped his riding crop against his leg twice. "Any loose ends I should know about, Colonel? I run a tidy ship. What about that spy business?"

"Shipped off to St. Louis for trial," Colonel Carter replied, keeping his answer short.

Edmonds snapped orders to the major and captain accompanying him, who followed him from the tent. Outside, he tsk-tsked about the disorderly manner in which Carter ran his entire command. "This whole operation is a mess," he grumbled in frustration. "Loose ends. Nothing but damn loose ends!"

CHAPTER SIXTEEN

CHEATING THE HANGMAN

Camp Dusty, Kansas

"I kill them!" Isaac shouted. "I kill Lawrence! I kill them all!"

The two Federal cavalry troopers, a sergeant and a corporal, dragged a disheveled, ranting Isaac into the large room where the tall, stoop-shouldered Colonel Roland Carter sat hunched over his maps. Isaac's uniform, wrinkled and torn from his near-fatal plunge into the rushing river on his desperate ride to Lawrence, was streaked with mud that had clung to him since he washed up on the bank. The disoriented man's eyes were wild, his hands shaking, his gait unsteady. The troopers had to support him for fear he would collapse.

"What is all this?" Colonel Carter shouted. "Silence!" he ordered Isaac, who stopped raving.

"Sir," the sergeant said. "Patrols picked up this man wandering around, lost. He claims he's with the Ninth MSM Cavalry, which was massacred at Lawrence."

The colonel examined Isaac closely, pulling at his long, salt-and-pepper beard, and then sat down heavily. "Get this soldier a chair before he faints."

The corporal pulled up a chair and thrust Isaac into it so hard his head flung back. Eventually, Isaac righted himself.

"What is your name, private?" Colonel Carter asked.

"Isaac."

"Isaac what?"

"I don't know. I don't remember."

The colonel met his sergeant's gaze, but all he received in return was a 'the-man's-lying' shrug. "You're with the Ninth MSM Cavalry, is that right?"

Isaac nodded.

"Is the Ninth a colored unit or a white one?"

"Can't you see me?" Isaac replied. "I been this color my whole life."

"I'll have none of your sass," the colonel growled angrily, and nodded to the sergeant, who squeezed Isaac's shoulder until he screamed.

Carter turned to his aide. "Bring me the Hurst case, will you?" The aide nodded, dug out the documents, and laid them before the colonel. That done, he saluted, spun about, and strode crisply from the room. Carter untied the papers and shuffled through them until he found what he wanted.

"Now listen, Isaac, I want to know what your regiment had to do with Lawrence. You said 'you killed everyone.' What the Hell did you mean? How did you kill everyone in Lawrence?"

"I never kill nobody, Colonel," Isaac pleaded. "I swear, I never kill nobody."

The colonel slammed his heavy hand down on the table in frustration, rattling the cups, pens, inkpots, and straightedges scattered around the maps. He leaned back, thinking, and then said, "Who was the captain of your regiment?"

"The captain? That was Durk. Durk Hurst."

"And were you with Captain Hurst in Mississippi, too; is that right?"

"Yes, sir. But what happen in Lawrence? Why won't nobody tell me about Lawrence?"

"I'll ask the questions!" the colonel interrupted. "All right. In Mississippi, what did this Hurst do?"

"Durk? Why, he be the white man for *DarkHorse*."

Colonel Carter got a puzzled look on his face. He took a moment to turn this comment over in his mind, then continued, "I know he's a white man, sort of: undoubtedly, part Indian. But what did he do in Mississippi? Did he own a plantation?"

"Yes, sir, *DarkHorse*. Won it gambling from a Chickasaw name a' Wounded Wolf. We all own it."

"You *all* owned...?" the colonel asked, confused and frustrated, dismissing this fool's story. His voice grew deep, angry, as he growled, "All right, private, how and where did you first meet this Hurst fellow?"

"I met him in the swamp."

"The swamp? And what were you doing there?"

"Sellin' corn squeezings to the Indians."

"So, you were a maroon?"

Isaac hesitated and then nodded affirmatively.

Colonel Carter continued, "And Hurst, did he manumit you?"

"Yes, sir, he done signed the paper."

"He did?" Carter said. "Let's see your document."

Isaac reached in his pocket, but when he withdrew his hand, the paper he held was soaked through and falling apart, its ink smeared and running, illegible.

He laid it on the table. Carter picked up the scrap between his two fingers as if it were contaminated, gave it a glance, then tossed it into Isaac's lap, and wiped his hand on his pant leg. The state of Isaac's uniform explained the ruin of his manumission papers. Though Carter wasn't particularly for or against slavery, having come from a free state and having no contact with the institution, he thought it sad that a man's freedom could be jeopardized by a fall into a river. Of course, if this colored soldier had become entangled with Hurst as he described, the manumission document was certainly invalid anyway. But that no longer mattered. By serving in the Union military, as President Lincoln had decreed, Isaac was forever free. Regardless, the colonel hadn't time to dwell on such ironies.

"Never mind Mississippi, let's get to the point: Lawrence, Kansas. What was your role?"

Isaac thought a moment, then broke down and began to cry. "I didn' mean to kill them peoples. I didn't mean it..."

Colonel Carter glared angrily at Isaac. "What do you mean, you killed them? Over two hundred people died. How did you kill them?"

"Cause my horse drown," Isaac sputtered, tears running down his cheeks. "My horse drown." He covered his eyes, weeping and sobbing as if his heart was breaking.

Carter nodded to the sergeant, who shook Isaac until he stopped crying. "What do you mean, private? What were you attempting to do?"

"I was tryin' to warn them people the 'whackers coming."

"You were trying to warn Lawrence?"

"Yes, yes, but my horse drown."

Colonel Carter examined Isaac's dirt-streaked and crinkled uniform, concluding that the man was telling the truth. He and the horse had been plunged into waters. The man was lucky he hadn't drowned, too. "And who ordered you to warn the town?"

"Big Josh. Big Josh and Durk."

"Durk? Captain Hurst, is that right? And what was Captain Hurst doing when he gave you that order? Why didn't he try to warn Lawrence himself?"

"He want to, but Josh tell him to ride off to Westport to tell the army."

Mortified, Carter sunk back into his chair. Deep in thought, he resumed stroking his beard, feeling contrite. "All right, soldier," he said, "so would you say Hurst acted responsibly, bravely in this matter?"

"Yeah, he want to save that town. They was hundreds of 'whackers, and we was only a few."

Carter slammed his large hand down hard on the table, making a startled Isaac jump. He may have accused Captain Hurst unjustly and was relieved that he hadn't had him summarily executed, though he had been inclined to. Carter had felt that Lincoln was attempting to tie the field officers' hands by insisting he review every court-martial capital verdict, but in retrospect, he began to see the wisdom of it.

"All right, Private Isaac, one more question. Antoinette DuVallier, do you know her?"

Taken aback by the question, Isaac blinked repeatedly. "Antoinette, yeah, sure."

"And she is connected to Captain Hurst?"

"That's right. She and Durk are..." He crossed his fingers together to make his point.

"And this woman, she has a number of Negro women and children with her?"

"That's right. They our women and sisters and children. Antoinette help us get them free."

Colonel Carter stared hard into Isaac's eyes, searching for reaction that would indicate a falsehood. "Isaac, is there a chance this woman is a spy for the Confederacy?"

"A spy! Is you crazy?"

"Calm down, down," the colonel said, quieting Isaac. He eyed the sergeant. "Get this man some food, rest, and a clean uniform. He's obviously hungry and exhausted."

"Yes, sir," the sergeant said, pulling Isaac to his feet.

Now Colonel Carter was in a quandary. It was likely Hurst was innocent and probably his female accomplice, too. But if that was the case, he knew his own position was imperiled, and General Barrett, Old Cannonball, would be furious with him for revealing it. He had a hard decision to make. A hard decision.

Well, he thought at last, *thousands of innocent men and women die in war. What's two more?*

***

Isaac woke up and rubbed his eyes, casting off the depth of a long sleep. It was pitch black. *Must be night.* He was lying upon an army cot in a tent, covered by an army blanket. *Where am I? How long have I been asleep?* Perhaps it was days, he'd been that exhausted. He tried to sit up, but it took a while. He was sore from head to foot from running, trying to get to Lawrence. His aching legs cried out, and his torso was weak and stiff, painful. Rising, he swung around and placed his feet on the ground. He leaned over and felt around the cot until he found his boots. In the darkness, he slipped them on. *I have to find Josh.*

He crawled out of the tent and looked around. The sky was clear, the stars and moon bright. Easy for him to be seen. The clearing between the rows of tents was littered by blackened fire pits and everyday scattered equipment, but no one was awake. Any guards or pickets the army had thrown out would be a distance from the heart of camp. Being as quiet as possible, he walked carefully first up one lane, then down another. Nothing but tents filled with sleeping soldiers.

There it was: Big Josh's uniform, hanging outside a tent. During the day, Josh sweated heavily, so he hung his uniform outside at night to dry. Isaac took hold of the sleeve and raised it. Yup, awfully big and slit to accommodate Josh's arms. This was Josh's tent.

Isaac paused to look about and around. Undetected, he entered the tent. Once his eyes adjusted, he slinked over Josh's cot and slowly shook him awake. When a startled Josh started to speak, Isaac quieted him. "Josh, it's me, Isaac," he whispered.

"Isaac, you alive," Josh said happily, rolling onto his side. "What h-happen?"

"I never made it to Lawrence. My horse drown."

"Not your fault, Isaac," Josh said sympathetically, sitting up. "N-nobody make it in time. The whole town was wiped out, my friend. I hate to say, but the m-men in the *DarkHorse* regiment we left behind, they all dead. Ever one k-killed."

The two were quiet a moment.

"What 'bout here?" Isaac asked.

"They is gonna attach us to another regiment, Isaac. Ain't gonna be no *DarkHorse* or no Ninth n-no more. New colonel come in today, and that's what he say. Least, he say we ain't under guard no more, so we got that."

"What 'bout the others who try to warn Lawrence? Long Lou, John Wilkens, Billy?" Isaac asked.

"You and Lou the only ones we f-find so far. Maybe the others lost in the woods — I hope," Josh said, shaking his head. He lowed his voice. "Look, Isaac, we gots a problem here."

"I know, Josh."

"It's Durk. They say he a s-spy."

"But they hang spies, or shoot'em, one or t'other," Isaac said.

"I don' know what we can do. I tried to go see C-colonel Carter, tell him the truth 'bout Durk, but he too busy to see a MSM colored sergeant. We ain't got no rifles to force our way in to see him, much less to save Durk. I'm afraid they gonna hang Durk before we can do anything."

Both men fell silent for a good minute.

Then Isaac asked, "What would Durk do?" He paused, thinking. "I know! We hang Durk ourself."

Josh looked through Isaac, not seeing the man before his eyes. "Or get ourself hung with him," he said.

CHAPTER SEVENTEEN

DIGGING HIS GRAVE

Beneath the star-speckled night sky, on the edge of the woods, Big Josh, Isaac, Long Lou, and Bammer dug quickly, trying to be quiet, but the rocky soil beneath their shovels and picks made silence impossible. They were already knee deep, breaking into the packed clay, shoveling and tossing.

A camp guard on his nightly rounds suddenly appeared, and the four stopped working. "What are you doing there?" the guard asked, leveling his rifle directly toward them.

"Diggin' a grave," Josh answered and then thrust his shovel in the direction of the guard. "Want to help?"

"I'm on guard duty," the man said disdainfully. "Get back to work." He shouldered his rifle and hurriedly continued on his rounds.

After a half hour of quick work, a man-length mound over two feet high marked entry to the nearby woods. Bammer finished patting it down with his shovel and sat on a stump, wiping the sweat on his brow. The others crouched down like country folk or sat propped against trees. They had been awakened from sleep in the middle of the night, and now that their labors were done, fatigue was rapidly draining them of strength.

Long Lou let out a deep sigh. "Some army we in! We been digging so many graves, but we ain't been filling none. And these guns they give us, they ain't gonna help much shooting 'whackers."

The others nodded, grumbling their displeasure at being issued such obsolete weapons.

"Any f-fight we in not gonna be no fair fight, that's for sure," Big Josh commiserated.

Isaac took a deep breath. "Well, we gots Durk buried. Now all we gots to do is get him hanged."

***

Chariton County, Central Missouri

Devereau French poked the burning embers with her stick, her eyes blazing hotter than the reflected campfire flames. Night was upon them, with stars in vast profusion, and the long day's ride had been arduous. They'd often had to circle off the main roads and detour through wooded hills and valleys to avoid both Union strong points and patrols and Confederate raiders. It was difficult being so far outside the law along the ragged edges of a war.

Squatting across the burning pit, an agitated Robert Sterling repeatedly flung his knife into the ground, retrieved it, wiped it on his pants, and then flung it again. After a number of repetitions, he sheathed the knife and sat back against a large maple. He stared at Devereau who first tried to shrug off Robert's attention.

All at once, she spoke sharply, "What do you want?"

"Dark Horse hasn't any treasure from Mississippi left now, if he ever did. I want to retrieve the slaves and take them south."

"We'll *do* that," Devereau replied.

Robert angrily threw a piece of rotting branch into the fire and admired how the sparks flew upward. "The rest of it, with Antoinette and Dark Horse, bears too much risk. Forget them."

"Forget them? You've turned weak in your old age," Devereau spit disdainfully.

At being called a coward, Robert's hand flew to his knife. He pictured Devereau lying with her throat cut, her skin pale, drained, blood soaking her fine suit and the earth around her. He took a moment to pleasure in the imagined sight, the release of feeling rid of her, free: the exhilarating wind in his face as he rode off on her white stallion. Yet he managed to wrestle his anger to the ground. He would need Devereau to acquire the women in St. Louis. There was also, of course, the small chance of gaining thousands of paper dollars. These were Confederate notes of uncertain value, of course, yet script that could be exchanged for horses. Both sides in the war were paying a premium for horseflesh, and he knew the beasts as well as anyone.

"You can't stop thinking about Dark Horse," he said accusingly. "You are mad with him. You want him for your own."

"You are mad with hate for him," Devereau retorted defensively. "You only want to see him dead. Let me tell you, Robert, he will not hang. I promise you that."

"He will. And trying to save him will only get *you* hung." He studied Devereau's sullen face. There was no advantage to pursuing this argument, so he chose another tact. "You only want Antoinette to hang because you believe she stole Dark Horse from you. But he never loved you, only her. He will *never* love you."

"How would you know? You're a liar," she countered, resting her hand on her pistol.

"Let me tell you, woman, Antoinette is very smart, smarter than you. She will find a way out of this."

"No, she won't. I'll see to that," Devereau replied.

"That's your sister, fool. Except for me, she is your only tie to this world. If her blood is on your hands, you truly will go mad, madder than your mother ever was. At least your mother wanted you both to live."

"Ha! Mother had plans to get me hung," Devereau answered bitterly. "But she couldn't fool me."

"Look, scheme all you want, Devereau, but I will save myself, no matter what. Let us just retrieve the slaves and let the army stretch their necks or not. I don't care."

Robert looked into Devereau's brown eyes but saw only a fierce enmity and a hint of desolate loneliness. He knew, at the moment, she was angry enough to kill him, but she needed him too much to murder him in his sleep, and he would sleep soundly. Not Devereau. Tormented by dreams of Durksen Hurst and the one night they spent together, she would sleep only fitfully, restlessly, if at all. Robert had often heard her crying in her blankets at night. Women were beyond understanding, especially this half-crazy one in man's clothing.

***

St. Louis, Missouri

The elderly jailer unlocked the cell with a loud clink and swung the rusty door open. The stench in the overcrowded women's section of the prison was a terrible soup of human waste and sweat, and both the jailer and the guard wore handkerchiefs covering their noses and mouths.

"Man from the provost marshal's office to see you, Mrs. DuVallier," the young guard announced. The jailer, a gray-haired old soldier with sad, deep-set eyes, didn't even place the cuffs on her. He saw that she was pretty, clearly a gentlewoman, and he was touched by her obvious distress.

Antoinette's eyes met the two women's remaining in the small cell, which was little more than a cage. She rose from the cell's single cot and walked into the hall. The jailer locked the door behind her, turned the key, and the three set off down the stairs. One of the distraught women remaining in the cell flopped on the cot and immediately closed her eyes.

Antoinette's cell was on the top floor of the Myrtle Street Prison. The imposing, two-story brick building had been a slave-holding pen for the active St. Louis market in human flesh before the war. The facility was ironically nicknamed "Hotel de Lynch" in honor of its long-time slave dealer owner, Bernard M. Lynch, one of two listed St. Louis slave dealers before the war, the other being Corbin Thompson at 3 South Sixth Street. Thompson had advertised that his slave pen had "a high and healthy location with ample room." Lynch made no such claim. His original practice was at 100 Locust Street, midway between Fourth and Fifth streets, advertising that he paid the highest market value for slaves, also sold on commission, and that he specialized in paying particular attention to the "selecting of homes for favorite servants."

He purchased the Fifth and Myrtle site in 1859, and immediately installed barred windows, bolts, and locks. Originally built for a hundred slaves, the Union Army, upon moving its headquarters to St. Louis, had converted the pen into a military prison, but martial law had not much improved the facility's conditions. Now the structure was badly overcrowded with one hundred fifty prisoners of war, political prisoners, deserters, and assorted Federal soldiers under indictment. The district martial law docket was invariably backed up, so the waits for transfer to larger, more accommodating prisons were often long, but proceedings for spy trials often shot to the top of the list.

Downstairs, as Antoinette passed the men's cells, she was badgered by scattered shouts and catcalls. She tried to ignore them, although they were coarse and intimidating. She started trembling, demoralized, not for the invectives, but for being accused of a capital crime, by her stay in the prison, and by her friends' plight.

The elderly jailer growled for the prisoners to remember their manners, which had a muted effect. As they continued down the hall, the soft-spoken, grizzled veteran talked calmly, sympathetically to her, as the two exchanged quiet, friendly words.

"Sorry for the accommodations here, ma'am," the jailer apologized. "It weren't made to hold no white ladies."

"It should not have been made to hold anyone," Antoinette replied.

When they turned toward the office, she pleaded with her two escorts to let her visit her friends being held in the cellar. The two guards talked over her request and came to the conclusion that a few minutes wouldn't hurt. The jailer explained that she wouldn't have much time to talk, though.

When they neared the end of the dank cellar, the pungent odor of too many souls crammed into a too-small, untended space overwhelmed her. She knew that she herself smelled none too fresh, but this was far worse. The light from the single window was so dim that she couldn't see more than a few feet ahead. Then, approaching their cells, she heard joyful and relieved shrieks and cries as her friends rushed to the bars on both sides. As her eyes adjusted, she at first saw their outlines, then recognized the faces of Auntie NeeNee and the others reaching hands out to touch her. Relieved to see they were alive, she grabbed Auntie's shoulders and hugged her tightly through the bars.

"Why they holding us here? You gotta get us out," Auntie NeeNee pleaded. Then she backed away as she took in Antoinette's disheveled condition. "What they done to you, honey?"

"Never mind me. I'm going to see the authorities now, Auntie. I'll try to get them to turn you loose."

"Ain't you got no paper for us to work for the army?" Auntie asked. "Just show them the paper Durk got you."

"The bushwhackers took it. We don't have any documentation at all," she confessed. Instinctively, Antoinette wanted to ask how they were being treated, but considering these crowded and dismal conditions, she held her tongue, stifling a sob.

Then the kindly guard gently took her elbow, and she allowed herself to be led quietly away.

"Please," Auntie cried after them. "We got sick children."

***

Captain Owen Whalen perused the case he'd been assigned to defend: a spy, Antoinette DuVallier. Attached was a handwritten note from the major informing him that General Barrett — Old Cannonball — had taken a particular interest in the case and that, though the evidence against the woman wasn't compelling, the Southern belle was presumably guilty. Whalen must appear to do his best to defend her, certainly, but Old Cannonball clearly wanted her tried and hung. And who was Whalen to question the hot-tempered general?

With a sneer, Whalen crumbled the memorandum and tossed it in the trash. Then he reached in his tunic pocket, slipped out his bottle, and pulled the cork. His hand shaking, he took two long swigs and sank back into his chair, feeling the burn slide down his throat. *Well*, he thought bitterly, *as far as losing cases go, they've sent the spy to the right man.*

He closed his eyes to enjoy the familiar relief of the alcohol-induced numbing cloud spreading throughout his brain. It irked him to no end that he was the final destination for the hopelessly condemned, invariably being assigned to defend the most vile cowards, deserters, and murderers. His reputation for ineptitude was so widespread, the other lawyers and military bigwigs often jeered at his proclivity to lose in court, branding him "the Hanging Judge," jeering that he'd killed more soldiers than Generals Lee and Grant combined. The insults against him were so pervasive, he had run out of retorts, and these days, he merely pretended he hadn't heard.

Barrett is an ignorant brute, Whalen mused angrily, always resentful of anyone who outranked him. *If I ever get the chance to defend that red-faced blowhard, I'll show him what the wrong end of a firing squad looks like.*

On Whalen's hierarchy of hatred, he despised generals more than anyone, and Barrett most of all. Fury rising inside him, he took a final swig, then corked and returned the bottle to his pocket. *Wouldn't Old Cannonball be shocked if I rose to my full powers as a lawyer and actually won this case. Imagine him getting that news!*

Then he sunk gently into his designated place in the scheme of military justice. He wasn't about to stick his neck out to save any of his clients, especially not a spy.

All in all, he did like representing female defendants; he had often taken advantage of their perilous situation by swearing that he would win their cases, promising to get them reduced sentences or to have them deported to their families in the South. Invariably, though, he cherished the instant when their verdict was read in court and they realized he'd lost their case. Particularly when he lay alone in bed at night, he got chills recalling the terror and disappointment flooding their faces. And the moments when harsh sentences, including death, were pronounced, an exquisite beauty! It was all he could do to pretend sympathy for them and hide his glee. He especially treasured the angry glare of injured disillusionment on the faces of his most cooperative clients as they were led off in chains. Until that moment, the silly creatures had lived their lives believing, or at least hoping, their beauty, charms, and precious favors, offered them grace. But upon hearing the harsh sentences imposed, they learned a hard truth, a truth he had been condemned to face about himself every moment of his own existence: there is no grace *or* justice.

I wonder what this one looks like, he mused, trying to imagine Antoinette DuVallier. *Interesting name. Will she be innocent-looking, of frail beauty, of porcelain face?* He loved those types the best, especially when they're condemned to a long prison sentence, or, even better, to die on the gallows. He had long-desired to witness such an execution but had never been strong enough to attend.

He thought over the current case and its ramifications, his anticipation unbound. *A death sentence often produces the most delightful and memorable distress on a pretty face. Oh, I can't wait!*

***

Downstairs, the old jailer broke off to attend to his other duties, while the young guard guided Antoinette into a cramped, musty office. Behind the worn, scarred desk, piled indiscriminately with legal documents, sat a nervous, black-haired officer wearing a disheveled blue tunic, its unbuttoned flap hanging loose below his neck. The man was extremely gaunt, his color only slightly more jaundiced than his documents. He had shaky fingers and a pronounced head jerk. Preoccupied with his paperwork, hearing the pair, he mumbled for Antoinette to be seated. When he finally looked up, he was taken aback. Seeing her, his face flushed a bright red, and his right eye twitched. "I will handle this, Private," he barked to the guard. "Wait in the hall. And close the door behind you."

Now alone with Antoinette, he rose and extended his hand. "I'm Captain Owen Whalen, ma'am," he said. "Provost marshal's office."

Antoinette looked the man over. There was something unsavory about him. He was exceedingly thin with bad teeth, darting eyes, thinning black hair, and a pock-marked face, unevenly shaven, and he reeked of alcohol. She took his hand, but when she tried to pull away, his grip tightened, refusing to let go. After three attempts, she was able to tug her fingers loose. This wasn't going to be easy, or by the book. Feeling rebuked, Captain Whalen gave her a hurt, angry look and sat back down. Studying her, his piercing eyes bore into her almost without blinking, and she steeled herself, straightening her back.

"You are Antoinette DuVallier, is that right?"

"Yes," she replied.

"You are to be tried for a capital crime, ma'am," Captain Whalen said perfunctorily, untying her documentation. "Therefore, I have been assigned to represent you. I'll do everything I can to help you."

"Thank you," Antoinette replied, concealing her discomfort.

"Who is your husband, Mrs. DuVallier?" the captain asked.

"I am a widow, Captain," Antoinette replied firmly.

His mood lightening, the captain fingered through the documents. "So," he paused, pursing his lips, before resuming, "how do you know this Captain Durksen Hurst?" he queried coldly.

"He is my fiancé," she said. Seeing the captain's eye twitch involuntarily, she repeated, "My *fiancé.*"

"Yes? And what did Captain Hurst do in Mississippi? How was he employed?"

"He owned a plantation. I've already..." She paused, realizing Whalen wasn't listening.

He studied her body closely, face flushed and hands trembling, so much so he laid down his pen and thrust his hand into his pocket. "I can see that," he said, forcing a limp smile, which disappeared in a moment. "That is what it would take to possess a woman like you."

"No one possesses me, Captain Whalen," she stated firmly. "*No one.*"

Chastised, Whalen sat back heavily, contemplating the situation, then cleared his throat and prepared to take another tact. "I'm sorry it took so long to get around to seeing you, Mrs. DuVallier, but the caseloads are backbreaking. Backbreaking."

"Not as backbreaking as the cot I share with two other women in a hole about a quarter the size of this room," Antoinette retorted indignantly. "One cot! We have to sleep in shifts."

"Oh, I know. You'd be fortunate not to die of disease here," Captain Whalen said offhandedly, avoiding her eyes.

"I know the perils of disease, Captain," Antoinette asserted. "I spent two years treating Union soldiers who died of every manner of illness, and this is my thanks."

The captain jotted a note. "Perhaps I can get you transferred south, depending."

"Depending? You misunderstand, Captain. I am not a rebel sympathizer," Antoinette objected. "I am very much an abolitionist. I *do not* want to be sent south."

"An abolitionist?" Captain Whalen noted, surprised. "You're an abolitionist, a Southerner?"

"Ask my friends whom you have locked up."

"An abolitionist?"

"If anyone harbors any doubt about slavery, a day or two at Hotel de Lynch will open their eyes," Antoinette remarked. "Speaking of abolition, Captain, when are you going to free those women and children? They've done nothing wrong. They're being held under worse conditions than I am."

"Well, that's another problem I wanted to discuss with you," the captain said, pulling the string to open a second case. He fingered through the new documents. "Now, Mrs. DuVallier, I am not against abolition myself, necessarily, but as an officer in the Federal Army, I have to follow orders. General Schofield doesn't know what to do with them. The law is problematic in Missouri, which is technically a slave state, s-so the general has ordered us to hold the subjects until their owner can claim them."

"Their owner!" Antoinette exclaimed. "These women aren't slaves. They were manumitted in Mississippi. I told the other officers I spoke with..."

The captain cut her off, flipping through the pages. "Yes, I see here that you've claimed they are free women. But the provost marshal's office has received notification from a man who claims the women belong to him. I've been wired that he's en route to St. Louis. So we must wait for resolution on that before they can be released. You understand?"

"That is a lie," Antoinette said, confused about this mystery man. "These women have been working for the army with me the last two years. Their men are in the Missouri State Militia. Can you at least board them under better conditions in the interim? You needn't lock them up. They have no place to go."

The captain listened, nodding.

"Look," Antoinette continued, playing another card, "if we are to work together, you must help me on this matter. I will not compromise their safety nor their freedom."

Whalen took a moment to size Antoinette up and plot his strategy. Finally, he affected another smile. "I'll send a wire this afternoon. I assure you, they'll be in better housing soon. Slaves or not, their people have seen enough of this sort of hospitality." He made notes.

"Thank you, Captain. I'm most grateful," Antoinette said, producing her own disingenuous smile. The man was at least pretending to be on her side, so she was determined to press her advantage.

"Now, as for you..." the captain began.

"This spy talk is absolute nonsense," Antoinette interrupted, adamant. "What evidence do they have against me? Doesn't *habeas corpus* still apply?"

"Not under Martial Law, not here in Missouri," Whalen replied.

"But surely you must be required to have some evidence to hold me. And there could be none because I am entirely innocent."

Whalen shuffled through the papers and withdrew a wire. "A General Thomas Barrett claims that you are an accessory to the spying activities of one Captain Durksen Hurst."

"Is Captain Hurst alive?" she demanded, realizing that perhaps she'd been lied to.

"I will check for you," he replied, clearly angry at himself for letting the Hurst cat out of the bag.

"Durk is no traitor," she said angrily. "I assure you, Captain. Do check on him. And wire to see if there are any men in his regiment left to vouch for me."

Whalen took a moment to think over his options. "All right, Mrs. DuVallier. I will."

"Thank you, Captain. Any one of them will verify what I am telling you."

Whalen took long moments to stare at Antoinette. His eyes began to twitch again, and his hands shook uncontrollably. Finally, he spoke. "Mrs. DuVallier, I can save your life. *If* you reveal your contacts and testify against Captain Hurst, we will agree to hold you until the end of the war. Then you'd be free."

"But Durk is innocent! So am I!"

"So, you won't testify against Captain Hurst?" he asked angrily.

"Neither of us are spies, and we can prove it," she insisted.

Captain Whalen held the telegraph wire where she could read it. "General Barrett says otherwise. Why would the general insist Hurst was guilty if it weren't true?"

"I-I can't imagine," a shocked Antoinette said.

"Hurst could perhaps help your situation, but spies are often killed under dubious circumstances. Understand my meaning?" he sneered. "I could intervene for you both, *if* you cooperate with me."

"Cooperate how?" She tried to stare him down, but his gaze never left her, and, uncomfortable, she finally lowered her eyes. He began breathing in short bursts, clearly inflamed. Growing increasingly nervous, she waited for him to speak.

Captain Whalen circled his desk, approached, and sat on the edge of the desk, legs spread to either side of her. "Any-any way you would like," he stuttered nervously.

Antoinette slid her chair back, but the room was shallow, and the wall halted her.

Her mind and nerves were suddenly consumed by feelings and memories that washed away her reason, her consciousness.

She was a child in bed in the darkness, and the door opened, as it had so many times. The wispy old man she had been forced to call "father" entered quietly. He approached, his slippers padding softly on the thick carpet, and sat beside her, making the bedsprings creak. He smelled dusty, like ancient furniture. Frightened, in despair, she pretended to be asleep, but he gently shook her shoulder. She tried to mumble him away, but he was urgent and would not be deterred.

She had been only three when he gained possession of her. That day, she was washed and dressed, her hair combed carefully, with long, loving strokes. One hand gripped her mother's white glove; the other clung to her mother's pink skirt. For most of her life, that was all she would remember about the woman: the white glove, the pink rustle, the intoxicating aroma of her perfume. The room was dimly lit by candles, dark, musty. As she watched, a check was proffered to her mother. Then her small hand was wretched from her mother's skirt and placed into the old man's, which felt dry and wrinkled, like parched leather. Within minutes, her mother was gone, and little Antoinette couldn't stop crying, couldn't stop.

She never saw the woman again until that awful night two years ago. That awful night...

Antoinette's vision cleared, furious. "I *have* cooperated," she insisted. "I've told you and the others everything I know. Durk and I are both abolitionists dedicated to preserving the Union. Now, your proximity is making me very uncomfortable, Captain. Please return to your chair or I will scream."

Flustered and shocked at her forcefulness, the captain returned to his chair and sat down. He rubbed his hands nervously, unconscious of the habit, and then made a decision, "I can't get you released immediately, Mrs. DuVallier, but I think I can get you transferred to better accommodations at the McLure Mansion within a couple days at most… if you can hold out. Mrs. McLure was aiding the rebellion, so we confiscated her house. We're holding disloyal female prisoners there until they can be shipped south, which is what became of Mrs. McLure. You'll still have to sleep on a cot, but it will be your own," he said pointedly. "Think about that."

"Well, if you can get me better accommodations, why don't you do that? I have served the army well! This is a great injustice, Captain. I do not deserve this treatment. Just ask the women you took prisoner with me; they'll tell you. You know *they're* not pro-slavery or pro-Confederacy!"

The captain was stunned to silence by her outburst. When he recovered, he nearly laughed. "Surely you don't expect the court to allow the testimony of chattel, madam? You're speaking nonsense."

Antoinette rose to her feet, a firm, haughty look on her face. "We will talk further at McLure's then, Captain. For the moment, you will return me to my suite in this fine hotel. We're done here, sir. Guard!" she called out.

CHAPTER EIGHTEEN

TOO FEW GRAVES

Captain Whalen took two long, hard draws from his bottle. He could not believe what he had just witnessed. The woman was magnificent. Her beauty and remarkable spirit were more than he could bear to think about.

He knew instinctively she would never weaken for him, never break, even if she was convicted and condemned to hang. But that was not what troubled him. He had often been unsuccessful in bending women to his will. But this one! Her hurt and shocked expression when he ultimately failed to free her would never be enough to satisfy him. No, he wanted to possess her forever, as his wife.

With a grand woman like her beside him, no one would ever disparage him again: never depreciate him with insulting names. He would draw strength from her, prestige, solidity. When he finally returned home after the war, he would no longer be known as the worst lawyer on the circuit. He might even be considered the best. He would be a great man, respected, a pillar of the community. For once, his family would be proud of him.

What a quandary his was in. If he was victorious in this case, General Barrett and the whole furious military establishment would come down upon his head. His life in the army would become a nightmare for as long as this unending war lasted. What would happen to him then? And even if he did his best, he was not the type to win in the courtroom. Could he find some inner strength that would lead him to success as her champion? Did he want to risk disapproval only to lose the woman, too?

He'd fallen helplessly into the most consequential decision of his life. Everything was at stake. He would have to ruminate over this deeply. He killed the bottle but was still no closer to resolving his dilemma.

One thing he knew for certain: if she were found guilty, he would definitely attend her hanging. The thought played on his imagination. The image of the rope being place around her neck was both frightening and titillating.

***

Camp Dusty, Kansas

With no shade under the glaring noon sun, the light breeze offered little comfort. The farmyard confiscated by the army was bare dirt, the long-gone grass and weeds trampled into oblivion by the repetitive boots of hundreds of marching men and the hooves of cavalry mounts.

Sergeant Josh Tyler led Bammer, Long Lou, and Isaac, a detail of four, marching up to the prisoner holding pen, once a plantation smokehouse. Their uniforms were buttoned to the throat, boots fastened, hats on straight. Rifles on their shoulders, they looked every inch soldiers in drill formation, albeit a tiny one. Josh neatly stepped aside and spun about, counting out repetitively one-two-three-four, as Isaac and Bammer as the front row, and Long Lou the second, were careful to keep their steps in synch. Training without any weapons in Lawrence, they had passed the time mostly by marching to and fro repeatedly across a barren field, the same field where most of their regiment, their friends, had been massacred.

"Halt!" Josh called out, and the four stamped to a halt in unison. Josh approached the two guards and saluted smartly. "Execution squad reporting," he said. Holding his breath, he tried not to show any emotion. If the guards asked for documents, they might be in real trouble. Real trouble.

The older guard, a corporal with a tobacco-stained beard and long, unkempt hair, eyed the other three suspiciously. He spit juice on the ground. "Who you here for?" the man asked.

"Captain Durksen Hurst," Josh replied crisply, head rigid, eyes staring straight ahead.

The guard glanced askance at his partner, gave him a sly grin, and then turned his attention back to Josh. "Hurst, you say?"

"Yes, C-captain Hurst," Josh stuttered.

This wasn't going well. The guard began to laugh. He looked at his partner, and both began to laugh.

The four *DarkHorse* soldiers maintained their erect pose, but they were shaken. A close examination would find them displaying slight facial twitches and trembling hands. "Is th-there a problem?" Josh asked tentatively.

"Real problem," the corporal said, still half-laughing. "Hurst's already gone."

"Gone!" Josh blurted with a gulp, feeling a burning rock drop into the pit of his stomach. Were they too late? Had Durk already been executed? They hadn't heart shots from a firing squad that morning, but a hanging would be quiet and not attract attention. "What you mean, 'gone'?"

"I mean, gone," the man gaffawed. "Gone, boy. Don'cha know what 'gone' means?"

"W-what?" Josh asked, perplexed. "What's it mean?"

"He was shipped out this morning for trial. President give that new rule. Got to be a trial 'for they hang you." He shook his head in derision. "Less, of course, you got shot escaping," he leered.

Taken aback, Josh finally managed to say, "I guess the paperwork got crossed. New colonel and all." He thought a moment and then decided to brave a question. "Where they s-send him?"

"A spy? They send him to St. Louie, 'course. Gettin' a free train ride." Then he guffawed loudly.

"Thank you, sir," Josh said formally, snapping a crisp salute. "About face!" he ordered. The other three spun about. "Forward, march." The four marched smartly away. As if they hadn't enough problems before, now Durk was being shipped to St. Louis — three hundred miles away.

***

Unbuttoning his collar, Big Josh sat heavily on a box, his face filled with despair. The other three sat on the ground around him, groaning and cursing. Their problem, saving Durk, was now markedly more difficult, likely impossible.

"Wh-what we gonna do now?" Big Josh asked, sighing deeply. "All we gots is a' empty grave and no body," he joked bitterly.

Numbed by the depth of their dilemma, the four mulled the situation over. Their minds fought to uncover some solution, any solution, no matter how farfetched, but they were overwhelmed by a dark despondency at Durk's cruel fate. Was there no way to save him? Their friend, who had often come up with schemes to rescue them, wasn't there to conceive a plan to liberate himself. It seemed a terrible irony.

"What can we do?" Long Lou mused.

"We got to just g-get started in the right direction," Big Josh said, trying to rouse their spirits. "Just take one step at a time. Ain't that the way we get to Missouri? Just start w-walking, and figure it out as we go along."

"He on his way to a prison way across Missouri," Bammer grumbled.

The group fell silent. Big Josh rubbed his chin, Isaac his brow. Bammer covered his eyes. Long Lou's head sunk into his arms. Hopeless, hopeless. Then Josh lifted his head, eyes shining.

"Our problem is," Josh said, "we only gots one grave dug. We needs four.

That's the first step… if you willing to chance going against the army."

"Against the army?" Bammer asked. "That's a hangin' offense, Josh."

Josh stared into Bammer's eyes. "Durk's our friend, our brother. Ain't he risk his life to save us more than once, when he coulda run off and save himself? He sure did. You seen it."

The remaining dozen survivors of the truncated Ninth MSM Colored Cavalry, the *DarkHorse* regiment, crowded around Josh, leaning in close to hear his urgent instructions. The soldiers believed they were all that remained after the others left behind in Lawrence were massacred. Neither Billy, the escaped slave, nor John Wilkens, the freedman volunteer, had been seen or found dead, and it was feared they hadn't survived their heroic attempt to warn the town.

"Here's what you gots to do," Josh whispered. "Tonight, you dig three more graves over by that one we dig last night. Make sure you pile dirt high on top so it look like a body down there."

"What if the guard come by and ask what we doing?" one of the soldiers asked.

"You burying four men from the Ninth who die of a fever. Understand? We die of typhus."

"What if they dig the graves up?" another asked, his voice trembling. "Ain't nobody gonna be in them graves."

"They won't dig up no colored troops die of sickness," Josh assured them. "They gonna stay far away as they can. Now, can you do that?"

The men exchanged anxious glances with each other; then, one by one, they reluctantly nodded their assent to carrying out Josh's plan.

"What you gonna do?" one asked.

"Only thing we can do. We gonna ride to St. Louie to save Durk. You dig them graves tonight, and we be gone in the morning. Understand?" Josh made eye contact with the men around him, showing them he meant business.

"How you gonna save him? They think he a spy."

"I don't know yet," Josh said earnestly. "But we gots to try to save our friend. Y'all don't know how many times he save us — and we save him."

"What's gonna happen to us, to *DarkHorse*?" another of the men asked, and a few grumbled their concern.

"Ain't no more Ninth: too few of us left. It's over. Next day or two, you gonna be sent to fill in other regiments. Listen," Josh continued, "once you gone from here, you gone. See? Nobody can ask you no questions about them graves. Far as the army concerned, Bammer, Lou, Isaac, and me dead."

Josh looked questioningly at the men around him, but they merely shrugged in resignation.

"Now," he said firmly, "give up all your money, everything you got."

"What you need our money for?" a man asked suspiciously.

"We not gonna steal chickens all the way across Missouri," Josh replied. "We'll have to pay to eat."

"White troops take what they want. Some leave vouchers, some just steal. Why can't you?" a man named Ike objected.

Josh gave Ike a critical stare. "We not gonna disgrace our brothers and sisters trying to be free by stealing no food from no farmers. Not wearing these uniforms, we ain't. You want people to be afraid of colored soldiers coming 'round? Sides, that would draw attention. We gonna have to make it to St. Louie without ruffling no feathers. See? Now, y'all give me your money, every cent, every one of you. Durk's life at stake."

The men dug in their pants and coats and filled Josh's big hands with coins and crumpled bills. When they were done, Josh stuffed the money in his pocket. "Now, we got any rifles?"

"No, sir," one of the men answered. "Any guns we had is long gone."

"You think you can save the captain?" another of the men asked anxiously.

"Our chance to just get across the state without winding up h-hung for deserters ain't very good," Josh said solemnly. He studied the faces around him, friends and comrades that he'd likely never see again, whether he succeeded or not. "So, dig them graves r-right. We may be needin' them."

***

Westport HQ, Kansas

Major Armand Benbow looked up from the documents and cast a bloodshot eye at Durk sitting across from him. The major's office was a simple, converted one-bedroom frame house on a side street he'd confiscated from rebel sympathizers, whom he'd exiled to Arkansas. He had seen traitors before, and the one sitting across from him was one of the worst. Not even a fully-white man, and a Southerner besides. If Lincoln hadn't issued orders to the contrary, he'd have had this man shot the moment he arrived. That would have saved him two men who would now have to accompany the prisoner to trial — two more good soldiers that he couldn't spare.

Tired and despondent, Durk slumped in the chair, absently gazing at, but not seeing, the heavy iron cuffs in his lap weighing down his arms. The wagon ride had jolted and slammed him about, and he was sore from head to foot.

"What are you going to do with me, Major?" Durk queried, resigned.

"When everything's in order, you'll be taken to the station to catch the train to St. Louis, Captain. That's where you'll stand trial. If you're guilty, you'll probably face a firing squad. It'll be quick, which is more than you deserve."

Durk gathered his strength and stated his case clearly. "Listen, Major Benbow, I've got proof that I'm not a spy. I just want to rejoin my regiment."

"Proof? What kind of proof?" the major asked skeptically.

"I was the man who warned your men about Quantrill's attack. Ask your own Major Danwell," he pleaded. "Just ask him."

Benbow took a moment to roll over the captain's claim in his mind, and then he said, "I'll do that, Captain."

Durk studied the major and saw a hint of openness that wasn't there when he'd first arrived. "Major, some of my men, they've been with me since Mississippi. They can vouch for me. All you have to do is wire Camp Dusty. They'll come and testify for me."

The major perused the documents. "Is the Ninth colored or white?"

"Colored, sir. I rescued many of them from slavery. Can't you just have them brought here for questioning? I trust your judgment, Major. You'll see. You wouldn't hang a good soldier if he's innocent, would you?"

"You want me to take the testimony of colored against the word of a general?" He rifled through the papers. "General Barrett?"

"Yes, they'll tell the truth. I swear."

"Well, Barrett is a bloated bag of wind." He scratched his head. "Wouldn't these men lie for you? Aren't you their former boss, their master?"

"They'd have no reason to lie for me. Why would I have freed them, if I was pro-slavery? Why would I have escorted them safely all the way to Missouri to join the Union Army? It makes no sense. A spy wouldn't do that."

The major took a long time to think over the request. While Durk held his breath, the major lit his pipe. He drew on it a number of times to catch the tobacco, then puffed on it thoughtfully, blowing smoke from his mouth and nostrils. Finally, he broke the silence. "All right, Captain, I'll wire to have them brought here. But if these men don't back up your wild story, I may save you that trip to St. Louis. Understand?"

"Yes, sir! That's all I ask."

"Understand, too, Captain Hurst, that the court will be weighing their testimony against the word of a general who, for some unknown reason, has malevolent intentions toward you. All right, what are their names?"

Durk started spelling out the names of his old *DarkHorse* partners who he believed were still alive. Any one of them would clear him, but would their testimony be accepted? Would he ever be safe? And what about Antoinette?

Then Durk was struck by another notion, devious, but it might serve as a last resort. He'd be willing to attempt it, even if it meant losing his lucky gold piece, which hadn't been so lucky lately anyway. It was time to attempt every trick he could think of, and some he hadn't.

He wasn't dead yet.

CHAPTER NINETEEN

THE CHARLATAN'S ESCAPE

St. Louis, Missouri

Captain Owen Whalen briskly organized his desk, readying for the day's activities. He preferred to shuffle his paperwork early in the morning before the office became unbearably hot. That afternoon he was to argue before a military court in defense of a number of female guerrilla sympathizers who were believed to have aided the rebels. His plan was to sway the court to deport them to the South rather than imprison or even execute them. But the "Hanging Judge" trial lawyer had lost far easier cases and expected no different now.

The exercise of such mercy would be no picnic for the traitors. The women would be forced to leave everything they owned behind. Exile often meant being shipped in reeking ambulances that hadn't been cleaned after transporting wounded from battle, with the floor still covered with blood and flesh from severe wounds. The usual route was from St. Louis to Memphis, Tennessee. From there, they were shipped to LaGrange, Tennessee, then to Holly Springs, Mississippi, where they'd be turned loose. At that point, survival was up to them. Often broke and friendless, they would face hardship, but at least their lives would be spared.

Seating himself, Captain Whalen noticed the wire that a night orderly had just dropped on his desk. He knew what it was about. Holding his breath, he stared at the brown paper rectangle, blankly contemplating nothing more than its existence. Then he began to consider the ramifications of the reply that might be contained within it. His mind tried to run through the legal consequences inherent in any exigency, but his thoughts were invariably drawn away from logic and the law to his client, Antoinette DuVallier. For two days, he hadn't been able to keep her off his mind. Finally, he found the courage to pick up the wire.

12 MEMBERS OF 9TH MSMCC REQUESTED BY COURT DECEASED STOP 8 KILLED LAWRENCE MASSACRE STOP 4 DIED DISEASE IN CAMP STOP COLONEL ROLAND CARTER US ARMY

Captain Whalen tossed the wire aside. All dead. Antoinette's best chance for immediate release had disappeared in the smoke and circumstance of war. He would have to give her this information: the question was when. He rubbed his forehead, trying to think through the startling news. He had expected at least one of the troopers to testify, at least informally. Now his case was weakened immeasurably.

In the meantime, he would have to wait for a second wire to arrive informing him of Hurst's status. Things were not going well. If Hurst turned out to be alive, the army would hang Antoinette. But if Hurst was dead, what evidence could they have against her?

He poured himself a large glassful of whiskey. After much consideration, he decided he would have Antoinette transferred to the McLure Mansion and visit her there. In the McLure yard, under the stars, he would commiserate with her on the unlucky turn of events plaguing his attempts to free her. He would show her sympathy, comfort her, and hopefully be a shoulder to lean on if she needed one. And he would bring her a clean dress. She could not help but be grateful for that small consideration.

***

Westport HQ, Kansas

Durk knew this was his last chance to free himself in order to save Antoinette from the noose. He heard the door being unlocked and set his tin plate and spoon on the crate by his cot. The guards' arrival meant that Major Benbow had likely received a reply to his wire to Kansas ordering Durk's partners be sent to headquarters. The major probably had spoken with his own Major Danwell, too. Durk rose and slipped on his tunic, brushing and straightening it. The blue uniform was wrinkled and smelled a bit ripe, but he would be attending no dance in the French Quarter that day. He stretched his arms, then his legs. Stuck for days in the windowless shack, he had been feeling despondent about his predicament. But he knew getting into the light would refresh his mind and spirit. He and his partners had often saved each other from harm, and Durk knew there was no chance they would let him down this time either.

Still, he had to fight against the terror screaming at him, the helpless feeling of imagining his hands bound on the gallows, of a rope being tightened around his neck. A familiar feeling since he'd beaten the odds to escape beatings and death many times throughout his life, yet the consuming fear that accompanied each perilous encounter never waned, never grew easier. This time, he knew he could not be held even tangentially accountable for Lawrence, nor for the absurd accusation of spying. Still, the prospect of imminent death hanging over him filled him with uncontrollable dread. In the middle of a guerrilla war, in a time of hysterical hatred, murder, and desperate panic, the daily toll of innocents alone was staggering. Why should he be an exception?

If worse came to worse, he would use his only remaining weapon to save himself: his talent to convince men and women that wealth, happiness, or power was within their grasp. When in dire jeopardy, a man always falls back on what he knows best. An army engineer, when surrounded, will engineer himself across a river. A newspaperman will attempt to write himself out of a hole. And Durk would spin a yarn.

He felt in his pockets. His lucky gold piece was there. Using the coin as a prop, he'd managed to win a plantation in Mississippi and pull off other schemes, both worthy — and a few shameful — and the gold piece had always landed back in his pocket. The coin had witnessed many a successful venture, and he hated to let it go. But to save his life, he was willing to chance parting with it.

When the guards entered, Durk held out his hands so they would clamp the cuffs on his wrist in front of him, not behind his back. "Let's go," he said hurriedly, "can't keep the major waiting on us." The guards, sensing the urgency in his voice, cuffed him in front, as he'd hoped, where he could still reach inside his pocket.

The clouds from the previous night's storm had nearly dissipated; the day would be bright. Exposed to the harsh morning sunlight, Durk blinked until his eyes adjusted. Then he was led to Major Benbow's office.

The moment he sat down and saw the major's face, Durk knew the news was grim.

"I received a return wire from Kansas," the major stated flatly, packing tobacco into his pipe. "Your four troopers died in camp. Disease. I'm sorry, Hurst." He showed Durk the wire.

"Died?" Durk croaked. "All of them?"

The major nodded sympathetically.

Durk's mind began to whirl, and for a moment, he thought he might lose consciousness. The best friends he'd ever had: men he could trust implicitly, men who had shared dangers and challenges with him. *All of them gone. Gone!*

For a time, he was unable to speak, to breathe. Finally, the despondency of his desperate loss was overwhelmed by the immediacy of his own peril. He fought to recover, to follow his alternate plan. He would have to speak for himself and to speak effectively, forthrightly: to somehow find the strength to put on the charm.

"Did you speak to Major Danwell?" Durk asked.

The major lit his pipe while considering his reply, and its consequences. "Yes, Captain. Not only did you warn us, but your hurrying back to Lawrence was nothing short of heroic."

"Look, Major," Durk said earnestly, feeling vulnerable. "Did you find any evidence in my record, any at all, that I am a spy?"

The major untied Hurst's documents and fingered through them, studying them carefully. Durk watched him, reading his face, brow creasing, seeing him grow more uncertain as he turned each page.

Major Benbow finished the last page and straightened up the stack. "There's really nothing here," he concluded. "Not a thing."

"Exactly. In point of fact, my men, those brave soldiers, no matter their color, should practically get a unit citation for attempting to forestall the massacre at Lawrence. We were unarmed, yet we risked our lives repeatedly. You know as well as I, a frenzy befouls the air when something like Lawrence happens. In this, I am a clean, blameless, loyal officer who was tainted by the stench. Can't you simply clear me and let me rejoin my regiment, or what's left of it?"

The major sat in deep contemplation, not speaking.

"Major, you know the army can be, and often is, dishonest in its machinations. You know, too, there is no way I will get a fair trial, that the whole device is geared toward getting me hanged. Without your help, I am a dead, innocent man."

"Captain Hurst, I believe you led your men with bravery. Yet, with General Barrett so deeply involved, I cannot free you without formal adjudication, which, as you know, can be unpredictable, and, as you've said, likely has no interest in providing you with justice."

Still at the mercy of an uncertain twist of judicial fate, Durk persevered. "Listen, Major, I have something important to tell you, but it's for your ears only."

The major concluded that Durk posed no threat and ordered the guards to leave the room. The two guards tromped out, shutting the door behind them. When Durk was certain they were alone, he reached into his pocket. His movement startled the major, but seeing Durk withdraw the coin, the officer settled back in his chair.

"You see this coin?" Durk asked, displaying the gold piece brazenly, giving the major a good, long look.

The majored nodded.

"This is from the infamous lost Confederate payroll. Maybe you've heard of it?"

"Can't say I have. Regardless, go on, Captain."

"Few have, Major Benbow, and that's to our advantage. You do know, in '61, in a surprise attack, the leader of the Union garrison, a man named Lyons, expelled the rebels from St. Louis. Most of the rebs were captured and paroled."

"Yes, I am aware of that."

Durk lowered his voice and began speaking in a confidential, conspiratorial tone. "The rebs were routed so swiftly, the Confederate paymaster had to bury the payroll so the Federals wouldn't capture it. The whole cache, which is still buried near St. Louis, is entirely gold coin like this, no paper money." Durk paused then locked eyes with the major. "The money never reached the rebel soldiers to whom it was intended, nor has it ever been located." Durk flipped the coin across the desk so Major Benbow could examine it.

"*Confederate* gold? You claim you are a loyal Union man, Captain," the major said, tossing the coin back across the table. "How would you know where the cache is hidden?"

Durk returned the coin to his pocket. "Because that very paymaster has been operating with Quantrill around Layfayette and Johnson counties. Last month, he was shot through the lung in an ambush. I gave him water from my canteen and tried to save his life. I staunched his wound with my bandanna."

"And…"

"Oh, he died, but not before he gave me the gold piece out of gratitude. In his delirium, he revealed to me the location of the payroll money." Then Durk whispered, "If you let me retrieve it, I'll split it with you."

"I don't know, Hurst. The whole..."

"Major, you said yourself I am innocent. If you send me to trial, you know very well I may even be acquitted on so little evidence and get the gold for myself. Or I'll be hung, and the money will be lost forever. This way, *you* acquit me and gain half the gold." Durk paused to gauge the degree of skepticism the major's face registered. "You know very well you can trust me. Wasn't I an honest captain of a colored regiment? Didn't the men in the Ninth, my friends, trust me enough to follow me all the way north? Didn't they give their lives for our country following my orders? Besides, what do you have to lose? It would cost you two good soldiers to accompany me to St. Louis, men you need right here fighting the bushwhackers."

Major Benbow thought long and hard. "I don't see how I can do it, Captain. The paperwork would lead right back to me. I would lose my commission at the very least, perhaps be charged with a crime myself."

"How about if you mark on those papers that I am deceased? Nobody's going to care about another dead man in this war. I'd be just another one of hundreds, thousands."

Durk had to suppress the urge to smile. With Durk officially "dead," the army would have to release Antoinette. They'd have no evidence against her and no co-conspirator to tie her to. Certainly, St. Louis was mobbed, overrun with 40,000 refugees from the brutal killing and, as military headquarters, with division upon division of army units and supply depots. Hell or high water, somehow he would find her there. He'd find Antoinette.

The major rubbed his chin. "I could declare that you were 'shot escaping.' That's so common, it doesn't mean a damn thing anymore. Maybe that would satisfy Old Cannonball."

"Major Benbow," Durk said, his eyes seeking sympathy. "What about my fiancée? Do you have to disgrace me, a loyal soldier? Can you at least give me an honorable death? 'Fallen in defense of his country,' that's no more than I deserve."

"But I received this query about you from the provost marshal's office in St. Louis. What will I reply?"

"Keep the story clean," Durk said. "Wire them that I died on the field of battle, defending the camp against a rebel raid." Durk thought a moment and then continued, "I think we best not seek a posthumous medal for me, too conspicuous."

Both men laughed.

"I don't know about putting my name on such a fiction," the major said, worried.

"Have your aide send it under his own name," Hurst suggested. "They won't bother to trace it back to you."

"Yes, I could do that. But how do we get you to St. Louis?" the major asked.

"Give me paperwork that says I'm wounded. Include me with the next batch of wounded men you ship to St. Louis."

The major thought this over. "What if someone checks on you? This paperwork," he indicated the pile, "says you're dead."

Durk laughed, then playacted as if the major was someone questioning him. "Paperwork error, sir. I recovered from a wound that the doctors expected would kill me. I mean, you can see me, can't you, sir? I'm here in front of you. I'm not a ghost, right?"

Major Benbow shrugged. "Fine, why not. We'll be shipping a group of wounded to St. Louis about mid-week. You'll accompany them. In the meantime, you'll wait in the smokehouse. At least there'll be no more chains for you, Hurst."

"See, Major, that document would prove my recuperating story. It would also explain how I am alive if there are ever any questions about my death, which, considering the condition of army records in all this chaos, will never arise."

"Why not, Hurst?" the major exclaimed. Breaking into a good belly laugh, he opened his drawer and took out a bottle of whiskey and two glasses. "Tell me, is this lost payroll real?"

"Oh, sure," Durk laughed and winked at him, knowing they'd reached the moment in some swindles when the gull knows he's been had and, to maintain his dignity, inexplicably aligns himself with the charlatan. "Next time you see me, I'll be bearing a great fortune, half of which will be yours."

Benbow filled the glasses. "Right," he joked, sharing the lie good-naturedly, "I'll be sure to quit drinking until then."

The pair laughed at the absurdity.

"One last thing, Major Benbow. Would you see that my regiment is cited for its bravery?"

"Of course, Captain, they deserve it." Major Benbow raised his glass. "Well, have a good visit with your lady in St. Louis. After what you've been through, you deserve time away from this Hell."

Durk downed the entire glass and smiled. Without him, the army had no evidence whatsoever against Antoinette. Hopefully, they would have to set her free. But the way army justice worked, there was no guarantee of that. None at all. He would have to find her.

***

St. Louis, Missouri

Captain Whalen examined the wire, his breathing short. Of all the wires that regularly appear on his desk, like artillery shrapnel from the smoke of battle, he knew this one would seal his fate with Antoinette.

CAPTAIN DURKSEN HURST FALLEN IN DEFENSE OF CAMP

STOP BURIED WITH HONORS STOP MAJOR ARMAND BENBOW US ARMY.

Whalen smiled broadly and placed the wire with Antoinette's file. His path to her heart was clear. Then he ceremoniously brushed back his hair and straightened his uniform, making himself presentable. Now how was he to approach Antoinette's imminent freedom?

CHAPTER TWENTY

AN UNWELCOME SUITOR

Westport HQ, Kansas

Durk lay on his cot, staring through the cracks in the smokehouse ceiling. The windowless room, always dark, was settling to pitch as the sun set outside. He had days to wait, and then he would be off to find Antoinette in the crowded beehive of a city at war. He was destined to find her. And, oh, he'd find her.

His thoughts went to his friends, digesting the words from the major that they were all dead now. Big Josh, Isaac, Lou, Bammer, as with about half the casualties of this grinding conflict, they had succumbed to disease: Little Turby and the rest, to bloodlust. The warmth he felt with them, the friendship they shared, gone from his life forever.

He smiled recollecting their first improbable, fateful meeting in the Chickasaw swamp outside Turkle. They were scared, as was he. As distrusting. As desperate. And as hungry and tired. He remembered their skepticism. They wanted to believe him but knew he could turn them in for a reward.

Then his thoughts turned inward, darker, more bitter, his grief distorting the past. He thought about the chances he'd taken that had put them in danger. It was vanity that drove him to risk their necks. Some friend. They deserved better. It wasn't purely greed that made him do it. It was simply that the *chance* was there to do something big, and he couldn't resist taking it, a fatal flaw deep in his soul. Vanity, the rash instincts of a lowlife charlatan, had overpowered him, destroying everything good they'd built together.

He missed them so profoundly, he couldn't endure it. In spite of all the hardship and loss he'd suffered throughout his life, he hadn't felt this deep sense of loss since his mother's death. Now he couldn't stop the torrent of tears running down his face — his whole body shaking. If it were not for Antoinette needing him somewhere in St. Louis, he'd rather be hung than feel like this.

He didn't care if the guards could hear him sobbing.

***

St. Louis, Missouri

The lock to her cell clicked, the door swung open, and Antoinette's name was roughly called. She immediately grew tense, and, remembering yesterday's meeting with Captain Whalen, her head began to throb. She was summarily led to the same cramped prison office as the day before. Was she again to face the captain with the wild eyes who had tried to intimidate her? How much more torturous humiliation would she have to endure?

When she was seated, Captain Whalen entered briskly, smiling awkwardly at her in a way that made her uncomfortable. Clearly, he had something up his sleeve.

"I've received responses to my inquiries, Mrs. DuVallier," he said, growing deadly serious. "I must warn you in advance, neither reply offers the best of news."

Antoinette's heart stopped, and then she caught her breath. "Yes. Please go on, Captain."

Captain Whalen slid Antoinette the telegram notifying him of Durksen Hurst's death.

Antoinette read the sheet. Then, her mind growing foggy, she tried reading it again, but its words and meanings were washed away by a black tide of despair. She felt lightheaded, and it took some time for her head to clear. *So Durk's really gone.* She was, once again, alone in a maelstrom of war, of killing. Alone.

They'd met by the forest stream: she a fugitive, a mariticide. His clothes were travel worn, his face animated with grand plans and visions for the future, his rush of words tumbling forth filled with wild claims. She couldn't decide whether he was mad, delirious, someone dangerous, even deadly, or vulnerable, as she was. What was it about him that so attracted her, the spirit and goodness that even his ridiculous bravado couldn't hide?

"I am sorry, Mrs. DuVallier," Captain Whalen said, putting on a cloak of sympathy, breaking her reverie. "Apparently, Captain Hurst died bravely. I hope you can find some comfort in that." He poured a glass of water and handed it to her.

Antoinette felt the urgency to cry but fought to control herself. Restraint was nearly impossible with her heart breaking, her hopes shattered. But she managed; yes, she managed. When she was finally able to speak, she croaked, her voice breaking, "I can. Yes. Thank you."

Whalen nodded. Then, without hesitation, he slipped the second wire to her.

She attempted to read it. Finally, she understood that all of Durk's partners, too, were dead. This second shock made her feel faint, and she nearly fell to the floor. It was some time before she could right herself.

"The loss of these men harms our case exponentially," the captain said.

"What about their women?" she asked, struggling to focus on the legal ramifications of her case. "We still have that."

"The men were soldiers," he replied. "That would give them some credibility. As for the women, their word wouldn't count for anything in a case of this magnitude." He paused and watched his comment register.

"Speaking of them…" she interjected, regaining some composure.

"As I promised, I have submitted the paperwork to transfer them to a much better facility," Whalen said, producing a smile. "Now, aren't you glad of that?"

Antoinette nodded, her head still swirling. "Thank you, Captain. Please, hurry it along," she said when she managed to piece her thoughts together. "You must get word to them about their men."

"I will see to it today," he replied, jotting a note for himself.

In his face, Antoinette saw that his promise and note-taking was merely a pantomime, meant to appease her. "And this claimant, who is he?" she asked.

"I'll try to find out. He hasn't arrived in the city yet."

Antoinette thought over her options. "If Captain Hurst is deceased, and you have no evidence against me, shouldn't you have me released?"

The captain placed General Barrett's wire declaring Durk a spy and Antoinette a possible accomplice on top of the other two he'd given her. "Not until the case is cleared through General Barrett."

Antoinette had already deduced what *that* meant.

She studied Whalen's face and knew he was lying, simply delaying her release to maintain his power over her. She was now Captain Whalen's prisoner, not the Union Army's. And judging by the man's burning eyes, his nervous demeanor, she knew the last thing he would ever do is set her free. She'd seen this look before. Clearly, he was obsessed with her and had abandoned all reason and mercy. She was trapped. It was time to take another tact.

She smiled. "Can you go over his head? To General Schofield? He would release me immediately if he knew my situation."

"A Major General? That would be impossible for a captain. There is a war on. However, I am making progress through channels."

"Well, then? When?"

Whalen folded his fingers on the desk. "That I cannot predict. I will do my best."

He had her. For now. "Listen, Captain Whalen, you said you could get me out of here. I insist that you keep your promise."

Whalen lowered his eyes and fumbled through her documents, hiding his thoughts. "I will get you transferred to McLure's by tomorrow," he said, trying to maintain a benevolent expression. "Mrs. DuVallier, do you mind if I call you Antoinette?"

"Not at all," she replied.

He reached for a box and handed it across to her. "Open it," he said with forced smile.

Unsure of what to do, she tentatively opened the box. Inside was a black dress. "What is this?" she asked incredulously.

"Black. So the court will see you as a mourning fiancée. I sent away for it. I thought it was appropriate. Do you want to try it on, see if it fits?"

"I-I can't take this from you," she managed to stutter.

"Consider it supplies from the army," he said with a wink. "What you're wearing has grown quite ripe in de Lynch."

"Have it sent to McLure's," she said haughtily. "I'll put it on there." She closed the box and shoved it across the desk.

"Antoinette, dear, as I said, I am entirely on your side. I will do everything I can for you and for the women you were with. I consider you more than a client. I am your friend. For the time being, is there anything more you need?"

"I wouldn't be adverse to a hot bath." As soon as it was out of her mouth, the captain's steel blue eyes lit up, and she was sorry she'd said it, even though it was the truth. "I can wait until I reach the mansion." Then she rose to leave.

Once Antoinette had been taken away, Captain Whalen slumped back in his chair, exhausted by the encounter and at his wit's end. He took several deep breaths, trying to calm himself. Still unsteady, he opened his top drawer and, with shaking hands, drew out a bottle and glass. Whiskey spilled when he pulled the cork, and more splashed when he poured. He took a deep drink, coughed, and set the glass down.

I've got her. But how will I gain her affections? She was nothing like the others he'd known, and that made her even more desirable, *and* more intimidating. She was no longer simply an object of his pleasure, but a perfect marble statue to enrich his life. All the others, the ones who had succumbed to his machinations, now seemed sordid, dirty, as was he. He wanted her for his wife, to prove he was, indeed, a man of substance. He wasn't a failed lawyer representing the scrap and waste of the war. He wasn't a failed human being, an ant, a humbug.

He located the document in her file that he'd completed the night before, a motion that could free her. He studied it, thinking over his options. He feared that once she was out of his grip, she would go on without him. What would she need him for? He knew he couldn't compete for her affections. He had to keep her at McLure's, where he could visit her evenings. Where his sympathetic warmth would draw her to him. Where she would learn to love him.

He folded the document and placed it into his coat. No one must see it until she was his, fully, wholeheartedly. He retied her file, now absent the conclusive motion. And with an eye twitching, he poured himself another drink.

***

Keytesville, Missouri

Devereau French spelled out the next name from the list printed in the newspaper to the clerk in the records office. The clerk, a man in his mid-fifties wearing wire spectacles, nervously wrote the name on the document, signed it on the bottom, and slid it onto the pile. He was well-aware of the Indian standing behind him whose reflection he glimpsed in the corner of his glasses.

"And the last one, Sally, a woman about twenty. It doesn't give a last name. Just write French like the others," Devereau said.

The clerk did as he was told, then straightened the pile of documents and handed them across the desk. "Can you pay me now," he stuttered fearfully. "I'm due home for supper."

Devereau nodded. "Pay him," she said, looking away.

Robert Sterling's knife quickly passed across the man's throat. Blood spread across the desk and down the clerk's shirt, and his head fell forward.

"Well," Devereau said, turning back to view the scene, "on to St. Louis."

"And off straight to Hell," Robert replied forebodingly. He wanted the women for the price they would bring, yes, but if Devereau tried to get them entangled with Dark Horse and her sister, his knife would grow thirsty very quickly. More quickly than her eyes could hope to follow.

CHAPTER TWENTY-ONE

GENERAL ORDER NUMBER 11

Randolph County, Central Missouri

Thinking of Durk, Devereau French's eyes glazed over as Robert Sterling led her on back trails eastward through the impenetrable woods and thickets of Central Missouri. Making their way across state to St. Louis would take longer this way, but they had to avoid the main roads, where Union patrols might confront them. There also might be authorities seeking the parties who murdered the clerk at Keytesville. And there had been other robbery victims, not to mention bodies, they'd left in their wake in their trek through Missouri, and even before Missouri.

"I decided," Devereau stated, a sob catching in her throat. "When we arrive in St. Louis, I am going to inform the authorities that Antoinette is wanted for murder in New Orleans." Blinded by a tear-distorted glare under the high sun, she wiped her eyes repeatedly in a vain attempt to clear her vision. "The Yankees have New Orleans now and can verify it. It may take time, but she will, nonetheless, not be released. Hell, she killed one of its leading citizens. They won't forget that so easily. They'll hold her in prison until they can ship her downriver for trial. We'll be rid of her for good, clean and easy."

Robert Sterling's face grew hard, his black eyes narrowing. He rode beside Devereau in silence for a quarter mile, contemplating this latest gambit by his unpredictable companion. Then he spoke, "Why are you so determined to get your sister hung? Hear me, woman, we're going to retrieve those slaves, sell them, and be done with it. That is first, last, and everything. After that, you'll be on your own to do whatever your want with her. I'm going my own way, and you won't see me again. If you want to kill the only remaining member of your family not already in Hell, and get yourself hung side-by-side with her, that's your business. I don't care. But if you think I'm going to let you steal my chance at that slave money because of a lingering vendetta, you do not know me well. I'd rather kill you and take your stallion. The white and that saddle would be small compensation for the loss of the slaves, but I deserve something for putting up with your female craziness all these years."

Devereau drew rein and stared daggers at Robert. "You are a fool, Indian. Antoinette's word is the only thing standing between us and possession of those slaves. If we discredit her in advance, our claim is a certainty. Don't you see that?"

"Dark Horse's word stands between us and the slaves, too," Robert retorted. "I would say that you have forgotten Dark Horse, but I know well he is never out of your thoughts. Why you are so possessed by such a man is beyond me. He is neither large nor fair of face."

The pair rode on without speaking, both angry, frustrated.

"Consider this, Robert," Devereau finally said. "Durk is being held on spy charges. He has no credibility with the army. With her off the table, too, there is nothing to stop us from taking the slaves."

Robert thought this over, instinctively massaging the handle of his knife. He didn't care whether Antoinette lived or died and would much prefer that Dark Horse did die, which he felt had been determined already by the Federal Army. No, it was the unnecessary risk Devereau was introducing into their scheme that troubled him.

A few hundred yards later, he growled, "I will consider your notion, French, but only as a last resort if we really need to dispense with her. You will have to get my agreement in advance, you hear me? You'll make no move without me." He glared at her menacingly. "And I want to hear no more about saving Dark Horse."

"Stupid Indian. Durk may have hidden the gold. Ever think of that? I'm sure he'd trade everything for his neck."

Robert knew this tact to be another of Devereau's lies but didn't feel like disputing the point. His voice grew low, steady. "If you cross me on this, Devereau, you won't have to worry about the authorities, the hangman, or anyone else. Keep in mind, I covet your stallion far more than I do your company. You understand what I'm telling you?"

***

Jackson County, Western Missouri

The four survivors of the *DarkHorse* regiment rode down the shade-dappled trail beside the heavily wooded forest, alert to their surroundings. The sounds of chirping songbirds and squirrels scurrying in the overgrowth seemed harmless, but the four knew there was danger around every bend. They'd already been riding through the dark for hours, and their uniforms, crumpled from sleeping in the brush, were coated with a dusty, chalklike film. The glare of sunrise temporarily blinded them, and they pulled their hats down to shade their eyes. It was going to be sizzling that day, but they had to go on.

Letting the reins hang loosely from his large hands, Big Josh sat back in the saddle, rolling with his mount's steady gait, but his mind was troubled. Desertion was a capital crime, punishable immediately — no court-martial needed for black soldiers. Why did he include the others in his scheme to save Durk, pitting their lives against insurmountable odds? How could they aid him in his hopeless task? He was more than willing to throw away his life. But why should they die, simply because they trusted him and he wanted them with him?

His thoughts drifted to Ceeba, and his heart burned like fire. Bammer, too, had lost his wife. Then his memories descended irrevocably along the path of sorrow to his darkest valley, to another time, another place… to his son, James. As always, he was tormented knowing that if the brave boy had been white, or if the girl James had tried to help had been black, or, God!, if Josh himself had been there, James would still be alive. His son would be a man in full now, maybe with a family, with Josh's grandchildren. Lost forever.

Josh always believed James' death had killed the boy's mother, Carolyn. Josh had watched her sit impassively for hours, staring into space. He'd tried to talk to her, to bring her back, but everything that ever made her a woman was gone, as if her life had been punctured and poured onto the ground. Finally, he'd watched her stop eating. Saw her grow sick and die without protest, without complaint. For many years, Josh had wished he'd died with her: that he'd joined the pair in oblivion, in peace.

His reverie was broken by frantic whispers from Isaac and Bammer. "Horses!" The four drew rein and craned their necks. Dozens of hooves were thundering toward them, clouds of dust arising in their wake. "We got to hide," Isaac said hysterically.

"It's too late," Big Josh said, grabbing Isaac's reins. "L-let me do the talking."

Josh saw the panic in Isaac's face, saw his eyes casting about, his agitated horse scuffling up dirt. The man was desperate to gallop away, which would be death for them all. "Isaac," Josh ordered, "if you run, we all dead. Understand? Isaac? These might be friends coming."

A company of men in blue was heading directly toward them in military formation, but pro-slavery bushwhackers, formerly regular Confederate cavalry, had taken to wearing Union uniforms as a disguise. The ruse proved an effective method of surprising Federal soldiers. Even when outnumbered, the guerrillas could get in close and overwhelm them with pistols and helter-skelter riding, often causing the Union troopers to panic, leading to a rout. Seeing their numbers, Josh realized that if the company headed their way was secesh, or Union Cavalry that questioned them too closely, their journey would end right there, right then. On the spot. They'd be rotting in a ditch.

An officer wearing a lieutenant's uniform rode up to Josh and saluted. "What regiment are you, Sergeant?" Lieutenant Langham asked.

Relieved, Josh crisply returned the salute. "Ninth MSM Colored Cavalry," he announced firmly.

Lieutenant Horace Langham, a barrel-chested man in his mid-thirties, with a week's beard from the trail, turned to a sergeant who had pulled up beside him. "Says they're the Ninth MSM Colored, Sergeant. Know anything about them?"

"Maybe, sir," the sergeant replied. He turned to Josh. "I thought the Ninth was wiped out at Lawrence."

"A few of us survived," Josh replied, looking back toward the other three, keeping steady as he could. He pulled from his coat his manumission papers, signed by Durk, and their assignment to the Ninth. "Here our papers, sir." He handed them to Langham.

The lieutenant examined the documents, then handed them back. "Where is your officer, Sergeant?"

"Killed. Sh-shot down by the se-secesh."

"Where are your weapons?" Langham continued.

Josh took a moment to think it over. "Bushwhackers surprised ever'body. Had to run without nothing."

The lieutenant looked the four over, skeptical. "Where you headed, Sergeant?"

"Headquarters," Josh replied, "to be reassigned."

Lieutenant Langham glanced at his sergeant, who nodded back. "Have you eaten today?" Langham asked.

"No, sir. Not since yesterday morning." Josh laughed. "I can afford to miss my vittles, but these others…"

"All right. You men come with us. There's a camp two, three miles up this road. We'll feed and arm you. You can rest your horses, if that's what you want to call those militia fleabags."

"Thank you, sir," Josh replied. "Then we'll go on."

"No, sir," the lieutenant said sharply. "You are now attached to my patrol. Going to need you. Order Eleven."

"Order Eleven?" Josh asked, puzzled and bewildered. "Eleven? I heard of Nine and Ten, but..."

"You only thought the border war was dirty," the lieutenant said. "Now headquarters issued Order Eleven. Welcome to the lowest ring of Hell itself, soldier."

***

The four huddled silently together in the chow line, facing in toward each other, as if trying to shrink themselves into invisibility. They didn't look about but rather glanced nervously at their surroundings out of the corners of their eyes.

The camp sat on a flat, barren lawn surrounding what had been the home of a large landowner. The property had been commandeered as a headquarters for the colonel that commanded the outposts throughout the Western Missouri county. Midday was already sweltering, and the poplars bordering the former homestead offered no shade by the cook fires, nor upon the flat spaces between the tents. Yet, the sun did not feel nearly as hot as the stares the four were receiving from the other soldiers in the food line and those eating nearby.

Shuffling forward together, the four followed the men in front of them, attempting not to seem too hurried, but not delaying the line. The aroma from the food made their mouths water. As much as their stomachs were growling, it was hard to restrain their anticipation. In front of them, two civilians, a bearded old geezer and a tow-haired young man, ladled stew from a pot, tore bread, and filled cups with water or hot coffee, while three other men tended the cooking fire, sliced meat, and chopped carrots and potatoes on a table. Meat, carrots, and potatoes, Josh figured the patrols had been cleaning out farms throughout the region. Otherwise, they'd be on hardtack and the other inedible military rations.

When the man in front of Isaac drifted away with a full tin plate and cup, Isaac stepped forward and held out his own cup and plate. The civilian geezer gave him a dirty look. "Go to the back of the line. White men get fed first."

Standing beside Josh, Isaac's eyes flared angrily. He started to opened his mouth, but Josh grabbed Isaac's arm before he could utter a sound and pulled him away to the back of the line, followed by Lou and Bammer. They would just have to wait until everyone else had been served.

***

"So, tell me 'bout this Order Eleven," Big Josh said to Lieutenant Langham. Both their stomachs were full, and the two men felt rested and relaxed. Josh's holster now carried a pistol, while sitting thirty yards away on ammunition boxes, Bammer, Lou, and Isaac held working rifles, with a supply of powder and ball at their feet.

"Lawrence was the last straw," the lieutenant confided to his new, albeit limited and temporary, Sergeant. "No half-measures. We're cleaning out four Missouri border counties and part of another."

"What you mean, Lieutenant, 'cleaning out'?" Josh asked.

"What do you think it means, Sergeant? Burn every house, barn, and field. Run everyone off. Everyone. Confiscate the livestock and slaughter what we can't take with us. No, sir, won't be no ear of corn to feed a crow in five counties, nor a shed left to shelter from the rain. And won't be nobody to aid the secesh. The whole district will be empty. Burnt."

After the Lawrence massacre, Federal General Ewing, head of the district, wrote Order Eleven, which was quickly approved by Major General Schofield. The Jackson, Cass, Bates, Johnson, and Layfayette counties would soon become known infamously as "the burnt district." Bushwhackers would have to shelter in Texas and join Confederate General Shelby south of the Missouri border, effectively ending the guerrilla war in Western Missouri. As a result, Shelby would be unable to attack Missouri in the west because there would be no friends, sympathizers, or provisions to gather along the way. As Napoleon said, "An army travels on its stomach." Then, relieved of the impossible task of guarding the whole heavily forested region, where two-thirds of the population supported the Confederacy, Union guerrilla hunters would be free to join General Grant on his attack down the Mississippi.

"You say 'everyone'? How you know who's secesh and who's not?"

"Everyone, Sergeant. Loyalists will be guided to the nearest camp, if they so choose. Rebel sympathizers will be escorted south, if they request it. Ewing and Schofield have had enough. We've got fifteen hundred good men swatting away a few hundred bushwhacker flies. Well, won't be no sugar left for them to suck on no more. They'll have to join the rest of the rabble down in Texas and Arkansas."

Big Josh leaned back against a tree, flabbergasted. "Kansas Jayhawker troops'll turn this into one big raid, take everything not tied down. You know how that Seventh Kansas Cavalry operates. They'll be after revenge killing and robbery."

"No, sir," the lieutenant said. "That would look bad. Ewing's order says any Jayhawkers crossing into Missouri will be shot. It's just us."

Josh hung his head, thinking. Finally, he tried to plead his case. "I don' know if my men can do such a thing, Lieutenant. After Lawrence? Watching their friends murdered? No, sir. We want to do what we can to win this war, b-but you can't have no colored soldiers burning down no white farms. Wouldn't look good for our side."

"Sergeant," Langham stated, "you and your men *will* accompany us. And you *will* do your duty. Understand?"

With a deep sigh, Josh rubbed his temple then wearily rested his forehead on his palm. He and his partners had wanted to fight, fight for freedom, fight for the Union, fight — even die — for Abe Lincoln. But setting fire to the hopes and dreams of farmers was not what they had had in mind. He knew war was cruel. He'd seen two years of that working in a Federal Army camp. But this ruthless mayhem wasn't war. Or was it, indeed, war in its purest form? He shuddered. He didn't know how he was going to order Isaac, Lou, and Bammer to burn down farms, people's homes and such, and force them to flee with their families down hardship road. The words would undoubtedly stick in his throat.

Numb and dumbfounded, Josh tread heavily to where his partners were sitting under a poplar, none of them speaking, as if lost, staring at a befuddling landscape at their feet in a world gone wrong. He sat down beside them silently. None looked up, as if they hadn't noticed him.

Josh picked up a stone and rolled it over and over in his hand, examining it as if it contained some property that would sort out the inexplicable. But the stone held no answers. In just days, they had been transposed from men with their boots on solid ground to whirlwind-tossed leaves. Was there no way to stem the merciless tides of war, to regain their footing on some facsimile of sane, reasonable Earth, to resist the unrelenting torrent of hatred and evil flooding the land? Or were men merely puppets at the whim of a malicious, dastardly fate?

He'd know soon enough, and he hoped the answer wasn't lethal.

CHAPTER TWENTY-TWO

HARDSHIP ROAD

Jackson County, Western Missouri

The sturdy log farmhouse lay peaceful on the land. Rooms had been added as children were born into the family, but now only the father and one frail, ten-year-old boy were left to work the soil, the mother having died in childbirth, the other five sons having joined in the warring: two on the Union side, three on the rebel. The two grown daughters had departed years before with their husbands. The property, reduced through hard times and tax-selling to only three acres, was surrounded by a sturdy fence made of saplings, enclosing fields of wheat and corn stalks emerging from the rich earth. Twenty yards back of the kitchen porch, chickens clucked in a well-kept pen, and the barn held several pigs and a plump milk cow. The farm's horses had been confiscated by raiders in 1861.

At Lieutenant Langham's signal, sergeants along the line shouted for their mounted troops to halt. Assigned as a rearguard, Josh drew rein, followed by his MSMCC cohorts, Isaac, Lou, and Bammer. They were escorting four wagons skinned by rough civilian teamsters who took orders directly from two traders wearing business suits. Of the traders, the smaller one, sporting a gold watch chain and an expensive bowler hat, sat on a wagon seat beside the teamster; the other mounted a strong chestnut.

Langham spoke orders to his nearby sergeant, who then shouted instructions that echoed down the line. As the balance of the column continued along the road, Langham led a patrol of six specially selected troopers toward the farmhouse, followed by two of the wagons, the two traders, escorted under his orders by Josh and company. The MSM Colored Cavalry would soon learn what their other duties entailed.

Langham gave an order. The six troopers dismounted and, as the two wagons arrived, checked their weapons. One trooper held their horses, while the other five quickly surrounded the farmhouse. Josh and his men dismounted near the wagons, while the pair of traders hid behind the wagons to shield themselves from any gunfire that might come from the house. Upon Langham's signal, two troopers broke in the front door and charged into the parlor, watched by the third man guarding the porch, while the two in back broke in through the kitchen door. In short order, two of the troopers forced the farmer and his son out of the house, pushing them sprawling off the porch head first into the dirt. The farmer, in his early fifties, with skin weathered and darkened and hands knotted by hard labor, rose painfully, favoring his left arm, visibly trembling with fear. He and the boy, living a hardscrabble existence without a woman's hand these many years, wore tattered work clothes. The rail-thin boy's long brown hair was uncombed, and his fingers kept sweeping the forelocks aside, out of his eyes.

One of the troopers shouted the all-clear, and the smaller trader with the watch chain headed for the house, quickly disappearing inside. Puzzled, Josh told Bammer to hold their group's horses, while he cautiously led Isaac and Lou out front to observe the activity.

It wasn't long before troopers started hauling furniture outside and setting it on the porch. "You, Sergeant," Langham shouted to Big Josh, "you and your men, load those into the wagons."

Lou and Bammer looked quizzically toward Josh, but he could only shrug. "Do what he say. Haul 'em to the wagon and load 'em up, I guess," Josh said. He figured stealing furniture was part of this nasty Order Eleven, and who was he to question an officer's orders. While Bammer and Lou each took an end of a heavy, old German chest and lugged it awkwardly through the yard, Josh lifted a large table onto his broad shoulders and, once it was balanced, strode right past them.

Langham dismounted and confronted the farmer. "Where do you keep your money hid?"

"Ain't got no money," the farmer replied, his face a mask of terror. "The war done broke us just like ever'body else in this town."

A pair of troopers struggled to carry a smaller chest out the front door, followed by the suit with the fancy hat. "The rest is worthless," the man with the watch chain shouted to Langham.

"Put it to the torch," Langham shouted, as the troopers began lighting pine knot torches and handing them around.

"Don't burn my house!" the farmer objected. "Please, sir, I beg you."

Langham withdrew his pistol from his holster and crashed it across the man's face. "I said, where do you keep it?" he yelled.

"I said we don't..." the farmer replied but was struck again with the pistol, knocking him back down to the ground.

"This is your last chance. Where's your money?" Langham shouted at the man lying at his feet, holding his bleeding cheek.

"I swear..." the man began, but Langham kicked him in the ribs, taking his breath.

"All right," Langham shouted, "burn it down."

Three troopers began setting the house afire.

"Line them up by the fence," he ordered. Two troopers dragged the farmer to his feet and hustled him and the boy to the perimeter fence, shoving them against the railing. Langham followed along behind them, and then stopped. He nodded, and the troopers aimed their rifles at the farmer.

"The money!" Langham demanded angrily, his eyes fierce.

"I told you," the farmer pleaded, "I'd give you everything I have, but we ain't got no money."

Langham nodded. The two troopers fired simultaneously, and the farmer fell in a heap, his face twisted in shock and agony. Immediately, the soldiers began to reload.

"Where did he hide the money, boy?" Langham barked.

"You yellow coward, Yankee bastard, murdering thief!" the boy shouted.

"Shoot the boy," Langham ordered.

Suddenly, Big Josh was beside Langham, his pistol drawn and pointed at Langham's midsection. "You w-won't do no such thing," Josh growled, stuttering. "That j-just a chile."

"Sergeant Tyler," Langham shouted angrily, "what the Hell are you doing? I gave orders..."

"No, sir," Josh stated firmly. "Ain't gonna shoot no boy for nothing he said. Not even for being no rebel sympathizer."

Behind them, one of the troopers approached fast from the house, his rifle drawn, but he stopped in his tracks when Bammer pointed a rifle at him. Around the burning house, everyone froze.

"Sergeant," a bewildered Langham said, "you are aiming that pistol at a Federal officer. That constitutes assault. I order you and your men to drop your weapons immediately!"

"No, sir, respectfully," Josh replied. "Won't do no such thing."

"Disobedience and threatening your commanding officer! I'll have you up on court-martial. In fact, if you don't drop that pistol now, I'll have you shot right here."

Big Josh paused, the realization of what he'd done condensing upon his mind. If he obeyed the lieutenant's order and dropped his weapon, they'd be shot on the spot. On the other hand, if they tried to run, they'd be outlaws — if they survived. "Get the horses," Josh shouted to Lou, as the four MSM soldiers, weapons still drawn, mounted.

"Boy, come here," Josh said. The boy ran to Josh and stood gaping up at the big man in the saddle. Josh stretched his hand toward the boy. The boy examined the big, black hand suspiciously and then looked over his shoulder. Seeing the fury on Langham's face, the boy turned back and grabbed Josh's hand. Josh pulled the boy up behind him. "Now y'all drop your weapons or I shoot the lieutenant. Go on, now. We ain't gonna hurt nobody."

Langham nodded, and the troopers dropped the rifles.

Josh looked the situation over. "Now, y'all stand over there. Go on." He waited until the soldiers complied. "You come after us, we gonna ambush you. Hear?" he shouted to Langham. Then glancing at his cohorts, he nodded toward the direction from which they'd come. "Le's ride."

Josh spurred his mount, and Lou, Bammer, and Isaac followed. As they rode off, shots whistled above their heads. Ducking, they reached the woods and plunged into the thickets, riding as hard as their poor MSM mounts could traverse the rough terrain. They didn't pause or look behind them until over an hour later.

They finally stopped to rest their exhausted mounts by a stream running through deep Missouri woodlands. As he dismounted wearily, Josh thought of how quickly their lives had narrowed to absolutely nothing. Durk was on his way to trial in St. Louis, likely to be hung for being a spy. And, as if their journey to rescue him hadn't begun badly enough, now they were deserters, too, supposedly dead, subject to immediate execution. How could things possibly get worse?

While the horses watered, Big Josh and the others splashed their faces in the creek, filled their canteens, and flopped down on the shady bank to catch their breath. They knew they couldn't rest but a short time. They had to come up with some notion of a plan. Nearby, the boy sat crying, his tear-streaked face a mass of hatred and hurt.

"Wh-what we gonna do?" a weary Bammer asked anxiously.

His mind still running faster than horses, Big Josh mulled their dilemma over. "First thing, what about these uniforms?" he posed.

Everyone began to express his own fears, rapid fire, one interrupting the other. "We better find some clothes and bury these uniforms before anyone see us," Bammer said.

"Get rid of our uniforms?" Long Lou objected hysterically. "The slave catchers will come after us."

"Yeah, Missouri slave catchers ain't so kind," Bammer agreed. "I seen that. Our papers won't mean nothing without our uniforms."

"We deserters," Isaac said. "We gotta get some real clothes."

"Where we headed, Josh?" Bammer asked. "Iowa or Kansas?"

Isaac, whose flaming eyes were seeing invisible terrors attacking from every direction, grabbed Josh by the collar. "Fools! The Confederates find us, we dead. The army catch us, we dead. Ain't nobody that don't want to kill us. Nobody! How far is Iowa, Josh? It's free territory. I think we should ride up there."

Everyone stopped to look to Josh, who brushed Isaac aside and paused to consider their options. It was true; their desperate journey to St. Louis would be like running a gauntlet. But then there was their friend, helpless except for his once-golden tongue. "No, we got to get to St. Louie to save Durk if we can. Can't leave him to just hang, can we?"

"So how we get there, to St. Louie?" Lou asked. "What we wear?"

"We maybe need the uniforms to get Durk out, Lou," Josh said. "Try to take him out to hang him like we did before. I think after we clear Western Missouri, maybe they forget about us a little. And with the war going, the army in St. Louie ain't gonna be looking for no four colored deserters. Hear me?"

Lou and Bammer nodded.

"Wearing these uniforms, maybe some Union loyalists along the way feed us at least."

"But what's the best way to go?" Bammer asked.

"We got to stay to the woods, keep off the roads much as we can. Least for now. It'll take longer, but it's our only chance. Isaac's right. Bushwhackers catch us, they gun us down. Right there. 'Cause of what the lieutenant probably say we done, Federals shoot us on the spot, too. Least won't no slave catchers come after us wearing them, though. Y'all understand?" He looked from face to face, and everyone appeared resigned to his plan.

"What we do with the boy?"

Hearing himself mentioned, the farm boy stared at Josh. "You ain't no better than those Yankees shot Pa," the boy growled. "You hear me, crow. I see any good Confederates, y'all hunks of crow stew."

"Leave him," Bammer said.

Josh thought this over. It was tempting to just abandon this nasty, young rebel sympathizer who was going to cause more problems than he was worth. On the other hand, when the troops caught up to the boy, they'd kill him on the spot. The boy knew of Lieutenant Langham's moneymaking scheme and, moreover, was witness to his murdering ways. "No, them soldiers kill him," Josh said, rising to his feet. "He coming with us."

"Le's kill him now," Isaac said. "He can't be trusted."

"I say he come with us," Josh said firmly. "You want to go off by yourself, Isaac, you go on."

Isaac hawkspit disgustedly.

Josh looked the boy over. "What's your name, boy?" he asked gently.

"None of your damn business," the boy spat out and crossed his arms over his chest.

"All right, le's mount up, try to put some miles between us and that lieutenant."

The men rose, brushed their hands, and climbed into their saddles. Isaac gave Josh an angry, resentful look. "This sure ain't getting us any closer to freeing our people," he growled.

Ignoring Isaac, Josh held his hand out to the boy. "You comin'?"

The boy looked back the way they'd come and rubbed his eyes clear. "I'll come," he said. "But we ain't friends. We never be friends." Then he took Josh's hand.

Dusk was falling, and the five were on a country road, the boy riding behind Big Josh. Being on this stretch with no cover was unavoidable because the whole area was nothing but cleared, flat farmland. The sun was setting over their shoulder, so they knew they were heading in the right direction, but, being in unfamiliar territory and having no maps, they weren't sure exactly where they were.

Just then, they heard the thunder of hooves and saw dust rising ahead, so they drew rein. Terrified, Isaac panicked, jerking his reins back and forth. His horse became wild-eyed, skittering circles in the dirt, until Josh could grab Isaac's reins and settle the horse.

"We got to run!" Isaac shouted at Josh. "We got to run!"

"You see them?" Josh asked Lou.

"No, sir."

"Then ride on ahead and signal. You got the fastest horse. If it's 'whackers, just start running. If it's Federals, come on back."

Lou spurred his horse and galloped toward the coming commotion, watched anxiously by the others. Finally, he drew rein and waved back that it was, indeed, troops in blue. Josh knew, of course, that if they were bushwhackers wearing captured Union uniforms, he and his friends had reached the end of the road. But, he told himself, at least they'd have tried to save Durk.

Lou rode back to rejoin the others, and they waited for the blue column to reach them. A company of thirty-five commanded by a captain in his late-twenties halted before them. Josh and the others saluted sharply. "Captain," Josh barked. "Josh Tyler, Ninth MSM Colored Cavalry."

"At ease, Sergeant," the captain said. He was a broad man with dark hair, dusty and unshaven from at least a week on the road.

"They're renegades!" the boy shouted. "Shot a Yankee captain back down the road."

The captain drew his pistol, and a sergeant and second lieutenant, pistols drawn, rode to flank the four.

"Now wait, Captain," Big Josh said, trying to calm the situation. "This boy's a Confederate sympathizer, just trying to cause trouble."

"Is that right, boy?" the captain asked.

"You goddamn right, and I'm gonna see all you Yankees dead, if it's the last thing I do."

"I tole you we shoulda shot him," Isaac growled to Josh. Isaac reached for his pistol, but the soldiers were aiming at his heart, and Bammer stayed Isaac's hand. No shots were fired.

"What the Hell is going on here?" the captain asked Josh, not lowering his pistol.

"These here slaves are renegades," the boy said, indicating Isaac, "and this one's crazier than a headless chicken."

"We taking the boy to his sister on a farm outside Jeff City," Josh said calmly. "Order Eleven. His whole family was killed."

"Don't listen to these cargo bucks," the boy said. "They're on their way to St. Louis."

The captain pointed to Isaac. "Your man there does seem a bit off."

"Oh, Isaac's crazy," Josh admitted, "but he a good man fighting bushwhackers. We got him under control."

The boy screamed, "Are you gonna believe that lying crow?"

"Captain," Josh said calmly, "please let us get rid of this little rebel and get on with our business."

The captain thought a moment. "All right, Sergeant, carry on." The two saluted, and then Josh and his group pulled off the road and lined up respectfully to let the column pass.

They'd escaped this one encounter, but Josh knew it was only a matter of time before wires went out alerting the army to their supposed "misdeeds." They had to move on and fast.

"You cowards," the boy shouted after the departing patrol. "You'll be laying in a ditch before I'm done with you."

Josh turned to the boy. "Where we gonna take you? You got family somewheres?"

"I wanna join Price in Arkansas. Two of my brothers are fighting with Price."

"We ain't taking you south to join no Confederate Army," Josh laughed, "unless we mean to join them ourself."

CHAPTER TWENTY-THREE

TWO WOMEN

Jefferson City, Central Missouri

The recently-deceased Captain Durksen Hurst waited at the back of a long line of wounded soldiers waiting to board the Pacific Railroad for the final leg of their journey to St. Louis. His head and left hand were wrapped in slightly bloodstained bandaging; his left arm hung in a sling. Volunteering to aid the medical staff had paid off in wrappings.

As the steam poured from beneath the huge iron wheels, a grizzly-bearded sergeant stood at the steps of the passenger car, directing the flow of wounded. The line moved toward him in good order, and when it became unruly, the sergeant barked at them, threatening to cancel their trip, which quickly quieted the anxious men. One at a time, each soldier stepped up to the sergeant, saluted as best he could, and identified himself. The sergeant then checked his list, put a mark by the name, and authorized the wounded man to climb aboard, personally helping those who were too badly injured to manage the climb alone. All the soldiers, disabled and ambulatory, wore smiles. Leaving a war zone is always euphoric, regardless of one's condition. Finally, Durk brought up the rear.

"Name?" the sergeant barked.

"Captain Hurst, Durksen."

The sergeant checked his list and then rechecked it. "I don't see you on my list, Captain Hurst."

Durk displayed his papers. "Must be an oversight, Sergeant. Major Benbow knows all about it."

The sergeant examined Hurst's papers closely and handed them back. "That don't look like any signature I seen before, Captain. Come now, did you bribe the clerk to get them transfer papers? You've got to be on my list to board this train."

"Ask Major Benbow, Sergeant. This is urgent."

"Well, there ain't time for that. Why didn't you get Major Benbow to sign them papers in the first place?"

"He was off inspecting, Sergeant. I can't tell you how important this is."

The sergeant looked Durk over with yellow eyes, suspicious of the man's appearance — *Clearly Indian blood. And his accent… Could be legitimate, could be a deserter or worse.* "Can't tell me? Or won't? What's your wound?" he asked, fingering about the bandages wrapping Hurst's pate. Seeing nothing on Hurst's head, he felt Hurst hand, feeling about carefully. "You ain't got no wounds."

Durk took a deep breath, his mind rushing. "I'll show you, Sergeant," he whispered, "but please keep it between us. It's embarrassing, very embarrassing. See…" He paused dramatically, then covered his privates. "See, a shell got me."

"A shell?"

"Yes, you understand?" He gripped his privates tightly. "Now it's done gone and got infected, too. Bad. If I don't get myself to the doctors in St. Louis quick, my wife won't have no kids. I'll be happy to show you, but I warn you…" Durk started to unbuckle his belt.

The sergeant thought quickly, then shrugged. "All right, Captain, no need to expose yourself. This ain't no Kansas City brothel. On board, and be quick about it."

With a mewing smile, Durk gratefully squeezed the man's shoulder and climbed aboard. The way to Antoinette was now clear. Or so he hoped.

***

Portland, Eastern Missouri

Naturally, she was unable to sleep. Devereau French poked the fire with a rotten branch that had fallen from the nearby maple. As the flames picked up, she added more kindling, then, when they caught, dropped another log on, which made showers of sparks fly high into the night sky. As the fire resisted the weight, flickering lower, she knelt and blew until it began to catch and build. A pair of boots crashed abruptly through the undergrowth and halted with a stomp next to her. When she looked up, a tall, heavy-set man in his forties wearing a brown suit was standing over her, aiming a pistol at her head.

"Don't move. Stay where you are," the man ordered. "Slightest move, I'll shoot. I'm the deputy sheriff of this county, and I'm placing you both under arrest." He gestured with the pistol to indicate the blankets covering Robert Sterling.

"Why are you arresting us, deputy?" Devereau inquired, rising to a sitting position.

"You two are wanted all over the state — robbery and murder throughout six counties we know of, and probably more downstate. Murdered the city clerk in Keytesville: slit his throat like a hog. Small man in a fancy suit with a' Indian sidekick dressed up like a white man." He indicated the horses tied nearby. "Yep, that's them: white stallion, brown mare. Y'all been spotted more than once't when these crimes been committed."

"Sir," Devereau replied firmly, "we are under the provost marshal's orders to return to St. Louis as quickly as possible."

"You can straighten that out with the judge back at the jail." Keeping an eye on Devereau, his pistol leveled at her, the deputy sidestepped over until he reached the pile of blankets. Glancing down, he nudged them with his boot and hopped back like he'd disturbed a sleeping snake. He waved his gun at Devereau. The moon was new, and with only dim light coming from the small fire, it felt as if the surrounding thickets were closing in around him. "You," he said nervously, "come on up out of there." The body under the blankets showed no motion.

"Crazy Indian was drunk last night," Devereau said. "Might be hard to wake him."

The deputy inched closer, his boot tapping lightly at the blankets once, but still no activity.

"I said, he's a drunk Indian. You'll have to kick a helluva lot harder than that," Devereau advised.

Frustrated, the deputy moved closer to the blankets and kicked again hard. When there still was no response, he gave the Indian a brutal kick. Again nothing. Then he drew his leg back to build real force and put all his weight into another attempt. When his boot was halfway to the blanket, a pair of arms emerged, caught his calf, and forcefully pulled his leg up. Completely off balance from the force of his attempt, the deputy fell heavily backwards, firing off a wayward shot harmlessly into the forest. The deputy landed hard on the ground, knocking out his wind with a grunt, as the back of his head struck the fire. He hurriedly struggled to sit up, brushing the flames from his burning, singed hair. As he flailed about, Devereau sprang up and quickly grabbed her pistol. In one motion, she put the barrel to the deputy's head and pulled the trigger. The bullet exploded loudly, as the man's blood and brains shot out onto the ground. Then there was quiet.

Robert Sterling cast off his blanket disgustedly. "This Indian does not drink."

Devereau stared in amazement at what she'd done, at the man lying beside the fire, head ripped open and gory. Plopping down hard by the fire, sick from shock, she began to wretch and vomit, shaking and sobbing. When she was empty, she crawled away from the man's body and lay on her blanket, covering her eyes.

Robert rose and crossed to the body. "You love a good killing when it's me doing the deed, but when it comes to your own, you're nothing but a weak woman," he spat disgustedly. He stared down at Devereau, but she could not stop crying. "We are on the wires now throughout the state. 'A man in a fancy suit on a white stallion and an Indian on a brown mare.' I ought to just ride off and leave you. They'll spot you on the white in a minute." He paused to think over their dilemma. "But we're nearly out of cash. We need to claim those slaves." Robert stuck the deputy's pistol in his belt and rifled his pockets, taking the man's watch and money and then stood over him, contemplating the body, admiring Devereau's handiwork.

Devereau cried for some time, arms wrapped around her head, covering her eyes. When she was finally able to speak, she confessed, "I don't know what to do, Robert."

Robert sat down heavily on the body, dropping his chin into his hands, deep in thought. "Run out of ideas, have you, woman?" Rising, he commanded, "Give me a hand with him; take his legs."

Wrung out, Devereau refused to rise. Robert grabbed her under the arms, lifted her roughly, and pushed her toward the deputy's feet. There, Devereau grabbed the man's ankles as Robert took him under the arms, and the two dragged the body off and deposited him in the brush. Then Robert disappeared into the woods. Seeing herself alone, Devereau returned to the fire, still shaking.

Soon thereafter, Robert returned leading a saddled paint by the reins. He tied up the paint near their own horses, removed its saddle, and dropped it on the ground. Then he untied the white, grabbed up its fancy saddle, and slung it over his shoulder. Without a word, he led the white into the woods.

Devereau watched these actions in stunned silence. If Robert was going to steal the white and run off, she'd still have the brown. She couldn't ride the paint with the deputy's saddle. That would be incontrovertible evidence of her crime. She stared at the spot where Robert had disappeared into the woods.

Then she heard her saddle crash into the thickets, as if thrown there. She sat up, wondering what was transpiring. Then a single loud pistol shot broke the night. Within moments, Robert reappeared in the clearing, sans saddle or white stallion.

"What have you done, Robert?" Devereau exclaimed in horror.

"Your white and saddle call attention to us. They'd be spotted a mile away. We'd never make it to St. Louis."

"You shot... You killed my horse?"

"I had to." Robert stomped over to Devereau and lifted her to her feet. "Come. While it's still dark. There's a town not two miles north of here."

"What are you thinking?" she objected, still horrified. "We've got to head south. We can't possibly make it to St. Louis, much less get possession of those slaves."

"Yes, we can. We will," he replied, dragging her to the horses. "Saddle up. Hurry."

***

It was easy breaking into the general store through the back door at night. Once inside, Robert Sterling's large hands pawed through stacks of ladies' dresses. He rapidly pulled them out one at a time and held them against Devereau, before casting each of them aside. Beside him, Devereau stripped off her suit, dropping it on the floor at her feet. Then under Robert's threatening glare, she removed the band around her breasts and flung it aside.

Finally, Robert hit on a simple gingham dress that met his needs. "Put this on," he instructed her quietly.

"Robert, this is crazy," Devereau objected.

"Put it on, woman, or you're on your own from here on. Hear me? Put it on or I'm done with you."

"This is ugly, and it's really rough," Devereau complained as she began to slip it over her head.

"You're not going to a ball," Robert replied acidly, still digging through the dresses. "You need to look like the homely woman you are."

When Devereau was dressed, Robert turned her by the shoulder and paused to examine her in the blackness. The dress met his approval. But then he examined her head. He brushed her hair disapprovingly twice. "Ugh, still a man's," he said. "You need to wear a bonnet till it grows out. Go over there and pick one out. Nothing fancy. Plain. And get me one, too."

"A bonnet? Never!" Devereau said with disgust.

"You'll wear one or they'll find your body lying on the floor wearing that farmwife getup." Robert flashed his knife. Devereau huffed resentfully but made her way to the ladies' hats. As she tried on hats, he continued sorting roughly through the dresses, holding one after another against his strong frame and throwing them aside, growing more frustrated by the moment. Finally, he found a simple calico that suited his purpose. He quickly changed into it, and Devereau rejoined him wearing a cheap straw bonnet sporting only a single artificial daisy. She held one arm behind her. "Did you find one for me?" he asked.

From behind her back, she produced a large bonnet, covered with mismatched patches of flowers and fabric, the foolish handicraft creation of a church-going widow. Gritting his teeth, Robert swiped it from her hand and tied it on his head.

Devereau looked him over, startled at his convoluted transformation, and fought to stifle a laugh.

"I'm armed," he warned, and she gained control of herself. "We'll abandon the horses about a mile from the depot."

"Can't we sell them?"

"Sell the missing deputy sheriff's horse and saddle? Are you insane? I'd let you try — especially wearing that outfit — but I'll need you in St. Louis."

Devereau pulled Robert to a mirror, where a sliver of moonlight fell on him. "You look like an Indian in a dress," she said. "This will never work."

He glared at Devereau and then studied his reflection. He paused to think. Without a word, he crashed through the store until he reached the potbellied stove. Swinging the door open, he reached inside for a handful of ashes, which he began to rub on his face and hands. Then he picked up a piece of tarp and, cleaning out the stove with his bare hands, filled it with the rest of the ashes. Satisfied, he ripped a string from his dress and tied up the tarp and returned to Devereau. "I will be your maidservant, Annie, from back home."

"Stupid Chickasaw. One word from your mouth, and they'll know you aren't any slave."

"Then I'm a mute servant," Robert replied. "You already do all the talking anyway."

He grabbed up two parasols and handed her one. Next, already in motion, he pulled her toward the back door where they'd broken in. "Mount up. We've got to get to the depot."

"You're the most contrary damn servant there ever was," Devereau said derisively. "I wish I could sell you, just to be rid of you."

"You'll be rid of me soon enough."

***

Portland, Eastern Missouri

Half-asleep, Durk sat near the window of the train, absently watching the bustling scene outside, as Union soldiers, officers, and assorted adjunctive civilians boarded from the platform, while others unloaded boxcars stacked with supplies and equipment.

He was about to close his eyes when he spied an odd pair of women near the engine, parasols held at an odd angle above their heads. They emerged from the ticket office and awkwardly, at a rocking gait, like horsewomen, strolled up to the passenger car reserved for civilian traffic. The larger of the two carried a weather-beaten bag in her oversized hands. At first, he dismissed the pair as harmless, just rural types with not much experience dressing for travel. Then, as they closed the parasols to board, something struck his memory, and he stared intently at the two.

Even from this distance, they looked familiar, very familiar. The small one with the plain bonnet appeared strikingly to resemble Devereau French. Impossible to believe, but he would have sworn to it. He brought the larger of the two, at first glance a slave woman of uneven complexion, into better focus. *My God! Except for the filth on her face, that could be Wounded Wolf.* He couldn't imagine what the Chickasaw chief would be doing here in Missouri wearing a dress and ridiculous hat, boarding a train to St. Louis, let alone accompanying Devereau French. But there was little doubt. The war couldn't possibly have ruined his eyes or addled his brain that much. *Why would these two even be together?*

He slunk down in his seat so that only his eyes and the bandaged top of his head were visible through the window. The pair appeared preoccupied in conversation as they climbed aboard, never glancing his way.

Yes, it's them! They're obviously trying to hide their identities. But why? If they knew he'd spotted them, Wounded Wolf would bring Durk's life and his attempt to rescue Antoinette to a sudden end. The army was no longer hot on his trail, but now he feared discovery by a murderous Indian and an erratic woman. If it weren't for Antoinette, he'd disembark and disappear. But she needed him.

***

Devereau halted to adjust her bodice and straighten her dress for the twentieth time since they'd reached the depot. She was terribly uncomfortable and self-conscious wearing a dress, unaccustomed to being without the band she typically wore to obfuscate her breasts.

Impatient that she'd stopped again, Robert set down their bag holding their clothes and gear and swiftly lifted her up to the first step. He pushed her rear upward to get her moving, then took up the bag and followed her onto the passenger car. Once on level footing, Devereau looked for the first row with two spaces available and took her seat. With a frown, Robert grabbed her shoulder and pushed her to the back of the car. At the rear, they quickly found two seats. Robert threw their bag against the window and sat down, followed by Devereau.

Two men in neatly pressed, light-colored suits climbed aboard, a sheriff and his deputy. The two paused at the entrance to inspect the car, spoke quietly to each other, then, led by the sheriff, moved single file down the narrow aisle, with the deputy keeping his hand on his pistol. They reached the last row of seats, stopping directly before Robert and Devereau. "I am the sheriff in this town, and this here is Deputy Rollins. I have an arrest warrant for a small white man traveling with a big Indian — murder and robbery. It's all over the wires. Your disguise isn't fooling anyone. Please stand up."

Devereau rose, and Robert slid across to her seat, his hand slipping to his knife. "No, sir, you're confused. That isn't us," Devereau said in a polite, slow Southern drawl.

"Oh? So who is this Indian with you?" the sheriff asked, indicating Robert.

"That is my maid woman, Annie. She's all the property I've got left, Sheriff."

The sheriff looked the two over from head to foot. "I think, maybe, you two match the description."

"But how could we be? We are not men, as you can see, Sheriff," Devereau giggled.

The sheriff eyed the deputy. "I think you two better come with me. I'll have my wife verify that. Now please open that bag."

At once, Robert lifted Devereau's dress with one hand, took the sheriff by the wrist with the other, and pulled the lawman's palm against Devereau's underwear. Then as the deputy drew his pistol, Robert, pressing hard, rubbed the sheriff's hand over Devereau's privates. When he released the sheriff's wrist, the lawman stepped back, aghast.

"I-I am sorry, ma'am," the sheriff stuttered, his face flushed crimson. "What about your maid woman here? I need to check her before we let you go on."

Robert quickly withdrew his knife and flashed it threateningly. Frightened, the deputy aimed his pistol directly at Robert's heart.

"Sir," Devereau said cheerily, "I don't believe that would be a good idea. Annie was badly served by a company of U.S. Colored Infantry and is very jealous of her privacy. I mean, hasn't she suffered enough from this war? Haven't we both?"

"Well..." the sheriff muttered, uncertain of what to do next.

"Sir," Devereau continued, "my mother is on her deathbed in St. Louis. Any delay, and I won't be able to send her to Heaven with her farewell kiss. You can't possibly deprive my dear mother her loving departure, her farewell kiss, now could you? That just wouldn't be right."

The sheriff took out his handkerchief and wiped his face, then wiped each finger as if drying them off. "All right," he said. "Clearly, you ain't no killers, far as I can tell. I'm very sorry for your loss. My condolences and apologies, ma'am."

"Thank you kindly, Sheriff. I know you were just doing your duty."

The sheriff nodded toward the door, and the two lawmen filed off the train. Soon the engines began huffing and puffing, the whistle blew, and the iron wheels began chugging and churning. Devereau and Robert settled themselves on the seat and, heads together, fell fast asleep. It had been a long sleepless night, but now they were on their way.

SECTION III

CHAPTER TWENTY-FOUR

PAST ACQUAINTANCES

St. Louis, Missouri

The stars glittered in vast profusion on the black canopy of clear night sky. Antoinette sat across the table from Captain Whalen in the once lush garden of the McClure mansion, now falling rapidly into disorder, with once-cultivated beds dying and wild plants taking root. Within view, a Union guard rested on a bench beneath the trellis entrance, his rifle leaning beside him. There was little chance of his prisoner escaping.

The breeze was blowing cold from the west, as Antoinette pulled her shawl tightly about her, to little effect. Seeing her discomfort, Captain Whalen gallantly offered his coat, but she politely refused. Antoinette wore the black dress given to her by the captain to replace her old, threadbare one, appropriate for mourning the loss of her fiancé, but she felt no pride in it, nor any obligation.

The captain took special care to look his best tonight, closely shaved, his long, dark hair slicked back with pomade, wearing his best dress uniform. Tall, nervously thin, the man remained hopelessly homely, and no amount of preparation could change that. She found the effort almost touching, humorous. That he'd arranged to discuss her case at night made her suspicious, but he claimed that his legal practice interfered with him finding time to see her during daylight, and she accepted that for the moment.

She noted Whalen staring unblinkingly at her. Uncomfortable, she averted her eyes, but when she peered back, his gaze was still fixed upon her.

"What *is* it you want, Captain?" she asked directly.

Whalen sat quietly, going over the speech he'd been composing in his mind. Finally, he cleared his throat. "I've been thinking about a solution to your situation — to both of our situations. And I've come to a conclusion. Mrs. DuVallier, may I call you Antoinette?"

She nodded approval.

"Antoinette, I wish that you would do me the great honor of becoming my wife, maybe not now, but at war's end for certain. I come from a substantial, not wealthy, family whom you'd be proud of and who would be proud of you. My prospects are good, and I would do everything within my power to provide you with a comfortable existence. How does that strike you?"

Antoinette stared at Whalen, dumbfounded. This is what she'd feared: the captain was keeping her held for his own purposes, not because of any legal complications. She mulled over how to reply. Of course, if her true background was ever exposed, Whalen's family would unquestionably be horrified. That would certainly free her from his advances. But to do so might expose the crime she was wanted for in New Orleans, and she could not breach that chasm, too much danger.

Were she to refuse him outright, would the care of her friends he'd promised be jeopardized? She had to think of their welfare, not just her own. If she had to remain a captive longer to aid them, then that was what she had to do. Still, Antoinette maintained a calm demeanor, a slight, demure half-smile fixed on her lips, as she listened to the contrived, honeyed words of his earnest proposal. Finally, he grew quiet, and the silence hung awkwardly between them.

"Captain, I am greatly honored and flattered by your proposal and will give it the serious consideration it deserves. However, I only just learned that my fiancé has died in battle. I am in mourning, naturally. Think of that, sir. It is far too soon for a woman like me to make such a commitment under these circumstances."

"So," he said, a dark shadow crossing his brow, "how long do you expect to ruminate over my offer? Can you provide me with an estimate?"

"You will have to give me time to grieve my loss, sir, and there is no certain period that is standard. You and I have known each other only a short time as client and representative. I will have to recover from my loss and adjust my thinking about you. Surely, Captain Whalen, my request is only reasonable."

Whalen silently drew himself in, a foul expression pinching his face.

"Captain," Antoinette continued, "you will keep your word about my friends?"

Whalen glared at her. "Yes," he replied finally, "of course. They'll be well taken care of."

Antoinette studied his face, but there was no way to discern whether or not he planned to honor his commitment. All she could do was hope that he would, merely to keep on her good side — and hope that he had no plans to punish her for denying him. He was clearly a man who knew how to pressure women under his charge.

***

Little Dixie, Central Missouri

The moon was old, and that was good for hiding in the thickets and caves of Missouri. Big Josh added a shard of hardwood onto the modest pit fire and blew on it to catch. He'd kept the fire burning low so that their enclave, hidden by a cave overhang, wouldn't be spotted from a distance. He knew, too, that good hardwood wouldn't smoke like green, soft, or rotten wood. This was just the way Durk had taught him to build his fires, small and orderly, the itinerant man's way. Now Josh was glad he'd listened to the man tell about his methods.

Josh took up his knife and cut the last of the cheese five ways, then handed the pieces around to Isaac, Lou, and Bammer. Then he held the knife forth toward the boy, the slice balanced on its tip. The boy stared at it suspiciously but seeing no choice, took the morsel from the knife and shoved it into his mouth, chewed ravenously, and swallowed it quickly. When it was gone, his stomach still cried hungry, as did all of theirs.

Josh chewed his piece and studied the boy. Scrawny, small for his ten years, his eyes filled with terror and sorrow, his cheeks flushed red. How was he to reach this youngster? Josh spoke calmly, trying not to spook him. "What's your name, boy?"

"None of your damn business."

"Look, we gots to figure what to do with you. You can't come with us. What you want? You got people somewheres?"

The boy simply stared at Josh, puzzling over the large figure reflected in the firelight. Finally, he said, "Why'd you save me? It don't make no sense."

"Cause it was wrong, what they was doing. Your Pa seem like a good man, a good man."

"What do you care? Now you're in big trouble. Big!" He gestured as if he was hung at the neck.

"You don't know the half of it." Josh rubbed his face, as if wiping away the stain of their predicament, but their situation couldn't be so easily dismissed. "Not the half. Now, young fellah, catch some sleep while you can. We maybe got two hours to rest, then we gots some riding to do. I can't have you falling off my horse."

"I ain't sleeping none too good."

"Me neither. Just try is all you can do. All any of us can."

***

St. Louis, Missouri

It was early dusk as the engineer blew the whistle and the train began to brake into the station. The loud blast and jostling of the seat woke Durk. He rubbed his eyes, trying to clear his head, unsure if they'd reached St. Louis or whether this was just another stop at a country town on the line. Keeping low on the seat, he peered through the passenger window. Yes, it was a large station. As he watched, the wounded soldiers in his car shuffled down the narrow aisle in single file and disembarked, clearly relieved with broad smiles on their faces. His cheek pressed to the window, he watched the passengers depart from the front car ahead. At the tail end of the front car, a final, well-dressed couple climbed down, then no one. Minutes passed. Did Devereau and Wounded Wolf decide to stay on the train or did they jump off earlier to avoid such a public place?

Finally, he saw the pair exit, the Indian carrying a sack, followed by Devereau, both still wearing dresses. He watched them pause, their eyes searching the station platform suspiciously. Then they continued. Durk hurried up the empty aisle and stuck his head out the door. From there, he saw the odd pair disappear, and he froze in place to give them time to leave the station. *Good riddance!* By the time he climbed down, the platform was deserted except for the remaining few civilians and soldiers hurrying to catch the next train.

Where to go? He strolled as nonchalantly as possible down the platform and into the main building, where people lined up at ticket windows. Others he passed sat in small clusters, some with children and luggage by their seats, as local men and women sold hot food and confections. The smell of the cooking victuals made Durk's stomach growl, reminding him of how hungry he was. Low on cash, he searched the food stands until he found one selling boiled nuts in a rolled paper cone, which might hold him over cheaply. He paid the vendor in Federal script and went on, eating as he walked. The first thing he had to do was find out where Antoinette was being held. Difficult enough. Then, who knew?

Outside the station, officers and groups of soldiers were coming and going up and down the street. The thoroughfare was crowded with carriages and wagons, with foot traffic finding its way into the station. Durk saluted officers that passed but otherwise avoided them. After two blocks, he spied two infantrymen sitting on knapsacks, passing the time whittling and talking. He stopped in front of them. "Can I offer you some nuts?"

They waved the nuts away.

"Can either of you tell me where the Army Provost Office is? Or the courthouse?"

***

The late afternoon shade stretched from the two tall brick buildings eastward, casting much of the street in shadow. Robert Sterling peered around the corner from the alley between them, his eyes searching up and down the avenue; then he disappeared again. He quickly dropped his sack and immediately began to pull the dress he had on over his head, tossing it aside. That done, he retrieved his suit from the sack and shook it out.

"Give me mine, too," Devereau said excitedly. "I'm sick of this thing."

Robert began to dress. "They're searching for two men, an Indian and a white man. I can't hide being an Indian, but you are a woman, in case you haven't noticed."

"We're in St. Louis now, Robert," Devereau said angrily. "Give me back my suit."

"We can't chance it. We're on the wires for certain."

"So I'm expected to keep wearing this frumpy rag? That doesn't make sense, Robert. My ownership documents for those slaves are for a man."

"No, they're for a Devereau French," Robert said, buttoning his pants. "That's you, man or woman."

"Don't joke about this, fool," Devereau said urgently. "I want my clothes! Give them to me."

"Those *are* your clothes, Devereau," Robert growled disdainfully, indicating the dress she wore. "And you best not call me 'fool' if you treasure your life." Robert felt around in the bag until he found Devereau's coat, from which he extracted the two phony documents — one Union, one Confederate. Next, he pulled his pistol from the bag, stuck it in his belt, and handed Devereau hers, waiting until her hands were empty before continuing. Then he took the sack of ashes out and tossed them into the alley. Finally, he struck a handful of matches and held them to the bag, blowing on it until it caught.

"Robert!" Devereau exclaimed, grabbing for the flaming sack. But Robert held it away from her, turning his back to keep his body between her and the developing fire. When he could see that the sack's destruction was irrevocable, he dropped it and let it burn.

"Let's go."

"You bastard. You'll pay for this," Devereau said venomously.

Ignoring her, Robert walked carefully to the end of the alley and stuck his head out to examine the street, busy with soldiers and civilians strolling in both directions. He quickly ducked back into the alley, signaling Devereau to stay back. Confused at being blocked, Devereau gave Robert a quizzical look.

"Dark Horse. He's there," Robert whispered excitedly. "In uniform."

"What, Durk? Where?" Devereau gasped.

"Walking right down the street, calm as you please. It's him." Devereau peered around the corner, then quickly ducked back. The two examined each other's face, with neither able to decide on a course of action.

"He must have escaped," Devereau conjectured. "I wouldn't put it past him."

Robert whipped out his knife. "I will end his life."

"Put that away, Indian. We want to capture him alive."

"Why alive?" Robert challenged.

Devereau paused, her face wrinkled in concentration. "Because he can help us acquire the slaves; that's why."

"How? You lie, woman."

"Trust me on this, Robert. You want those slaves, right? We need the money?"

Robert nodded uncertainly.

"If worse comes to worse, we can trade Durk for them."

"What if he hasn't escaped?" Robert asked. "What if he talked his way free? You know Dark Horse."

"Then we offer to free him if he signs over the slaves to us. We win either way." Devereau waited until Robert reluctantly agreed. "Now put your knife away. We're stalking game in a city, not a swamp. We'll trail him… from a safe distance."

Robert sheathed his knife and then carefully scrutinized the street again, as if peering around a tree in the forest. Reassured, he nodded for Devereau to follow and stepped onto the sidewalk, instinctively treading lightly.

Devereau is lying! Disregarding her convoluted logic, Robert determined that he would end Dark Horse's life at the time of his own choosing. Devereau would have nothing to say about it. This street had too many soldiers about to find him easily. Dark Horse seemed to be heading north, where city activity would undoubtedly thin out. If so, a satisfying resolution to the man's very existence, long an irritant, could be imminent. Relishing the prospect of seeing Durk bleeding at his feet, Robert smiled for the first time in a week. "Follow me, woman, and do as I say. I will show you how to track prey."

CHAPTER TWENTY-FIVE

A DISTASTEFUL AGREEMENT

Durk strolled as casually as he could northward on Twelfth Street, hoping to avoid attention. He passed officers and soldiers, couples and businessmen in fine clothing, men in work clothes, and women with parasols. Men on horseback and others skinning mule- and horse-drawn wagons navigated the busy cobblestone street. Suddenly, he stopped. *Could it be?*

Durk broke into a run. After a block, he caught up with a tall, elderly black man in neatly-tailored attire ambling ahead, eating a sandwich wrapped in brown paper. "Moses? Is that you?" he exclaimed excitedly. It was, indeed.

"Durk?" the startled man said, nearly dropping his sandwich. "What you doing here?" The two hugged, and then both became self-conscious, searching the street to see if anyone had taken notice of their greeting.

"Let's go talk somewhere," Durk said.

"There a park two blocks that-a-way," Old Moses said, nodding west.

They reached the one-block square green before sundown. The park was quiet except for the muted chatter of soldiers lounging about, their backs to maples, their knapsacks beside them. Seeking privacy, the pair found an isolated bench, situated themselves, and began to talk in whispers.

"You all bones," Moses tsk-tsked. "You need vittles?"

"Yes, I'm starving," Durk replied.

Moses tore off a large hunk of his sandwich and handed it to Durk, who ate hungrily. "Where the rest of our partners?" Moses asked.

A shadow came over Durk's face. He swallowed the food he was chewing until he was able to speak. "Dead, Moses," he said sadly. "You heard about Lawrence?"

"Ever'body has." Then the old man caught the connection. "Oh," his voice dropped.

"The ones the bushwhackers didn't get, the typhoid did."

Moses hung his head and spit. Recovering, he looked Durk in the eye, tearful. "So why you here?"

"It's hard to explain," Durk replied.

"Ain't ever'thing these days," Moses agreed. "So?"

"So I was arrested for spying."

"Arrested for...? Why that's crazy!" Moses exclaimed, slapping his thigh. "An' how you get here?" He paused as Durk tried to piece together his tale. "Never mind, I know you, Durk. You talk your way here. But why St. Louie?"

"That's just it, Moses. They've charged Antoinette with spying, too. I'm just trying to find her. I'm terrified they'll hang her before I can free her." He paused. "See, they think I'm dead."

"Ain't this another mess *DarkHorse* into," Old Moses said and whistled, shaking his head wearily. "News gets worse. The women and young'uns being held in prison by the army. I been trying to get them out, but what can I do?"

"How come you're not being held with them, Moses?"

"See, when the 'whackers take the train, I hid behind boxes. They all drunk, so somehow they miss me. Didn't come out 'til I seen the women being rounded up by the cavalry. Been trying to get to them ever since. Maybe you can help."

"Maybe we can work something. I'll do what I can." With a deep sigh, Durk shook his head. "And you, Moses? You're looking prosperous."

"Well, I'm working for Pelagie Ailotte Rutgers. Yes, sir. Woman of color is one of the richest people in St. Louis, owns property all over town. Rents to white businessmen tenements and business buildings and such. Yes, the money be coming to me, my friend, sure is."

***

Crouched low, Robert Sterling peered over a wagon left at the curb, then ducked into the storefront where Devereau waited. "Talking to that old man. There're soldiers in the park."

Consternation crossed Devereau's face. "What can we do?"

"We have to wait for him to break cover. Then track him till he's alone." Unaware he had done it, Robert's hand went to his knife.

***

Night was falling, and Durk was getting tense. He glanced over his shoulder. "I think we're being followed," he whispered to Moses. "I thought so before, but now I'm sure."

Old Moses looked back but didn't see anything. He knew, of course, that Durk's vagabond days gave him a special sense of such things. "I' take you to my place. You can tell me what happen."

The two walked faster. "Where are you staying, Moses?"

"They calls it Nigger Colony." Secessionist Governor Claiborne had given it that name. When his forces were defeated, he escaped to Texas to be replaced by a loyalist, but the name stuck. "I just calls it home."

"Is it far?" Durk asked.

"Just north of here." He grinned broadly. "If'n you don't mind staying 'round black folks."

Both *DarkHorse* partners laughed. "The rabbit don't mind the briar," Durk said.

***

The night was falling outside the window. Captain Whalen rose to light a candle and then returned to his chair across from Antoinette. A small room, holding just four chairs and two tea tables, had been converted from a servant supply room adjacent to the McLure Mansion kitchen into a place for lawyers to confer with their accused clients. He stared at Antoinette intensely.

"Yes, Captain," she said at last, "I will agree to marry you." Clearly surprised and relieved at her acceptance, Whalen's startled face broke into a broad grin. "Under three conditions."

Captain Whalen, now deflated, searched her eyes, suspicious. "Yes? And those condition are?" he queried.

"One, that you release the women and children. This is not negotiable. No ceremony can take place until that is done."

"And the other two?"

"That until they are released, they are relocated to proper conditions. Proper. With air, light, and no bars. And, of course, the third is that I, too, am freed relatively soon. You know very well I am innocent of these charges."

Smiling triumphantly, exposing his brown-stained teeth, Whalen pulled a document from his coat and slid it across the table. "Here is the motion I filed with the provost to free you for lack of evidence. I am waiting for the prosecutor to respond. I believe our chances are excellent."

Antoinette examined the document. It was dated two weeks earlier. Playing her cards closely, Antoinette merely nodded, revealing no approval or disapproval. Captain Whalen's expression told her that her case may have been dismissed already and that he was purposefully holding her captive until his marriage proposal was resolved. Now the only thing holding back their wedding was her friends' internment. "And my other conditions?"

Whalen placed another document before her, clearly pleased with himself. "Your friends are to be transferred to Camp Jackson here in the city within the week. They will be housed in proper barracks to serve as adjunctive labor to the military, in the kitchen, laundry, and so forth. They will face no bars, but they are not yet free to leave the facility."

"And their freedom?" Antoinette asked flatly, as if negotiating a deal.

With a deep sigh, Whalen snatched back the documents he'd given her, folded them, and placed them in his coat. "There is a claimant for them. I've told you. There is nothing more I can do until that is resolved. General Schofield's direct order."

Antoinette stared at her hands folded in her lap, wondering what tactic to take. "All right, Captain," she said coldly. "Then there is an addendum to my first condition. There will be a hearing on this man's claim, am I correct?"

"Yes, certainly."

"Then I want to be at that hearing. Can you do that for-for us? Will you represent them? And me?"

Whalen shrugged, obviously distressed by the promise he was being forced to give. "Yes, Antoinette, I will attempt to arrange that." He slumped back in his chair. "And if they are freed, or matters are resolved to your satisfaction, you will marry me? I want your commitment."

Antoinette studied the captain's face. Clearly, he cared little whether her friends were free or handed over to this mysterious claimant, but she needed him to do his utmost to represent their interests. "My word of honor. Regardless, my demand still stands. I want to be at the hearing, and they must be freed by adjudication or our engagement is off. Is that clear, Captain?"

Distraught, Whalen rubbed his face in thought and then sat up straight. "I will do my best, my dear. In the meantime, I have this for you." He reached into his vest pocket, withdrew a ring from its velvet case, and placed it on the table before her.

Antoinette studied the ring, a large, deep-red ruby set in 18-carat gold. Her best guess was that he'd taken it in payment from one of his clients, or as a bribe from some Confederate female prisoner in deepest distress, perhaps her wedding ring.

The fine quality and size of the ring shocked Antoinette. Nevertheless, she continued to play her part, a serious actress holding true to a role at odds with the tragic farce in which she found herself trapped. "This is a remarkable work of crafted jewelry," she said with practiced admiration. "You never cease to amaze me, Captain. How can you possibly afford such a thing on *your* salary, a captain's?"

"Oh," he replied with a conceited smile, "I have my ways."

"Now, now, you're being modest. You must be open with your future spouse. You know we can't begin our lives together in the great debt a piece like this would require."

"I owe nothing," he said smugly and launched into expansive braggadocio. "Antoinette, dearest, I own enough jewelry to complement your beauty for the rest of your life — our lives. When we are married, it will all be yours. I will present it all to you, my whole hoard."

"Jewelry? You clever man! But how could you come across such a treasure? In wartime, no less."

"My clients paid me for special attention to their cases, which often saved their lives," he declared proudly.

"Oh, I'm surprised. Does the army allow you to charge your clients like that?" she asked demurely, trying to sound like a layman asking a university professor to explain a twist in an obscure law.

Watching his face, Antoinette saw Whalen struggle to answer. Then he replied haughtily, "I assure you, my dear, the practice is quite widespread and entirely legitimate. I think I know military law. Remember, the women who gave me these baubles were Confederate sympathizers." He studied her face for a reaction, but her expression never wavered from one of starry-eyed veneration. "You will look lovely wearing them. Now, give me the honor of placing this on your finger."

Antoinette held her palm up toward him in a 'halt.' "I will not wear this yet, Captain Whalen." She took the ring from the table and slipped it into her pocket. "I will keep it to hold you to our betrothal, but you may not place this on my finger until our wedding. And we will not have a wedding until those women and children are set free. Understand?"

"I-if the case g-goes against us, I-I cannot afford to buy them," Whalen stuttered. "You must realize the legal difficulties I will face."

"What if you sold your jewels in order to buy them, husband?" she suggested, eyes fluttering. "I'd admire you much more if you set my friends free, rather than shower me with such riches."

"Th-there is no market for them currently," he said cautiously. "N-not until war's end. Believe me, dear, I've long considered selling my jewels, b-but…" He fell silent.

"All right, Captain Whalen. You know my conditions," Antoinette said firmly. "I expect to be at that hearing." She waited until Whalen nodded agreement.

Satisfied, Antoinette rose to her feet and raised her hand to attract the guard's attention. It was time to go back into captivity upstairs.

To the captain's chagrin, there would be no long-anticipated, tender kiss to seal the betrothal.

***

Robert Sterling broke from the alley and slipped behind a carriage sitting by the curb. With a wave, he signaled Devereau not to follow yet. She waited.

Like stalking a deer, Robert tiptoed quietly around the back of the carriage, then, crouching low, hurried forward to hide behind a pile of crates. From there, he advanced rapidly to take cover behind a stationary wagon and crossed the street to pause behind a horse-drawn phaeton, before taking a final sprint to light behind the corner of a two-story brick building. He removed his hat, with its red feather, and peered around the corner. Satisfied, he waved for Devereau to follow, which she did using the path he'd blazed.

Ahead, Robert saw Dark Horse and the old black man nearing a densely populated neighborhood. Though dusk was rapidly approaching, the streets were filled with black people selling fruits and vegetables, all manner of clothing, trinkets, and knickknacks. Well-dressed men and women, and others in work clothes, talked in clusters, while children ran and played games in the street, avoiding traffic as best they could.

When Devereau caught up to Robert, he turned to her. "We can't follow him there."

Catching her breath, Devereau examined where the Indian was pointing. She looked at him quizzically and then smiled. "But I know where he's going, Robert. Not tonight, but tomorrow or the next day."

Robert nodded knowingly. "You're right. Let's get some rest." He flashed his knife and smiled broadly. "Then we can find a blind to set our trap. We've got Dark Horse now."

CHAPTER TWENTY-SIX

BITTER FRUIT

Montgomery County, Eastern Missouri

Over the trees ahead, the brightening sky announced the sun's imminent arrival. Within the hour, the flaming sphere would begin its daily journey, steady and strong, unconcerned with the consequences, neither asking nor giving quarter.

Big Josh drew rein, the boy clinging to his back, and his three partners pulled up beside him. They had ridden east through the night, hoping darkness and inactivity would provide a degree of camouflage and solitude. Now they were exhausted and, being out of food, their stomachs pinched. Their horses, pressed to the limit over the unrelenting journey, were losing strength by the hour, in little shape to continue.

"We got to stop, Josh," Lou said. "These animals about to drop dead."

"I'm about dead, too," Isaac complained.

Josh surveyed the road east. "That stand of trees yonder make a good place. Right around this bend."

"I'm hungry," the boy grumbled. "I ain't ate since yesterday morning."

"We all hungry, boy. We get some food later today," Josh promised, not convincingly. "Somewheres."

The boy spit and watched it fall to the ground. "We could eat one of the horses," he said sarcastically.

"We may have to," Josh chuckled. "Be b-better than the army feed us when we was digging forts and laying road."

As the four cajoled their mounts to continue, the newly evident ball of sun projected rays directly into their eyes. They pulled their hats down, leeching what shadow the brims could offer, and lowered their eyes to stare blankly at their horses' necks. The bareheaded boy hid his face by leaning against Josh's broad back. Thirty yards down, the road angled off to the left. On one side lay a fallow, burnt field, a tableau in black ash: on the right side, a rich thicket. As they raised their eyes to look for a likely place to hide, the five saw it, stopping them cold.

Two mature maples flanking the road had been "decorated" in the night. Immediately overhead, from strong outreaching branches, hung four black soldiers, blue uniforms stained by generous profusions of blood. Three of the soldiers' faces were smashed in; two were missing eyeballs; one had a hand cut off at the wrist. The morning air was quiet except for swarms of buzzing flies. The four bodies dangled limply, motionless. Shocked, sickened, and unable to recover from the terrible sight, the five sat their horses breathlessly, staring at the gruesome spectacle above them.

Josh thought of the four men, soldiers just like they were, with fathers and mothers, perhaps wives and children. All tortured bloody, murdered and mutilated, to what end? To the perpetrators of this atrocity, these four hanging before their eyes weren't men, weren't even human. You wouldn't treat a pig or dog this way.

"My God," Josh whispered. "Welcome to Little Dixie." He turned to see if the boy was all right, but the child had covered his eyes with his hands. "Don't look if you don't have to, boy," Josh said. "They's bad, bad men done this. They's bad and good men on both sides."

"They's Federals," Bammer observed, noting the victim's uniforms. "Infantry."

"We gots to get out of here, Josh," Isaac said, his eyes growing wild. "Bushwhackers."

"Them 'whackers ain't staying 'round so the army can catch them," Big Josh surmised. "Ain't no place safer than right here. For now."

Isaac's head swiveled desperately. "We got to git."

"No, Isaac," Josh said calmly, grabbing Isaac's reins. "We can't leave them like this. They soldiers just like us. Y'all tie up your horses over there. We gonna bury them."

"You crazy, Josh?" Bammer exclaimed. "Patrol come by, we be hangin' from them trees ourselves."

"Tie up them horses like I said," Josh ordered, spurring his horse toward a heavy patch of the thicket. "Come on, we got to cut them down."

Reluctantly, the three followed Josh, dismounted, and tied their reins beside him. Josh helped the boy down and then climbed down himself. The boy's face, filled with horror, had turned deathly white. "You okay, son?" Josh asked, lifting the boy's chin so they were eye to eye.

It was as if the boy neither heard nor saw Josh. With no reply, the boy dropped his eyes to the ground again. "You lay over there," Josh said, nudging the boy toward a shaded area across the road from the horses. He paused, thinking. "You won't run off, will you?"

The boy ignored the question. Once he reached a soft grass, he laid down. In minutes, he was sound asleep.

The four men returned to the pair of maples. "Bammer, climb up there and cut them down."

Muscular Bammer secured his knife between his teeth and shimmied up the nearest of the trees. When he reached the branch where two soldiers were hanging, he slid out along it, took the knife from his teeth, and cut them loose.

"You two," Josh said to Lou and Isaac, "carry them to that bush." Finished with the first pair, Bammer jumped down into the road. Then he climbed the second maple and cut the other two down. Once that was done, the men hurriedly dragged the last two off the road, across a ditch, and, at Josh's instruction, the four began digging graves, even though they'd be seen from a distance.

As they worked, they heard horses approaching, and by the time they spotted the Union patrol, it was too late to run. A young sergeant with light brown hair, fair skin, and pink cheeks, leading a dozen troopers, drew rein before them.

"What's going on here?" the sergeant asked crisply.

The four MSMCC men stopped digging to salute. "Bushwhackers, sir," Josh said. "Must have been last night." He indicated the pair of maples, which still had the ends of rope hanging.

"What unit are you?" the sergeant inquired of Josh.

"Ninth MSM Colored Cavalry, Sergeant," Josh replied crisply.

"Where is your officer?" the sergeant asked.

"Captain went on ahead. Left us to bury them, sir."

The sergeant examined the poor state of the four, their crumpled uniforms, their ashen, drained faces. "How long you been on the road?"

"M-must be a week, Sergeant," Josh answered.

"You look awful' tired, in bad shape."

"Yes, s-sir," Josh replied. "We is that. Been riding all night."

The young, fair-faced sergeant spotted the boy sleeping in the brush. "Who's that?"

"A' orphan we pick up, sir. Family all dead."

The sergeant thought this over. "All right," he shouted to his platoon. "Help these men bury those soldiers." The soldiers dismounted and began to tie up their mounts. He turned to Josh. "You men hungry?"

Josh smiled and shook his head. "We powerful hungry, Sergeant. Powerful hungry."

"All right," the sergeant ordered his troopers. "When you're done burying those soldiers, feed these men. Then we've got to be off." He had a final thought. "What about the boy?"

"You wanna take him?" Josh asked.

"Can't," the sergeant replied. "Want to feed him now, too?"

"I don't wanna wake him just yet," Josh said.

"We'll leave you with some grub."

"Thank you, Sergeant," Josh said, relief flooding his face. "We is grateful."

"Keep up the good work," the sergeant answered.

***

St. Louis, Missouri

Old Moses ambled down the marble hallway, keeping as quiet as possible.

"You there! Where you think you're going?" the guard demanded, snapping his rifle across his chest.

Moses stopped in his tracks. "Going to clean the general's office. General Schofield."

"The regular man was here this morning, old timer," the guard said skeptically. "Who sent you?"

Moses set down his bucket, soap, and rag. "I' the detail man, sent special by the boss. I does all the corner work, under the desk, 'round the walls."

"So? I asked who sent you."

"I tole you, the boss. Don't remember his name right off the top of my head, but he ain't changed it none."

"You can't go in there. The general's having his supper."

"General be awful' mad if'n he don't get his detail work done," Moses cautioned. "Awful' mad."

The guard shook his head in frustration. "All right. But be quiet. Hear me?"

"I surely be that." Moses tapped on the door and, without waiting for a reply, entered. There, at his desk sat Schofield, just as he'd been described by friends of Moses who'd seen him. Schofield's head was round, with a balding top broken by few independent strands of hair, but with side hair pouring into a lush beard that reached halfway down his tunic. His eyes were steady, clear.

Upon seeing Moses, General Schofield ceased chewing mid-bite. He watched as the old man's eyes searched the room, then knelt down on the floor and began scrubbing a large stain on the heavily-worn carpet, itself a long-time victim of the heavy boots of anxious men reporting, map conferences, and misdirected chew spit and spills.

"Who are you, boy?" the general asked.

"Detail man, General," Moses replied, not looking up from his continuous rubbing.

Schofield shrugged and resumed eating.

Building his courage, Moses put his shoulder into his methodical work, eyes fixed on the irredeemable blemish, his efforts having no effect on the rug. Finally, he stood. "Um, 'scuse me, General."

"Yes?" the general asked, looking up, a potato suspended from his fork. "What is it, man?"

"Sir, I-I gots to tells you a story. A' important story, but it ain't no tale…"

***

The city was bigger in the sunlight than anything any of them had ever seen, with tall brick buildings everywhere, framing the narrow streets like an ominous, orderly canyon. Josh hesitated, drawing rein. These monster monoliths looked ready to fall down on his head. Then, gathering his wits and courage, he spurred his mount on.

The four passed wagons and carriages bumping along the cobblestone, people gathering or walking down the sidewalks, soldiers on leave drifting, all manner of curious activity. Finally, they came upon a black man sitting on a crate, wearing a long apron over his clothing.

"Excuse me, sir," Josh said, drawing rein. "We just getting to town. Can you tell us where we can get some sleep and a bite of food? We ain't got but a bit of change in our pockets."

The man in the apron stood and examined them. "What regiment you in?"

"W-we the Ninth MSM C-colored Cavalry, Western Missouri." Josh tugged the identifying patch on his shoulder.

The man studied them closely. "You a far piece from home, ain't you?"

"Y-yes, sir, we is. We just be here a day or two, then head back. Wanna see our wives and children. Can you help us?"

"You not lookin' to rob nobody, is you?"

"No, sir, we wouldn't."

"About six, eight blocks that-a-way. They calls it Nigger Colony. Anybody there can afford it will take soldiers in, rest you, feed you vittles."

"Thank you. How do we get there?"

***

Old Moses sauntered down the deserted side street whistling a tune. While he'd been inside Union Army headquarters, a cloud cover had rolled in and, with the wind blowing strongly through the canyon of buildings, the hot day had cooled. He felt good.

"Moses, wait," a voice behind him called, startling him. Moses turned to see Durk emerging from his alley perch where he'd been keeping watch from behind a stack of barrels. Durk ran to where Moses waited. The two gripped hands, then strolled together toward the Colony.

"You get to see Schofield?" Durk asked anxiously.

"I did. Tole him everything."

"That's wonderful, Moses! And? Did he say anything? Anything at all?"

"He ain't say much, but I seen him write on a paper."

"What?" Durk urged. "What did he write?"

"I can't read no upside-down scratching. You think my eyes in backwards?"

Durk continued walking, realizing that Moses probably couldn't read. "Did he ask you anything, Moses, any questions?"

"Yeah, he ask me 'bout things. Ask me plenty."

"That's good, real good!" Durk exclaimed, his eyes lighting up. "Do you remember any of his questions?"

"None in particular. The whole discussion just kind of flow. Know what I mean?"

"I do." Durk's stride picked up. "Anything else?"

"Talk to two men I know who live over to the Colony near me. They say they gonna help me find out about Antoinette. They the ones tole me our womens lock up. They good men, gots friends work upstair. Don't worry. We find out, Durk."

"I hope we do soon," Durk said. "Did you tell them we want to know when they set her trial?"

"I did. One of the upstair fellas gets all them papers. He be watching. He say he' tell us when he learn 'bout it."

Durk made a tight, determined fist, biting his lip. Now they had a chance!

"Say, Durk. She go to trial, what you gonna do? You going? They see you alive, they wanna hang you just for tricking them. You know them peoples."

Durk merely kept walking, unable to answer. Now that he'd gotten this far, what was his plan? What could he do, realistically, to help Antoinette? Anything? Or would his appearance hurt her chances? If he was somehow able to make her trial in time, would he possibly be throwing away his own life? And perhaps hers, too? It weighted on him.

They turned the corner and headed down a deserted narrow avenue. Daylight was in full retreat, and a chilly wind whipped between the hulking brick structures surrounding them. Still carrying his bucket and rags, Moses pulled his jacket tightly around him.

Durk crossed his arms for warmth. Striding forward, staring blankly at the sidewalk, his thoughts were a jumble of demon questions and fears. The corner of his eye caught movement in an alley they passed, and he glanced aside. A dark figure suddenly came lunging at him, knife poised. Moses was knocked to the ground, sending his bucket clattering along the stones.

Instinctively, Durk ducked away as the knife sliced at his neck. He instantly felt a sharp, cutting pain in his shoulder and fell sideways, hitting his ribs on a curb. Blood flowed from the wound. When he looked up to identify his attacker, he saw Robert Sterling regaining his balance, preparing to spring again. Durk hurriedly scuttled backwards, crab-like, and Robert stabbed downward, but Durk threw his feet up, deflecting Robert's body. When Durk rolled over and away, the knife hit the ground. Then Durk heard a shout.

"It's Durk!" Isaac shouted, appearing from around the corner, spurring his horse directly at them.

Undistracted, Robert grabbed Durk's tunic with his powerful left hand, holding him in place, and raised his knife. But before his hand could drop, Isaac leaped from his saddle directly onto Robert, and the two tumbled to the ground, Isaac on top. Robert slashed one final time, pushed Isaac off, and sprung up. He immediately saw Lou, Bammer, and Josh, a boy clinging to his waist, riding swiftly toward him. The sound of two shots split the air. Not hesitating, in a flash, Robert dashed back into the alley from where he'd come and ran away.

Lou and Bammer pursued the fleeing Chickasaw, but Robert had already disappeared into the city warren along an escape route he'd planned in advance. Bammer and Lou, their horses blocked by a dead end, dismounted and chased after him, but was as if he had vanished into thin air. When the pair returned to the avenue, they found Durk kneeling in the street, Isaac's head cradled in his lap. A crimson flood poured from Isaac's belly.

"No," Bammer cried, "his guts are all out of him!"

Standing over the pair, Josh covered the boy's eyes.

"Isaac," Durk said quietly, "you saved my life."

In great pain, Isaac grimaced, and then he managed to speak. "Don't get no idea I like you, Durk." Isaac attempted a smile on a face twisted in agony.

"Isaac, you're my brother."

Isaac managed a nod as blood gurgled between his lips and poured from his mouth. The light left his eyes, and he became still.

"Isaac," Durk pleaded desperately. "Isaac." But there was no reaction.

Josh knelt down beside them and put his ear to Isaac's lips, then to his chest. "I think he g-gone, Durk."

Durk carefully laid Isaac's head on the ground and then stood above his motionless body. It took him a few moments before he realized he was seeing his friends. "You're alive! Josh, Bammer, Lou, you're alive! They told me you were dead."

"We was, Durk," Josh said. "We *is*."

CHAPTER TWENTY-SEVEN

WOUNDED IN SORROW

Only two candles kept the night from dominating the squalid, second-floor room. The four stained walls retained much of the day's heat. Added to the bodies of five hard-traveled men and a boy, even with the single window fully open, the room was stifling, oppressive, pungent. Their hand-scrubbed uniforms, tunics and pants, were spread haphazardly on the rusty stove to dry, the washtub leaning against the wall. Durk's tunic, although scrubbed with lye soap, still bore a residue of darkened blood stains. The knife tear, repaired imperfectly by men's hands, was a mass of cross-stitches in hardly any discernable order.

They ate in silence, the memory of their dead friend fresh in their memories, hungrily gnawing clean every morsel from the ribs Moses had managed to scrape together, and devouring the last of the greens. Throughout the truncated meal, the sight of the four mutilated, hanging black Federals tortured their thoughts. As deserters themselves, was the fate those four innocents suffered a stark rehearsal of their own? Only their extreme exhaustion would allow them to sleep, although nightmares would trouble even that modicum of rest.

Big Josh wearily plopped down next to Durk, who sat pensively against the wall, hand to his slashed shoulder. The wound had been expertly washed and wrapped by Moses' neighbor lady, and sewn up by the street's doctor-dentist-soothsayer. Josh could see from Durk's face that the wound still stung and throbbed. As long as gangrene didn't set in, with some luck, Durk would retain only a deep scar to remind him of his deadly encounter that afternoon.

They'd been fortunate. A friend of Moses had alerted them that General Schofield had issued messages to bring Antoinette and the women and children to him tomorrow. The friend hadn't learned the exact site of the special hearing, but there were a number of lower-level allies seeking that information, and they believed they'd have it by morning. That meeting might be their only chance. Chance at what? They had no idea.

"Wh-what you gonna do, Durk? You gonna go there?" Josh asked.

Durk nervously brushed back his hair and then rubbed his hands together. "I want to. I want to see Antoinette. To meet this absurdity face to face. But…" He fell silent, pressing his shoulder wrappings.

"If you stay away," Josh cautioned, "they ain't got no evidence against her. They g-gots to let her go. But if you shows up, maybe both of you hang."

Durk let go of his shoulder and fiddled with his bootstrap, thinking. "I just don't know, Josh. I know you're right. I should stay away. But my heart, my heart tells me…"

"Well, I can't tell you what to do."

"How about you?" Durk asked. "Y'all are deserters, too."

Josh expelled his breath heavily. "I knows it. The sensible thing is to stay put at Moses' place till the trial's over. But we can give evidence she innocent, Durk. 'Sides, Lou want to see his wife and children. Bammer's wife kill in that raid, you know, but he want to see his daughter. So, I don' know. We gonna have to talk it over in the morning."

Durk indicated the child sitting motionless, staring aimlessly out the window into the black sky. "What are you going to do about the boy?"

"Don't know that either. Since he s-seen the hanging, it like he deaf an' b-blind. Ain't said one word. Don't speak when I talk to him, nothing. Least he ate."

About them, the exhausted men were already crawling wearily into their arrangement, sleeping six people on the cramped floorboards. Without further word, Josh broke off and nestled into his area between Bammer and Lou, and Durk laid down beside Moses. Moses blew out the candles, enabling the darkness to prevail. Within minutes, snoring was the dominant sound.

Durk tossed and turned in the heat, knowing he would never sleep. His shoulder ached, and sweat was making it itch under the wrappings. His thoughts rushed in all directions, like quails fleeing a starving wolf. He pictured his friend Isaac expiring in his arms. He sensed the Chickasaw lurking on some unknown street. He conjured up the army gallows standing above them like giant wooden vultures. He imagined Antoinette in the general's office in all her glory, yet terrified of her fate.

Durk rose quietly. Leaving his boots behind, he tiptoed between the packed bodies to the door and then softly made his way into the hallway, down the stairs smelling of ochre and pork, and into the street. There, he sat on the stone stoop, awash in the familiar, comforting sounds of laughter and talking wafting up and down the street through the cooling night air. He stretched his sore body, wincing at the sudden sharp pain in his shoulder.

Without warning or sound, the boy appeared and sat beside him. Durk's tormenting thoughts mercifully broken by the intrusion, he examined the boy, whose eyes seemed to be staring aimlessly ahead, unseeing, at the building across the street. The child was all ribs and bones. After a week on the road, his worn and patched bib jeans were grimy and mud-spattered. His bare feet were filthy; the long sandy hair was a tangle. Who knows when it was last combed, let alone washed?

"What's your name, son?" Durk asked.

The boy didn't even blink at the question, as if he were, indeed, deaf.

"Josh told me what happened to your pa."

Still no reaction.

The pair sat in silence, both staring ahead. Durk knew tomorrow was going to be trouble and danger enough. What were they to do with this mute ball of anger and despair?

"I guess you're about ten, right?" Durk asked.

But no reply or acknowledgement was forthcoming.

Durk tried to think of what to say; then he came up with an approach. "Look, boy, I lost my pa, too, when I was about your age. My ma was already dead four years."

Durk waited, but the boy didn't even turn his head toward him.

"Pa was a hard drinker," Durk mused, "a mean drunk, but he was still my pa, and I loved him." He waited, but the boy could have been made of marble. "Unfortunately, he was also an abolitionist who couldn't keep his mouth shut when he was in his jug. Back home, abolitionist talk could be lethal, even for preachers, especially for preachers." When the boy again failed to react, Durk leaned back against the door, stretching out his legs and crossing his hands behind his head. He stared in the clear star-speckled sky.

"Pa was burned to death in our cabin. It was a horrible sight." Durk's eyes fell to his feet. "By folks in a pretty nice town, too, a pretty nice little town. If Pa had just kept shut, I'd probably still be living there among those people. Farming, owning a general store maybe. Who knows?" He broke off his tale, ruminating on what might have been.

Living in Turkle would have been a whole different life, he mused. *Another whole life. And I'd likely be a whole different man. Perhaps with a wife and children of my own. Happy, maybe.*

At times when he'd been alone, a solitary figure riding an endless, deserted country road with no sure place to land, or sleeping in dusty blankets beside a field

— conditions he'd endured frequently — he'd often pictured himself sitting at a kitchen table, enveloped in the comforting aroma of home cooking. His loving wife knitting, sons and daughters reading or playing. Sometimes he couldn't get the scene out of his head.

He studied the scrawny, sad, disheveled boy. Life was going to get hard for the child — and soon. With so many refugees pouring into St. Louis, there were many orphans on the streets, at the mercy of hunger and strangers, and this boy was destined to be one of them. Durk felt a pang of regret, realizing that, had the Chickasaws not taken him in when his own daddy was murdered, he'd have been in the same hopeless position. And his life had been hard as it was.

"Real nice people," Durk muttered, remembering Turkle fondly… and bitterly at the same time.

***

In the makeshift courtroom, Antoinette sat stiffly upright at the defendant's table, her black dress newly cleaned and pressed, a guard with a rifle at her shoulder. Captain Whalen sat at her right, fingering through his brief, a helplessness expression on his face. The room was neither a courtroom nor an office, but a large auxiliary room set up in General Schofield's headquarters for his convenience. Soldiers were stationed throughout the chamber. Detracting from the decorum, boxes of office supplies, canned meats, and random cleaning materials were stacked about on perimeter walls. Two prosecutors whispered together at Antoinette's left; to their left, a smaller table was set up for two, which was presently unoccupied. In the far corner, forty empty chairs waited in neat rows. At the front of the room, a desk had been set up for the general facing the room.

The sun poured through the bank of windows on two sides, making every detail of the room clear, light, distinct. An anxious Antoinette absently fretted with a loose thread on her sleeve, smoothing her dress repeatedly. She stared at the room's side door, from which General Schofield would emerge at the time of his own choosing to hear her case and also make a determination of her friends' fate. Captain Whalen had advised Antoinette to remain silent and let him speak for her, but she was determined to speak forthrightly in defense of herself, and so end this charade, this ridiculous nightmare to which she'd been subjected. She wasn't going to leave her fate in the unsteady and unreliable hands of a man she didn't trust.

There was commotion in the hallway behind her, and she turned to see the main doors open. Into the room, herded by four soldiers, came Auntie NeeNee,

Sarah, and the other women and children. Their clothes were in a better state than when she'd last seen them, but their faces were grim, lined by fear and uncertainty. Seeing her, the children immediately ran between the soldiers to surround Antoinette, hugging and kissing her until the guards shepherded them back to their mothers. The whole group was then seated, with the children being settled and quieted by loving hands.

Antoinette's eyes met Auntie NeeNee's. Doubt and mutual encouragement flowed between them. Shrugging, Antoinette turned to Whalen to discuss her case. She wanted to feel out his legal approach and to gauge his degree of confidence. After a brief discussion, she concluded that Whalen's shaky grasp on both was not reassuring. She swallowed hard.

The door at the side of the room opened, and the Federal officer over the entire Department of Missouri, Major General John McCallister Schofield, entered, followed by a pair of aides and a corporal. The room quieted; everyone became alert. The general's tunic was buttoned to the neck, partly covered by his long frizzled beard. As he took a commanding seat facing the room, an aide placed a stack of documents before him, untying them. His other aide slipped several papers by his left hand.

General Schofield cleared his throat. "All right," he spoke aloud, as if to himself. "Let's straighten out this convoluted mess."

He examined the room until his steely gaze lit on Antoinette. Then he announced in a clear, deep voice for all to hear, "I am overseeing this trial myself because of its connection to the horrific tragedy in Lawrence, Kansas, and all that it implies. Today, we have two issues at hand: the charges against Mrs. Antoinette DuVallier and, as a corollary, the disposition of these persons." He nodded toward the corner where the women and children sat.

At that moment, Devereau French and Robert Sterling entered abruptly through the main doors. Devereau was still wearing her simple print dress and flowered hat, Robert a suit. They paused inside the door to study the situation. Then Robert handed Devereau a stack of papers and nudged her toward the general. Hesitant at first, Devereau took the documents and crossed the room to stand behind the prosecutors, nervously teetering back and forth from foot to foot. Robert waited by the door, standing erect. Ever alert, his eyes ceaselessly roamed the room.

Antoinette examined Devereau wearing her print dress and ridiculous hat, shocked to her core. She had never seen Devereau in anything but a man's suit, but she quickly concluded that this was, indeed, her half-sister. She didn't know what the woman's presence at her trial meant, but she surmised that Devereau didn't mean well for her or for her women friends.

The two women glared at each other.

"And who are you?" the general's aide asked.

"My name is French. Devereau French."

"Ah," General Schofield remarked. "The claimant. Let's get this matter out of the way." He waved for Devereau to come forward. Devereau hesitated, glanced back at Robert, who nodded, and approached. "Do you have documents?"

Devereau laid the forms on the desk and stepped back, as General Schofield fingered through them. He kept one and slid the rest aside for his corporal to examine. The corporal studied them and then whispered into the general's ear. The corporal held one paper to the light and then whispered to the general a second time.

A stern expression came over the general's face. He whispered angry instructions to the corporal, who selected one of the documents and hurried from the room. Devereau didn't like the look on his face, nor the fact that the corporal had been dispatched on some mysterious mission.

"Now, Miss French..." the general said, "It is 'Miss'?"

"Yes, General."

"Miss French, go sit over there." He indicated the small table beside the prosecutors. Devereau complied tentatively. "Miss French, are you a citizen of the state of Missouri?"

"No, sir. Mississippi. I own a plantation there, *FrenchAcres*. But I am not a secessionist."

Antoinette shouted, "Mississippi is a state in rebellion. Slavery is illegal there!"

"Yes," Devereau shouted back, "but we are in Missouri. These slaves are mine. This woman, this spy, this thief, this *murderess* has no say in this matter."

The general's aide barked, "You will both be quiet until the general tells you to speak or I will have you gagged. Understand?"

Devereau and Antoinette fell silent, sheer enmity passing between them.

"Now," the general continued, "these documents are from Keytesville, Missouri. You said your plantation is in Mississippi."

"Yes, sir, but I plan to establish a plantation in Missouri, near Rocheport. Slavery is still legal here. Just ask these women, General," she said, indicating the group crowded in the corner. "They were all French slaves until *that* woman,"

Devereau pointed at Antoinette, "stole them from my family. See on those papers how many are named 'French?' That's *my name*. They'll tell you."

The women in question erupted all at once, their angry shouts comingling into incomprehensible babble. Antoinette's lawyer, Captain Whalen, broke his silence, jumping to his feet, interjecting, "Murder is not one of the charges against my client, General. I ask that this woman's statement be stricken from the record."

It took a while for the general's aide to quiet the room.

"Now," the general said to Devereau, "we will not get sidetracked with unrelated charges. Murder is not relevant to our purposes."

Whalen sat back down and turned to Antoinette, a smug grin on his face declaring his first victory as her champion. She forced a grateful, encouraging smile, which quickly disappeared.

"So, Miss French," the general proceeded, "you say these women belonged to you until they were stolen by Mrs. DuVallier and taken by her to Missouri. Is that right?"

"That is correct, sir," Devereau replied. Again, there was commotion from the back, but guards moved in to surround the area, and, intimidated, the group quieted down.

"Miss French, these documents you presented to me are Missouri documents, dated recently. Do you have papers from Mississippi that prove you owned these people?"

Devereau's face reddened, and her hands became fists. In a fury, she spat, "That woman, Antoinette DuVallier, killed my mother, and then she burned down my home, destroying any documentation we had." She gestured toward Robert Sterling. "Robert and I have been in pursuit of her ever since. Now I learn from the newspapers that she has been spying for the Confederacy. General, I know her to be a vocal supporter of Jeff Davis and would do anything for the rebellion. Antoinette DuVallier is a scourge upon the land. My property must be returned to me and justice meted out to her."

Antoinette rose angrily. "That is a lie, General Schofield. This woman killed *our* mother, Mrs. Marie Brussard French. It was Mrs. French who owned these women. She authorized me to sell them, which I did under proper authority." Devereau and Antoinette began to yell simultaneously at each other, but the general's aide quickly shut off their spat.

"Quiet, both of you," the general ordered. "Sit down, Mrs. DuVallier. If either of you speak to the other again, rather than to me, you will be bound and gagged. Do you understand?"

Both women nodded agreement, mumbling a contrite 'Yes, sir.'

"Good. You will both keep to the point. Accusations of spying against Mrs. DuVallier are not relevant to the current issue, which is the disposition of these slaves. Now, Mrs. DuVallier, you claim you are this woman's sister..."

"Half-sister," Antoinette interjected.

"Half-sister. And your common mother gave you permission to sell these women, correct?"

"Correct, General."

"She's lying, General," Devereau shouted. "She was a fugitive from justice for murdering her husband in New Orleans. My mother took her in, but she is no relation to us. Legally, the plantation was, and is, mine. So my mother had no right to sell or give permission to sell any chattel on my property, including these slaves. They are mine!"

"She knows better, sir," Antoinette replied.

"Yes, I do," Devereau said. "Ask her who she sold them to and for how much! And ask her how *she* came to be in possession of them in Missouri."

"All right," the general said. "Mrs. DuVallier, assuming you did have authority to sell these women — an issue very much in doubt — who did you sell these slaves to?"

"I sold them to-to Durk... to Durksen Hurst," Antoinette replied haltingly.

Schofield thumbed through his notes. "Your supposed fellow conspirator in espionage, Captain Hurst. And my notes read Hurst is — or was — your fiancé, correct?"

"Yes, that is true."

"And how much did you sell them for?"

Antoinette hesitated before answering, "A symbolic amount. One dollar."

"One dollar! For more than a dozen slaves, counting the children? To your fiancé? That certainly smacks of self-dealing, don't you think?" The general stroked his long beard. "It looks to me like you have mishandled Miss French's property to your own advantage, perhaps without proper authority. Unless compelling additional information is presented, I am inclined to rule in Miss French's favor." Cries of deep angst shouted forth from the back of the room, and it took some time to quiet the women down.

"But, General," Antoinette pleaded, "these women were the wives and mates of Durk's men. I sold them to him so they could be together. Durk's men were mustered into his regiment to serve the Union cause: the Ninth Missouri State Militia Colored Cavalry. It's there in the record."

"This is another of her fabrications!" Devereau exclaimed. "She stole those slaves from me."

"Quiet!" the general ordered sternly, fingering through the case documents. He paused to read one of the papers. "They are the women of these original dozen members of the Ninth? The colored soldiers you requested give testimony on your behalf in the spy trial?"

"Yes, yes, that's the men," Antoinette replied urgently. "These are their women and children."

The general slid the paper he was reading to the top of the stack and then faced the seated black people in the corner. "I don't know if you've been told this, folks, but I am sorry to relate to you that those dozen troopers are all deceased. Eight were killed at Lawrence in defense of their country, and the four survivors died of typhus at Westport."

Loud, heart-wrenching cries rang out from the back corner, as the women and children, already deeply traumatized by their long incarceration, plummeted into abject blackness. Emotionally devastated, the women screamed, flailed their arms about, and fell to the floor. General Schofield could only wait hopelessly for order to be restored.

Captain Whalen turned to Antoinette. "It's looking more hopeless by the minute."

Unhearing, Antoinette could only stare in horror at her friends' reeling in chaotic, hysterical despair: their last chance, their men, their children's fathers, their only hope, buried under the dirt far away and gone forever. In a country that was creating widows by the hundreds of thousands, none were more desolate and alone, nor felt more doomed, than these.

CHAPTER TWENTY-EIGHT

CONVERGENCE

Durk ran frantically along the street, blind to the attention his desperate flight was attracting. If anyone stopped him, he'd resolve that then. The sun was high in the sky, glaring, so he knew the day was half over. Mid-morning, when he'd decided he couldn't stay away from the hearing, he'd rushed to the military courts building. There, he learned the session was being held elsewhere. Terrified that he'd be too late, he'd spent valuable time tearing around the building, questioning everyone, before he found where he needed to go. Now the clock on the tower ahead read 12:30.

He stumbled to a stop. Breathless, bent over at the waist, he gulped air, gasping, holding his side, afraid he'd missed his chance. Then the boy appeared at his side, winded also, and halted next to him. He must have been following since Durk left the Colony.

"What are you doing, boy?" Durk growled angrily. "I told you to wait with Moses." As before, the boy remained silent. "Go back! Do what I tell you." But the boy didn't move.

Disdaining to deal with this child further, Durk started running again as soon as he could. When he glanced over his shoulder, the boy was still right behind him. "Go back, boy!" Durk shouted. He stopped, and when the boy caught up, he grabbed and shook him. "Wait for me at Moses' place." But his instructions had no effect. Durk merely shrugged and continued onward, trying to ignore the bare feet slapping the cobblestones behind him. Nothing he could do about it, he had to get to Antoinette before it was too late.

***

Every window in the improvised courtroom was open, yet the air was stifling. That morning, with the proceedings disrupted by the women's lamentations, General Schofield had called a recess and left for his office to attend to pressing duties. After all, he had a war to run. In the interim, all the participants had been fed out back. The women and children were sent to a military facility a few blocks north of the general's office to mourn their dead and recover, leaving only Auntie

NeeNee to be their spokesperson. The other participants returned to the courtroom.

Now Antoinette sat at her table between Captain Whalen and Auntie NeeNee. As before, the two prosecutors sat to Antoinette's left, with Devereau French at her own smaller table to their left. Robert Sterling took his watchful post near the doors at the back of the room, his eyes surveying the number of armed guards scattered about. With nothing to do but wait, Antoinette, Auntie NeeNee, and Captain Whalen silently watched the side door for Schofield's return, with her life, and her friends' freedom, hanging in the balance.

After the interminable, nerve-wracking delay, the general entered with his two aides and seated himself. "All right," he said, "let's get this over with. You," he said, indicating Auntie NeeNee, "what is your name?"

The black stick of an emaciated old woman straightened her dress and red headscarf. "Me? Why, I'm Auntie NeeNee, General, um-hum."

"And what is your last name, Auntie?"

"Mine? Why I can't rightly say for sure. People just been calling me Auntie, um-hum."

"All right, Auntie," the general said, jotting a note. "Now, did you belong to this French family? Did you live on *FrenchAcres*?"

"Goin' onto seventy year, yes sir. I was sold to old Mr. French as a young woman. He long dead now. That be my third plantation since I got sold away from my mama, um-hum."

"And who owned *FrenchAcres* when you lived there?"

"*FrenchAcres*? Why, ol' Mrs. French, of course, an' Mr. French, her son." She pointed to Devereau. "I don't know who this girl sitting here is, General."

The general stared at Devereau and directed his comments her way. "A *Mr.* French? And how do you explain this, madam?"

A look of panic overtook Devereau, and then she stood and barked, "An old field slave wouldn't know such a thing, General Schofield. It is neither legal nor proper to take the testimony of a slave in such matters."

The general looked confused, checking the documents and his notes. "I'll decide who can and cannot testify. Now," he scanned the room, "can anyone explain this discrepancy?"

"General," Antoinette interjected. "Devereau French has been masquerading as a man for most of her life. You can't trust her. People around the plantation called her *Mr. French*, but I knew better."

Schofield studied Devereau closely. "Please take off that hat, Miss French," he ordered.

"My hat?" Devereau questioned, alarmed. She paused and then took off the flowered bonnet, revealing her man-cut auburn hair. "Yes, General," she said bitterly, "to do business in Mississippi, it was necessary for me to act in the personage of a man to get the respect I needed. I was the owner of the largest plantation in Lethe Creek County. Everyone knew me as *Mr.* French, thought I *was* Mr. French, and I felt and acted as Mr. French would. That's just a fact of life in the South."

"All right," the general concluded, shaking his head in puzzlement. "I will accept that. Be that as it may, Auntie..."

"Yes, sir," Auntie replied.

"When you were last at *FrenchAcres*, who was running that plantation?"

"Why, Mrs. Antoinette," Auntie answered. "Mrs. French have *her* run the place. Mr. French ain't so good at no business dealings, you see, um-hum."

"And it was Mrs. DuVallier who sold you to Mr. Hurst, is that right?"

"That's right, General. Sold us to Mr. Durk so we could be with our menfolks who work over to *DarkHorse* plantation. Been together with them ever since, um-hum."

The general sat back in his chair, stroking his beard. Finally, after long deliberation, he slammed his hand down on the stack of papers on his desk. Nodding toward Auntie NeeNee, he said, "This woman would have no knowledge of the legal ramifications of such a sale, whether Mrs. DuVallier had any authority to sell these slaves or not. However, she *has* verified that Miss French here did, indeed, have ownership, a point not contradicted by any party. Furthermore, the putative owner, Captain Hurst, is deceased and, thus, cannot testify on his own behalf about his own claim. In fact, if Hurst were alive, he would be put on trial as a spy for the Confederacy. Therefore, with no evidence to the contrary, I must rule that..."

Suddenly, a loud commotion erupted at the main door, and all eyes turned toward it. With their hands raised to show they were unarmed, Big Josh, Bammer, and Long Lou, pushed their way into the room, restrained by the two Union soldiers who'd been stationed in the outside hallway. Upset at the disturbance, one of the general's aides shouted, "What is this intrusion? Who are these men?"

Big Josh froze where he was, and his two companions halted, as well. All three of the interlopers saluted sharply.

With the guards distracted by the intruders, Robert Sterling, seeing who the interlopers were, bolted from his place near the doors and, knife in hand, ran out of the room.

"He kill Isaac!" Josh shouted after him. "Somebody stop him! That's Wounded Wolf!"

They could hear Robert's feet clacking as he ran down the hallway.

"Have that Indian placed under arrest!" General Schofield ordered.

"Chase after and arrest that Indian!" Schofield's aide bellowed, and one of the guards ran out of the room hollering for others to engage in the pursuit.

"You ain't gonna catch him," Josh said dejectedly.

In shock, Antoinette rose from her chair, her eyes meeting her friends. "Josh," she cried, "you're alive!"

"The defendant will sit down," the general's aide ordered.

As she was taking her seat, Antoinette blurted, "Josh, Ceeba was killed! Marcy Darcy and Melody, too."

Knowing this already, Josh merely nodded sadly.

"The defendant will be quiet," the aide commanded, and Antoinette fell silent.

Devereau French rose from her chair. "This matter is settled. Please let me take my property and go, General."

"I haven't ruled on that yet. You will sit right there until I tell you you may leave. Understand, *Miss* French?" Devereau nodded and sat down, her fingers nervously tearing up the artificial flower on her hat.

"Now," the general said when order was restored, "who are you men?"

"W-we' soldiers of the N-ninth MSM Colored Cavalry, the *DarkHorse* regiment, General Schofield. Sergeant Josh Tyler reporting, sir. These two, Lou and Bammer, are privates."

"What do you mean, breaking in here?" the general snapped angrily.

"S-sir," Big Josh replied, "we come to testify for Antoinette, Mrs. DuVallier. A great injustice is being done at her. And we wants to get our wives and childrens released. S-sir!"

"Durk manumitted these women and children, General," Antoinette exclaimed but was ignored.

The general conferred with his aides, who shuffled through his stack of papers. Finally, one aide laid two documents before the general. Schofield said pointedly, "One of these documents reads that you men are deceased. Subsequently, after your supposed deaths, an order was issued on the wires to have you men arrested. This is all very confusing to me. Please, Sergeant, give the Captain here your orders."

"I' s-sorry, General," Josh stuttered, "we-we ain't g-got no orders."

"So, in effect, you three men are deserters, is that right? Plus, there is this latest arrest order."

"If I could explain, General," Josh pleaded. "Please..."

"You'd better, Sergeant," the general said. "Mind you, desertion is a serious offense — the most serious in wartime."

"See, General Schofield, after Lawrence, we was commandeered by Lieutenant Langham, Horace Langham, to help they patrol with Order Eleven. We didn't have no choice, what with our regiment practically wipe' out."

"Yes, go on, Sergeant," the general said.

"See, first farm we come to, the lieutenant say to burn the place down: Order Eleven, but he have two civilians with him, who kinda seem in charge along with him. Anyway, they bring a wagon and a ambulance skinned by civilians. Next thing we know, the civilians bust into the farmhouse, and they was telling the soldiers what they want to cart out to the wagons, to keep."

"And what were you three doing?" the general asked.

"The lieutenant tell us to load what they stole into the wagons. We didn't want to, but we had to follow orders."

"So Langham and these civilians were, in effect, robbing the place?"

"Yes, sir, General, they was. Cleaning out the barn, too, before they burn them both down."

"Go on. What happened next?"

"They drag the farmer and his boy out the house. Kick and punch him. They demand he give them his money. But the man say, he ain't got no money. So they shoot him down like a dog. Like a dog, General! Man was a Union loyalist, too, or so he said."

"This is very serious," the general said. "Go on, please."

"They was gonna shoot his boy, too, just like that. That's when we pull our rifles, to save the boy. We been on the run ever since, General, 'cause I know Lieutenant Langham gonna say we did something terrible, to get us in trouble, and cover himself up."

With a grimace, General Schofield exhaled deeply and sat stroking his beard thoughtfully. "This is what I was afraid of," he said, "that the Order would lead to instances of outright robbery and murder. I issued explicit instructions, established harsh penalties against any such horrendous misdeeds. I even went so far as to forbid any Jayhawker troops from entering Missouri, knowing the ravages they'd inflict on Missouri.

"However," the general added, turning to the guards, "an accusation by these men is not proof. I want these three troopers arrested immediately. Sit them back in the corner for the time being." He indicated the now-empty rows where the women and children had been seated that morning. "Now, where was I?"

Before the proceedings could continue, the door burst open. Durk ran through and came to an abrupt stop. Frantically, his eyes searched the room, lighting on Antoinette. So relieved, his whole body deflated, and he made his way hurriedly to her table, as she rose and collapsed into his arms. The two embraced deeply, entwined as if to shut out the horror of a hostile world they found themselves trapped in.

"They told me you were dead," Antoinette whispered tearfully.

"I'm not," Durk whispered reassuringly, breathlessly. "I'm here for you."

"What is this?" General Schofield demanded. "Who is this man?"

Durk released Antoinette, who returned dutifully to her seat. Durk saluted sharply, still winded. "Captain Durksen Hurst, Ninth MSMCC, *DarkHorse* regiment, sir."

The general conferred hurriedly with his aides. One placed a telegraph wire down before him. He read it over once, twice, and then laid it aside.

"Has the Second Coming arrived?" the general exclaimed quizzically. "We seem to be confronted here with a massive resurrection of the dead! Hurst, you were reported to be killed in battle. What the hell is going on?"

"Sir," Durk said, "I have, indeed, recovered from my wounds, as you can see. Reports of my death were clearly made in error."

"What nonsense," the general grumbled, slapping his palm down on the wire. He looked the disheveled Durk over, noting the bandages and bloodstains on his shoulder.

Just then, the boy stumbled loose-jointed from the hallway into the room and fell to his knees, gasping for air. As one of the guards helped him to his feet, the general examined this new invader. The boy was scrawny and dirty, as if he'd been dragged through a swamp. "What are you doing here, boy? How did you get here?"

The boy merely pointed to Durk.

Josh rose from his seat in the corner and cried out, "That' the boy who' daddy was shot by Lieutenant Langham's men. That's him, General!"

Schofield surveyed the room. "That woman," he said, pointing to Auntie NeeNee, "escort her back with the three troopers." A guard helped Auntie from her chair and guided her to sit in the corner with Josh and the others.

"Captain Hurst, you will take her seat beside Mrs. DuVallier. Both of you are on trial for treason."

"Yes, sir," Durk responded and sat down beside Antoinette, taking her hand under the table. "I am ready to defend our innocence and our patriotism."

Devereau French stood to address the general, glaring at Durk for several long seconds. "Sir, my business is done here. Please let me take my slaves and leave."

"You will stay right where you are," the general snapped. "Sit down, French. I'm not done with you."

Devereau sat, lips pinched, glaring at the defendant's table.

"Now, bring that boy up here."

A soldier guided the reluctant boy to the general's desk. "Now, son, what is your name?"

"Ain't your business, Yankee," the boy said with sullen anger.

"Oh," the general mused, "seems like we have a little rebel here. Okay, son, just tell us in your own words what happened."

"Them murderin' Yankees come to the house, start stealing ever'thing. Then the officer ask Pa where's his money, but we ain't go no money. So's they shoot him. They gonna shoot me, too, but them there crows —" he pointed to Josh and the others, "grab me up, and here I am."

"So Lieutenant Langham was going to kill you, too, is that right?"

"Damn right. A bunch of murderin' Yankee cowards is what they was."

The general stroked his beard, contemplating what he'd just heard, then turned to his aide. "Have this Lieutenant Langham and his civilian cohorts taken into custody, Captain. This could be very damaging to how our efforts in this godforsaken war are perceived. We need to get to the bottom of it."

"Yes, sir," the aide said, making a note to himself.

"Now, take this child back to that corner," the general ordered.

Devereau shouted, "What about my claim, General?"

"Just hold your horses, French. I'll get to you soon enough." He studied Durk and Antoinette. "First, let's get to the bottom of this spy trial…" he said thoughtfully, "and all these soldiers suddenly and mysteriously risen from the dead."

CHAPTER TWENTY-NINE

TAINTED EVIDENCE

General Schofield's aide handed him the document with the main evidence listed; then he placed the stack of supporting proof and other evidence beside it. The general took a moment to examine the materials and then turned his attention to the prosecution table. "You may begin, Captain Stanford."

Captain Randall Stanford, who was shocked at all that had taken place so far, settled his spectacles on his nose and rose to approach the bench. The day had taken a momentus turn, for which he was not prepared.

Stanford was a tall, narrow-shouldered man in his mid-thirties, fair of face, with short, clipped blond hair. Stanford had been a respected lawyer back home in Iowa before he volunteered his services to the Union cause and joined the army.

He cleared his throat and spoke in a dignified, deep baritone, "General Schofield, members of this special tribunal, I intend to prove that this pair of defendants, Captain Durksen Hurst and Mrs. Antoinette DuVallier, have engaged in espionage in the service of the rebellion. Their reconnaissance contributed to one of the most heinous crimes in this country's history, the burning of Lawrence, Kansas, and the blatant murder of the town's innocent residents. The evidence against these two is unambiguous and substantial. Because of the critical part they played in affecting these unspeakable crimes against the United States of America and its citizens, it is only just that they both face the maximum penalty under military law, to be hung by the neck until they are dead."

At the defendants' table, Durk glanced aside at Antoinette, drawing on her nearness to calm his raging fears and to strengthen his tenuous resolve. This was the second time in two years he'd taken a reckless, seemingly hopeless gamble to intervene for her, the second time he'd put his life on the line to come to her rescue. His being in the courtroom, consciously choosing to risk what he suspected were impossible odds, defied all logic, certainly for the coward he'd always been. He could have ridden away. Moreover, he could have simply stayed at Moses' and been safe; the army would never have found him in the Colony. Yet, troubled as he'd been by his dilemma the night before, when he was exhausted and wounded and in despair over Isaac's death that morning, he'd had few qualms about what course of action to take. He simply could not bear the thought of Antoinette being sent to the gallows alone, could not stomach the notion that she would feel so abandoned. He reached under the table and took her hand.

Antoinette felt his touch and squeezed his hand reassuringly. She'd been shocked enough when Big Josh and the others appeared, after being told they were dead. And then Durk arrived! Foolhardy, possibly suicidal, he should never have come. But she could not help feeling relieved that he was beside her. If they had to die in this war, it was best that they die together.

Captain Stanford returned to his table, a pleased expression on his face. His fellow prosecutor smiled his approval. The general nodded toward him and then turned to the defendants' table. "Captain Whalen," he said. "Let's hear what you have to say."

Whalen stood nervously but seemed uncertain of his approach and so said nothing for several moments. Finally, the general prodded him. "Captain Whalen, it's your turn."

"I-I think we ought to resolve the slave matter first, General," he stuttered. "I haven't made my arguments in th-that case yet."

"You will do what I tell you, Captain. We are addressing the spy charges right now. They are the most important."

Still looking flustered, Whalen said softly, "General, members of this tribunal, I haven't yet had time to confer with the second of my clients. I ask..."

"Captain Hurst," the General interrupted, "do you want to meet with Captain Whalen before we begin? Would you prefer another representative? If so, we can try the two of you separately."

"No, sir," Durk replied. "We are both innocent, and we want to end this nightmare as quickly as possible."

"It's your choice," the general said. "All right, Captain Whalen, begin."

Whalen cleared his throat. "Yes, well, I hope to show that both of my clients are innocent of all charges and should return to their duties." He paused to shuffle through his papers. Then, seemingly hesitant, he sat back down.

Durk stared at him, incredulous. "That's all you have to say, lawyer? You have two innocent people sitting here accused of a capital crime, and that's the best you can do?"

Whalen merely averted his eyes from Durk, his face reddening.

The general waited for more, then shrugged, and turned to Stanford. "All right, Captain, begin the prosecution."

Stanford rose to his full height, then paced back and forth, hands locked behind his back. He presented his case coldly, methodically, making one point at a time, as if ordering supplies. He introduced the records of Durk's attachment to a contraband labor force: a report from Colonel Rowland Carter placing the blame for the Lawrence massacre on Durk's betrayal, false statements Hurst had made and signed about his own men, including his attempts to get them on the payrolls as a white regiment, and the list went on and on. The fact that he'd been a Southern plantation owner before the war and Antoinette the daughter of a wealthy planter appeared damning in and of itself. These points all seemed to tie up neatly when it was revealed that on the morning Quantrill burned Lawrence, Captain Hurst was suspiciously absent, safely en route to Westport. Furthermore, Antoinette had sweet-talked her way into sending multiple wires both before and after the massacre, using a military communication facility that was normally off limits to civilians. The case was fairly cut and dried. In wartime, people had been executed with far less evidence than was being produced against either one of the defendants.

Despondent, with eyes downcast, Antoinette merely stared at her table, hands folded in her lap. The darkness at the back of her mind, often held at bay, now consumed her. The prosecutor's voice merely droned on; she didn't even hear his words. She had spent two years sacrificing for these people, losing sleep, giving of her spirit to poor, brave boys who knew they were to be dismembered and disfigured for life, and comforting others on a slow, painful journey to oblivion. Yet in spite of her service, these mad fools were ready to march her to the gallows.

Durk, growing angrier and more frustrated by the second, shifted nervously in his chair as if sitting on an anthill. He blurted an objection aloud at one point but was cautioned to keep quiet and wait for his turn to speak. He laid his hand on Antoinette's knee, but, lost in her own thoughts, she didn't respond to his touch. He turned to look at her face, but all he saw was despair. He placed his arm around her, and she leaned in to him. He thought about declaring his own guilt to somehow get her acquitted, but that might implicate her. Under these conditions, their destinies were inextricably entwined. She pulled away, and he removed his arm to let her descend into her dark, private space alone.

Seeing them together, Devereau, who had been watching the trial fearfully, sunk in her chair as if to hide and cut daggers at the pair. Her entire life had been a barren desert where she dwelt alone, unloved, unwanted, with no friends, no one with whom she could share her burdens, no one. Now, to see the man she'd wanted for so long with her half-sister, who she wanted dead, consumed her with a despairing, jealous rage. If she had a gun, she would shoot them both dead right here; damn the consequences. That would be worth dying for.

Captain Stanford neared the conclusion of his case. "And last, and most damning, is General Barrett's statement and the documents attached to it accusing *both* defendants of spying, which enabled the Lawrence massacre. You'll note that the first of the intercepted messages is addressed by Captain Hurst to Quantrill, who led the raid on Lawrence. In it, Captain Hurst writes that his men are the only force currently stationed there. The second message is to Bloody Bill Anderson, written in Mrs. DuVallier's hand, to tell him that Federal forces have no immediate plan to bolster the Kansas border garrisons. Together, they form a dastardly, indelible link between these two and the active guerrilla forces in Western Missouri. There can be only one inescapable conclusion: the two are guilty as charged."

"These are lies," Durk yelled, but the general's aide shouted for him to be silent and wait his turn. All Durk could do was glare at the prosecutor, fuming. In shock, Antoinette merely shook her head.

Without warning, Devereau jumped to her feet. Reaching into her purse, she pulled out a sheet of paper and waved it above her head. "General Schofield," she called out nervously, "I have proof of Antoinette's guilt. And it proves she duped Captain Hurst, too, who is innocent of all charges."

The room fell silent, stunned at the unexpected intrusion into the proceedings. Antoinette turned angrily, as every eye fell upon Devereau.

"What do you have there, Miss French?" the general asked angrily.

Devereau's face flushed, as she realized she had exposed herself to scrutiny. "Never mind. I'm sorry, sir."

"No," the general said skeptically. "Read your note, please. I'm sure we're all interested to hear what it says. If you can resolve this case for me, I'd be most grateful. Then you can take your slaves and go."

"It's nothing, General," Devereau replied, glancing back furtively at the room's main door.

"Read it," the general ordered. "Now."

Devereau took a deep breath. "It's a message to a man named Quantrill." She paused, swallowing with difficulty. Then, prodded by Schofield, she continued. "It reads, 'Lawrence unguarded. Has only an unarmed colored regiment in training for defense. Regimental captain unaware.' And it's signed, 'A. DuVallier.' That's all, General."

"That's a fabrication," Durk shouted.

Flabbergasted, Schofield said, "Where did you get that note, Miss French?"

"Robert, the Indian with me, found it. He was going through a dead bushwhacker's pockets, probably a messenger. Anyway, that's all Robert said about it."

"This is quite extraordinary," the general mused, adding after a pregnant pause, "if it is, indeed, genuine."

Just then, the corporal who had been dispatched by General Schofield that morning to send a wire to Keytesville, returned with the reply. Seeing him enter, the general held up his hand to quiet the courtroom. The corporal hurried over to the general, dropped the wire before him, and whispered to him. Startled at first, the general regained his poise. "Bring that note up here, Miss French."

Hesitantly, Devereau walked up to the general's desk and handed him the note. The general examined it closely. "Oddly enough," he said, "this handwriting is different from the message General Barrett attached to *his* report. That note is also supposed to have been written by Mrs. DuVallier and sent to Quantrill. How do you explain this?"

Devereau merely shrugged. "Robert gave it to me. That's all I know."

"Coincidentally," the general continued, holding up the wire, "my corporal here just returned with the reply from the authorities in Keytesville. It seems the clerk who signed your Missouri slave ownership confirmation papers met a sudden and deadly end. How do you explain that, Miss French?"

"I-I don't, don't know," Devereau sputtered.

"Yes, well, apparently a local woman got a look at two strangers leaving the clerk's office together about the same time he was murdered. A big Indian and a small man wearing an expensive suit. French, you did say you've masqueraded as man. Quite regularly, in fact."

"It wasn't me," Devereau blurted, frightened. "I've never harmed a soul. I swear it. The clerk was alive when I left him."

"His wife and orphaned children would dispute that," the general retorted. "Your Indian friend seems to reach pretty readily for his knife. Empty out your purse, French. Let's see what other mysterious documents you've neglected to reveal."

"You can't search me without a warrant," Devereau objected.

"Write a letter of complaint to President Lincoln. In the meantime, this is my courtroom." The general turned to the nearest guard. "Seize her purse." The soldier ripped the purse from Devereau's grasp and handed it to Schofield, who opened it, reached inside, and withdrew two official-looking documents, which he examined in depth.

"Fascinating," he commented, stroking his beard. "A letter to Quantrill signed by General Hindeman, the *Confederate* General Hindeman. And, lo and behold, a letter from Colonel Dupré of the Cairo provost marshal's office, only Dupré's been stationed in Kentucky for over a year. He must have an awfully long reach in order to sign this paper in Cairo. Even more compelling, they're both signed in the same handwriting. Could it be that Hindeman and Dupré are one and the same?" The general turned knowingly to his aides, who grinned back at him.

At a loss for words, Devereau began to tremble. She tried to speak, but it was as if the words caught in her throat. Finally, she croaked, "With all that's going on out there — the whole state is overrun with killers — a woman, a woman's got to protect herself anyway she can. Any way. You think I wanted that filthy Chickasaw to accompany me? Do you? He's not even interested in women. Can you imagine? Could I help it if he murdered people when I wasn't looking? I never saw him do it, but I'm willing to testify against him. I know he's guilty."

The general thought this over. "Place this woman under arrest," he said. "She'll have a chance to explain herself, although I can't imagine she'll be able to invent a story to explain what she's been a part of."

A guard took her arm in hand.

"Hold her for trial. Right now, she needs to make a written statement about the Indian's misdeeds and her participation in them. Forgery is one matter. With the documents she had, she may well have been in position to sell information to the rebels. There is also the matter of accessory to murder, or in her own words, *multiple* murders. If she helps us to convict him, perhaps she can escape the hangman. But she appears, indeed, culpable in numerous capital crimes for which she will be held accountable with her own life."

Sobs erupted from Devereau, and her whole body began quaking. She wiped her eyes and nose with her sleeve but couldn't stop. The tears ran down her cheeks, and she covered her face.

"Now, Miss French, I'm curious," the general asked dryly, "why did you produce this phony letter implicating Mrs. DuVallier, your own flesh and blood, and exculpating Captain Hurst? You took quite a chance."

"I love Durk. I have for years," she cried, trying to compose herself. "He couldn't have spied for the Confederacy. That level of duplicity just isn't in him. He's too simple for that."

The general stroked his beard. "But why implicate Mrs. DuVallier in this?"

"The woman is evil! Evil! She tricked Durk into loving her. He should have been mine."

"All right, enough," the general barked, "hold her with the others. Miss, you are now under arrest on multiple, serious charges. I don't think you'll be romantically involved with anyone in the near future, if ever. Take her away."

The guard led Devereau back to the corner of the room, where she was seated with Auntie NeeNee, Josh, Lou, and Bammer. She crouched down and covered her eyes, crying hopelessly and trembling like a small child, hurt, scared, damaged beyond repair.

"Let us continue," the general stated formally. "We still have a spy trial to conclude."

CHAPTER THIRTY

WITNESS IN EBONY

Captain Whalen stood shakily, his right hand trembling. As if the presence of General Schofield wasn't frightening enough, he had no strategy to win this case. The evidence against his clients seemed incontrovertible, overwhelming.

"General Schofield," he said hesitantly in a subdued voice. "I know," he cleared his parched throat, which was screaming for the bottle, "I know the prosecution's argument seems convincing, b-but I hope to show that this woman is innocent. And this officer, too. Regardless, I hope I can offer enough doubt to avoid the maximum penalty."

The general gave Whalen a foul look. "Not a very strong opening statement, Captain. These people's lives are at stake. Can't you do better than that?"

"I'll try, sir. I'll certainly try."

Durk stood. "I'll defend us."

Whalen appeared puzzled and then looked toward the general for guidance.

General Schofield nodded. "Captain Whalen, these people have the right to a defense, any defense, and that's not what you are offering. Mrs. DuVallier, do you mind if Captain Hurst speaks for both of you?"

"That is fine with me, General Schofield," she answered, relieved. *Durk has always been my saving grace. He can do this.* She looked up at him, giving her approval.

"All right then. Captain Whalen, you can speak if you have something to add. Understand? Otherwise, keep your mouth shut."

"Yes, sir," Whalen replied.

"Then sit down."

Whalen complied.

"You may proceed, Captain Hurst. I know you're not a lawyer, so I'm going to give you a little leeway with your presentation, a privilege I will extend to the prosecution as well. But please don't get off track with this thing, gentlemen. It has already taken too much of my time."

"Thank you, General Schofield; I won't," Durk said, as he began to pace, giving himself time to gather his thoughts. "Let's look at the logic of this first, shall we? We have two innocent people here — and a prosecutor's case that makes no sense whatsoever: a case based on false evidence, besides.

"First, much seems to be made of the fact that I was a Southern planter. The prosecution infers there are no planters who are abolitionists, which is not the case. Such a stand Antoinette and I took against slavery was not popular. In fact, it made us pariahs, eventually costing us dearly. But ask the men I brought north with me to fight for the Union, three of whom have survived, their brothers having died to defeat the rebellion. They will affirm that I freed them back in Mississippi, even gave them a cut of the plantation's profits. Now isn't that more than Northern factory or mill owners provide their workmen? Sir, if you will allow it, I would like to call the sergeant and the two privates in the back to prove my assertion," he said, indicating Big Josh and the others in the corner. "They can tell you everything about my conduct in this war because they were there with me. They risked their lives to get here. Their testimony will, in fact, prove Antoinette should be honored for her loyalty, not be subjected to this parody of justice!"

At that moment, Big Josh spontaneously rose and, waving his manumission document, shouted, "The man set us free. How much more proof you need?"

Bammer and Lou joined him, waving their manumission papers. In a sharp voice, Schofield's aide ordered quiet, threatening that any future outbursts would see them locked up. They were again seated and order restored.

Prosecutor Stanford stood and intoned in his deep voice, "I object to even the possibility of such testimony, General Schofield. You cannot allow Negros to testify in a capital trial. It is unheard of."

General Schofield thought this over. "I realize there is little precedent for it, Captain Stanford, and we should be guided by established standards in these cases, but this is an unusual hearing. I will decide on that point later. In the meantime, Captain Hurst, you may resume."

Durk took a moment to ponder what direction he would take. "Sir, Antoinette, Mrs. DuVallier, served our country selflessly as a nurse for two years, making great personal sacrifices for little recompense. You will grant that she had no access to current military information from the sick and dying. Therefore, her only value to the rebels, if she were a spy, would have been to transmit any information that *I* had gathered. Will you concede this point, Captain Stanford?"

Stanford nodded. "I grant the point, Captain."

"Good. Therefore, if I am proven to be no spy, Mrs. DuVallier must be completely blameless."

"Agreed," Stanford said.

Durk smiled, pleased with himself. If he could somehow evade conviction for himself, then Antoinette would automatically go free. He knew this was a difficult proposition, but facts and the truth often overcome falsehoods: albeit, sometimes too late to save the victim. Even if he were found guilty, perhaps he could get the charges against Antoinette dismissed. Inexplicably, he felt a warm feeling wash over him, knowing that he'd done the right thing to put himself in jeopardy for her. If he had to die for someone, she was worth it. He continued, "Even if I were a spy, which I am not, you will grant it is possible that Mrs. DuVallier had no part any such activities."

"I grant that, too," Stanford said, "but there is substantial evidence against you both. We'll see where this leads."

Durk had the case where he wanted it. Now if he could get himself found not guilty, Antoinette would automatically go free. So his own innocence had to be his next objective.

"All right," Durk said, "let's get to the crux of the matter. These brave men were eager to fight, even die, to free their people and to preserve the Union. I was merely their go-between with the white authorities. So, admittedly, the bravery is theirs, not mine. But you must understand, my neck was no less at risk than theirs. As a white officer of a black regiment, you know what my fate would have been if the bushwhackers or even Confederate regulars had caught me. So let's not talk of cowardice; we're all afraid of dying. But my actions, while certainly not heroic, were hardly cowardly."

Captain Stanford rose. "I object. Captain Hurst's cowardice is not the issue here. I will grant that he took a substantial risk, but that risk was taken to further the interests of the Confederacy… as a spy. The same for his co-conspirator, Mrs. DuVallier."

The general chastised Durk, saying, "You will keep to the point, Captain, or I'll put Captain Whalen back in charge of your defense."

Durk nodded his consent. "First, the prosecution has inferred that my being a planter would automatically make me disloyal to our country. Right now, I want the prosecution to confirm that there were, indeed, abolitionists in the South. In the twenties, there were many abolitionist preachers. My pa was one of them. And because of their preaching, a number of planters were inspired to manumit their slaves. But these preachers were beaten and chased north; some were even killed. In Turkle, where I lived, there was a deacon who railed against slavery. The man and his daughter, Ellen, knew I was of like mind and can confirm this."

"What was their last name, Captain?" Stanford asked.

"I never learned it." Durk sighed.

"We can't send a fact-finding mission to Mississippi, so that cannot prove your contention," Stanford countered. "Any spy might claim the same thing."

"The claim is unproven," General Schofield ruled. "Continue, Captain."

Durk gathered his next step. "Now, as to papers I signed. I admit I sometimes called my men manumitted slaves; sometimes I claimed they were escaped contrabands. And yes, I admit these two assertions are contradictory. But I did it so they could work for the army on behalf of the Union cause, which is all they desired, nothing else.

"Now, as to my getting the *DarkHorse* regiment established as a white one, I would like to ask General Schofield how many colored regiments have been formed under General Sparks?" He waited, but there was no reply. "You know very well, sir, that General Sparks is an avowed charcoal, against even *freeing* the slaves, and he will not permit a colored unit under his command. Isn't that so, General?"

"Yes, Captain," General Schofield replied wearily. "General Sparks has made that abundantly clear to me."

"General, sir, my men wanted to fight; that's all. And President Lincoln has said the army must accept colored troops. So General Sparks is placing his own prejudices above the country's interests, even defying the president's stated policy. Isn't that so? So how else was I to get these good men into uniform but to lie? There was no other way. They deserve our thanks, not condemnation. And, frankly, neither do I. More to the point, if I was a spy, I was safe doing manual labor and training horses. Why would I take the risk of joining the active military? It doesn't make sense."

Durk looked to Antoinette, who nodded her approval. He considered his next approach and then began to speak. "General Schofield, I want to call the men from my regiment as witnesses. You know full well they're not pro-slavery, nor pro-secession. I call Sergeant Josh Tyler to the stand."

"I object," Captain Stanford said. "There is no precedent for a Negro testifying in a military trial."

"General Schofield, these men have suffered extreme hardship to aid the

U.S. Army, as much as many white soldiers. They have seen their best friends slaughtered and mutilated by bushwhackers. They have no reason whatsoever to lie for me. Please," Durk pleaded "let the truth fall where it may."

General Schofield sat back in his chair, rubbing the nape of his neck, and looked to his aides, who bent over to confer with him. After a brief conversation, the general leaned forward, placing his hands together on the desk. "I will allow this one exception, but only the sergeant, a man in authority. The others are irrelevant to our purposes. Have Sergeant Tyler brought forward and sworn in."

A guard guided a determined Big Josh to the witness stand, where he placed his hand on the Bible, and raised the other. The guard asked, "Do you swear to tell the truth, the whole truth, and nothing but the truth, so help you God?"

"I s-swear to God," Josh said, his stutter more pronounced than usual.

"What is your name, rank, and regiment?"

"Josh Tyler, S-sergeant, Ninth MSM Colored Cavalry."

Josh sat uncomfortably, settling his girth in the witness chair, and Durk stepped close to question him. "Now Sergeant Tyler, would you lie to protect me or Mrs. DuVallier?"

"No, sir. I done swore to G-God. And I don't n-need to 'cause you two are innocent."

"Good. Now, we've been together how long?"

"Neigh on to four year. Since M-miss'ippi."

"All right. Now, when we left Mississippi, what did I want to do? Where did I want to go?"

"You? You want to go out w-west. Say we' be s-safe there."

"But you and the others, what did you want to do?"

"We want to join the Union Army, fight for President Lincoln. We all want to, even Isaac."

"But y'all ended up in Missouri, serving the army, and I was with you. You must have persuaded me. How easy was that?"

"It was h-hard. You smart, but you ain't no man to be doing no shootin' an' k-killin', that's for sure. We t-talk and talk. An' after all this spyin' and trial and such, I wish we let you go west. You sure don't deserve this. Antoinette, neither."

Stanford interrupted, "Let's have no more opinions from the witness, General."

"Yes," Schofield said to Josh, "just answer the questions, Sergeant."

"Yes, sir. I'm sorry."

Durk became more aggressive. "Okay, I'd like to make a point here. If I were so intent on spying for the Confederacy, why would it be so difficult to convince me to work for the army? That doesn't make any sense."

Stanford interjected, "Sergeant, how long *did* it take you to convince Captain Hurst to come north with you? Minutes? Hours? Days? What?"

"Days. We had to decide fast. We was on the r-run."

Stanford approached the witness chair, leaning on the general's desk five feet from Durk. "So you had to leave in a hurry; is that right?"

"That's right. Th-they coming to kill us and h-hang Durk."

"They? Who do you mean, 'they'?"

"Everyone. Turkle, the whole town. They wants to string up D-durk, Captain Hurst."

"And why would that be?" Stanford asked.

"Why? 'Cause they say he a traitor."

"A *traitor?* Which is what we are contending here," Stanford said pointedly. "And why did these people believe that?"

"Why? 'C-cause he try to stop them mens from running off to fight. Tole them to go home to they families."

"So I was called a traitor to the *South?*" Durk interjected. "Against the war? Is that right, Sergeant?"

"That's right. You couldn't keep shut and leave it alone. Almost g-got us killed."

"So, General Schofield," Durk pointed out, "if I was against the war, against slavery, why would I come to Missouri to spy for the Confederacy? That, too, makes no sense."

"All right, Captain Hurst," General Schofield said. "Go on with it. There's still much evidence against you. People change their minds, for whatever reason. A traitor to one cause might become a traitor to another."

"A final question, Sergeant Tyler," Durk said. "You've been with me in Missouri for two years. Did you ever see anything that made you suspicious that I was spying for the rebels?"

"No, sir. I'd-a known it if you done it."

"Thank you, Sergeant. That's all the questions I have," Durk said, returning to his seat.

"Hold on a minute," Stanford said. "I have questions. Now, Sergeant Tyler, did Captain Hurst own you back in Mississippi? He told us he signed manumission papers for you."

"No, sir, he never own n-none of us."

"Ah," Stanford exclaimed. "So these manumission papers he signed, they're a subterfuge. In other words, they're invalid. Captain Hurst couldn't free you because he never owned you; is that right? General, see, that's another of his tricks. Captain Hurst seems to be a man full of tricks and schemes, like when he swore in writing that these colored soldiers are contrabands, or manumit slaves, and more importantly, a *white* regiment. Now don't lie, Sergeant. You're under oath. The whole truth."

"That's true. He weren't never our master. We just pretend he was when f-folks come 'round. See?"

"So who *was* your master, if not Captain Hurst?"

"Man from Tennessee folks call 'the general'."

"And what happened to this 'general'?"

"He was murder' by that Chickasaw run out of here, by Wounded Wolf."

"But how did you men end up with Captain Hurst?"

"M-met him in a sw-swamp."

"And what was Captain Hurst doing in a swamp?"

"Don't know."

"Never asked?"

"No, s-sir. Figure that's his business."

"All right," General Schofield said impatiently. "That's enough of this nonsense. Return the sergeant to his seat."

"B-but I g-g-gots more to say," Josh said.

"Wait," Durk said. "We've yet to ask him about Lawrence. Isn't that what this trial is about?"

"All right, Hurst," the general replied. "But confine your questions to Lawrence, and make it fast."

"I will, sir," Durk said. "Now, Josh, Sergeant Tyler, much has been made of my being absent when Lawrence took place. You were with me then on the way to Westport. What was our purpose for that excursion?"

"Why, we went to get g-guns. Didn't have n-none that work the whole time we was training."

"Good," Durk said. "Now, why wasn't our regiment supplied with working firearms?"

"Regular shipments weren't coming."

"That's right, Sergeant. Can you tell us why?"

"Why? 'C-cause it too dangerous. 'Whackers done raid the wagons. Colonel complain we can't even get mail regular. Run out of food once't."

"And nobody wanted to chance it to supply a colored regiment, correct?"

"Objection!" Stanford said. "The captain is speculating on motives he has no knowledge of."

"Agreed," General Schofield said. "You will refrain from speculating, Captain."

"Yes, sir," Durk said, returning to the witness. "While we were en route to Westport, what did we encounter?"

"Saw them 'wh-whackers heading west. Musta been hundreds of them."

"That's right," Durk said. "Quantrill's men on the way to Lawrence. What did we do under those circumstances?"

"W-we was just a few men. You sent four to warn Lawrence."

"Four men who didn't make it in time?"

"Yes, s-sir. Still don't know what happen to two of 'em. They lost, probably dead now. Then we hurry to warn Westport."

"Good. Now, Sergeant, once we warned Westport, what did we do?" Durk turned to Schofield. "Notice, General, Quantrill had us outnumbered twenty to one."

"Why, we got guns and head back to Lawrence fast as our horses can take us. But we too late. Most all our friends are dead."

"Enough of this," General Schofield said. "At the behest of a man named Moses, I wired a Major Danwell at Westport, and he confirms this testimony. Let it be put on record that Captain Hurst and his regiment displayed real courage in a nearly impossible situation. All right, Hurst, get to your main point and quickly. There is still critical evidence implicating both you and Mrs. DuVallier, and I'm nearing the end of my patience. Step down, Sergeant." He turned to the guard. "Take this man back to his seat."

Josh returned reluctantly to the corner with Lou, Bammer, and Auntie, frustrated that he hadn't been permitted to say more. When he sat, his three friends came up to hug and reassure him. He nodded his gratitude but then remained withdrawn into himself, sullen and angry.

CHAPTER THIRTY-ONE

JUSTICE IN EQUAL MEASURE

"In conclusion," Durk said in his most sincere tone, "the only remaining evidence against Mrs. DuVallier and me are Colonel Carter's statement and a supposedly intercepted message from me to Quantrill. That and, most powerfully, General Barrett's report and *his* evidence depicting Mrs. DuVallier and me as spies. Taken by themselves, in isolation, these appear to be damning. But let's examine the situation more closely.

"These two messages — one unearthed in Kansas, one in Eastern Missouri — how were they obtained? Were they discovered on another pair of dead bushwhackers? On captured Confederate messengers? And, miraculously, both just in time for our trial. What are the odds against such an unlikely, but highly convenient, coincidence? Their timely appearance smacks of more precise military coordination than either of these two officers ever displayed on the battlefield." There were snickers from the prosecutors' table and even from Schofield's aides, but these were quickly suppressed. "And of these two," Durk continued, "neither Antoinette nor I have ever been stationed anywhere near General Barrett's headquarters, yet he seems to know so much about us, which is plain ludicrous. Doesn't this all seem incredibly unlikely?

"On the other hand, fortunately, all the documents in our case have been collected here in one place, in your comprehensive file on your desk there, General Schofield. Please examine the handwriting on them. You have official documents with my signature on them, acknowledged by me. Do any of them match the note Colonel Carter sent to you from Camp Dusty, the one I supposedly wrote? No, they do not. Clearly, that note is a forgery."

Out of nowhere, Captain Whalen interrupted, "Colonel Carter is Barrett's toady. He'd report anything he was told." He smiled, very pleased with himself for insulting a superior officer on record and ingratiating himself with Antoinette.

"Thank you, Captain," Durk said. "That explains one falsehood.

"And the message purportedly written by Antoinette, transmitted to you from General Barrett's command? General Schofield, you have Mrs. DuVallier's statement in full, in her own hand. Does that match the writing on the 'intercepted' note provided by General Barrett? Clearly, it, too, does not. Mrs. DuVallier spent two years, day and night, as an angel of mercy in service to our country's wounded and dying... and now, to put her through this, facing the possibility of a rope around her neck. I have my flaws, and they are legion, but Antoinette is as honest and pure of heart as anyone you will meet in this lifetime. To hang such a beautiful soul on the basis of a forged document would be worse than a sin. Such a travesty would besmirch our whole war effort.

"And finally, we must ask ourselves: Why would General Barrett fabricate such a fiction? Did he feel culpable for Lawrence? Was he merely looking to deflect blame elsewhere for his own failures?"

"One second, please, Captain Hurst," General Schofield ordered, holding up his hand. He and his aides went through the stack of papers, comparing the supposedly treasonous notes to the official documents in the stack. Then Durk overheard him confer confidentially with his aides, telling them, "Damn political generals. I know Barrett spends all his time protecting himself first, but committing forgery is beyond my limits. The idiot's been nothing but a burr under my saddle since the day he arrived here! I'm going to relieve Old Cannonball of his duties as soon as I can replace him. Bring me the files on Generals Holland and Maple. On second thought, also on General Graff."

"Yes, sir," one aide said. "Do you want to press charges against the general?"

"No, don't bother," the general replied. "Sending the fool back to Ohio will aid our cause better than adding a battalion to our forces. Addition by subtraction."

"Do you plan to replace Colonel Carter, too?"

"No. The fool isn't competent enough to do much harm." The general turned to the courtroom and spoke in his most commanding voice. "All right, Captain Hurst, you've made a convincing case. It is clear, in black and white, that the only substantial evidence against Mrs. DuVallier and you are forgeries. Therefore, I hereby dismiss the charges. You and Mrs. DuVallier are free to go. Furthermore, I am going to recommend a citation for the outstanding service, above and beyond the call of duty, for both of you. And let me say from my heart, I apologize on behalf of the army for the unwarranted and undeserved injustices foisted upon you both. As compensation, defendants will be accorded back pay."

Exhausted, Durk collapsed into his chair. Antoinette threw her arms around him, and they wearily embraced. But Durk wasn't done yet. When he regained his composure, he asked, "General Schofield, what about my men? We can't leave their fate up to chance. They have served the Union nobly, even risking their own necks to attend this trial and prevent judicial murder."

General Schofield didn't hesitate. "You make a strong point, Captain. When I approved Order Eleven, I included strict prohibitions against any such criminal behavior as these men encountered. Therefore, I rule that these soldiers acted properly, with their disobedience being fully justified under the circumstances."

General Schofield turned to the prosecutor, Captain Stanford. "I want these men and the boy to remain in St. Louis so they can testify against Langham and the others — colored or child as they might be. You will make suitable provisions for them. When they are no longer needed for their testimony, they will be returned to duty. The boy's fate will have to be determined later."

"As you say, sir," Captain Stanford acquiesced reluctantly.

"But, sir," urged Durk, "their manumission has come into question."

An aide whispered to the general, who pronounced, "Under the president's current policy, as active members of the military, these men are forever free. Captain Hurst will sign new documents for them stipulating this."

"And what about *their* back pay, sir? These men suffered and practically starved to get here from Eastern Kansas."

"They shall receive any monies due to them, as well."

"And the women that were with Mrs. DuVallier?" Durk challenged. "They've been treated brutally since the train raid."

"I agree. Miss French's claim for them is hereby denied," the general ruled. "Their Missouri registration was completed under compulsion. Therefore, Devereau French will be held for trial as an accessory to murder."

"No!" Devereau screamed, shocked by the realization that her crimes were coming home to roost. "I'm innocent!"

"You will have a fair chance to prove that in court," the general concluded, "which is more than you and your Indian gave that country clerk. Take her away."

In tears, and resisting every step, Devereau was led off by the guards, as Durk watched her with pity. She paused at the door to cast one final pleading glance toward Durk, and then she was gone.

"Hurst," Schofield continued, "these women have reverted to your ownership, per testimony in this court. Do what you want with them."

"Thank you, General Schofield," Durk said, taking a long moment to consider his reply. "Since the authorities are now paying slave owners three hundred dollars for each manumitted slave, I will manumit these people, and in compensation for their extreme abuse, I will turn over the three hundred dollars to each of them. It is the least we can do to uphold the honor of the Union."

"That's the new policy," Schofield chuckled. "Captain Stanford, you will make arrangements to accomplish these transactions."

"Yes, sir, General," Stanford said offhandedly as he collected his briefs.

Back in the corner, tears began streaming down Auntie NeeNee's cheeks as she wept silently. In all her many decades of life, she'd never been truly free. Even the last few years with the *DarkHorse* men, she had technically been a slave, with fear of discovery and a return to bondage her daily dose of gall. Now, with all that behind her, and some money to get started on, her heart was near bursting. Momentarily, the whole group was bittersweet happy.

"If there are no other matters…" the general began, rising to his feet.

Antoinette stood. "There is one final matter, General Schofield," she said, straightening her black skirt. "My representative, Captain Whalen, has betrayed his trust in a most scurrilous and dastardly manner."

Irritated, the general sat back down. "What are you claiming, Mrs. DuVallier? Be brief; I have no time for shenanigans."

"I shall, sir. If you question his former female clients, most of whom are most likely in prison, I think they will attest that Captain Whalen made a practice of demanding intimate favors and other inappropriate compensation from them. Not that his work for them was ever exemplary or to their advantage."

"Did Captain Whalen make such demands on you?" General Schofield asked, disgusted by the suggestion.

"Yes, but I refused him."

"Captain Whalen," the general said, clearly detesting the inference, "did you make such demands on this woman?"

"I did not, sir," Whalen replied, his nervous eye-twitch becoming pronounced. His hands began to shake so, he pulled them under the table.

The general shrugged. "I am sorry, Mrs. DuVallier, while such a practice would be unconscionable, you offer no proof. It is your word against the captain's."

"But I do have proof, sir." She withdrew the ring Whalen had given her from her pocket and held it high for all to see. "Besides their favors, Captain Whalen also demanded jewelry from his female clients. He gave me this engagement ring from what he bragged was a large stash of jewelry he possessed, personal valuables, which I think you will find he extorted from his clients."

"Why would he give you this ring, Mrs. DuVallier?"

"So that I would agree to marry him, General. I merely accepted the ring so that I could present it in court."

With a sneer, General Schofield examined Whalen more closely, as if he had bitten into a rotten apple. "Are these accusations true, Captain Whalen?" he demanded. "Did you give this ring to Mrs. DuVallier? Do you have a stash of jewelry that was acquired by unethical demands?"

"I-I didn't give it..." he stuttered. "I mean, y-yes, I did give her this ring for her hand in honorable marriage. But I p-purchased it... You s-see, General..."

"Have you extorted valuables from your clients, Captain?" Schofield demanded.

"N-no, no one would say that. N-no..."

"There is a simple way to resolve this," the general concluded, rising to leave. "Captain Stanford, have guards accompany Captain Whalen to his quarters. There, the captain's room will be thoroughly searched. If he is hiding a cache of jewelry, have him arrested on professional misconduct and any other charges you feel are appropriate. And see to the cases he represented. Unfortunately, we cannot return convicted defendants from the gallows, but we can see if there were other irregularities. We are done here." General Schofield strode briskly out the side door, glad to be finished with this unpleasant duty, followed closely by his aides.

"But, General," Whalen shouted after him, "the jewelry was given to me in gratitude for my services. Gratitude!"

With the general gone, the guards not assigned to further duty hightailed it out of the stifling building, their workday mercifully ended.

As guards surrounded Whalen, Antoinette turned to face him. "I don't believe you will be free to marry any time soon, Captain," she said with some glee. "Therefore, sir, I must disengage our pending betrothal. Forget me as quickly as you can, Captain, because I certainly will forget you." Then she took Durk's arm, and they crossed the room, triumphant, to join their friends in celebration.

Out of the corner of his eye, Durk noticed the boy. It was as if the child had sunk into himself, sitting with his bare heels on the chair, arms wrapped around his knees, his eyes on fire, staring at Durk resentfully like a wounded animal. Durk contemplated this small, emaciated figure: ragged overalls, torn shirt, shoeless. This could have been Durk himself at the same age. He'd never pictured himself held back by anyone, much less a child. But, inexplicably, he felt elated by the prospect. It made him feel like a man.

Certainly, Durk was free to run from this terrible killing and destruction. He had money in his pocket and was listed as "Killed in Battle" in the army records. He could start over anywhere. All he needed was a riverboat ticket west. But there was the question of Antoinette… and the boy. He gazed with profound admiration at the lovely Antoinette, her weary face so relieved from the strain of her ordeal. Then, with a silent nod, Durk brought the child to everyone's attention. "What are we going to do with this boy?"

CHAPTER THIRTY-TWO

THE PRODIGAL CHICKASAW

Indian Territory, Mississippi

Under the night skies, dimly lit by an old moon, he skirted the bayou, guiding his mount around a moccasin-infested backwash. His city suit was mud-spattered with rips and tears, his hat long lost on the trail. The horse hesitated at a blind ridge, and he urged it on slowly through a tangled stretch of vine and undergrowth. Regaining his bearings, he continued circling the slough, lying black in the darkness, the horse stumbling through creeper and flood debris. Finally, he came upon the riverbank where the oracular Great Tree had once stood.

He drew rein and slid deftly from the saddle. As he had planned, he slipped the bridle from the horse's mouth, unhitched the saddle, and tossed them aside. He patted the animal's nose, said a few gentle words, and let it wander where it would. It had served its purpose.

He turned to examine the familiar clearing, a mere five miles from the main Chickasaw tribal encampment. The Great Tree, once so proud and tall, lay uprooted and far into rot, like a giant beast slain. Its long black carcass, with bark torn and wasted, stretched across the wild forest floor, home to colonies of termites and ants, to insects and rodent nests, to a whole world thriving upon its corpse. Farther upstream, its brittle, bleached top branches draped above the current like Mother Death washing her hair.

"You finally succumbed to Brother Wind," he solemnly told the downed oak.

He pulled his shovel from the saddlebag and dug a fire pit in the soft soil. Then he set about gathering driftwood, haphazardly grabbing whatever came to hand: for the first time in years, unconcerned that smoke from rotten or green wood would betray his presence. No man would be within miles of this place. After gathering a heaping polyglot of hardwood and bug-infested branches, he dumped the choicest shards into his pit and got a large bonfire burning. Satisfied, he stood close to its edge to watch the flames catch, warming himself against the night dampness.

Then he began. First, he removed his right boot and threw it into the river; then he did the same with his left. Next he removed his suit coat, threw it into the fire, and watched as it caught and burned. Next, he removed his pants and did the same. Satisfied that his old existence was being consumed, he stripped off his shirt, underclothing, and stockings and dropped them into the flames. The resultant sparks flew off into the black void above.

Standing fully naked, his spirit soared as the fire burned Robert Sterling from his heart, and Wounded Wolf the Chickasaw reclaimed his own body.

He took up the shovel and dug a second, smaller hole, placing his knife and sheath ceremoniously in the new hole. This he covered with dirt, patting it down into a grave-like mound. Satisfied, he rose to his feet again and casually tossed the shovel into the water, its splash frightening the frogs into leaping from their floating log.

"My knife died gorged with blood," he cried. "Truly, this is every drunkard's fate."

As he had envisioned, he turned to where the moon hung above the stark stand of cypress across the river, tears in his eyes. Firmly planting his legs apart, he raised his face toward the sky, spreading his arms wide as if accepting an embrace from the eternal spirits encompassing the forest.

"Father Sky!" he declared in his deepest voice. "I will kill Man no more. Forever!" He stomped hard once on the knife mound, leaving his footprint in the dirt like a monarch's seal on an official decree. He was done with it.

Truly liberated, he shouted a single sharp yelp and, laughing wildly, ran down the bank, his bare soles not feeling the stones and thorns littering the mud. When he reached the water, he dove in headfirst, feeling the icy shock when he struck the river. His plunge carried him gliding swiftly underwater, then, rising to the surface, he began to stroke with all his might, swimming the chill away. The distance to the middle of the Chickasaw branch was great, but he continued stroking against the current, determined to reach the farthest point from either shore. Halfway there, his legs and arms began to feel like lead: aching muscles crying out for rest. He had difficulty keeping his head above the surface, more and more frequently swallowing water when he tried to breathe, yet he would not turn back. Finally, when he reached the river's deepest point, he gulped a last breath and, kicking his legs skyward, dove like an arrow into the depths. Unafraid.

And so, as foretold in his dream, his rapid descent into the rushing waters peeled away the reptilian skin of foolish civilization, sending the dead husk of memory sinking to the riverbed, there to be devoured by catfish, sucker, sturgeon, and countless other bottom-feeding scavengers.

CHAPTER THIRTY-THREE

BELONGING TO THE AGES

April 16, 1865. "The Burnt District"

Spring was in high step, with the land showing off its new green coat. In the East, General Lee had surrendered his forces at Appomattox Courthouse only six days before, and calm had begun to settle upon the rich farmland. Careworn civilians wearing threadbare clothing were filtering back home to work their once-abandoned soil with new hope in their eyes.

In the western sky, the striated layers of gray clouds rippled above the horizon, dispersing eastward like debris from a waterfall, their underbellies glowing bright pink from the setting sun. With dusk's arrival, the robin's egg blue slowly drained from the sky, but no rain was anticipated.

Durk rode beside Josh at the head of the *DarkHorse* regiment, heading back to the militia outpost that had been their home for five months. Since the big news had reached Missouri, he hadn't suffered the dread of impending ambush that had gripped him during their daily patrols the past two years. Rather, the surrounding thickets and woodlands had shucked their ominous terror, and Durk allowed himself to luxuriate in the familiar symphony of creaking leather saddles, clopping hooves, and melodic birdsongs.

What a celebration they'd had when word of Appomattox first arrived! Laughing and crying and hugging, indulging in double rations of tin meat and fresh greens, dancing around the fire throughout the night, even drinking local moonshine. At the time, they thought they were in the first moments of an untroubled future, but good portents can be followed by bad.

In contrast to Durk's lightheartedness, Big Josh bore a serious mien. "So the colonel tell you *DarkHorse* being transferred to Oklahoma?"

"Yes," Durk replied, pulled back to reality. "To Fort Towson near Doaksville. Stand Watie's Cherokee Mounted Rifles are still fighting as if the war were in full bloom. We're supposed to hold him in check until he agrees to make peace."

Josh spit. "W-war ain't over till the last dog is dead, and I don't want to be that dog." There would be more hard fighting. And with the danger that riding the barren, scorching reaches of Oklahoma would bring, any one of them could still be killed.

"When we supposed to go?" Josh asked.

"Next week at the latest."

"Stand Watie? Brigadier general? I hear of him," Josh said. "They good fighters, mostly Cherokee, some Creek, Muskogee, and Seminole."

"At the Battle of Cabin Creek, Watie captured a million dollars in Union supplies," Durk groused.

Avoiding thought about what awaited them in the Southwest, the two rode in silence, trying to pull the new feeling of impending peace around them like a soft blanket they didn't want to shuck on a cold night.

"Hey, Josh, have you decided what you're going to do when the war's finally over?" Durk asked, attempting to break the gloom.

"I been thinking. I wants to start a school for black chiddren. They gonna need that to get along now they free. But where and how I ain't figured yet. Wh-what you gonna do, D-durk?" Josh asked.

"I haven't talked with Antoinette yet, that is if she's still willing to have me. A city would be her first choice. But she's wanted in New Orleans, so it's going to be the rural life, if we have any at all. I have had a thought, though. This may sound farfetched, but…" Durk said, pausing.

"Let's hear it."

"I still have papers on the *DarkHorse* property. Much of the land is raw, but there's so much of it! My claim is still registered with the Federal Indian agent, at the county seat, and at the Honor Store, too."

"Back to Miss'ippi? Turkle?" Josh asked, taken aback.

"It won't be easy," Durk continued. "I'm sure the bankers, lawyers, and politicians already have the parcels divvied up one way or another, temporarily at least. And you know they'll remember us." He ruminated over the possibilities. "Of course, with the war about over, things down there would be in a state of flux, even chaos, I'd bet."

Josh mulled this over. "The folks in Turkle tried to kill you, D-durk," he uttered with a graveyard chuckle. "It could be pretty dangerous. For both of you."

"Sure," Durk exclaimed, growing increasingly enthusiastic, Josh's concern barely registering. "We could chop up the properties into farms, sell out lots cheap, on credit, like a mortgage. We could mix up Negro and white farms, like a chessboard, see? Folks could be independent, former slaves and 'croppers, too. That way, living side by side, they could learn to be neighbors instead of being afraid of each other."

Josh smiled benignly at him. "Whoa! Slow up, Durk. You gonna have plenty of Big Ideas 'fore you own a thing. That notion though, knowing how people is 'bout such things? So soon after the war? That may not work out the way you figure it. L-listen to a f-friend."

"We'll, see," Durk added sheepishly, "I'm thinking *FrenchAcres*, too. All that land, that old plantation, sitting there…"

Josh shook his head. Once the man started in on one of his fancies, there was no stopping him.

"Sure," Durk continued, seeing Josh's skepticism. "French could sign the papers over to Antoinette. It's as much Antoinette's as hers. We know where to find French." He chuckled. "She can't run away from a Union prison. With *FrenchAcres* documents, we'd have two shots at getting possession of something."

Josh sighed, his eyes looking heavenward. "But French hates Antoinette. And you, too. She'd never give the place over to neither of you."

"Yes, but she hates me *because* of Antoinette," Durk argued. "Maybe I could convince her to sign. It would be worth trying."

"You'll come up with something, Durk. You always do," Josh said offhandedly, his mind already off to other subjects.

"Why don't you come with us, Josh? Bammer and Lou, too? We're still partners. Everybody has an equal cut like before."

"I'm just thinking on my school," Josh stated, cutting off the discussion. "If you can help me with that, I'd be most grateful." They continued in silence, their minds in flight to divergent destinations.

***

The outpost was eerily calm, more than it would soon be. Antoinette dragged herself to the long benches and collapsed, her elbows leaning on the rough, makeshift table, and dropped her head into her hands. Shock and sorrow were etched into her face. Bloodstains marred her dress, but she was too weary and consumed with her thoughts to change. Nearby, Auntie NeeNee stirred the pot simmering over the fire, trying to decide whether or not to approach her, to try to comfort her. Choosing rather to leave her in peace, Auntie busied herself with making do for supper, her eyes avoiding her friend.

Durk rode up to the nearby men's cabin, drew rein, and dismounted. He tied his horse by the trough, removed his saddle, and tossed it onto the porch, too hungry and sore to tend to his horse before supper. Durk and the rest of the regiment had been riding hard on patrol since before sun-up, having saddled their mounts by lantern that morning, a daily regimen. But all their enthusiastic galloping and exuberant high-jinx throughout the day were more a lark celebrating the war's impending end than any serious effort to seek diehards among the bushwhackers who once plagued this mostly pacified district.

Arriving with him, Josh followed suit. The big sergeant wore the medal for bravery that had originally been awarded to Durk, the regimental captain, who in turn had pinned it on Josh, the man everyone agreed really deserved the honor. At the time, Durk had promised to get the military paperwork corrected in Josh's favor, but they'd long since grown fatalistic about their chance of setting things right. Josh felt it was enough that the regiment recognized his actions.

Josh threw an arm around Durk's shoulders, and, following their noses toward the stew, the pair strolled beneath the maples toward the common area tables. These the regiment had constructed from pine harvested in the woods across the road. Their steps were lighter these last few days. For the first time in years, Durk felt like it was only a matter of time… If only he could survive this war a little longer.

Durk plopped down on the bench across the officers' table from Antoinette, and Josh settled his large frame beside him. Uncharacteristically, Antoinette didn't look up; clearly something was troubling her. Durk resisted the urge to console her, seeing the state she was in, and he waited for her to ascend from the dark place where her thoughts had fallen. Finally, Antoinette raised her eyes toward him, but they were vacant, staring right through him.

"Wh-what is it, Antoinette?" Josh asked, his expression grave.

It took a moment for her to focus. "There is news, bad news," she managed to say. "Last night. President Lincoln was assassinated. Shot dead in cold blood."

Incredulous, Durk slammed his hand on the table. "No!"

"Are you sure?" Josh asked, flabbergasted.

"The president's dead. Abraham Lincoln's dead."

Josh's head sunk into his hands. "It's 'cause he promise Negros the vote," he grumbled, his voice cracking. "I g-guess we never gonna get that vote now. Our friends d-die for him; now he d-die for us."

The three stared at each other, but words wouldn't come. Meanwhile,

Auntie NeeNee placed bowls and spoons on the table, as the other colored cavalry troopers filtered in by twos and threes. Tiny was the first corporal to limp in to their table. He was the bravest, most foolhardy man in the regiment, having already suffered four gunshot wounds charging into rebel ambushes. Then came Yeller Joe and Bradley Peak, laughing and talking together. Without a word, Auntie filled their bowls and retreated to her fire, where she sat with her back to everyone, having overheard Antoinette's revelation. She'd cried often in her life, but no one had ever seen her do it, and she wasn't going to let them see her now. When the new arrivals saw how morose their leaders were, they, too, became quiet.

When Josh informed the others about the president, the men stopped chewing in mid-bite, spoons suspended in mid-air. Courageous Tiny began to weep, his strong heart broken. He covered his eyes and ran from the table into the woods, leaving his bowl behind. Joe and Bradley simply picked up their vittles and disappeared around back, not a word said.

After they'd left, the boy ran in from the woods, mud stains on the knees of his new britches. Still preoccupied with whatever he'd been doing, he offered a brief 'hello' before seating himself. Then he hurriedly emptied his bowl, barely chewing as he gobbled down the stew. Finished, he wiped his mouth with his shirtsleeve and hugged Antoinette, who said a few quiet words to him. Then he managed a 'see ya' before returning to the woods.

Durk shouted after him, "Don't go too far. Hear? There might be bushwhackers over the hill." The boy merely kept going, waving perfunctorily to acknowledge that he'd heard.

By the time they finished eating, it was dark, and Durk lit the bug-splattered lantern. The three took up their bowls and utensils and carried them to Auntie, and then they returned to the table. Josh pulled out his knife and shard and began whittling hard to assuage his anger and frustration.

"I've got other news that ain't so good neither," Durk told Antoinette.

"What is it?" Antoinette asked.

"The Ninth is being sent to Oklahoma," Durk said. "By next week." His eyes met Antoinette's, the understanding that they would have to separate once again passing between them, and that there would be more killing, with the chance that Durk could be among the slain.

The three talked about Oklahoma for a while but soon ran out of conversation. Durk studied Josh, but his friend looked as low as he'd ever seen him. "Josh," he said softly. "Don't be discouraged. It's temporary. Temporary, you hear? Why…

Why, someday you'll get that vote — and that school. I really believe it; I do."

The three talked quietly, and soon the cloud hanging over them thinned out a touch. Slavery was dead; they'd wrung its neck. There would be brighter days ahead, fraught with pain, conflict, suffering, but somehow brighter.

Josh took his leave and headed to the bunk cabin, offering to take care of Durk's horse and saddle, leaving Durk and Antoinette alone.

The pair took a stroll hand-in-hand in the moonlight down the dirt road: thick Missouri pine forest and brush on their right, abandoned farm acres fallow on their left. After a hundred yards, they turned off the road onto a deer path familiar to them, accompanied by the nighttime croaks of frogs and the rapid chatter of insects. The path led to a clearing they'd retreated to on the rare occasions their duties allowed them time together. Finally reaching their private little refuge, they paused and sat together on a fallen oak, holding hands and gazing at the stars, silently contemplating the country's fallen champion in Washington.

Durk had never felt so uncertain, so confused, so at a loss for ideas or any desire to pursue them. He longed for quiet, yet he knew his heart would never let him pay the inescapable price for peace — obscurity. He still believed he was born with a special calling to change the way people thought, to make the country right, to make his mark on the world. He knew the end of slavery didn't presage the end of injustice, but would only alter its form.

In every direction, the great land lay torn and scarred by the steely machines of mass murder and destruction. Its people only now waking as if from a feverish nightmare. His thoughts drifted wistfully to home, to Mississippi, as ever, drawn to the unremarkable hamlet of Turkle. He couldn't conjure why that place, of all places, held such a grip on him. Its citizens, from a general sense of outrage more than anything, had twice tried to kill him: had taken his land and the fruits of his and his friends' labor. Yet, inexplicably, he missed it. Moreover, he missed the old Chickasaw squaw who rescued and raised him as a boy and wondered if she was still alive.

Durk fixed his eyes on Antoinette, her chiseled, tanned features accentuated by days spent under the glaring sun. *Perfection*, he thought. Her trials had etched more than the six years he'd known her into her countenance, as they undoubtedly had into his. The loss of her son, her traumatic life in New Orleans, the Frenches, and now the war, four years of insufferably long days and nights caring for the sick and dying. All his dreams were wrapped up in the hope that when he returned from Oklahoma — if he did — she would still be there for him. That his face could be draped once again in her long black hair, his battle-scarred body wrapped in her arms.

Weary, they had to return to their separate bunkhouses to catch what sleep they could. Tomorrow would be a rough day, as had all the others that had gone before. They rose, embraced a final time, and kissed lovingly, longingly. Arms around each other, they made their way back to camp.

Overhead, a dark cloud passed before the moon. At once, the irregular forest pathway was a blind, twisted tangle of vines and fallen branches underfoot, of unseen gullies and stumbling sinkholes. Finding their way was difficult now, and it would never be easy, even with the war over, but they desperately tried to convince themselves that their lives would soon be somehow better. Better. That nothing would ever separate them again. That Durk would return whole, not torn and repulsive to the eye like so many poor souls had. That they would share quiet moments together again, someday.

ACKNOWLEDGEMENTS

For Jeanie Loiacono at Loiacono Literary Agency and Sheri Williams and the gang at TouchPoint Press for their trust, belief, and encouragement. And for the many fine historians whose work informed my research for this novel, including the following:

BLASSINGAME. John W. *The Slave Community: Plantation Life in the Antebellum South* (Oxford University Press)

CODDINGTON, Ronald S.; foreword by J. Matthew Gallman. *African American Faces of the Civil War: An Album* (The Johns Hopkins University Press)

ERWIN, James W. *Guerrilla Hunters in Civil War Missouri* (The History Press)

ERWIN, James W. *Guerrillas in Civil War Missouri* (The History Press)

ERWIN, James W.. *The Homefront in Civil War Missouri* (The History Press)

GERTEIS, Louis S.. *Civil War St. Louis* (University Press of Kansas).

GILMORE, Donald L.. *Civil War on the Missouri-Kansas Border* (Pelican Publishing)

PISTON, William Garrett, Editor. *A Rough Business: Fighting the Civil War in Missouri* (The State Historical Society of Missouri)

REDKEY, Edwin S., Editor. *A Grand Army of Black Men* (Cambridge University Press)

WINTER, William C. *The Civil War in St. Louis: A Guided Tour*. (Missouri Historical Society Press, for the Civil War Round Table of St. Louis)

WRIGHT Sr., John A. *African Americans in Downtown St. Louis* (Arcadia, Black American Series)

CPSIA information can be obtained
at www.ICGtesting.com
Printed in the USA
LVOW11s1801120418
573254LV00002B/452/P

9 781946 920317